Ace fighter pilot Smilin' Jack Rawlins has seen his share of the horror and folly in Vietnam, done his share of the killing and somehow managed to complete his tour and return to civilian life emotionally unscathed. At least that's what he used to think. Back home, however, Rawlins's fortunes start fading fast when he signs on with VVAPS, an aerospace manufacturer whose bureaucratic excess stands second only to that of the US government.

Mordantly funny, viciously satirical and written in the irreverent tradition of *Catch-22* and *M*A*S*H, Pettibone's Law* is the story of one man's and one nation's journey to the heart of darkness and their tentative steps back towards the light. It is a hugely entertaining *tour de force* and Keene moves effortlessly from the ribald to the profound, bringing together a gallery of colourful characters, telling a hilarious and horrifying story of a misbegotten war.

PETTIBONE'S LAW

JOHN KEENE

BLOOMSBURY

First published in Great Britain 1992

Copyright © 1991 by John Keene

This paperback edition published 1992

The moral right of the author has been asserted

Bloomsbury Publishing Ltd, 2 Soho Square, London W1V 5DE

A CIP catalogue record for this book
is available from the British Library

ISBN 0 7475 1038 5

10   9   8   7   6   5   4   3   2   1

Printed in England by Clays Ltd, St Ives plc

For the elves and the dwarves and the gremlins,
one in particular; and CDVM.

The characters and events in this story are entirely fictitious; if anyone should find any similarity between these and real characters or events, the author will be flattered.

And you will cry, "I am alone!" The time will come when that which seems high to you will no longer be in sight, and that which seems low will be all-too-near; even what seems sublime to you will frighten you like a ghost. And you will cry, "All is false!"

—*Friedrich Nietzsche*

Prologue

Colorado, 1980s

It was a time of returning. Once, while shoveling a path from the cabin to the woodpile, Rawlins was able to think about things with a clarity that he hadn't managed to summon before. Still he had to wonder if everything had happened as he remembered. Had he dreamed part of it? Embellished or diminished the truth? Fabricated history? And what about the gaps—periods of crucial decisions of which he had no recall? Yes, a time of returning, of trying to reexamine the life that had slipped away. To somehow make sense of it. To look closely at the things he had done and the thing he had become, and try to draw some kind of conclusion. To understand some of it. He was sober, he was back in the high, clear air of the mountains, where perhaps he had always belonged. There was the fresh smell of pine and spruce, and sometimes he could hear the silence. This was the place, and now the time, that he might piece some things together, if indeed he could ever hope to. It was a time of returning and of clearing chemicals and sociological soot out of the memory. It was the time to look closely and wonder why.

When the brash kid from the sawmill up the road first came around, Rawlins shied away from his friendly, outgoing manner. He had to be alone, to devote all his energy to searching the past. He could not afford to have friendships, to be diverted from his quest.

But the kid grew on you. One day as Rawlins was digging his pickup out of the snow, the kid said, "I could run up here with my blade every so often and keep this open for you." He cackled recklessly, and with a note of good-natured defiance. "I ain't s'posed to, but I reckon I could, jest the same."

That innocent remark made Smilin' Jack Rawlins smile for real, something he had not done a lot lately. How many times had he done what seemed like the right thing, even though it was against the rules? Or done the wrong thing for the right reason? Yeah, he liked the kid's attitude. "I expect you'd want an arm and a leg," he said with a wink.

"Shoot no, mister. It ain't no skin off of my butt. 'Course if you got extra money, I could always use some." They both laughed.

So Rawlins ended up slipping the kid fifty bucks to keep the road to his cabin clear. It was fifty bucks that Rawlins couldn't really afford, but he decided the boy needed it more than he did. The kid was an orphan and the man at the sawmill gave him room and board, bought him a few clothes, and sent him to school. But he paid him precious little, and that irregular. Rawlins handed him the money, and all the shoveling he had to do after that was from the cabin to the woodpile. When he saw the kid in a new mackinaw, with gloves instead of the overlarge red-knuckled hands protruding from the sleeves, he figured he had done right.

And that, he had determined, was a lot of it: doing the right thing. Or doing the wrong things. He thought sometimes of the war, and the war within the war. When an airplane would fly over, tracing conden-sation trails in the high blue sky, he sometimes felt a pang. He thought of the so-called defense industry. Missiles to go all the way to Russia. Nuclear fish prowling every coast but ours. Multimegaton bombs for what shores? And cities aswarm with their lemminglike throngs. Salvadorans, boat people, migrants, wretched, forlorn, homeless. Roving gangs, grid-lock, desperation. The seemingly random murder and mutilation and ca-tastrophe throughout the world, that never stopped, but only moved around. He remembered his wingman pickling a Mark-77 napalm bomb, five hundred pounds, into a trench, and the liquid fire running its course, around corners and everything, like water in a ditch. It was the Phleg-ethon of Hades, guarded by a three-headed dog that permitted all spirits to enter, but none to return. The time he punched Slocum out to save his fucking life again, and got his own ass chewed for it; when he stayed on the target too long, because they needed him there, and then ran out of fuel; flying hops and popping Zunis. He mused on the annihilation, by the Vietnamese, of millions of Laotians and Cambodians. And Afghani-stan. And Central America was just getting started.

And he thought about all the girls, the false promises. There was the pleasure principle, the booze, the endless good time, and the refusal to acknowledge responsibility. And where did it all lead? Back to the moun-tains? He threw another log on the fire and pondered these and other things. There was nostalgia and a peacefulness about the smell of smoke and pine tar and the crackling as the flames licked and flickered in the old stone fireplace. He squirmed and stretched in the warmth, stared at the fire, heard the hiss and pop of the pitch, and listened intently to the stillness that surrounded him. Yes, he was sober for a while, and it was a time of returning.

1

California, mid-1960s

Mrs. Master Gunnery Sergeant O'Flynn stepped her largish pump down on the accelerator of the '59 Plymouth wagon. She had a heavy foot. Attached to a stout leg, the folds of which caressed the top of the pump. It was the day that a limited number of Hummel figurines would go on sale at the Marine Corps Exchange, and Mrs. Master Gunnery Sergeant O'Flynn meant to be the first in line.

As the Plymouth accelerated, so did the F-8U Crusader piloted by the unsure hand of Lieutenant R. R. Jones, who had just tapped the afterburner as he crossed the beach. R. R. stood for Roy Rogers. Roy Rogers Jones. Everybody called him R-square. One supple mind had altered that to pi, as in πR^2, but mostly he was R^2. Lieutenent R^2 was currently the laughingstock of the squadron because the week before he had gotten a little slow on the tanker while attempting to plug in for air-to-air refueling. A little slow. He stalled the F-8, put it in a spin, and only just managed to straighten things out as the Little San Bernardino Mountains came barreling up at an alarming rate. The rest of the four-plane division he was flying with nearly crashed because they were laughing so hard at the R^2 display of precision airmanship. Even the KC-130 tanker was seen to yaw around a little, as if the pilots weren't paying complete attention to business. Several pungent remarks came over the radio, but when they got back to the ready room, the comedians really hit their stride. As the CO remarked aside to the operations officer, the old maxim that every Marine was basically a rifleman was nowhere better demonstrated than in the case of Lieutenant Jones. He might have made a hell of a tank driver, too.

So R^2 was the laughingstock of the squadron. But then, he was per-petually the goat. It had partly to do with hand-eye coordination. Gold-

finger, the flight surgeon, said there was nothing wrong with his hands
or his eyes, but somewhere in the ganglia and telencephalic tissues that
connected those things, there seemed to be a bottleneck. The Doc figured
it might be an underdeveloped *pons Varolii*, but he wasn't sure. He was
going to be a gynecologist when he got out and that's what he read about,
mostly. Pussy.

Anyway, R² wasn't too swift, but by God he was going to show them
today. He was going to come into the break so hot that every fighter
pilot on the base would be impressed. R² flipped a switch to open the oil
cooler door, making the F-8 scream even louder.

Colonel Creed was in General Jefferson's office getting his ass chewed
because some of the pilots in his group had been flat-hatting around the
countryside and there had been a noticeable rise in the daily complaint
calls from the retirement community over the hill. Old people and low-
flying jets did not mix very well, but the developers only sold the con-
dominiums on Saturday and Sunday, when nobody was flying except an
occasional cross-country, so they didn't care. Business was brisk. But
when flight operations started up during the week, complaint calls got
pretty brisk, too. One old gentleman wrote to the Commandant of the
Marine Corps making references to the possibility of a class-action law-
suit. The Commandant did not like the idea, so he spoke to some other
generals, who spoke to some other generals, who spoke to General Jefferson. And he was about to speak to Colonel Creed. Oh, *was* he about
to speak to him.

Colonel Creed did not like General Jefferson because he had once been
senior to him, but Colonel Creed was passed over for the coveted star
and Jefferson got it. Now he worked for Jefferson. That was one reason
he didn't like him. There were several others.

General Jefferson did not like Colonel Creed because he considered
him a second-rate officer and Creed's wife's family had more money than
Jefferson's wife's family did. Creed wasn't too respectful either, sometimes, frequently even, forgetting to address him as "General."

Before the bloodletting, General Jefferson offered Creed the custom-
ary cup of coffee. Kind of a last request. Creed didn't smoke.

Lieutenant R² Jones called Point Alpha for landing, still in burner,
the airspeed building right along. He was descending to pattern altitude,
with a light load of fuel. R² had forgotten about the afterburner and
hadn't noticed the airspeed for a minute because he was concentrating
on his steeliest, suavest, debonairest radio voice as he chatted with the
tower. And he wanted to come in hot anyway.

"Tower, Whiskey, Whiskey one zero, Point Alpha, one for landing."

"Roger, one zero, call the numbers."

The cherubic little Hummels with their baskets and umbrellas and geese and things were displayed on a series of glass shelves. The exchange system was able to import only a limited number of these bric-a-brac items at German wholesale prices, and the sale of the available figurines was rotated from base to base each week. Mrs. Master Gunnery Sergeant O'Flynn never missed one. Neither did fifty or so other avid collectors. The scene was grim, but O'Flynn was at the front of the line and, miraculous delivery, one of the figurines that she most fervently sought was right there at the front of the shelf.

As Mrs. Master Gunnery Sergeant O'Flynn approached the Hummel display, Colonel Creed picked up the Pyrex coffeepot that General Jefferson always kept within arm's reach. That scene was already a little grim, too. Creed knew he was going to get another ass-chewing, and he wanted to suffer through the embarrassment and frustration and injustice of those troubled waters as rapidly as possible, so that he could pass it on to Lieutenant Colonel Al "Shaky" Morgenkrank, the squadron CO of the offending jet drivers, who would pass it on to Major Poltroun, the executive officer, and so on.

Creed leaned across the general's lap to refill his cup. It was done with the adroitness of a steward at the officers mess. Career military men develop an enviable skill with the coffeepot. "May I warm your coffee, sir?" he asked a little weakly.

But Colonel Creed was cut off in his subservient gesture and only just missed scalding the general's well-manicured hand as he placed it over his coffee cup and stared moodily at the wall. This was to be a goddamn ass-chewing and he didn't want any goddamn tea-party atmosphere filching his thunder.

Even the poise of that venerable pot-handler Charleston Clifford Creed was strained in this situation. He hovered awkwardly over the khaki-clad lap of his superior officer with the steaming pot's motion arrested in midpour, feeling a little stupid, or as Private Parton, one of his clerks, would have said, "like whale shit, man."

Master Gunnery Sergeant O'Flynn sat, as was his habit, in the line shack with a cup of coffee and a copy of *Naval Aviation News*. He tilted his chair back precariously, spit-shined boondockers planted in the middle of the gray metal desk. He was savoring the letters in Grampaw Pettibone's column, which described various crashes and maintenance fuckups. In twenty-six years of aircraft maintenance he had never tired of reading Grampaw Pettibone. O'Flynn loved the crashes and maintenance fuck-ups of other squadrons, particularly Navy ones. He did not even consider the Air Force, dismissing them as being so wholly incompetent as to be unfair game.

But crashes in his own squadron he did not condone. Well, crashes maybe, so long as they were caused 100 percent by pilot error. But Master Gunnery Sergeant O'Flynn, the maintenance chief, did not have maintenance fuck-ups in his squadron. They were not tolerated.

Lance Corporal DeVille Hoggins had just opened a five-gallon can of Lubriplate grease. He was going to lubricate some objects, which had originally been designed as moving parts, on number 12, the old hangar queen. These parts seldom moved, however, because number 12 was never flown, except for test hops, after which it was always downed and sent back to the hangar for more surgery. Hoggins set the bucket of grease down behind the Top Sergeant. O'Flynn clamped his Marine Corps–issue teeth down on an unlit cigar and teetered on the legs of his chair. He was reading Grampaw Pettibone's reply to an anonymous letter describing how a pilot coming into the break at five hundred knots had narrowly missed having a midair collision with a transport that was in the pattern.

"Land a goshen," wrote Grampaw. "Only a dadburned idiot would fly into the break at five hundred knots."

R^2, doing something over eight hundred at the moment, had acknowledged that he would notify the control tower when he was over the identifying numbers painted on the end of the runway, whereupon the tower would clear him to "break." That meant he would turn smartly to the left, fly around in a racetrack pattern, slowing and transitioning to the landing configuration, and land near the same numbers that he had just passed. In R^2's case that would be a rather large pattern, in that he had around Mach 1 of extra airspeed to bleed off.

R^2 hit the break at Mach 1.2, 20 percent faster than the speed of sound. At low altitudes and high speeds the F-8 makes a lot of noise. Especially with the oil cooler door open. The severity of the shock waves of a sonic boom being relative to the altitude at which it is initiated, R^2, supersonic at around a thousand feet, would make more than noise. He would make waves. Make a lot of waves and not only shock waves.

Jack Rawlins had already had *his* ass-chewing for that day, administered by Lieutenant Colonel Al "Shaky" Morgenkrank because Rawlins had saved Slocum's life twice the day before. The first time was in the air, on the last hop of the day, with Slocum leading and Smilin' Jack flying wing. They had been out over the ocean intercepting each other for an hour or so, then turned in and commenced a twisting, shuddering air-to-air hassle, bending their airplanes around in all kinds of crazy gyrations as they vied for a firing position somewhere around the other one's six o'clock. Rawlins began to get the better of it, and Slocum tried a high-g barrel roll as an evasive maneuver. Rawlins, with extra airspeed, yo-yoed high, reversed, and moved in for the kill.

He keyed the mike. "Bang, bang, you're dead, Dash one."

They broke it off and, being low on fuel, joined up and headed for the barn. They dropped down to a couple hundred feet and smoked toward home, scoping out the pleasure boats bobbing on the blue Pacific. Rawlins, the wingman, looked always at his leader, maintaining position, so he never really saw the helicopter; saw only a blur out of the corner of his eye. It was Slocum's responsibility to watch where they were going—the trouble was that he didn't see the helicopter either. He had squandered a mite too much scrutiny on the female crewmembers of a motor sailer that was just below them, and somehow, in the light haze, that chopper just sneaked right up on him.

When Rawlins saw the blur, he reacted instinctively, jamming the nose over violently and yelling at Slocum. "Dash one, break left, break left! Traffic at twelve!"

Actually there were two helicopters; Slocum went right between them, observing for a split second the plan view of one that seemed only inches away. Rawlins sailed under the whole mess, but only by pulling two or three negative gs, causing all the maps and charts and approach plates and other residue to float up against the canopy, adding to the confusion. Slocum, on the other hand, hurtling through the fray, felt that he couldn't have come any closer to that chopper if he'd been riding in the goddamn thing. He just plain, flat scared the shit out of himself.

When they had got their frazzled nerves in hand and wobbled back to the base, Slocum was still shaking. But for Rawlins's warning, Slocum would be wearing a helicopter suit. It had been a closer look at death than he really cared for; the only thing for it was to hit the club and start forgetting.

They did that, and old Slocum was hell-bent on this forgetting business. He went for it whole-hog, and by the middle of the evening he had managed to forget all but the most rudimentary aspects of how even to walk.

There was, in the officers clubs of that day, a nonsensical ditty that was often to be heard. Upon learning of Slocum's near miss and observing the zeal with which he undertook therapeutic measures clubside, the boys at the bar sang it:

Old Joe Slocum used to own a grocery store,
He used to hang his meat upon the outside of the door.
All the little children used to run and shout,
"Old Joe Slocum, your pork is hanging out."

Shortly after the song, Slocum drained his drink, dropped the glass on the floor, stood abruptly, swayed, nearly fell, described a 360-degree turn while pursuing equilibrium, caught it for the moment, slapped his piss-cutter crookedly on his head, said "Good night, ladies and gentlemen," and staggered out of the club, colliding with the doorjamb on the way. Rawlins followed him out, figuring he was in as much danger now as he had been flying through the thicket of helicopters.

"Hey, Sloc," he said very carefully. "Let me run you home. Might get a ticket or something, you know."

"No, no. 'S awright, Jack. You save m' life t'day, buddy. Don't have t' take me home. I'm okay."

"Well, you know those fucking cops and all. Why don't you ride with me? I'll pick you up in the morning."

"I can drive anything I c'n start." Slocum then dropped his keys and spent a few minutes crawling around in the dark finding them. He struggled back to his feet, teetering and swaying, and Rawlins knew there was no talking him out of this.

He took a deep breath, said "Sorry, old pal," and hit Slocum on the jaw as hard as he could. Slocum jerked precipitously to the left, overcorrected back and sat down awkwardly. He snorted, rolled his head, and then lay back supine.

Rawlins said, "Man, I didn't save your young ass up in the big blue sky today just so you could go out and waste it on the fucking highway." He grabbed Slocum by the ankles, dragged him around to the passenger side and, with some difficulty, loaded the dead weight into his car and headed off the base. There was only one sinister development: Major Poltroun had observed the brief fisticuffs. He made a mental note. Officers fighting at the club would not be tolerated.

Rawlins knew the general neighborhood where Slocum lived, but he didn't know the address. He had only been there once, at a drunken party, and didn't remember what the apartment looked like. Slocum was by now soundly passed out, dead to the world. He kept falling over on

Rawlins, who finally had to prop him up against the window with one hand and drive with the other.

When they got close to where Rawlins thought they were going he stopped and shook Slocum. "Hey, where do you live, man? What's the address?" Nothing.

Rawlins slapped him a couple of times. "Come on, Sloc, what's your address?"

Finally Slocum mumbled, "Ten sixy sis Elum Street." Then he lapsed into a deeper coma and would not be roused further until he'd had his sleep.

Rawlins drove around and around looking for Elm Street, but it was not to be found. Finally he drove to his own apartment, walked around the car, and opened the door. Slocum came tumbling out. Rawlins grabbed the ankles again, dragged the corpse in the front door, threw a blanket over it, and went to bed.

In the morning, after the repentant Slocum had been provided with aspirin and coffee, Rawlins said "Where the hell is ten sixty-six Elm Street?"

Slocum thought a minute, then brightened and said, "That's where I used to live in St. Louis."

When they got to work that morning, Rawlins was told to report to Major Poltroun, who made some predictions about the dire consequences of his ungentlemanly conduct, and ushered him into the skipper's office.

"We can't have this shit, Rawlins," said Al "Shaky" Morgenkrank. "Fighting at the O club is tantamount to conduct unbecoming an officer and a gentleman. You know that."

"Yes sir, I know that."

"And it won't be tolerated. You know that, too."

"Yes sir. I know that, too."

"All right. I'm going to fine you a hundred dollars for this incident. Is that clear?"

"Yes sir. Very clear."

"And don't let it happen again. Understood?"

"Yes sir. It won't happen again."

"And stay out of the club for a week, understood?"

"Understood, sir."

"All right, that's all. You're dismissed."

"Aye, aye, sir."

So Rawlins had already had his ass-chewing for saving Slocum's life, but Colonel Creed was still awaiting his. And R² Jones was at that moment absolutely *screaming* into the break, surrounded by shock waves and sonic booms and producing a screech and roar beside which the very hounds of hell would pale.

Mrs. Master Gunnery Sergeant O'Flynn bustled toward the glass shelves and reached out a quivering, liver-spotted hand toward the delicate porcelain doodad of her choice.

Across the dual runways, on the other side of the field, her husband sat in his line shack, balancing on two legs of a chair above five gallons of Lubriplate. He chewed his cigar and scratched the close-shaven stubble on the back of his thick red neck. It was haircut day.

General Jefferson congratulated himself on the strategic move of placing his hand over his coffee cup. Creed stood there looking stupid. The general had established full control of the interview. The ass-chewing would commence. And still the idiot stood there holding the fucking coffeepot and looking pained. General Jefferson savored the moment.

R^2 Jones called the numbers, which he noticed had come up rather suddenly. Everyone, it appeared, was in for something of a surprise.

2

Southeast Asia, 1960s

The four Phantoms screamed off the end of the runway in Da Nang, South Vietnam, and began a gentle turn as they joined up. Well, three of them did. The last one staggered off like a pelican with an albacore in the bomb bay. Major Poltroun was leading, with Cavendish on his wing, Moon Dog was the section leader, and Smilin' Jack was tail-end Charlie. Rawlins was flying double zero, old double nuts, which had just come out of check. They were so short of aircraft that he was supposed to do a modified test hop on the way to the target and, if everything seemed OK, then he would go ahead and bomb the heathens. The airplane seemed all right now that he had airspeed and was cleaned up, but it had been a little dicey getting it off the deck. He was pretty heavy, with a dozen five-hundred-pounders and full fuel, and on the takeoff roll his burners didn't light. Gripe number one on the test checklist, but he didn't have time to write it down right then. He cycled the burners a couple of times, but no joy. No big problem, there was lots of runway, so Rawlins pressed on. It took a while to get flying speed, and maybe a fresh set of skivvies for Warrant Officer C. Ross Culpepper, the radar intercept officer in the back seat, but they finally mushed off. The nose was awfully heavy but Rawlins kept trimming and watching the airspeed, still groundspeed really, and the runway markers.

"What the fuck's wrong with this fucker?" piped Culpepper. He spoke with a nasal twang, highly agitated at the moment. He had some pretty colorful expressions from his Oklahoma boyhood. "Come on, Jack, let's fuckin' abort this motherfu—"

Rawlins reached down and switched to cold mike. He had already rotated. Nobody likes a two-man airplane after he has flown single-seat.

Smilin' Jack stayed under fifty feet and let the airspeed build. The

F-4 was a big, heavy hog, but if there was anything it had it was power, and the elephant grass became a blur at that altitude as they picked up speed. C. Ross Culpepper's asshole was clamped shut tighter than a bank vault with a forty-eight-hour time lock. They were doing three hundred knots about forty feet off the ground when Rawlins started his climb.

The Daily VC Harassment Detail was kicked back behind an old paddy dike, invisible in the grass, just about where Jack Rawlins pulled the nose up smartly. A pair of J-79-GE-9 engines, even without afterburner, pump out 21,800 pounds of thrust at full power. And a lot of noise and heat. The Daily Harassment Detail—two dudes totaling ten feet eight inches and about 250 pounds, including a launching tube and three rockets—was knocked on its ass by Rawlins's jetwash. Also startled somewhat. It flattened the elephant grass, blew them up against the dike, singed their eyebrows, sent their conical hats rolling like grounded Frisbees, and scared the shit out of them. They hadn't seen or heard him coming. They babbled and spat and shook their fists. This was a shit detail to begin with, because you had to sneak up near the base before light, wait a while, shoot a rocket inside the perimeter, then haul ass in broad daylight, undetected, to a new spot, wait, shoot another one, and so on. They hated the noise of those goddamn airplanes and this was the closest they had ever been to one and the first time they had been scorched, and they were pissed. As soon as they had got their shit together they looped a rocket into the air base that scored a direct hit on the Marine Air Group-22 officers club, which was closed, so all it destroyed was a thatch-roofed hootch and five cases of Falstaff that had been flown in from Ubon, Thailand, in a center-line baggage tank that morning. The warhead detonated inside the beer cooler and, miraculously, not too much else was damaged.

Rawlins could see the rest of the flight, hardly more than specks now, owing to his lack of horsepower, but the more visible because, having come out of burner, each of them trailed a thin line of black smoke.

"Condone seven flight, is everybody aboard?" It was Major Poltroun, wheezing slightly in his oxygen mask.

"Two roger."

"Three roger."

Rawlins keyed the mike. "Four negative. My burners won't light. Stand by one."

"Condone seven flight, switch two six niner point seven." Poltroun again.

Rawlins saw in the remote channel indicator that the RIO had switched from the back seat. Well, Culpepper was alive and functioning.

"Condone seven flight, radio check." Poltroun.

"Two's up."

"Three's up."

Culpepper keyed the mike. "Four's up."

Poltroun keyed his mike. "Waterboy, Waterboy, Condone seven dash one, flight of four fox-fours checking in for your control. We have twelve delta-twos per aircraft, over."

Major Poltroun thought he was very professional. He had two Air Medals already. Of course he had not yet been shot down by Tran Van Ban. Rawlins thought he was a pain in the ass. Of course Rawlins had the leisure to think so, because double nuts was performing as advertised, except for the afterburners, which he wouldn't need since there weren't any MiGs where they were going. He didn't yet know about Gunnery Sergeant O'Flynn's maintenance fuck-up.

Well, actually Staff Sergeant Hebblethwaite's fuck-up, but Gunnery Sergeant O'Flynn had signed the aircraft off and was ultimately responsible, as maintenance chief. Anyway, neither of them knew about the fuck-up. Only the apocryphal Murphy knew as yet. But they would all find out. Even Grampaw Pettibone would find out. And God knew he would tell every living soul in Naval Aviation.

O'Flynn had been summarily demoted from master gunnery sergeant to gunnery sergeant even though everyone from Lieutenant Colonel Al "Shaky" Morgenkrank to General Jefferson had hated to do it. Even generals didn't fuck with master gunnery sergeants unless they had to. But it had to be done, because O'Flynn had inflicted seventeen small but potentially dangerous scalp wounds and a fracture or two upon the skull of Lance Corporal DeVille Hoggins with a one and seven-sixteenths-inch box-end wrench, and was increasing that number like a metronome gone berserk, until they pulled him off. That was after the episode of the five gallons of Lubriplate.

The brothers Fiske, of Newark and Toledo, good citizens, industrialists, and taxpayers, giving their all to the war effort, had certainly never intended their fine Lubriplate grease to be used as a tonsorial supplement, or in any other way to be applied to the head, but that surely happened, for, as was revealed in testimony at his own court-martial, Lance Corporal DeVille Hoggins had "with willful neglect and disregard" placed the bucket of grease behind O'Flynn's chair. Al "Shaky" Morgenkrank had Hoggins busted to PFC not so much because he put the bucket of grease down in "dangerous proximity," as the record said, to O'Flynn's teetering chair, as because he failed to move fast enough. Al "Shaky" Morgenkrank didn't give a shit about the grease, Hoggins, or even the phantasmic specter of an apoplectic, bellowing, red-skinned Irishman, whose shaven head was daubed, smeared, covered with thick, phlegm-colored petrochemicals, on top of, astride, a tall skinny black lance corporal, smiting him repeatedly on the head with a box-end wrench. It was only the resultant wounding that Al "Shaky" Morgenkrank cared about. And he only cared because one of the LAWS, an article of the Uniform Code of Military Justice, said that no noncommissioned officer shall strike, attack, or otherwise physically abuse a man of lesser rank.

There was another article that said you could also not beat up a man of higher rank. You could maim anybody of the same rank as yourself in a private dispute, but that wasn't written down. Woe, though, unto the master sergeant who fucked with a lance corporal, or vice versa. Skull fractures, even minor ones, lead to sick bay and then medical reports, inquiries, investigations, and the first thing you knew, you were forced to take disciplinary action. Al "Shaky" Morgenkrank thought of promoting Hoggins to master gunnery sergeant on the spot, thereby to avoid Official Interest, but that was no good. The article of UCMJ that was not written, *it was well established by legal precedent*, the article that, had it been written, would have condoned at least limited violence between people of similar rank, *clearly stated by omission* that the combatants had to be of equal rank *at the time* that the nonviolation was not committed. So promotion for Hoggins was out.

Demotion, it looked like, was in for O'Flynn. Nobody wanted to bust a master sergeant, especially a maintenance chief, because it might piss him off, *would* piss him off, and then aircraft maintenance might suffer. He might be pissed off enough to slacken somewhat in his duties. If you got less pay and privileges, you should be expected to do less work, right? Maybe the maintenance chief would only work his troops eighteen hours a day. He might quit hoarding the parts that they desperately needed, that the three-M supply system said they could not hoard, but that it could not provide when they were required. A pissed-off maintenance chief was a liability. He might even refuse to cannibalize all the airplanes that were in the hangar for check to get enough black boxes and servos and gyros to keep the other airplanes, which were not in check, flying. And maintenance was the key. The airplanes had to *fly* in order to drop the tons of bombs and pile up the tons of bodies and log the thousands of hours that made up the records of majors and colonels and generals, and that made majors into colonels, colonels into generals, and so on.

And aircraft maintenance was the thorniest pustule in the side of Marine aviation. The goddamn planes were always down, and how could you fly a record number of sorties in a given time or deliver more ordnance than another other outfit if your fucking airplanes wouldn't get off the ground?

So nobody wanted to bust O'Flynn, but then there was the LAW and that was paramount. A master gunnery sergeant had attacked a lance corporal, inflicting bodily harm, and something had to be done about it.

So they busted O'Flynn back to gunny, although Al "Shaky" Morgenkrank called O'Flynn into his office and assured him that he would be reinstated as soon as militarily feasible.

But Lieutenant Colonel Morgenkrank was *goddamn* sure that none of it would have happened if Hoggins had moved fast enough. If, when the Big Boom of R² Jones, which turned O'Flynn literally and the rest of the base figuratively upside down, hit, if that shitbird had got his young ass, or in this case, young skull, the hell *out* of there quicker, there would have been no mishap. So Morgenkrank ordered a court-martial for Hoggins and busted him to PFC.

It was argued by counsel that it was the teetering chair that was the proximate cause of the incident, not the placement of the grease. The prosecutor deftly established, however, that O'Flynn had teetered in similar chairs in similar line shacks, with his feet on similar desks for more than twenty years without misadventure.

On the first charge, that Hoggins had "recklessly endangered" another Marine, defense counsel Second Lieutenant DeWayne Ludlow, who had two years of college, argued brilliantly that Lubriplate grease, in and of itself, although messy and perhaps degrading, was not inherently dangerous, and the court found Hoggins not guilty.

The second charge, however, that Hoggins had been negligent in the performance of his duties, was tougher. Hoggins was always pretty negligent. They got him on that one and Lance Corporal Hoggins became Private First Class Hoggins again.

But Lieutenant Colonel Morgenkrank, Colonel Creed, and General Jefferson were all a little sad that they had had to bust a man who everyone agreed was the finest maintenance chief in the Marine Corps.

Well, almost everyone agreed. Rawlins might have argued the point when he discovered that O'Flynn had signed off double nuts for a test hop without noticing that Staff Sergeant Hebblethwaite had installed the trim actuator yoke upside down, so that everything was cool until you lowered the gear and flaps and then instead of an automatic ten units of nose-up trim, you got ten units of nose-down. That cost the taxpayers two million dollars and very nearly cost Rawlins his life, which he valued even higher. In truth, though, it wasn't entirely O'Flynn's fault. He didn't know, Staff Sergeant Hebblethwaite didn't know, *nobody* knew the yoke would fit upside down. That was Murphy's LAW, though. If it would fit in there upside down, someone would install it that way.

But Rawlins didn't know about the trim actuator yoke yet and he was sailing along on God's own mission, which at the moment was trying to catch up to the rest of his flight. And finally he did, charging up to the formation with about fifty knots closing speed. He pulled up sharply off to the side and popped the speed brakes, doing a modified whifferdill to bleed off more airspeed, and settled in forty or fifty yards off Moon Dog's wing.

Moon Dog's head was moving back and forth in jagged, arrhythmic motions, which meant he was singing one of his country and western hits to himself. Hang Dog was in the back seat eating a sandwich. Moon Dog wouldn't fly with anybody except Hang Dog. He didn't like most of the RIOs, or pretended not to, but Hang Dog was his buddy and they went everywhere together, in the airplane or out of it. Moon Dog was a cowboy from Wyoming, short and designed along the lines of a concrete block. His other name was "Built by Republic" because that's what the Air Force pilots had inscribed on the massive brick-and-concrete barbeque outside the DOOM club in Da Nang, and Moon Dog looked like the same engineers had designed him. The inscription was on the barbeque because the Air Force was flying F-105s and they were built by Republic and reputed to handle much like a ballistic safe when airborne. At least after a loss of power. The nickname for the 105 was the Thud, which Moon Dog's asshole buddies in the Air Force called him. Thud.

The reason you had to have some asshole buddies in the Air Force was because they had the Da Nang Officers Open Mess—DOOM club— and Marines were not allowed to go there except expressly as guests of Air Force officers, so you'd better know somebody's name in case Major Poltroun jumped out of the bushes and caught you frying a steak on old "Built by Republic." And they *had* steaks. It was the only game in town, twice over. They even had a package store where for a dollar or two you could score a bottle of Bushmills to lull you to sleep or improve your singing voice.

And Poltroun *did* lurk in the bushes, just beyond the glow of the firelight, and watch for Marines with a piece of meat on a paper plate, sidling up next to old "Built by . . ." He would slide out of the brush with a deadly smile and a gait somewhere between a lynx and a snake and say, "Lieutenant/Captain, I'd like to know who your sponsor is. Whose guest are you?"

Eight times out of thirteen there would be an Air Force pogue standing there with a long-handled fork who would smile and say, "Why, he's my guest, Major. J. D. Heggenberger here. Yes sir, we're sure right glad to have you folks drop over when you can. Have you had your supper, Major?"

Whereupon Poltroun would stalk back into the bushes as if he were walking on punji stakes.

And the lieutenant/captain would buy his counterpart a drink and remark to himself that there was some justice left. But sometimes there was no Air Force pogue standing there and then you had to say, "Oh, good evening, Major. Yes, I'm the guest of Captain/Lieutenant Hank Doggett, an old friend from back home." (That phrase always helped because "back home" was second, third, or fourth only unto God, mother, Demolay, and etc.) "He just got a call from his outfit, but he'll be back shortly." Then you threw your New York cut casually onto the blackened grill, made by a subcontractor for Republic, no doubt, and Poltroun did his walk on eggs back into the cover of darkness.

There are those who would jump to conclusions and say, "What a bummer. Why wouldn't the punkish-assed Air Force let the Marines come to their club?" right? Wrong. Dead wrong. The Air Force welcomed their bedraggled hobo counterparts from across the field with open arms. Come and enjoy the facilities, the Air Force said. We're all in this good-deal war together, we'll share. No, it was the *Marines* that wouldn't let the Marines go to the Air Force club. See, the main higher-command-type general didn't want the Marine pilots, who lived on an Air Force base, with the Air Force, to live *like* the Air Force did. He reasoned that that might be seen as coddling his men. This general was, of course, a grunt and had no use for the air wing anyway, and as long as there were grunts living in foxholes sharing their blood and body heat with an infinite population of leeches and getting their ass shot off in the daily ambush or booby trap, no air-wing pogue was going to have it easy.

So the hoboes were not allowed to go to the DOOM club except as guests. They would not be spoiled or allowed to get soft by having good food and a drink with ice in it and other epicurean shit like that. So after the fourth straight day of "red death" (an institutional food having a consistency somewhere between corned beef and Spam, packed in barrels of ketchup) breakfast, lunch, and dinner, the troops boycotted the mess hall. They said fuck it, they'd rather eat C rations because at least Cs had some variety.

And all the world's greatest fighter pilots started making heavy overtures to their inferior counterparts over on the Air Force side of the base. Of course the Air Force couldn't fly, but they did know how to run an officers club, and all those perfect Marines, who subsisted largely on false pride, were able to humble themselves and get downright friendly with an Air Force pogue if it led to sinking their canine teeth into a piece of grade-A beef.

Being a poor relation to the Navy and depending upon them for everything, the Marine Corps always got by with less than they really needed. The Cong had blown up the docks at Da Nang and sunk a few junks in the channel, so even though the Navy had supplies floating around the South China Sea, they couldn't unload them. Some congressman had got word that the Marines were short of bombs and raised a stink in Washington. It was true. "Not true!" said the Navy. "We have, at this moment, umpteen thousand tons of ordnance in the area. There is no shortage." In the area. Except all that stuff was piled on the docks in the Philippines with no way to transport it to the hoboes, because they couldn't get their ships into the harbor.

So they were running out of parts and food and now bombs. Not exactly carte blanche for the war effort. But, like everything else, it would get a lot worse before it got better. They would soon be launching four airplanes, each fairly bristling with two measly 250-pound bombs, when one plane could have carried all that ordnance plus double the amount and saved gas. They would fly this quadruple effort, of course, to amass the flight time that would get Al "Shaky" Morgenkrank an outstanding fitness report from Colonel Creed because Creed wanted his group to fly more sorties and more hours than anyone else did, even though they didn't have anything to deliver.

But things weren't that bad yet, so on this Blue Blazer mission they each had twelve bombs, five-hundred-pounders. Hang Dog had finished his sandwich. Hang Dog was an acne- and fist-scarred Irishman from New York, who was two-and-a-half-feet taller than Moon Dog and didn't weigh anything. He was always making up jokes and songs and skits, and was at this moment creating a lyric to be sung to the tune of "Brazil." He sang it into his oxygen mask a couple of times and then pushed the mike switch to OVERRIDE and interrupted Moon Dog's wailing.

"Dog. Go hot mike, I got a new song for you."

"Ah, roger, Dog. I'm just all ears waiting for that little ditty."

Hang Dog cleared his throat and crooned: "Da Nang, Da Nang. There is no poontang in Da Nang. . . ."

It was true, too, at least in a sense. Oh, there was poontang all over Da Nang, place was crawling with it. Only the Marines were not allowed off the base. The Army, Navy, and Air Force could go to town, even *live* in town, but thanks again to that fair-minded grunt general, the Marines could not, and that's where the poontang was. The Air Force even had their own whorehouse on their side of the base, only it was patrolled by APs and it was off-limits to anyone in uniform. The Marines were forbidden to wear, even to *have* civilian clothes, so that was the name of that game.

General Jefferson had been terrified of syphilis ever since he had seen the VD films in boot camp, so he felt the only humane thing to do for his Marine Air Wing was to keep it from any contact with women, whatsoever, and that is what he did. As for the other services, let them die imbeciles' deaths with huge gangrenous lesions, brimming with spirochetes, all over their you-know-whats. Not the Marines. In the matter of the Air Force whorehouse, the brass was just as happy not to have Marines rutting with their ladies. They were nice clean girls, inspected by the flight surgeon every week, and who knew what bacterial oddities those grubby animals from the hobo camp on the wrong side of the runway might introduce? Sharing their steaks was one thing but pussy was another matter.

So General Jefferson was convinced that his was a healthy, moral contingent and he said so at Sunday morning services whenever the Sky Pilot asked him to give a guest sermon. He and Colonel Creed only fucked Red Cross girls, and only white ones at that. Of course one of them did give Colonel Creed the clap, but for various reasons he never got around to mentioning that to General Jefferson. In fact he secretly hoped that the general might take a shine to that very girl.

Besides all that, General Jefferson had unimpeachable intelligence, garnered from a vast, billion-dollar network of spooks, spies, agents, and other flakes, that the Communists were methodically infecting their most attractive (although how a gook could be considered attractive was beyond the general) women with viruses and gonococci and such, and posting them to Da Nang in a very fifth column of physical and spiritual decay to undermine the Armies of Freedom. So he knew he had done the right thing.

Of course there was the old aircraft-washing boondoggle, where you got to fly a bird over to Clark AFB in the Philippines and get it washed.

The hoboes couldn't believe they were still getting away with that one. Moon and Hang were due to go next. Woooo doggie! Not only was the town full of whores, the base was full of stews. Nice jiggly light-complexioned round-eyed American stewardi. Hang Dog was ready and then some. He didn't know yet that aircraft availability had fallen off for the month, so Al "Shaky" Morgenkrank had restricted all aircraft to combat flights only in order to keep his combat sorties up and keep the checks on that fitness report in the right column.

Waterboy handed them off to Flashpan Alpha, an airborne forward air controller, so they switched and called up the FAC.

"Flashpan, Flashpan, this is Condone seven dash one, flight of four fox-fours for your control, over."

"Roger, Condone, Flashpan Alpha. I'm presently two two zero at thirty-five, channel forty-four, over."

"Ah, roger Flashpan, we'll be there in about two minutes at seven thou. Flight go trail." They dropped back into a twisting line a few hundred yards apart, gaining airspeed as they descended to seven thousand feet. Rawlins watched the three airplanes in front of him, each with its telltale smoke trail, bouncing along through the cuttingly clear blue sky with occasional fluffy white clouds. The scene was always so peaceful as they went to war. The jungle was bright and verdant, the color of an emerald. This was lush country where the C-123s had not defoliated it and the B-52s Arc-Lighted it to rubble and everybody else burned and scarred it, and so on.

"Condone seven, Flashpan Alpha. I'm on the two one five at thirty-seven, just south of a sharp bend in the river."

"Tallyho, Flashpan. We're descending at your seven o'clock." Everybody knew that Goldberg, Poltroun's RIO, had spotted the FAC. Poltroun was lucky to make out the visor on his hard hat on a clear day. Goldberg had been washed out of pilot training because of eye trouble, but he could see better than any pilot in the squadron.

"Condone, do you have the stone building with the red roof in the village across the river?"

"Affirm, Flashpan."

"Well, I'm taking a lot of small arms fire out of that ville. Let's start at the red roof and work your way through. Run in to the southwest across the river."

"Roger, Flashpan." They flew around in a semicircular pattern, taking interval, and Rawlins checked his bombsight setting at 105 mils. He reached down to the dogbone, or multiple weapons control panel, selected

SINGLE BOMBS, ARM NOSE AND TAIL, and moved the master armament switch to ARM. He cycled the stick quickly left and right, like a wrestler shaking his arms and shoulders before he engages. "One's in hot."

"Two's in."

"One's off."

"Three's in."

"Good hit, One. Flight go ahead and drop your first one in the same place." Hot doggie, they had a real target today! Usually it was just a suspicious stand of trees or a dirt road or some ominous shit like that. But a real building with a tile roof, hey, that was something. Even fucking blind Poltroun had hit it.

"Four's in." In a thirty-degree dive with airspeed building, Rawlins tracked the pipper up to the rubble that still had pieces of red roof visible. As Culpepper reported three thousand feet, five hundred knots, he pickled a Mark-82 and felt the thump as the bomb kicked off the airplane. "Four's off." Rawlins hauled back on the stick to grab some altitude, g-forces pressing him down into the seat.

"That ought to be a bull's-eye, right there," he said, pleased with the run.

"Well, get some, Doggie! Kill some fucking Cong!" was Culpepper's excited reply.

"One's in."

Rawlins zoom-climbed back to pattern altitude and followed Moon Dog around the imaginary racetrack. Then he saw that super-dumb-shit Cavendish, self-proclaimed future Commandant of the Marine Corps and generally ham-fisted plumber when it came to aviating, had leveled off a thousand or so feet below pattern altitude and started his run from there. That made for a long, low, shallow run, which totally screwed up the pattern for everybody else and put Cavendish well within the envelope to pick up fragments from his own bomb. And the rest of the flight, flailing around the sky, trying to maintain interval, because Cavendish was taking forever to get off the target, sincerely hoped that Cavendish *would* pick up a frag. And he did. It knocked a hole in his right aileron you could stick your arm through, but didn't hit anything critical. So though he felt the airplane bounce in the concussion of the bomb, he didn't even know about the frag until the ground crew found the hole while post-flighting the aircraft. And then, because Captain Cavendish was asshole buddies with all the majors and colonels, they said it was caused by hostile fire and put him in for another Air Medal instead of pulling his wings like everybody knew he deserved.

Well, it just wasn't Cavendish's day, but then neither was it going to be Major Poltroun's or Rawlins's. After pelting that village with enough bombs to level a small city and getting a Bomb Damage Assessment of five structures destroyed (one a Catholic church, but they didn't mention that) and twenty suspected killed-by-air, the boys were on their merry way back to Da Nang. This was a little more respectable than their usual BDA of "suspected enemy position destroyed," or "road cratered." As they crossed a river south of the field, they all started looking for Major Poltroun's hostile fire. If you observed hostile fire on any hop, it counted two points toward your next Air Medal instead of just one.

Major Poltroun observed enemy fire on every hop he ever flew, including test hops and ferry hops. The amazing thing was that other members of the flight would see it too. If you flew with Poltroun, you could expect to get shot at. It was as if some phenomenal VC were conducting a personal vendetta against the man. Of course it didn't really matter because the Cong almost never hit anybody and even when they did, the small arms fire was so spent by the time it got up there it usually just dented the skin or left small holes and didn't really hurt anything. Helicopters were a different story. They moved slowly at low altitudes and made a nice fat target. They were always getting the shit shot out of them, but the jet drivers didn't even worry about small arms.

Sure enough, Poltroun's sniper opened up. He spotted some tracers coming from a tree line and warned the flight. Ho hum. Only this time, incredibly enough, the line of tracers jerked over very close to Poltroun's airplane. This happened, though none of them knew it, because Tran Van Ban, the man firing the tracers, had tripped over a branch and sat down with his weapon on full automatic. Ping! One of the bullets entered the left engine of Poltroun's airplane and shattered a turbine blade. The pieces of that one began shattering more blades and very shortly that engine was spitting out a barrage of red hot hunks of titanium in all directions, and little explosions began to occur with worrisome frequency. And they grew louder and shook the airplane. Poltroun pointed the nose out to sea and told Goldberg to stand by to eject.

"Mayday, Mayday, Mayday," Poltroun came up on guard channel. "Condone seven dash one, ten miles south of Da Nang. I've been hit by enemy fire, have fire warning lights on both engines and am experiencing explosions and control problems."

His instrument panel was lit up and blinking like a pinball machine run amok. He was having all those control problems because he had lost power and was about to stall out, but he didn't realize that.

Poltroun was a nervous man, fearful that nature and everybody else were out to get him. While his life was not at that moment actually flashing before his eyes, still he was alert to a certain insecurity inherent in his present situation. "Omigod," he said to himself with sinking heart. "What is happening here? What have I got myself into. OH—MY—GOD."

Then came a kind of roar and the airplane shuddered and Poltroun had had enough. He jerked down on the face curtain and shot out of there, strapped to his Martin-Baker seat, without saying shit to Goldberg in the back seat. Goldberg, however, had an agile mind, and his next decision, after seeing the pilot go, through a billow of smoke and fire, did not require a lot of time. Goldberg was right behind. Later Major Poltroun would claim that the fire must have knocked out the intercom because *of course* he instructed the RIO to eject first. They had the old Martin-Baker seats with a shotgun shell for propellant. Otherwise Goldberg might have been cooked by rocket blast.

The rest of the flight was following at what they considered a safe distance when they saw more smoke, some external flame, and then two white chutes.

Moon Dog came up on guard: "Mayday, Mayday, Mayday. This is Condone seven dash three, ten miles south of Da Nang. Condone seven dash one has ejected. Two chutes observed. Request SAR, over."

"Condone seven dash three, Da Nang tower. Search and Rescue helicopter has launched and estimates your position in four to five minutes. Request you stand by and observe downed personnel, over."

"Seven dash three, roger." So they orbited around in a gaggle and watched the chutes descend.

"Hot damn," gloated C. Ross Culpepper, "I hope that motherfuckin' Poltroun lands his nigger ass in the biggest shit ditch in Southeast Asia. Hee hee. Whataya say, Jack? Face down for that dirty cocksucker, huh? In the slimiest shit ditch in this slimy fuckin' country. Hee hee hee."

"Shit," Rawlins chuckled. "Number fucking one. I can't think of a nicer guy to land in a shit ditch." Of course Rawlins didn't know, nor did Culpepper, how prophetic those words might be. That was because they didn't know about Gunnery Sergeant O'Flynn's maintenance fuck-up. But they would find out soon enough.

Poltroun's airplane was trimmed up pretty well and flew itself east, descending, then blew up and buried itself in the South China Sea.

When the helicopter had picked up Goldberg and Poltroun, and the major was not scared anymore, he realized that he was something of a goddamn *hero*. This would definitely be good for his career. Probably an

Air Medal, maybe a DFC. On the other hand, he was furious at being shot down, because he might have been hurt or captured, God forbid! Still, everything had worked out pretty well, considering. But then that was only the first time Major Poltroun got shot down.

As the SAR chopper started to leave, the rest of the flight lined up in parade formation and flew into the break.

Rawlins was hot mike and had been chatting with Culpepper during the excitement. "Nothing like a little diversion to keep you awake during this undeclared police action," Rawlins said as he banked sharply to the left and popped the speed brakes.

"I still wish the dirty motherfucker would of landed in a shit ditch," Culpepper said, genuinely disappointed. At that moment they were directly above the Da Nang River, which accepted the sewage of the entire city and the base too, and might have been described as the granddaddy of all shit ditches. Rawlins had just lowered the gear and now moved the flap handle to the down position. When the flaps came down, Murphy's LAW took its full effect. The old upside-down trim actuator yoke moved the wrong way and inexorably programmed in ten units of nose-down trim. The bottom fell out. The nose plummeted like Tommy John's best sinking fastball, down toward the river, and Rawlins couldn't hold it.

"Eject, eject, eject!" he screamed, sensed Culpepper and seat leaving, then yanked on the face curtain. He last saw the river looming, magnifying, guaranteeing instant death as he plummeted. Rawlins felt a terrific jolt.

3

California, 1960s

Things, it seemed, just happened to Rawlins, for the most part. He was not much at making them happen. Neither did he take great measures to avoid the occasional unpleasantry. He just drifted, mainly, figuring life would take care of itself, and he would live it as it came up and not waste a lot of energy worrying and planning. It was an intellectual laziness shared by many of his peers: Life, in its essence, was just flying as many hops as you could.

So it was some years after the war, and the war within a war, and even the war within a war within a war, that Rawlins began to suspect that any of it might have had an effect on him. At first it didn't seem to have any effect on anyone. All the old fighter pilots who were still around got together in the same bars and retold their war stories, swilling whiskey and talking with both hands. Most of them got airline jobs and stayed on at the beach. They regularly threw all-night drinking marathons, where often dozens of people would show up. They were quasi-heroes to the once or still hawkish girls, whom they most frequently met in their circle of ex-Marines, airline people, school teachers, and aging beach bums. But even with the new generation of chicks, decidedly antiwar, the pilots became acceptable. The participants in the national atrocity were generally considered to be only pawns of an evil government and were not held individually answerable.

So things went on much as they had three or five years before and no one seemed to change much. At first. Oh, there came to be girlfriends, then wives, members of the informal group, who were appalled, infuriated, would not listen to the boys talking about napalm, crispy critters, killing Cong, and strafing villes. But the pilots usually only mentioned those things among themselves or in safe, select company.

Many of them joined the Reserves, as did Rawlins, because flying was one hell of a lot of fun, and if you could do it and get paid and avoid nearly all the paperwork and military bullshit of the Regulars, that was one good deal. So they practiced the same skills, bombing, strafing, and dogfighting—which they called hassling—out in the desert or over the Pacific, and they got together at happy hours in officers clubs and talked about naping and strafing, and the fraternity was intact. The ones who had been in the Reserves all along or had had noncombat duty couldn't hear enough about it; the boys who had been there couldn't tell them enough.

And there were the cross-countries. Some of the older Reservists had stayed in just so they could get away from their wives on weekends and for two weeks active duty in the summer. And the younger ones lacked no appetite for strange stuff, so almost every weekend a bunch of the boys would fan out across the country in taxpayer's jets, with unlimited fuel chits, in search of whiskey and secret ladies. Proficiency training. And there was usually no shortage of either. Fighter pilots had groupies too. Back at the base in the Regular Marine Corps, where several squadrons would be deployed overseas at any time, unaccompanied by dependents because the Corps did not believe in dependents overseas, there was a maxim: If a group of officers' wives came to the club for dinner, it meant absolutely nothing. Stay away. If one or two of them came back alone, it was a lock-on dead-sure thing.

Rawlins had saved some money in Vietnam because there was no place to spend it and it was tax-free, and he had made a little more gambling, so he was pretty well-heeled when he got home. He got in on the tail end of the bull market and then got lucky in commodities for a while and had some real money. For a while. He turned down a job with a domestic airline because he thought it would be more glamorous to work for an international carrier. And everybody was hiring, or was expected to. There would be time. So he decided to go back to school first and complete his degree. Rawlins had been in and out of school a couple of times in his youth. He liked campus life, was fascinated by some subjects and authors, but didn't give a hoot about others. His grades were average or a little below, though somehow he never stuck around long enough to finish. But he was always lured back. Something about books and serious thinkers attracted him.

It occurred to Rawlins that, having kept a half-assed journal for a while, he might try to write a book some day, so he got into an English program and began reading everything he liked and skimming the rest.

Between that, heavy reliance on *Cliffs Notes*, making up some of his quotes and footnotes, and borrowing an idea here and there, he got by. It was a good life. He arranged his schedule so he never went to school more than two or three days a week. The rest of the time he would either lie on the beach and read (not so intently as to interfere with hardbelly watching) or go fly somewhere for the Reserves and get paid for extra man-days. The Reserves loved Rawlins because he was always available. He had no job, no family, no real responsibilities. If somebody broke down in Texas and needed a part, they could call Smilin' Jack. Day or night, if he was sober and not with a lady, he would go. If they needed an airplane ferried to Florida or one picked up, Rawlins was ready. So he made pretty good money from the Reserves. The GI Bill paid for school, plus he could borrow sizable amounts through the Federal Student Loan Program at low interest rates, which he then invested in stocks that would yield dividends greater than the interest he had to pay. He had money in the bank and a good stash in the market. His Corvette was paid for, and he had a cheap apartment two blocks from the beach, with a stone fireplace, a comfortable bed, and a stereo system he had acquired in Japan, whose designer had been thinking more along the lines of concert halls than one-bedroom apartments. There were plenty of girls and plenty of sun. He just wanted to enjoy life and this seemed like the way to do it. Jack Rawlins was thirty, but he had not really changed or matured much in ten years. He still didn't know that life would not stand still, that it must be pursued and exploited and reckoned with.

"Hi there. I like your frown," Rawlins said in his most engaging manner to the slenderish girl on the next stool.

She raised an eyebrow, but otherwise her expression did not change. "Hello," she said. Rawlins returned to his drink for a minute. She studied hers also.

"I know this is highly irregular," he said, returning his attention by way of her legs, which were long and tan and pleasantly curved, with trim ankles and knees. "I don't wish to seem impertinent or unseemly, but purely as a scientific observation, may I say that I think that's the shortest skirt I've ever seen."

She smiled. She liked the little speech. That was good. Communications were open. "Yeah," she said. "You have to wear clean underpants with this outfit. Do you have a light?"

Rawlins chuckled and fired up his Japanese Zippo with the enamaled tiger's head from his old squadron. "Thanks," she said and smiled again, exhaling. Something in her pale blue eyes when she smiled sent all kinds of impulses running through Rawlins's mind and body. He began to suspect that fate had been kind once again.

"Weren't you just sitting at the other end of the bar?"

She took a drag and gave him a long look. "Yeah."

"Why'd you move down here?"

"I like the company better," she smiled, the eyes smeared with implicit invitation.

"I seem to detect a message here," Rawlins said, gazing. "Can I buy you a drink?"

"No. Let's go somewhere else."

"Okay. My name is Jack." He drained his drink.

"I'm Nora." She was stirring the ice in her drink with a finger.

"Why'd you pick me out?"

The pale eyes stared. "You looked right for me." Rawlins couldn't quite believe this was happening.

In the car he said: "Do you have any place in mind?"

"Why don't we just go to my place. It's not far. I have scotch."

"If you are saying what I think you're saying, this, ah, boggles the mind, is how we might put it. *Are* you saying what I think you're saying?"

She turned and put a hand on his thigh. "I think I like you, Jack. You come on home with me and I'll give you the best blow job you've ever had in your life." She squeezed his thigh and Rawlins managed not to veer off the road.

Her apartment was fancier than he expected, with a lot of brass and teak and things from the Orient. "Where'd you get all this stuff?"

"I was married to a naval officer and we were stationed in Japan for three years." Oh, yeah. The Navy pukes got to take their families along when they went overseas. The Marines did not. Only the Corps, he thought.

She filled an ice bucket and put glasses on the bamboo bar. "Why don't you fix us a drink while I get comfortable? I like a little water."

"Coming right up. I didn't know you were uncomfortable."

"Shut up." She disappeared and he started pouring. A few minutes later she slid in wearing only a short dusky blue satin robe, which was translucent and trimmed with lace. It was loosely belted. He could see that her breasts were small, but provocative, with raised aureoles around the nipples, as if they were slightly swollen. They moved nicely when she walked. He let his gaze run over those legs. Rawlins was really aroused. She put on some music, walked up and put both arms around him, and kissed him long and with an insistence that meant business. They drank their drinks with him sitting on a bar stool and her standing beside him, always touching or fondling him, rubbing his ear or the back of his neck, pressing a breast into his arm, running her fingers along his ribs. She was giving him no opportunity to forget either her presence or her purpose.

He cupped a breast in his hand and kissed it slowly. "You're gentle," she said. "That's nice." She clinked her glass against his. "Let's go in the bedroom."

Several candles burned and flickered, giving a dim, wavering light to the room, which was also furnished with Oriental things, except for the king-sized bed. She began to unbutton his shirt. "Take off your clothes, honey. I want to get a couple of things."

Rawlins undressed. He was fairly certain he had gone to heaven only he didn't remember dying. Rawlins sat on the bed and grinned.

She came back in carrying a jar of something and a steaming cup of water. She gave him that strange smile again and said: "You just lie down, baby, and I'll blow your fucking mind."

She began by kissing his nipples. At this point Rawlins was not at all sure he would even make it to the high point of the demonstration. Presently she began to rub his cock with the stuff from the jar, Vaseline, maybe. Or Vicks VapoRub. It had a cool, menthol sort of feel on his skin. He immediately had even less confidence that he would be able to endure past the preliminaries, but she seemed to cease each activity just in the nick of time and then start doing something else. Finally she sat up for a minute and drank hot water from the cup. She swirled it around in her mouth, gargled some, drank some more, and then quickly slipped her mouth over his hypersensitive member. The combination of the grease on his skin and the contact with her heated mouth and tongue produced a sensation he had not experienced before. As she moved deeper he could feel her epiglottis and then she moved methodically, caressing, teasing, tantalizing, *sucking*, and in less than ten seconds he jerked and shuddered and trembled through the most memorable garden-variety orgasm he had ever had.

She sat up, wiped her mouth with a Kleenex, and gave him the funny pale-eyed smile. "Wasn't that something?"

"You're in a class by yourself." He could see that she was genuinely proud of her little trick. She should be. He squeezed her and nibbled on her ear. "Really, that was so fine."

They had another drink, smoked a joint, and then moved on into one of the strangest nights of Rawlins's life. They went through every orifice, stroke, position, and combination that either could think of. Sometime near daylight they got an hour or two of sleep.

Rawlins had to fly at seven in the morning and by the time he stumbled down to the flight line, Jack was not smilin'. But in those days he could still hack it and once he got strapped into the airplane and on 100-percent oxygen, things were all right. He even got four bull's-eyes on a rocket hop, and boy did he have some shit to talk about at happy hour. That broad was too much. And that was but a day, in a week, in a month, in years that were slipping away, but he had nearly forgotten the past, didn't think of the future, lived for the moment.

So that was life in the early postwar Rawlins period—just flying hops—and he figured it would go on that way. Things were already changing, though. He just didn't realize it. The world was moving ahead and he was falling behind. He was near the end of his flying career, but he didn't know it. Happiness is not a constant and he didn't know that either. "Life will not stand still," Rawlins would later state, "we should know that from Darwin's LAW."

But at that point Rawlins hadn't thought a whole lot about Darwin's LAW. Or anything else that mattered much. He was immersing himself in a contentedness that was a bit too shallow, something less than genuine. And pipers, unfailingly, will be paid.

4

California and Japan, 1950s

He remembered saying to himself sometime in the fifties, "Shit, I don't have a war. How can I amount to anything?" Without combat there were no heroes and how else could you distinguish yourself in a boring world? The generations before him all had wars to serve in and survive and talk about and Rawlins was fucked. Cheated. He could look forward to a life of Cold War peace. He had hated every job he ever worked at, and he was not about to spend the rest of his life going to the same office or factory or some shit every day for thirty years. He had to find something that was exciting, where he could prove himself and get a little respect, maybe a little envy.

Rawlins drifted into college because he was sick of construction jobs, drifted out of college because he wasn't interested in anything in particular, and then, one day, drifted into the Marine Corps because he would be drafted soon anyway and, what the hell, he might as well give the Marines a try. That night about midnight, at the Marine Corps Recruit Depot in San Diego, a short, oppressively squared-away drill instructor punched Rawlins square in the gut and knocked all the air out of him. He slumped against the wall where he had been standing at attention, made an effort to keep from crying, determined right away that he was not fond of DIs, and wondered if he had made just the right decision.

That was still the relative *old* Corps, before a staff sergeant drowned a few of his shitbirds in the swamps of Parris Island, South Carolina, the East Coast recruit depot, and caused a complete revamping of the recruit training procedures. They could still knock you around in those days and nobody ever heard of "brutality."

They formed up into a platoon and Rawlins continued to float for a while, doing as little as he could get away with and just getting by. It was easier for Rawlins than the others because he was a good athlete, he had wrestled in high school, and the physical stuff was no problem. He had hunted and cleaned and handled guns since he was ten, so the rifle bullshit wasn't much either. One day a runner came and told him to report to Sergeant Dunson, the senior DI. Rawlins ran to the duty hut (recruits were not allowed to walk anywhere) and pounded three times on the bulkhead beside the hatchway. The Marine Corps didn't have doors or walls.

"I can't hear you!" came a roar from the Quonset hut. Rawlins pounded three more times, as hard as he could pound, fearing he might break a hand. "Get in here!" came the roar. Rawlins marched in and stood at attention in front of the desk.

"You call that the proper procedure for entering my duty hut, maggot?" It was close to a scream. "I don't allow pussies in my duty hut and that's just the way you came in here, Private, like a goddamn cunt! Now get the fuck out of here and by God when you come back in you better do it right!" All in a screaming bellow.

"Aye, aye, sir! Will that be all, sir?" Rawlins yelled it out. Every word to be spoken in boot camp is to be yelled.

"Get out, shithead!" Even louder. "And when you come back in here you better act like a Marine, even though you're not one!"

Rawlins thought he had it. The DI hadn't heard his heels click when he halted in front of the desk. Take one step to the rear with the right foot, swivel, and march out the door. Close it, pound three times. "I can't hear you!" Pound three more times. "Get in here, maggot!"

He repeated the entry, thumping his boondockers together loudly as he came to a halt at stiff attention.

"Sir, Private Rawlins reporting as ordered, sir!" Yell it out.

The DI glanced through the pages in a manila folder. "Private Rawlins, I see by your service record book here that you went to college for a while. Is that correct?"

"Yes sir!" He belted it out.

"What did you say to me, shitbird?" The DI had risen from his chair and was screaming with his red face and bulging eyes less than six inches from Rawlins's face.

"*Sir*, yes sir!" Rawlins amended.

"By God, you *better* call me sir, Private Rawlins, or I'll run you out of this platoon so fast your fucking eyeballs will spin. Do you understand me, Private?"

"Sir, yes sir!"

"So you went to college," he sat back down. "And you were a wrestler in high school, is that right?"

"Sir, yes sir!" Rawlins wondered what this was leading to. It had to be bad.

"So you've been to college and you're smart." The DI shuffled papers. "And you're a goddamn ath-a-lete. Well, I doubt if a little feather merchant like you could hack it." He was silent for a moment. "But just maybe you might make a squad leader. Do you think you've got what it takes to be a squad leader in my platoon, Private?"

Rawlins made a terrible mistake. Some kid he had talked to who had done some time in the Marines, and probably had an undesirable discharge, had told him never to volunteer for anything. And had told him if they offered him right guide or squad leader or anything, by all means to turn it down, because those guys were held responsible by the DIs for all the fuck-ups of the rest of the platoon and then they had to lean on the other guys and pretty soon everybody hated them and their life was miserable. From what he had seen of the Corps thus far, it seemed like sound advice.

"Sir, Private Rawlins doesn't know what being a squad leader means, sir. Private Rawlins isn't sure he could do it, sir."

Sergeant Dunson leaned back in his chair and snorted. His eyes bulged again, though Rawlins did not see it because he was at strict attention and looked straight ahead. "Sure?" Dunson asked in the low, terrifying voice of an assassin. "You're not sure? Well, let me tell you, Private, you're not *sure* of anything in this Marine Corps. Being a squad leader means working twice as hard as anybody else and kicking your squad's asses into line and busting your fucking hump, Private!" His voice had risen to a roar again. "Now do you want a chance to try to be a squad leader, or not? I don't want to hear any more fucking questions. Yes or no, Rawlins. Do you think you've got what it takes or not?"

Rawlins sensed that his answer was the wrong one. He knew it would piss off the drill instructor, but still it seemed to be the better course over all. He didn't want to stand out. He wanted to be anonymous, just another member of the cast.

"Sir, no sir. Private Rawlins doesn't want to be a squad leader, sir." He would never be anonymous again.

"I didn't think you had it in you, you fucking scumbag. I don't think you have what it takes to be a Marine. I'll be watching you real close, Rawlins. Now get out of my sight!"

"Aye, aye, sir. Will that be all, sir?"

"Get out!" he screamed. Back with the right foot, turn, march. Haul ass. The refusal had endeared him to Dunson forever.

Sergeant Dunson stayed off him for three or four days, checking his shoes, checking his rifle, checking his locker, but not saying much. Rawlins began to think he had done the right thing. Maybe he could drift back into obscurity and not be an issue. Then one day they had an hour to square away their gear. The members of the platoon sat around on their footlockers, some with open cans of dark brown Kiwi polish, a little water in the top of the cans, white T-shirts wrapped around index fingers that described small, rapid circles on the spit-shined toes of shoes. Others probed the openings and clefts of the mechanism of the M-1 rifle with pipe cleaners, banishing motes of dust. A few of the most squared away used the time to hand-rub hundredth coats of linseed oil into the stocks of their already spotless M-1s.

Rawlins got up to go out to the tap for a few more drops of water in his shoe polish lid. These times for working on their gear were the closest thing to relaxation they got during their waking hours. Even church was no time to kick back and skate. Because you were *watched.* Constantly. Sergeant Buch usually sent them off to church.

Sergeant Wadislaw Buch, the junior DI, whose entire family had been massacred by the Russians, and who himself had escaped as a young boy, had no ambivalent attitude toward Communists. Upon arriving in this country at seventeen, he had immediately joined the Marine Corps, thinking to pop over to Korea and kill off a few Reds. But he had not reckoned with the humanistic snares of a "free" society. He was, alas, only seventeen, and at that officially tender age, he could, within the maze of statutes of, for, and by the people, with the consent of his sponsor and guardian, an uncle, join the Corps. He could not, however, by mandate of the people, be sent into combat until he was eighteen. It made no sense to Wadislaw. All he wanted to do was kill some goddamn fucking Communists, and they wouldn't let him. But he was such an exemplary Marine that they gave him a meritorious promotion to corporal and sent him to drill instructor school. By the time he finished his first tour as a DI, and was old enough to satisfy their rules, they called off the goddamn war, gave him meritorious sergeant, and kept him in San Diego.

On Sunday mornings he would have the platoon fall in. "All right," he almost piped, his voice was so high and thick with accent. "All you goddamn pipple want to go goddamn church, fall out on goddamn road."

The right guide was a devout Catholic, which was often the case, and at least one of the squad leaders was a devout some-kind-of-Protestant, which was always the case, and they would form up separate details and march the troops off to their preferred places of worship. Wadislaw never went. Rawlins went a couple of times but it was dangerous. You were, indeed, *watched*. And it was hot in there and the chaplain's voice droned on and if you nodded off, the DI found out about it. And you paid the price, maybe running laps *around* the platoon, while the platoon *ran* to chow. And back. And so on. But if you stayed back from church, you got some shit detail: trimming the ice plant, raking the sand, field-daying the hut, *some* shit. Sometimes the DI would have them pour buckets of sand on the deck and then field-day that fucking hut until it was white-glove-spotless and that was less fun than church. So you were fucked if you went and fucked if you didn't and Rawlins began staying back at the platoon area, because at least you didn't have to march anywhere to get fucked over. He found out the Jews got to go off the base to some tabernacle or something and he was tempted, but he reasoned that they would have figured out ways to make that deal even worse, so he stayed back at the hut and did his Sunday shit detail.

But this particular day was not a Sunday, and Rawlins was walking out to get some water in the lid of his shoe polish can and was as close to relaxed as he ever got and not paying a whole lot of attention to anything. As Rawlins stepped across the threshold of his Quonset hut home with his right foot, he plunked his utility cap on his shaved head, because it was ultimate LAW that when you were outside you would ALWAYS have your cover on and when you were inside you would NEVER have your cover on. The first indication that he was suddenly in deep shit came as Rawlins, who was looking at the deck, noticed a perfectly spit-shined left dress shoe, at the end of a green, flannel, winter-service-alpha trouser leg, coming in the building as his own right foot went out. There were several new, perhaps eccentric behavior patterns inscribed on Rawlins's brain. One of the foremost was that when a drill instructor entered any area, the first recruit to observe him was to *immediately* freeze at attention, and scream out the order for everybody else to do likewise.

"TennsshhHut!" bellowed Rawlins, pillar of stone. There was perhaps a second and a half of low background noise, muffled thumping, springs creaking, clothes swishing, as the platoon came to attention. A rifle, left in too precarious a position, clattered to the deck with the, to them all by now, sickening sound of steel bouncing on concrete. Oh, God, would somebody pay there.

The sharp point of a shined, copper-jacketed .30 caliber bullet, attached to the end of a swagger stick, came up painfully under Rawlins's chin.

"Private Rawlins, what are you doing?" Dunson's voice was low, flat. "Didn't I make it clear to you that you will be covered only when outside? Don't you know that you *never* wear a cover inside except when you are on duty and under arms?"

"Sir, yes sir!" Scream it out.

Dunson backhanded him hard on the side of the head, knocking Rawlins against the bulkhead. He recoiled automatically, without thought, to attention, his ear red and hurting. He was filled with terror and anger. The adrenaline flowed, but, amazingly, no thought, no fleeting impluse, *not even the consideration of retaliation* entered his mind. Rawlins did not consciously perceive it, but he was already converted. In a few short weeks, the harassment, the embarrassment, the forced impotence, the herding and oppression, and the constant reminders that terrible consequences awaited anyone who, ever, for any reason, tried to buck the system, had broken his will. He was brainwashed, in the thrall of the vast inscrutable military establishment. Though ignorant of it, Rawlins was already in a state of psychological bondage. He stood there and quivered.

Dunson yanked the cap down over his eyes and ears. He could not see. "What are you doing with your goddamn cover on inside this hut, Private?" Dunson had practiced his "tirade, type-one-each," so many times it was second nature to him. His voice rose gradually, increasing at the same time in intensity, volume, and rapidity of speech. He could work himself into a state of genuine anger in no time.

"Do you hear me, Private? I gave you a direct order not to wear your cover inside and you disobeyed me. Now why the fuck did you do that, Private? Why did you disobey a lawful order, you scumbag?" He was yelling now, his face close to Rawlins.

"Sir, Private Rawlins was going outside, sir. To—"

Dunson slapped him again. "Yeah, but you weren't outside, Private, you were inside and you had your goddamn cover on in defiance of an order. Now, do you have any excuse for that shit?"

"Sir, no excuse, sir," he yelled.

"Yeah? Well I've had all your 'no excuse, sirs' I want to listen to, you shithead." Dunson had him by the lapels of his utility jacket now, shaking him, banging him against the doorjamb. Rawlins looked like an idiot with his cap pulled down over his eyes, trying to stand at attention, while another kind of idiot kept smashing him against the wall, but he did not lift a hand.

Years later he would really begin to wonder about that. Why didn't he protest? Defend himself? At least speak out? He did nothing.

Dunson had worked up an estimable rage by this time, and it seemed to feed on itself and grow. He had not intellectualized it but he was hating and beating Rawlins for several reasons. Rawlins was really pretty squared away, because it was relatively easy for him. He was intelligent and had less trouble running, swimming, doing calisthenics, memorizing orders and historical facts, dismantling and reassembling his rifle than others did. And he did just enough to keep himself out of trouble. That is what enraged Sergeant Dunson. The little bastard was fucking off. He was not giving 100 percent and that would not be tolerated. That amounted, in Dunson's mind, to silent contempt. That smart-assed little motherfucker had refused to be a squad leader. He did not try his damnedest every minute to excel. He didn't care. He didn't give a shit about Dunson's Marine Corps and that was unforgivable. That attitude had to be broken.

And it was true. Rawlins never *did* try very hard at anything because he really didn't care that much. He was getting a little pissed at this fool pounding him against a wall, but it wasn't really hurting him, it was just embarrassing. He offered no resistance. He was to go through life that way, working or trying just hard enough to get what he wanted or thought he needed.

Sergeant Dunson was determined, at least for the next few weeks, to change that approach. He slammed Rawlins against the wall once more, then jerked him out the door. "Yes, I'm sick of you, Rawlins, you fucking pussy." The tirade, type-one-each continued. "So I'm gonna get rid of your miserable ass. A fucking germ like you can infect the whole platoon, so I'm gonna lock your smart-aleck ass in the brig for a week and see how you like it there, Private." All this time Dunson was dragging Rawlins across the street toward the Company Office. The utility jacket was starting to tear so Dunson got a better grip and continued to shake him, at intervals slapping him hard on the cover, which was pulled tightly down over his eyes and ears, boosting him along with a knee, jerking him back and forth. The seams of his jacket chafed under his arms. And the tirade went on.

"And if the brig doesn't send you to Casual Company to wait for your undesirable discharge, then I'll set your young ass back and get you out of my platoon forever."

The operative words here were *brig* and *set back*. They all knew, sensed, even dreamed about the brig. Where you scrubbed the deck with a toothbrush all day long, could never speak unless spoken to, got no breaks, no mail, were methodically tortured, and so on. No, the brig was no way out of anything. And to be set back was almost worse. The one thing in the mind of every recruit in this asylum was that if you could somehow just hold it together, take any abuse, just *make* it, in thirteen weeks it would all be over. You would be *out*. You could actually go into town two or three Saturdays a month. Buy a hamburger, have a beer. Maybe even talk to a girl. To get out of here was everything. But if you got set back . . . First of all you had at least one more week in hell, but that was just the beginning. If you were set back for any reason, you were regarded as the lowest kind of malingering shitbird, despised by everyone. That made it real easy to get set back again. To be in that place, not progressing but going backward, was the worst punishment of all. There were recruits with walking pneumonia, dragging themselves around with 103-degree temperatures, who would not report to sick bay for fear they would be hospitalized, miss some training, and be *set back*. It was a psychological killer, and the poor bastard who broke a leg or suffered some serious illness knew a terror that others could only imagine.

Rawlins was getting scared. This maniac seemed to mean it. Dunson dragged him up the steps to the Company Office, his voice dropping now to a fierce whisper. This was officer country. Rawlins's shirt was in shreds now and his nose was bleeding. "And you by God better take that fucking cover off when we enter, Private."

The captain was a chubby young man with pink cheeks and an almost imperious air about him. Mostly what he did all day was sit at his desk and practice his looks. He had a grave look, severity, incredulity, and so on.

Dunson explained that Private Rawlins was an incorrigible lawbreaker and mutineer and that locking him up seemed to be the only thing for it.

The captain rubbed his eyes. "Well, Private, what do you have to say for yourself? Are you in the habit of wearing your cover indoors?"

"Sir, no sir. Private Rawlins was just coming out of the hut, when—"

"But, you *were* inside the hut and you *did* have your cover on, is that right?"

"Yes sir, but—"

"No buts, Private," the captain looked hard at him. This was his piercing look, but it was wasted because Rawlins stared straight ahead and saw nothing but the wall above the captain's head. "I don't want to hear any of your damned whining excuses. You were covered while inside, in direct defiance of an order. Tell me, Private, have you said 'sir' every time you were supposed to? Every single time?"

Rawlins was not at all comfortable. He was beginning to believe this was happening. "Sir, no sir. But not intentionally, sir."

"Intentionally? Damn you, mister, I asked what you *did*, not what you *intended* to do.

"I see what you mean, Sergeant. I think a little brig time might be just what this boy needs. Let me call over there."

"Sir, Private Rawlins requests permission to speak, sir."

"Shut up, Rawlins." The captain began dialing.

Intellectually, Rawlins knew they couldn't do this. In our society you cannot be put in jail for wearing a hat. Or not wearing one. But then, the Marine Corps is not of our society. And they *were* doing it.

"Yes. This is Captain Bravehart here. How are you, sir?" He listened a moment. Rawlins was, in a vernacular not unknown in boot camps, starting to shit. This phone call was official. They were really going through with it. "Is that right, sir? Ho, ho. I'll tell the colonel when he comes back. Yes sir, he's golfing this afternoon.

"Sir, I've got a small problem. We have a young troublemaker down here who doesn't want to go along with the program. Sergeant Dunson thinks maybe you folks could square him away a little bit."

Rawlins was now shitting bricks. How could this happen? Well, a lot of things happened in this place. Why had he just stood there and let that oaf slap the self-respect out of him? Because if he had resisted, he *knew* he would go to the brig. They had learned that the first week. There was a big, scarred, bad-looking black recruit in the platoon named Anderson. Rawlins had never heard him say a word. He just acted kind of surly and kept to himself. Nobody wanted to fuck with him. Even the other blacks didn't mess around with Anderson. You got the impression that he wasn't real swift, but also wasn't used to being pushed around and didn't intend to get used to it. Dunson got on him right away, pressing and needling. Anderson didn't say anything, just looked defiant. They had only just formed up into a platoon and the behavioral patterns were not really established yet. The second day, Dunson had them fall in on the road for a speech.

"Some of you people may think you're tough. Well, you ain't tough. You are just a bunch of skin-headed pussies. You're not civilians any more, but you are a *long* ways from ever being Marines. What you are is scum. The lowest kind of scum. You are lower than whale shit, and that's at the bottom of the ocean. But some of you may think you're tough, and I'm gonna give you a chance to prove that. Anybody think he can whip me? Huh? Who's tough? You!" He grabbed the tallest man in the front rank by the shirt. "You think you can whip me?"

"Sir, no sir."

"You better believe it, Private." Dunson shoved him and prowled on down the rank. "How about you, Anderson? I'll bet you're a bad motherfucker, ain't you?" He knew his name already. Anderson said nothing.

"Yeah, a real hardcase. I'll bet *you* think you can kick my ass, don't you? Huh? Don't you look at me shithead, you're at attention! Now tell me, Anderson, do you think you can whip me?"

"Yeah."

"Yeah? You said 'yeah' to me? Well, I'll teach *you* when to say 'sir.' " He grabbed the private by the arm and jerked him out of ranks. Anderson pulled away and stood, angry but hesitant. Dunson still had the psychological advantage, though it was wearing thin.

"All right, Private, you march around behind that hut and that's an order. Move it! NOW!"

They disappeared behind the Quonset hut. The platoon heard voices, then scuffling. The sounds of combat. More voices, thumps, feet sliding on gravel, but too many feet, Rawlins thought. Heavy breathing and the sound of fists on flesh, then Anderson in a long, choked wheezing, desperate outpouring of unintelligible words and profanity. An animal scream that sounded like the last gasp. Then silence.

Dunson walked back around the hut with a bright red welt on his jaw and skinned knuckles on his right hand. He inquired if anybody else wanted any. There were no takers; the point was made.

They never saw Anderson again. Rawlins figured afterwards that the whole thing was a set-up. There could have been two or three or a dozen more DIs back there, but that didn't matter. What mattered was that *they did it.* They could do any damn thing they wanted to and get away with it.

He was never more aware of that than at this moment when the almighty Captain Bravehart casually discussed his fate over the telephone, along with the colonel's golf. Rawlins was shitting tombstones now. He knew they couldn't do this, but he also knew that they *could* do it.

The captain replaced the phone and told Dunson to march his prisoner away, they were expecting him.

"Sir," Dunson cleared his throat. "I've just been thinking. If this man would *bust his hump*, I think he might be able to make it. Maybe we should give him one more chance."

"What? After I called the brig and all? Are you sure you want to fool with him, Sergeant?"

"Captain, I would be willing to give him one chance. With the understanding of course that if he fouls up, he goes to the brig."

The captain extracted Rawlins's word of honor that he would give 100 percent in the future and told Dunson to get him out of his sight.

"And if you ever come back in this room again, Rawlins, I'll run you out of the Corps, so help me God I will."

Rawlins always thought it was just an act to scare him, but he never knew for sure, because they could have done it. They could do anything they wanted to. He never gained any respect for the military establishment, but he never completely lost his fear of it. Also he never completely trusted a superior officer again.

Rawlins stayed scared and pretty squared away for over two weeks. About the time his cynicism and laziness returned, they started the thing that really saved him, and that was the rifle range. Rawlins was a good shot and when he scored expert on the first day of firing they began to look at him in a different light. High scores reflected well on the DI, the platoon, the battalion, and everyone. They coddled that sort of thing and suddenly nobody bothered him anymore. He ended up shooting the highest score on the range on qualification day and made PFC out of boot camp.

In spite of the bitterness, this strange and unexpected pride thing manifested itself. As he marched past the reviewing stand in the *honor* platoon, the band played the "Marine Corps Hymn" and he felt the skin tighten on his head and the back of his neck. In years to come regardless of disenchantment and the gradual eroding of illusions, he would not lose that feeling completely. Even while flying hops.

Rawlins had joined the Marines not even thinking about airplanes, but he figured out pretty quick that he didn't want to spend the next four years walking around with a pack on his back and a rifle over his shoulder, so he put in for Basic Aviation School and ended up in the Air Wing. It was two years later when it suddenly hit him. The thing he had been looking for. The glamour shot. He was assigned to a small detach-

ment of a helicopter squadron in Japan, and one day, as he stood on a
Marsten matting airstrip at the base of Mount Fuji, he saw his future,
or part of it. Two FJ-4 pilots were out boring holes in the skies of the
rising sun and they remembered that one of their pals was consigned to
driving ignominious helicopters around Camp Fuji, so they called up for
a low pass. The tower passed the word and everybody lined up beside
the strip to watch.

They came in hot, maybe 450 knots, about fifty feet off the deck in
close parade formation. They absolutely thundered over the little gaggle
of onlookers and Rawlins was transported. He could even see the pilot
of the lead aircraft wave as they roared past, his face covered by hard
hat, sun visor, and oxygen mask. The noise, the rush of air, the movement. These guys were showing some class. They pulled up over the
shoulder of Mount Fuji in a series of slow rolls, the wingman hanging in
tight, sun glinting off their canopies. God, it was cool! There it was.
Excitement, respect, a real shit-hot line of work. For one time, Rawlins
knew what he wanted. And he was serious. Sort of.

5

Southeast Asia, 1960s

Colonel Creed tended to look upon every event that befell him in the light of how it might enhance his career. It had been difficult, at first, to divine even the remotest sign of enhancement from the episode of the steaming Pyrex. He searched his agile brain, but was unable, for some time, to discover just how pouring a pot of coffee in General Jefferson's lap was going to help that career. Oh, R² Jones's sonic boom may have mitigated the act somewhat, but still, it was Creed's own hand that held the pot.

No, the first discernible results of the incident were fairly negative. General Jefferson had orders cut within thirty minutes and gave Creed twenty-four hours to be on a plane out of Travis AFB headed toward Southeast Asia, and, Jefferson hoped, the slimiest slough of despond that the region had to offer.

Jefferson knew he would never see Creed again because he had just finished an overseas tour himself and had made general and didn't have to go to that shithole to enhance his fucking career. The Republicans were already touting him to resign and run for the Senate. He wished his stupid wife would have had the brains to come from a more prominent family, one with a little older money, and a little more of it, but he knew that he would prevail against all adversity. Had he not always done so?

General Jefferson was the only Marine aviator in that august body to have been in more wars than he had combat missions. He was a certifiable, incompetent lunatic at the controls of an airplane, which was no big deficit in his rise through the ranks, but made combat duty the shits. Jefferson had been shot down on his first mission in World War II and spent three years in a prison camp, giving his name, rank, and serial number and eating fish heads and rice. He was also shot down on his first mission in

Korea and spent the ensuing year and a half in another prison camp, a sphere of existence to which he was by now well accustomed. At that point he was even: two wars, two hops. Then along came this idiotic Vietnamese flap. General Jefferson was tired of prison camps, had lost his taste for fish heads and rice, and didn't need the points, so he didn't have to go to this war to participate; for income-tax purposes, though, he *did* have to go to this war *officially*.

Under the Great Society, tied in with the Tonkin Gulf Resolution, no doubt, was a widely heralded legislative package that exempted the poor boys who had to do the bloody business from paying income tax. Which was a beautiful gesture and did a great deal of good by assuaging the intolerable guilt that burdened thousands of vital politicians and bureaucrats, and allowed them to go on waging the war more efficiently. Only by the time the military lobby got through writing amendments to the bill, it exempted nearly as many boys who *didn't* have to do the bloody business as boys who did. It was immediately seen that transport crews who flew in-country maybe two or three times a month had a fine opportunity to be killed in the war and must be covered. Likewise the B-52 crews who lived in Guam or Thailand, but popped over to South Vietnam for an Arc-Light run at thirty thousand feet every so often. And what of the supply officer from Headquarters, Fleet Marine Force Pacific, in Hawaii, who had to fly in and give a lecture on the new accountability form for 782 gear at Wing, Division, and I Corps Headquarters? Was he not in some danger of being overrun and brutally murdered? Was he not serving his nation in a hostile zone? And so on.

So the LAW that they came up with said that anyone who spent a specified number of hours, forty-eight or seventy-two or something, within a combat zone, on official business, in any given month, would be exempt from taxation for that entire month. Thus began what Moon Dog and Lance Major Slocum called the biggest boondoggle in air travel, dollarwise, since the Berlin airlift. Lance Major Slocum was the most senior captain in the squadron. He was also the most dumb. Slocum had been selected for major, but he would not accept the promotion. He was so dumb he thought Moon Dog was intelligent and that was why he always espoused all of Moon Dog's theories and ideas, like the one about the Berlin airlift. Moon Dog *was* intelligent, but he took great pains never to let anyone discover it, probably because if the wrong people got the idea that he was intelligent, they might try to make *him* a major. So no one ever knew, except Slocum, and he only *thought* he knew, and for all the wrong reasons. Lance Major Slocum would not accept his promotion because he could never be *absolutely* convinced, never 100-percent certain, that Naval Intelligence or somebody did not whisk all candidates for field-grade rank away to some secret hospital ship, disguised as an oil tanker and flying the flag of Panama—probably the same one that harbored those tortured souls who were dying of unnamed and incurable veneral diseases—and perform the prefrontal lobotomies that everyone knew were prerequisite to becoming a major.

Oh, he could laugh about it, with the terse, cynical humor of the fighter pilot, but somehow he was never entirely sure. Slocum did not feel ready to become a major.

Moon Dog didn't either. He knew that the month-end influx and subsequent exodus of a few thousand military experts on important business was not nearly so large a boondoggle, dollarwise, as had been the relocation, for an indefinite period, of even the first regiment to land in Vietnam. He only said that as a joke and so as not to appear intelligent. The trouble with Slocum was that he often thought serious things were a joke and always took the jokes too seriously. It occurred to Moon at one point that maybe Slocum wasn't so dumb after all.

Still, the influx/exodus was a sizable boondoggle. All the generals and colonels, most of the majors, several warrant officers, and not a few master sergeants would begin arriving at the end of each month, on all manner of high-priority missions, just in time to log the required number of hours in-country for that month's tax shelter and stay long enough to satisfy the requirement for the following month. So, toward the end of each month, control towers around South Vietnam would begin receiving inbounds from Japan, Korea, Okinawa, Taiwan, the Philippines, Hawaii, CONUS, and points in Western Europe. Then, a week or so later, all the transports with the strange markings would be gone and they would have room to open up the bases for combat operations again and have a peaceful twenty-eight–day cycle of war.

So that was what drove General Jefferson's batting average so far down that he would have been waived by the New Mexico Military Institute if the armed forces had had an efficient farm system. For tax purposes, officially, he had to spend some time in Vietnam. And there it was: three wars, only two hops. He was the only aviator in the history of the sport who held both a DFC and a Navy Cross, but did not yet have an Air Medal. His war record was a sore spot with the general. Every time he heard laughter echoing down one of the endless halls of the Pentagon he knew it was some dirty son of a bitch who *did* have an Air Medal. He stayed away from the Pentagon as much as possible.

General Jefferson had fucked up in his handling of Colonel Creed after the Pyrex incident. What he had done wrong, in his agitation, was to ship Creed off to the sinkhole of Southeast Asia before he had time to write him an unsatisfactory fitness report. Anyone who got an unsatisfactory fitness report, by LAW, had to read it, rebut or accept the evaluation, and sign it. Otherwise no one ever saw his fitness reports. Creed was gone, so Jefferson could not make him sign. He knew better than to trust such an important matter to military channels of correspondence. Oh, he could have saved the unsat report and hand-delivered it on his next bimonthly tax run, but he had just returned from Chu Lai on business and didn't have to go back for nearly two months. In addition, he was contemplating taking a thirty-day leave to Washington and New York so his wife could have a shopping spree, and he could confer with the power elite of the party about campaign matters. And this at great personal sacrifice. It appeared that the trip would interfere with the next duty tax run. He would likely lose two months' tax exemption by vacationing in the East instead of the Far East. General Jefferson accepted this with the stoic equanimity of the professional soldier, however. For nearly thirty years he had lived by the Code of an officer and he knew that it was the professionals, the dedicated few, who were the backbone of the military and who bore the onus of those unfortunate wars fought by the young and ingenuous, the foolish, and also of the caprices of politicians and their tax legislation. It would cost him money, but he couldn't make the trip this time—could not deliver the fitness report for signing.

So, though it pained him to be so lenient, he wrote Colonel Creed another fitness report, merely below average across the board, which was, in the best tradition of damning with faint praise, the kiss of death anyway, and sent it through channels to Washington. It was the kind of compromise that a career officer, considering the big picture, the greater good, sometimes had to make.

Only "channels" in this case were Corporal Parton, who had been promoted, transferred to Station S-1, and happened to be the duty clerk when General Jefferson happened to forget to tear up the unsatisfactory fitness report and passed them both along to Parton. Parton didn't tear up the unsatisfactory report for the general, but he did tear up the below-average one. He reasoned that the general, in his infinite benevolence, had at first glance been overly indulgent of Creed and only rated him as below average, but then, recognizing the painful reality and in the cold, lonely arena of command, had readjudged him unsatisfactory. God knew the man *was* unsatisfactory. Murphy knew, Grampaw Pettibone knew, *everybody* knew. Certainly Parton knew, because he had just worked for Colonel Creed for over a year, and the only reason Parton was now a corporal and now assigned to Station was because he had stuck his own meritorious promotions and requests for transfer in Creed's IN basket with piles of other paperwork and the stupid son of a bitch signed everything that Parton put in front of him.

So Parton tore up the below-average report and sent the unsatisfactory one to Da Nang by guard mail. However, the unsatisfactory report did eventually get torn up too, disproving the old adage that says if you want a thing done right you have to do it yourself. It got torn up some months later when Colonel Creed got it in his official dispatches one day, along with a note from Parton, requesting him to read it, sign it, and return it. Creed tore it to smithereens, tore it up as well as even the general himself could have done.

That was how Colonel Creed finally came to look upon the incident of the steaming Pyrex as being beneficial to his career. There was more than one happy circumstance owing to the spilling of that coffee. Not only was he no longer under Jefferson's thumb, but he now had a comfortable combat command where he would blackmail Al "Shaky" Morgenkrank and the other squadron commanders into flying more hours and more sorties than anybody else did and score innumerable points. He would get his fucking star yet. Best of all, he had known that Jefferson was going to give him a bad fitness report anyway, had indeed spent several sleepless nights in his office, his field glasses trained on the windows of the Women Marine barracks, worrying about it. Under Jefferson's command there was no way to avoid that bad fitness report, but now he was in another theater of operations and the offending document, it seemed, had been lost in the mail.

And now yet another great blessing had come in disguise when the Daily Harassment Detail from the VC blew up the sorry little thatch-roofed hootch that MAG-22 called its officers club. Creed would have another one built. The first thing he did was call the Philippines and divert a C-130 hauling fresh frozen meat to the group. He had the meat off-loaded and the plane sent to Hong Kong to pick up a load of cement and order a three-by-four-foot engraved brass plaque, which was to read:

OFFICERS MESS

Built by the officers and men of Marine Air Group Twenty-two

COL. CHARLESTON CLIFFORD CREED *Commanding*

He would build a goddamn lasting monument to himself for all the free-world military to see. Now that was career embellishment. Nothing ostentatious, call it simply the Officers Mess. The OM club. Colonel Creed could see that graven record of his command shining through the Asian sun of innumerable future campaigns. The name Creed would be as familiar to later generations as Clive of India, Pershing, Patton, and Chesty Puller. Colonel Creed needed himself a Kipling or a Pyle, but a brass plaque on an indestructible stone building in a soon-to-be-free Southeast Asia was good enough for starters.

He got on the phone to the commanding officer of the Seabee detachment and offered him half a plane load of fresh frozen meat, which was scheduled to come in the next day, in exchange for postponing the rebuilding of the docks for a couple of days while his men completed working drawings and poured the slab for a high-priority building to be erected in the MAG-22 area. Colonel Creed figured it didn't matter that the scheduled plane would be carrying mortar for the high-priority building instead of fresh frozen meat, because everything always took a day or two longer than they said it would, and by the time the Seabees *really* expected to get their meat, he could send the plane back for it and deliver right on time. He knew that the Seabees were not eating red death in *their* mess hall anyway, because they were allowed to go to town, and since everyone had more money than he could spend, they were eating in French restaurants every night. Besides, the OM club was his most crucial project, right then. What he had to do now was get the motor pool and sufficient working parties to start hauling the stones from the partially destroyed Buddhist temple outside the gate to the site of the new edifice.

This gave Creed what Captain Cavendish liked to call a "raisin de etra." Cavendish knew that you couldn't talk convincingly about war or politics without throwing in quite a bit of French, so he was always "reconnoitering" things and establishing "lay-i-zon" with other numskulls. But the OM club did give Colonel Creed a project in which he could fairly taste the career enhancement, and he accepted the challenge with all the good humor of the career Marine. His decision was made.

It was not a major decision as such things went in the thick of combat, but it was one that would cause Nguyen Van Dan to get his ass shot off, cause Hang Dog to be the star defense witness at Lance Major Slocum's court-martial, and cause Moon Dog to blow a drop of sweat off the end of his nose and say: "What the fuck is this bullshit, Smilin' Jack?"

Moon was perched on hole number three of twelve, gazing at the flight schedule for the day. Rawlins sat next to him, tiger suit bunched around his ankles. Morning call at the twelve-holer had become a veritable symphony of liquified flatulation after the first week of red death. As C. Ross Culpepper said, "By God, I could shit through the eye of a needle at twenty paces."

"What's that?" Rawlins asked, moving some flies down the line with a copy of *Stars and Stripes*.

"Look at this here." Moon Dog was puzzled.

"Let's see."

"It says you and I have to report to the O club at ten hundred. We're not flying this morning."

"What are you talking about?" Rawlins took the schedule and looked. "Well, you got it right, Doggie. Why, that's terrible! They're ordering us to go to the club, probably to sample fine porters and lagers from around the world. That's a damn shame, man."

"You think it's one of them humanitary gestures?" Moon grinned.

"Couldn't be anything else, Dog. We'll get there early and launch at ten hundred. Couldn't be anything else."

It was something else. "You guys don't have the latest word," said Cavendish, who was playing the eleventh hole, on the back side. "They'll tell you all about it at the AOM."

AOM. All Officers Meeting. Seldom, if ever, has so much been said about so little by so many. Cavendish, assistant operations officer and ham-fisted, self-proclaimed future Commandant, was giving a lecture on how not to overstress your aircraft.

"Say, Candy," Moon Dog had on his sly country-lawyer smile. "Don't you reckon you ought to be tellin' how *to* overstress instead of how not to? Seein's you've dropped more rivets on the enemy than the squadron has bombs?" Those who were awake cracked up a little. The laughter woke C. Ross Culpepper, who hadn't heard the joke and so let his small, bulging eyes dart around the ready room, suspecting that the humor might be at his expense. Satisfied that he was not implicated, he returned to sleep.

Cavendish blushed. He was furious. He did not enjoy the sobriquet "Candy," which was short for Candyass, any more than he liked the reference to the rivets he had popped out of the undersides of airplanes while overstressing them as he pulled up too sharply from bomb runs.

Candy had this nagging fear that he might hit the ground some day. His ears and all the baby fat around his cleft little chin turned pink. "Well, then I guess I ought to know about overstress, ha ha ha," he said desperately, but no one was paying attention anymore and his laugh failed to convey much mirth.

Cavendish forged ahead into his speech, still smarting. He would have made a fine pamphleteer, because his lecture style was a study in telling them what he was going to tell them, telling them, then telling them what he had told them. "I'm going to tell you perhaps the single most important cause of overstress in the F-4, apropos of the type of operations we are conducting here . . ."

"Hey, Jack," Moon Dog had perfected a special stage whisper for AOM lectures. "What the fuck does 'apropos' mean?" General laughter.

This brought a withering look from Major Poltroun and Moon shut up, but he loved it. Candyass turned a little redder in his anger and embarrassment, but blundered on. "Trim, gentlemen. These high-g pull-outs are the result of improper trim settings. We have studied all the data and we have ascertained that trim is the culprit." Cavendish never found anything out, he always ascertained it.

"Trim, trim, trim. As you all know, we often loiter at two hundred and fifty knots, trimmed to a high angle of attack, waiting to get on the target. We then roll in, accelerate to four hundred and fifty, creating a radically different trim configuration. . . ." Cavendish droned on. Captain America appeared to listen attentively, and took an occasional note.

Captain America was always attentive. He was always pleasant. He was always charming. The majors and colonels all loved him because he was always politely interested in whatever bullshit they were proponing or proposing. But, funny thing, all the captains and lieutenants liked him too, because he was always sunny and genuine and politely interested in whatever bullshit they were complaining and caviling about. Of course they also hated him, because he never, ever fucked up. Captain America did everything by the book and he did everything right. His was a charmed existence. Everybody liked and hated him, but that was okay. Everything was okay. Life was an infinitely enjoyable experience and if you did everything right what was there to worry about?

So joyous and harmonious was Captain America's relationship with his squadronmates that all of them, even the more bigoted specimens, such as C. Ross Culpepper, had completely forgotten that he was black. Culpepper would occasionally spew out some pejorative about fucking niggers this or fucking niggers that, but even that didn't bother Captain

America much, because he knew that Culpepper had forgotten he was
black and didn't mean anything personal by it. And anyway—Father
forgive him, for he knows not what he does. Captain America was like
that. In fact the only people who remembered that Captain America was
a Negro were Captain America himself, who was quite comfortable with
that fact, and Corporal Parton, who wasn't. Parton liked Captain America
so well that he got out his service record book and changed the race-
block entry to "CAUC." He was pleased that he had done this, and told
one of his buddies about it over a warm beer.

"Goddamn, Parton. That's goddamn white of you to do a thing like
that without even being asked," the Marine replied with real admiration.

So technically Captain America was white now, but he didn't know it
because he had no reason to look at his qualification jacket. So he was
content, and still thought of himself as being black, even though he wasn't.
He smiled attentively. Hang Dog worked a crossword puzzle, and Culpepper began to snore softly. Rawlins yawned, scratched his ass, and
wondered idly about torture in the prison camps. Maybe they just had
their own Candyass Cavendishes and held endless AOMs, day after day,
until the prisoners were reduced to writhing, glossolalic loonies.

Some hours later, Cavendish finished telling them what he had told
them. Poltroun got up and said a few thousand words about how scraggly
and unmilitary the young troopers looked with their adolescent attempts
at mustaches and how Colonel Creed had been overheard remarking on
that same hirsute felony and so henceforth all facial hair for officers and
men would be forbidden. And so on.

Finally Al "Shaky" Morgenkrank took the podium. "Gents, I've got
some good news and some bad news. The bad news is that we're not
going to Japan." A great groan reverberated through the room. The
squadron had been scheduled to rotate to Japan for a few months to patch
up their airplanes, re-man with newly arrived personnel, drink, and fuck.
It had seemed too good to be true—and it was.

"The good news is, think of all the money you can save and all the
Air Medals you can collect." He grinned at them. "Well, that's horseshit,
but seriously, our replacement squadron is on maneuvers with SEATO
in the Philippines for three months."

Just then the congregation in the chapel hootch, which was right next
to the ready-room hootch, burst into a lively rendition of the hymn that
was number one on the Naval Aviation hit parade. It was Sunday. The
Sky Pilot's wavering tenor led the way and the singers drowned out Al
"Shaky" Morgenkrank. For a minute. Then he roared through the open

sides from hootch to hootch, "Padre! Can you hold it down for a minute? We're trying to conduct a briefing here."

The singing was modulated down to a soft accompaniment to Al "Shaky" Morgenkrank's remarks, sounding a little like the Sons of the Pioneers behind Roy or the Jordanaires backing up Elvis. A hushed counterpoint.

"So while those assholes play war in the Philippines . . ."

"Oh Heavenly Father, hear my prayer . . ."

"We bomb the piss out of the Cong for the next three months."

"For those in Perrill in the air . . ."

"Well, what the hell. Let those pussies do the war games and we'll do the war. Major Poltroun, make a note to have that chapel hootch moved somewhere else. That's all men. Oh, as you were. Colonel Creed wants to build a new officers club. We don't have enough troops to spare, so he has requested two officers to work on the club every day. We'll, that is, you'll do it in shifts. Under each launch on the flight schedule there will be two men assigned to club duty for two hours. Report over there to the slab and somebody will tell you what to do. Okay, Padre, we're finished. Hit it." Al "Shaky" Morgenkrank walked away from the lectern, and the next chorus of "Heavenly Father" swelled melodically in the heavy tropic air.

Moon Dog and Rawlins trudged over to the club site. Colonel Creed had some asshole buddies in the grunts and he had managed to commandeer a young brown-bar second lieutenant from the Engineering Battalion, complete with transit, level, slide rule, plum bob, and lots of string. He was the honcho of this construction lash-up. The journeymen were two captured Vietcong bricklayers, who weren't bricklayers at all, but they had built lots of bunkers for the Cong, so a four-thousand-square-foot club shouldn't be too hard. Nguyen Van Dan only said "yes" when they asked him if he knew anything about masonry because he always answered "yes" when the prison chasers asked him something. They all did. It was the best answer, even if they didn't understand the question.

"You want some more red death?"

"Yes."

"Hey, Luke the Gook, you likee boom boom 'nother boy-san?"

"Yes." (Laugh.)

"Slope-san, you think the Phillies will win the pennant?"

"You betcha." It was always what they wanted to hear.

The second lieutenant of engineers put Moon Dog and Smilin' Jack to washing rocks. They had a hose and scrub brushes and half an engine can for a water tank. As fast as Colonel Creed's work parties, with their compressors and jackhammers, could disassemble the rest of the Buddhist temple, and the motor pool could haul it in, Moon and Jack were supposed to wash the stones and pile them next to the masons.

Nguyen Van Dan became perhaps a bit overenthusiastic in his self-appointed role as foreman of the crew. He was a take-charge man.

"Hey, boy-san. Di di! Mo dock, mo dock!" He was calling for more rocks.

When Moon Dog heard the command, he ambled over toward its source, heisted a twenty-pound stone over his head, and let fly. It smacked into the damp earth just where Nguyen Van Dan's size-six bare foot had been before he sized up the situation, retreated behind his wall, and reassessed his role as foreman.

Rawlins grinned. "Shame on you, Moon Dog. You ought to be more careful. Why, you might have injured that poor child, throwing them big old rocks around and all. And him a trustee from the prison camp, who is learning the American way, too. Tch, tch."

Moon took the damp chamois from around his neck and wiped the sweat off his face. "You know, Jack, I come over here to kill them cock-suckers, not work for 'em. If that little son of a bitch says about two more words to me, I might just shoot his ass. You know, if he was to try and escape, like." Moon beamed.

So Colonel Creed began to build his career-oriented dream house in the midst of chaos. And that afternoon the ADs, twenty-four old propeller-driven attack planes of the Vietnamese Air Force, came droning into the pattern. They swarmed like some kind of time warp from World War II, broke, landed, and taxied off the runway, not five hundred yards from Creed's monument. Without even calling the tower. Nobody knew it, except maybe Murphy and Pettibone, but the war within a war had started.

6

Colorado, 1960s

Smilin' Jack Rawlins discovered mortality a month before his thirty-second birthday when he took off from Buckley Field in Denver in a Reserve A-4, on the day after Christmas. He climbed to 26,000 feet, headed west on J-60, reported his altitude to Denver Center, and, for the first time in his life, felt that he was going to faint. At flight level two six zero, alone in the tiny cockpit of an A-4, looking down at the splendor of the Rocky Mountains, the twelve- or fourteen-thousand-foot peaks of the Continental Divide glistening white with snow, unconsciousness translates directly to mortality. Asleep is dead. To pass out is to buy the farm.

Rawlins knew real terror for the first time. The debilitating fear that seems to inhibit breathing, that saps strength instantaneously. Rawlins finally realized that he was going to die sometime. And it looked like a whole lot sooner than he had planned.

"Denver Center, Marine five lima one three, cancel my instruments. I'm returning to Buckley. I think I've got bad oxygen, over." He jerked the mask loose from one side of his hard hat, pulled the power to idle, and turned back to the east, diving for the deck. The sense of dread deepened instantly, pervaded. He felt panic coming on for the first time. Worse, he was so *afraid* of panicking that he might just as well have panicked. He flew with one hand on the face curtain, hoping for some brief warning. He pictured himself yanking that curtain, hauling on it with his last conscious effort, jerking it down over his face, and launching again on the rocket-powered magic carpet. The aviator's ultimate answer. The way out of any can of worms. Rawlins remembered punching out into the Da Nang River. The sharp jolt of the old Martin-Baker seat with its shotgun-shell propellant. The sting of the air, the tumbling, then separation from the seat and a tremendous jerk as the chute popped open. Of course if he really were to pass out, it would happen too fast, he would not have sufficient warning, wouldn't have a chance to pull the handle. But still, at the bottom line, in the worse case, when all else failed, you thought of the seat.

He clung to the handle. Then the next level of worry gripped him. Here he was, hurtling earthward, strapped into this small metallic meteor, which, but for his constant control, would plunge headlong into the hard dirt of eastern Colorado or the granite of the nearest mountain outcropping, and he felt faint. Why? It must be a heart attack.

No, no. His oxygen was contaminated. That was it. Bad oxygen. He had heard of that for years. True, neither he nor anyone he knew had ever experienced it, but that must be it.

"Marine five lima one three, Denver Center. Descend below flight level two four zero and proceed VFR. Squawk one six zero zero. Contact Buckley tower three four zero point two."

"Five lima one three, roger. I'm out of two four zero, switching."

There was a tightness in Rawlins's chest and he was sweating. Strangely, it seemed to be the altitude that worried him most. Altitude was supposed to be the fighter pilot's best friend, but it was like he was so alone way up there in the sky and really scared for the first time. He belched, he farted. He stamped his feet on the deck and squirmed and flexed and clenched his hands and tried every way to whet his will, to steel his concentration. To stay conscious. As he got closer to the ground his anxiety eased somewhat. The denser air increased the pressure in the cockpit and he felt slightly better, but the terrible dread of that unknown something was still there. Once felt, it would never entirely leave him.

No sound had ever brought such relief as the rapid clunk, clunk of the wheels hitting the runway. As soon as he turned off he opened the canopy, sucked in the cold mountain air, wiped his brow on a sleeve. Whew. He was alive. The panic was gone. But the fear wasn't; wouldn't ever be again.

He told the ground crew to purge the liquid oxygen system and refill it. Once out of the airplane he was okay, if weak and shaken by this little affair of the mind. He needed sleep. He had been whooping it up for two days and nights with an old friend who ran a sawdust-on-the-floor and tinkling-piano joint downtown. And a new friend, who was a married lady from Texas and who saw to it that he didn't sleep much those nights.

She was a feline ectomorph, with long, slender, gorgeous legs, long arms, long neck, long nose, even longish tits. Under a tawny hide, which had half a tan even in the middle of winter, lithe muscles ran; the flesh was firm. She was blond all over and had greenish eyes that seemed to change shades with her moods.

She didn't talk much, uttering a quick, humorous remark every so often, but many times just smiling and remaining silent. In a room at the Holiday Inn, sometime before dawn, through half-closed eyes, Rawlins saw her smile with content and run her finger along his jaw. She seemed almost to purr. She had demanded all the energy remaining in his abused body, had thrilled him even beyond what he anticipated, wrapped her arms and legs around him and squeezed, rubbed, seemed determined to have every inch of her skin in contact with his; had raked, in passion or in the attempt to affect passion, her long nails across his back. She had taken his all and now seemed satisfied and held him as he began to sleep. She would waken him again within the hour.

She carried a bottle of vodka in her purse and a case in the trunk of her car. She must have been a little drunk all the time, because she didn't seem to change much over the course of an evening. She was his kind of girl.

Rawlins had never worried about being an alcoholic because he never had hangovers. Oh, once in a while a headache, but aspirin fixed that. And he could always struggle up after an hour or two of sleep and do whatever was asked of him. There had been veiled threats and denuded entreaties and dire warnings from assorted majors and colonels, but everybody, including God, knew how much majors knew, so forget that. Rawlins liked his whiskey.

But now this fainting bullshit changed things some. He would have to reassess and figure out what the hell was wrong with him. He sent a message to the Reserve detachment that he would remain overnight, got a little room with a sink on the wall in the transient BOQ, and collapsed.

When he woke up, late in the afternoon, he felt okay, but hungry. He dressed and walked over to a cafeteria in the Operations building, where an expressionless 250-pound girl burned a couple of cheeseburgers for him. He read the log of her shift on the bulky white apron that enfolded her. Some eggs, a lot of spattering patties on the grill just above waist height, a few bowls of chili, and so forth. She had a cold and kept sniffing and wiping her nose on the back of her hand as she flipped the burgers.

Rawlins went back to the BOQ, bought a couple of beers out of a machine, watched some black-and-white TV, then went up to his tiny room, wrenched the handles of the sink in an attempt to silence the drip, and crashed again in one of the two narrow, springy marshmallow beds. He woke up at six, raring to go. Sort of. He felt fine, but the dread was there, as henceforth it would always be. He did not know why this thing had happened in the airplane yesterday, and, not knowing the reason, he was afraid it would repeat. He did some push-ups and felt fine.

He returned to the Ops cafeteria and had breakfast. If you were to believe the proselytizing of the Navy's Bureau of Medicine, 80 percent of all aviation accidents were caused by the pilot's not having availed himself of a good, healthy, wholesome breakfast and eight hours of sleep. The other 20 percent were caused by arguing with your wife before a flight. Rawlins had had the sleep and there was no wife to not argue with, so now he ate the breakfast. He hated it. He never ate breakfast and had no appetite at all in the morning, save for coffee and cigarettes, but he ate it anyway.

Rawlins, in recent years, had fallen out of the habit of making preflight inspections. He trusted the enlisted men who took care of the aircraft and reasoned that, since they spent their whole day going over these planes, they had looked a lot closer than he had time to do, and if anything was wrong, they would have found it. His standard preflight, therefore, was of the variety known in the trade as "kick a tire and light the fire," only he usually didn't bother to kick the tire.

On this day, though, he checked the forward section of the fuselage and both wings. He checked the aft fuselage and tail section. He looked long into both main wheel wells and noticed the underside of the fuselage, the cockpit area, and the nose wheel well. He looked for wrinkles, cracks, and popped rivets, leaks, frays, and corrosion. He checked every air bottle in the plane, measured strut extension, peeped into the external fuel tanks, moved the slats and control surfaces. When he got to the cockpit, he gave the ejection seat a meticulous going-over, although he didn't really remember all the intricate mechanical points for which he was supposed to be looking. When he couldn't think of anything else to check, it was time to strap in.

When he was tied in, the first thing Rawlins did was snap his mask on and plug in to 100-percent oxygen. If there was anything wrong with it, he wanted to know before he got airborne. He went through a modified prestart checklist: emergency speedbrake knob NORMAL, emergency fuel transfer OFF, drop tank pressure OFF, fuel control PRIMARY, manual fuel shutoff NORMAL, throttle OFF, speedbrakes CLOSE, exterior lights OFF, flaps UP, airstart OFF, altimeter SET, radar altimeter OFF, emergency stores select ALL, arming switches OFF, tailhook UP, UHF radio OFF,

TACAN OFF, IFF OFF, SIF SET, compass SLAVED, interior lights OFF, emergency generator bypass NORMAL, cabin temp SET, windshield defrost HOLD.

Going through these mechanical checks had taken his mind off worrying and he felt fine. When he'd worked his way around the cockpit he glanced out at the plane captain standing by the starting unit.

Rawlins held up one finger. The plane captain nodded and gave him a thumbs-up. When the external power was connected, the instruments that jammed his little cockpit began coming to life. Lights flashed, dials rotated, needles quivered. Rawlins glanced at a couple of the gauges, then looked at the plane captain and held up two fingers. The plane captain flashed two fingers back, then a thumbs-up, and threw the switch for the high-pressure starting air. The Wright J-65-W-16A began to turn and a low whine emanated as the RPM built up. Rawlins always marveled at the intricacy of sounds when he started an airplane. Every gyro and servo and amplifier contributed its peculiar hum or whine and the result was like a muted musical arrangement conceived by some extraterrestrial Moog synthesizer. The most impressive sound in his life had been the high-pitched whine of the turbines the first time he started a Grumman F-11. It had been his first supersonic aircraft and the screaming of that paltry engine had been as awesome to Rawlins as the roar of the Saturn rocket must have been to the first Apollo crew. He was always inspired by the rhythms of the hundreds of minute mechanisms meshing, synchronizing, coming up to speed to form the whole of the airplane—a congress of components that produced stunning results when everything worked as advertised and terrifying ones when a part or two didn't.

Rawlins counted silently, "One thousand one, one thousand two, one thousand three, one thousand four." He moved the throttle around the horn to IDLE and monitored the engine performance indicator for exhaust gas temperature and RPM. As the RPM rose to the halfway point between START and IDLE, he held up three fingers, then held the fingers of one hand against the palm of the other and moved them abruptly apart as if pulling a plug. The plane captain cut off the air and moved under the aircraft to disconnect the external power and starter probe. When the engine had stabilized at idle, Rawlins checked the RPM, EGT, oil pressure, and fuel boost. He turned on the radios, checked the air start switch, warning lights, fuel and oxygen quantity, and started the clock.

The plane captain appeared in front of the aircraft and gave a thumbs-up. He then held his fist in front of him and moved it around in a horizontal circle. Rawlins moved the stick and rudders through full travel. The plane captain gave a thumbs-up and held his hand in front of him, palm down, opening and closing his thumb and fingers in alligator-mouth fashion, then crossed his index fingers in a plus sign. Rawlins lowered the flaps, then raised them to one half. The plane captain signaled thumbs-up again, then repeated the alligator-mouth and Rawlins cycled the speed brakes. Their silent ritual completed, he gave a sign to pull the chocks, then hit the mike button.

"Buckley Ground, Marine five lima one three for taxi, put my clearance on request, please."

"Marine five lima one three, Buckley Ground Control, taxi runway two five, altimeter two niner niner eight. Clearance on request, sir."

As he taxied out to the runway, he busied himself with compass, altimeter, fuel quantity, and the rest.

"Marine five lima one three, Buckley Ground Control with clearance. Ready to copy?"

"One three, go."

"Roger. ATC clears Marine five lima one three to the Los Alamitos Airport via flight planned route. Climb and maintain flight level two six zero, squawk one one zero zero, contact Denver Center three two one point one when airborne, over."

Rawlins read the clearance back and switched to tower frequency. He checked the trim, harness, canopy, and flaps.

"Buckley tower, Marine five lima one three, takeoff."

"Marine five lima one three, wind is light and variable. Cleared for takeoff."

The familiar rush of acceleration, scan the gauges, rotate, lift off, gear up, gauges, flaps up at 170 knots, trim, gauges, accelerate to climb speed, switch the UHF radio.

"Denver Center, Marine five lima one three, airborne, squawking one one zero zero, climbing to two six zero over." He was on his way.

Once Rawlins got everything cleaned up and squared away, was on course and on climb schedule, with nothing to do for the moment, the fear came back. He thought he felt queasy, but was not sure if he really felt queasy or was just afraid of starting to feel queasy. There seemed to be a tightness in his chest, as if something were putting pressure on his heart. But he wasn't sure. He had never fainted, never been unconscious in his life except for an occasional crash-and-burn at the bar or at a party, so he didn't know what the signals, if any, for an impending blackout would be. He was worried. He was starting to sweat, so he turned down the heat. He was scared shitless, actually, but he had to figure out what this thing was.

Old Smilin' Jack was not smiling now, but he stayed on course out of habit and trimmed automatically. The airplane was now forgotten. Instead of scanning the instruments, he was monitoring his vital signs. He was ready to abort the flight, step over the side, go to the Big Sleep, or whatever was on the old metaphysical flight schedule for the day, but he had to examine things, diagnose, posit, find out what the fuck was wrong with him. Or seemed to be wrong.

As he climbed higher, the cockpit pressurization decreased proportionately and what he perceived as the squeezing of his heart and lungs became more pronounced. This was his first inkling of a theory that he would propound, deny, question, experiment, and struggle with for years: that some internal plumbing or sealing defect was allowing gas from his stomach and/or intestines into the wrong compartment. As external pressure diminished at higher altitudes, the gas expanded, bringing to bear on those most vital organs the forces that caused him to think he was passing out. It was a sound theory and he was right, partly. Rawlins would later take an airplane out and test his theory. He would fly around at low altitude and feel relatively okay, physically, though the fear, the hint of dread, would always be in the back of his mind now, but when he zoom-climbed to twenty thousand feet, he could feel the pressure inside his chest build. Or thought he could. Then the queasiness, the shortness of breath, the obscure message from his cerebellum to his brain stem, saying "Hey, send out an SOS. We're not getting enough oxygen up here." And then, even through the fear, as he tensed his muscles and strained, concentrated, fought against the oblivion, he would expel gas, relieve pressures, and adjust and compensate and feel somewhat better, though not entirely comfortable, as the angst was still there.

Rawlins thought he might have a hole in his diaphragm, which was not far wrong. He was, in fact, developing a hiatus hernia, but that would not be accurately diagnosed for some ten years. What he didn't know, but should have suspected, was that the ravages of cigarettes and whiskey and general abuse were having a telling effect on his nervous system as a whole, and that while his imagination was being honed to a higher perception of incipient evil, his natural sense of well-being was steadily eroding. It was nature's inexorable reminder that she was going to kill him anyway, that he was terminal and it was only a matter of time. In later years he would come to reflect that perhaps there were other factors at work in the distintegration of his perfect, innocent self. Maybe guilt, maybe survivor's syndrome, maybe the emotional residue of a less than idyllic childhood. He would even come to give reluctant recognition to some of the myriad traumata that all card-carrying psychologists prattled about: That the irrational acts he had seen and done had possibly left a little undetected scar tissue.

Not the least of these was murdering seventy-five people with napalm one afternoon, simply because they were trying to murder some other people on the other side of the familiar triangular perimeter of a Special Forces camp. Only the seventy-five people were on *their* home turf and nobody needed any goddamn graffiti or other ground spoor to recognize that, and the other people were from five thousand miles away somewhere and were shooting at them, so why the hell *shouldn't* they murder them? And so on.

Only when Rawlins finally arrived at his war, the war he once felt he would never get, had been cheated out of because he was born too late, but the one that he got after all, was not cheated out of—only now, at this stage of his career, it was the war he did not want at all—when he got there he saw that he had better rationalize it some way and get comfortable with it. He was going to be here and take part for a year, like it or not, and if he didn't want to go crazy or go to the brig, and he didn't, or live the remainder of his life in disgrace—because he was a child of the fifties, the last generation of crew-cut American chauvinists who believed in democracy by aggression and Dulles diplomacy and not chickening out even if the alternative was checking out, so it *would* be disgrace if he didn't play—if he didn't want these things to happen, then he'd better learn to live with this war and resolve any difficulties.

So Rawlins did. His rationalization was simple enough. He reasoned that if, through no fault or action of his, but rather from some incomprehensible demographic compulsion, two people were trying to kill each other for any number of reasons, most probably unknown to either of the combatants, *but*, if they stood there blazing away at each other with an M-16 and an AK-47—and one was a red-haired, blue-eyed kid from California with "Devil Dog" tattooed on his left arm and "Yea though I walk through the valley of the shadow of death, I shall fear no evil, for I am the baddest motherfucker in the valley" scrawled on his flak jacket—and the other was a swarthy little fellow with black teeth and black pants and no tattoos except the scars of infant smallpox vaccinations, grown up with the man, and Rawlins had the Solomonic choice, then it was easy. He became the *deus ex machina*, greased the gook, saved the farmer from Kansas or the sausage maker from the Bronx who could then go out another day to step on a claymore made in the USA but pilfered from an overrun ARVN ammo dump by the Cong. Rawlins could collect his medals and march on to greater glory, endless happy hours, and oxford-cloth shirts with button-down collars.

And Rawlins never looked back. He and his wingman pressed on in at five hundred knots and pickled off cans of napalm that tumbled into the tree line only ten meters from the friendlies, creating instant piles of crispy critters and scorching the survivors out into the open, and didn't miss. Then they made long, shallow runs up the one street of the ville, where the bad guys were running for the hills, squirting off five-inch Zunis with their swirling smoke trails. Mucho KBA. Killed By Air. The colonels loved it, the generals loved it, and those Special Forces pogues inside the triangle, with their green beret–topped bodies most recently stuck down in the dirt so tight they could run over the rosary beads strung around their necks just by *pulse beat* for Christ's sake—they *really* loved it because it bought them another day.

So Rawlins and his wingman pushed on in there, low and fast and right on target, their airplanes screaming like the ghouls of a thousand hells, raining fire and death by asphyxiation even before you were cooked, the ugly, blunt-nosed Mark-77 cans tumbling off and igniting the entire goddamn sky, sucking the oxygen right out of your lungs. Even the friendlies couldn't breathe, there was so much fire, but the ten meters between them and the tree line was the difference. They had been perhaps one minute away from being overrun and having their balls cut off and stuck in their mouths, but only half that minute later, they peeped one eye over the sandbags and all that confronted them was the scorched, fried, devastated stalks of jungle forestation, with small fires burning here and there and not one living, moving, fucking thing in sight.

When those boys got back to regiment with their eyebrows singed off, but their balls still hanging where they belonged, they were *grateful*. One of them called up the 3rd Marine Air Wing and talked to General Jefferson's aide.

"Hey," he said, "those guys in the Condone flight saved our *ass*. Why don't you get 'em a medal or something?"

The aide spoke to the group awards officer, who was combing his cornsilk mustache. "Any colonels on the flight?" he asked.

"No."

"Silver Star's out. Any majors?"

"Nope."

"DFC's out. Senior captains?"

"Let's see here. Hmm. Not very senior, oh nine oh seven two six?"

"Single mission Air Medal's out." He held up a hand mirror, liking the way the white-blond mustache set off his dark eyes. "Tell the general to write 'em a letter."

"Good idea, Captain," said General Jefferson when his aide had told him the idea that now was his. "Write 'em a letter."

"Me, sir?"

Jefferson arched his eyebrows and, archly, scrutinized each corner of the room. He then trapped his aide with a heavy stare. "Unless our position has been infiltrated," he said, "I believe you are the only swinging dick in this office besides me."

"Uh, yes sir. What would the General have the letter say, sir?"

The general arched brows again. "I would have it say what the fuck they all say, Captain. You know. 'It is with a great deal of pride, etcetera, etcetera, aggressive airmanship, accurate delivery, blah, blah, blah, highly commendable, blah, blah, my personal congratulations for a job well done,' and sign it."

"Aye, aye, sir."

So Rawlins got a note from the general that was really from a captain, and was a minor hero for a day or two until he got drunk and overslept and missed an AOM and was back on Major Poltroun's shit list again, where he was more comfortable.

But Rawlins never thought about the other side of the tree line. Neither during the war nor for several years after did he pay much attention to, or even consciously recall, most of the things he had seen and done. It needed some years of imagined suffering, disappointment and disillusionment, and watching his feet turn to clay—brittle, impure clay at that, clear up to his ass and then some—before he would reach the point of frustration and desperation at which he would timidly begin to grasp at straws like psychological scar tissue, or give credence to such harebrained tenets as the idea that the past determines the present and even, to some degree, the future.

But on the day that Rawlins flew for the first time with the angst along, the monster of dread, perched up there on his shoulders in the tiny cockpit, the war, he felt, and the war within a war, were far behind him. And all the questioning was ahead.

It was rough, that first time, maybe the roughest of all the times because it was all new. Even though it got worse as time went on, worse to the point that he would one day find himself sitting in his apartment drinking scotch, with Miles Davis's "Concierto de Aranjuez" cranked right on up there, pondering the .357 magnum that he cradled in his lap—still it came to be a familiar presence, however terrifying. So the first time may have been the roughest. Stuffed into the airplane, five miles above the planet that he longed to get his feet on, but that was nonetheless unfriendly in his immediate situation, someone had set a safe on his chest, and his ears and little fingers seemed to be numb and maybe a couple of other fingers and was he light-headed, or did he just imagine it? The first thirty minutes were one entire age of man, worse than anything he had done. Worse even than towing that son of a bitch, muscle-bound little sinker three lengths of the pool for the lifesaving test in preflight. He flew with his left hand fingering the face curtain and nothing to do but worry, but conjure up more demons. When Denver Center handed him off to Salt Lake Center he had a short respite, something to do, something to occupy him for a few seconds. Two things were paramount. He must fight this thing, find out what it was and confront it, beat it. And no one must know about it. He couldn't breathe a word of this to anyone. Bad show. Weakness.

After a while it got a little easier. It was still there, but nothing had happened and the stark terror was dulled a little. By the time the controller, with his clipped, flat, monotonous, but still cheerful, reassuring voice, just like a thousand other controllers, had started him down, just before Cajon Pass, he busied himself in the cockpit and got his mind off the monkey. He felt almost normal. The anxiety was nearly gone. It would come again, though.

Mortality.

7

California, 1960s

Mrs. Gunnery Sergeant O'Flynn had become disaffected with the Vietnam conflict. This condition did not stem from any creeping humanism or knee-jerk liberal-socialist leaning, it was simply that her husband was over there involved in the thing and through some idiotic caprice of the gods of war, he had been demoted to gunnery sergeant. This, in itself, did not concern that redoubtable lady because she knew that he would do exactly the same thing regardless of his rank—very little. No, as she adjusted the flower-spangled hairnet that was to conceal most of her curlers while she made her weekly foray to the supermarket, she reflected that Ex-Master Gunnery Sergeant O'Flynn's demotion concerned her because he made less money, and her monthly allotment check had gone down accordingly. Mrs. O'Flynn was feeling the well-known economic crunch. If things got any worse, she would have to consider accepting some kind of employment to supplement the purchase of Hummels and other works of art, and support her insatiable lust for church bingo games. And what was an uneducated, unskilled connoisseur of daytime television to do?

Of course Vietnam had nothing to do with O'Flynn's demotion. What had to do with O'Flynn's demotion was R^2 Jones coming into the break supersonic and DeVille Hoggins's refusal, in an act that Al "Shaky" Morgenkrank considered tantamount to sedition, refusal, *failure*, to move his black ass out of that line shack before the begreased Master Gunnery Sergeant O'Flynn could crack his skull with a box-end wrench. It was DeVille Hoggins who was almost solely responsible for the uncelebrated demotion, but somehow Mrs. O'Flynn associated all her troubles with the Vietnam flap. The politicians said the war was a great burden that all citizens must bear; the economists said the war was uneconomical; the moralists said the war was immoral; and the humanists said the war was inhumane. Everybody said the war caused inflation and was debilitating to our servicemen. Mrs. O'Flynn said the war sucked. Actually she didn't say that, because Mrs. Gunnery Sergeant O'Flynn did not use profanity or vulgarities. She only thought it. Corporal Parton would have said the war sucked, except that Buck Sergeant Parton did not by any means think that was the case. He loved the war because it was good for business, if you were a military man, and he had managed to sneak another meritorious promotion across the old man's desk with a pile of papers for signature and had become a buck sergeant almost before the ink was dry on his corporal's warrant. He had the lowest cutting score in history, but he took his promotions meritoriously, so it didn't matter. Buck Sergeant Parton had already decided to ship over and was considering a Marine Corps career.

But Mrs. Gunnery Sergeant O'Flynn blamed everything on Vietnam and she thought the war sucked, even if she didn't say so.

When Gunnery Sergeant O'Flynn got busted to staff sergeant for killing the wrong man for the right reason, and Mrs. O'Flynn's allotment check was reduced even further, she took a job with Dulcie's Dynamic Catering Service and vowed to do everything within her power to end this tragic war. It had cost her dearly in service-related remuneration. She was further deprived of the second income that her husband made, when he was stationed stateside, by overhauling people's cars with the complete set of tools that he had pilfered from the base over the years. Enough was enough, and Mrs. O'Flynn went into the catering business with some vigor. She entered into the antiwar movement with the same determination.

Dulcie was an altruistic hedonist, a radical moderate, and a liberal capitalist. Because of her contacts she was widely used by rich California liberals who were always throwing bashes in those big tents, all aflutter with banners and pennants that put them in mind of Camelot or something, around their swimming pools, to raise money to send doves to Washington and end this terrible war. Mrs. O'Flynn spent many balmy nights under these canopies. Her husband spent every night in a tent. They would have Dulcie and Mrs. O'Flynn catering up the crab salad, finger sandwiches, and caviar *en croute*, and Rene, the French Canadian deserter from that peaceful army to the north, pouring the Chardonnay. Ismael, the Mexican waiter, would be busy rat-holing enough chow to feed his family of seven. His were the skinniest kids in their school because their diet was mostly cocktail shrimp, watercress, and brie cheese on stone-ground wafers.

Then Barbi Belheur would strum the three chords she knew and start wailing out a protest song. Barbi was a folksinger whose records all became platinum after her haunting, soulless rendition of "We Shall Overcome" hit the top of the charts. Oddly enough, that was the same day that Moon Dog slipped out the gate for some black-market shopping in the sewer of Dogpatch, and there, among the miniature Vietnamese flags, miniature electric fans, full-sized Zippo lighters, and other items stolen from the PX, he found a neat black button, with red lettering that said, "We Shall Overkill." The eleven-year-old all-around Merchant of Venice who was hawking these goods, among other things, only wanted fifty cents for the button, but Moon thought it was worth at least a dollar, so he paid her that. He took the lieutenant's bar off his camouflage utility cover, tossed it to the peddler as a tip, and replaced it with his shiny new button, which he wore for the rest of the war. So with very nearly the same motto, the fighter pilot and the folksinger prospered through those tumultuous times. Moon Dog collected body counts and Barbi Belheur collected money.

The corrupted girl-woman who sold Moon the button, in all her accelerated wisdom, could not fathom the inscrutable American. If a painted tin button was worth a silver-plated bar *and* a dollar, what price might other trinkets command? She made a mental note to stock more beads, mirrors, and other bright objects. One reason she had to concern herself with trade goods was that her prepubescent body was not yet sufficiently filled out nor cleaned up to be very marketable.

And Barbi Belheur collected more than money. She began to garner acclaim, renown even, as a revolutionary philosopher. As her records became hits and the attendance at her concerts rose, it was perceived by the teenaged constituency of the nation that she spoke far more profound truths than did literate reactionaries, apologists, politicians, and other pigs over thirty. Moon thought that he should kill as many Cong as possible, that being, *de facto*, a deterrent to the Cong's killing of his teammates in the game of war. Barbi Belheur felt that the Cong should kill as many Americans as possible because that would reduce the probability of the fascist conspiracy being able to sully and undermine the glorious Communist victory of the people. And Barbi was listened to more and more by the bright young (or old) ideologues of the Left, primarily because she could draw a larger crowd than the average graduate student or radical politician. Barbi became a sought-after speaker on campuses around the country. Her fee grew to five thousand dollars.

Barbi was often asked to entertain at the parties that Dulcie and Mrs.

O'Flynn catered. There was usually a Black Panther security force, all in their little leather berets, to guard against Nazis, John Birchers, Republicans, surfers, and others who might seek to crash the party. The featured speaker was usually a senator from South Dakota, who would speak for a half an hour or so, in a quiet, sincere, slightly effeminate voice, against this awful war. Quite often he would be followed by the mayor of Los Angeles, who would stand up, blustery, and talk *for* the war for thirty minutes, in support of the president, thereby canceling out the senator. Except that most of the minds present were predisposed against the war, so, ironically, the ravings of the hawkish, maverick mayor in fact *validated* the senator. But they were congenial speakers and good solid party men, and funds were raised. The guests nibbled their canapés and sipped their white wine, applauded politely, joined in a song or two, and got out their check books.

Mrs. Staff Sergeant O'Flynn had been hot-housed inside the military cocoon for all the twenty-odd years of her marriage and had never heard anyone talk *against* war before. War was the *raison d'être* (as Candyass Cavendish would have said), the ultimate legitimacy that succored her world. Everybody wooed and caressed it, believed in it, and sang the ballads of the ages, all festooned up with the glory of the good fight.

But as surely as Staff Sergeant O'Flynn's dress blues, with the red stripe running down each leg, signifying the bloody battle of Chapultepec, seduced him to the way of the warrior, Mrs. O'Flynn's black nylon dress and white Chantilly lace–trimmed apron won her to a different march. As she shuttled the silver salvers and heard the rhetoric of the Left at party after party, it began to ring true. She found herself humming some of Barbi's catchier ballads. Especially as her husband continued to get himself busted, and her allotment checks dwindled, Mrs. O'Flynn was converted to the cause of peace. She began to synthesize into her own meager musings the prophetic insights of Barbi Belheur, who was educated at Pasadena City College.

Mrs. O'Flynn found herself watching the six o'clock news with stirrings of urgency. Night after night she saw the medevac choppers hauling off the blood and guts that remained of America's youth. It seemed that was all they ever showed. They would slap the compress bandages on sucking chest wounds, strap the muddy, sweaty, grimacing boys to stretchers, stick lit cigarettes in their mouths, and haul them away. It occurred to her that one evening on Channel 7 she might see her husband swathed in muddy, bloody gauze, with a plasma bottle dripping into his remaining arm. She knew they all died as soon as they got off camera.

That would really fix the allotment check. And Dulcie did not pay her enough to live on. Not by a long shot. Besides, she liked O'Flynn sometimes. Didn't he take her to the Staff NCO club every Sunday?

And so another mother for peace emerged. Maybe not in the strictest sense, since Mrs. O'Flynn was childless, but then Buck Sergeant Parton would almost certainly have called her a mother.

8

Southeast Asia, 1960s

Shortly after the incident of the steaming Pyrex, before even his scalded balls had peeled and healed, General Jefferson found himself in hot water again. Only two days had elapsed since Lieutenant R² Jones's supersonic pass over the adjacent retirement community en route to the hottest break in Marine aviation history, when the results started coming in. The first tally included a dropped Sparklett's water bottle and resulting crushed seventy-nine-year-old foot, which might have to be amputated. There were two cardiac arrests and a suddenly mute, catatonic wife who had shown no deficiencies in the talking department during the first fifty-two years of her marriage. There were cracked bay windows, dead parakeets, and blown-out hearing aids. And so on. There was as yet no firm assessment of damage to pacemakers, but several of their wearers were ensconced in oxygen tents, being monitored by other machines too big to carry around. The claims were mounting, and the worst part was that they were not just coming to General Jefferson. Many were going straight to the Commandant and beyond. The Department of the Navy. God knew Lyndon wouldn't have anyone fucking with his senior citizens!

The Commandant of the Marine Corps was, of course, a grunt, because they always are. As a ground pounder he had neglected to expand and refine his appreciation of the inherent humor in flying stories. The veteran of only a few years of happy hours at air base officers clubs can see the classic comedy in nearly any anecdote having to do with flight, but the Commandant could not. When he spoke to General Jefferson he did not seem to be amused at all. Commandants tend to be a little stuffy.

What the Commandant told General Jefferson, in a general way, was that if one more complaint, of any nature, were received from his sector, it would be curtains. He was given a direct order to preclude his base and all its personnel from offending anyone. Anyone! If one octogenarian heard an airplane and didn't like the sound of it, if one drunken Marine brushed his red-knuckled hand with the bitten-down fingernails along the panty line of a waitress in a beer bar and it didn't feel good, to her that is, Jefferson was sunk. One complaint would be evidence that the general had disobeyed a direct order in time of war. He would be stripped of his command, court-martialed, and shot, any of which might dash his political hopes.

So General Jefferson closed his base. He summoned all the group commanders and all the squadron commanders to his conference room within the hour and gave them their instructions. All airplanes and all pilots were to be sent away immediately. Extended cross-countries, weapons training deployments, TAD, he didn't care what kind of orders they were on, just get them out of California. They would operate from the transient flight lines of other bases, UFN. They would be issued unlimited fuel chits and the transport outfit would be dedicated to supporting them by shuttling maintenance personnel and equipment wherever they were needed. All yellow sheets and other substantiating paperwork were to be telexed back to General Jefferson daily, so that he could continue to report normal flight operations and take credit for business as usual. Only there would be no incidents. Not in his sector.

He then put all the enlisted swine on port and starboard duty sections and declared indefinite restriction to base for all personnel. Every morning at the changing of the guard, the half who had not been on duty were issued weapons and orders to shoot to kill, then posted at hundred-foot intervals around the perimeter of the base. The other half of the troops had the day off to shine shoes or brass and go to the club, the PX, or the bowling alley. No one left the base and no one came on it and there were no incidents.

The plan worked so well that a few months later, when the Commandant was casting about for a new idiot to replace the other idiot, who had been relieved for fucking up the conduct of the war, General Jefferson was a shoo-in candidate. Flat-hatting incidents actually increased in several other areas of the country, but there was not one report from Jefferson's sector.

So, by closing his base, General Jefferson became such an effective base commander that he was put in charge of the war, the last place on earth he wanted to be. General Jefferson's LAW: The likelihood of your being sent to a particular duty station varies directly to the square of how much you don't want to go there. Several long-term military planners surmised that General Jefferson would use the same formula for success on his war as he had on his base, and close it down, but that was not to be.

"Just so, Jeff," said the Commandant. "I expect you to take charge of your post and all government property within view and run it just like you've been running your base. No incidents, no complaints. I want happy citizens in that war zone, just like you've got in California. Understand?"

"Yes sir. This is quite an honor, General. Uh, do I have permission to close it down, sir?"

"Close it down? Close what down, General?"

"The war, sir. Just pack it in. We're sure to eliminate complaints that way."

"General, don't talk like a damned fool. Must I point out to you that this is the only war we've got? Would you waste all the effort it took to get this far? No, Jeff, don't talk nonsense." The Commandant gazed out the window, contemplating the necessity of war to a business like his. You had to have wars regularly to remind the people that war was inevitable in a civilized nation, so they would pay the taxes to fund the insurmountable military organization that would ensure that those inevitable wars did not occur and would then, of course, go fight those wars when they sprang up. General Jefferson tugged at the shoulder strap of the Sam Browne belt that he always wore. "Another fine mess you've got me into," he was thinking.

"Sir, I was only thinking of the complaints. If you wage war on a civilian populace, in their own country, even if you bomb them into submission, there may be resentment. I would venture to say that airplanes shooting cannons and rockets invite more complaints than just airplanes making noise."

The Commandant ran an index finger along his pencil-thin mustache. "Be that as it may, Jefferson, we must keep our war. I want you to go out there and run the damn thing the best way you know how. I want you to bomb those slope-headed Communists to their knees and bring freedom to the masses of Asia. Then we'll set up a democratic government and show 'em how to run it and the Commies can crawl back to Red Russia with their tails between their legs. You're the best man for the job, General, and remember, when you've got 'em by the balls, their hearts and minds will follow."

So that was how General Jefferson inherited the war he didn't want and came to be the only aviator in history who had fought in three wars and only had two missions. The political stratagems he had devised would have to be put off for a year. Indeed, they would be put off for several years, but he didn't know that yet. He was not pleased by this turn of events.

Someone else who was not pleased by this turn of events was Colonel Creed. Try as he might, he could not see how the transfer of General Jefferson could possibly enhance his career. Indeed, the return of Jefferson as his commanding officer spelled disaster. And while Creed was lamenting his involuntary return to the thrall of General Jefferson and the unsatisfactory fitness report he was sure to get for the next period, another problem emerged. Troubles always came in bunches. It seemed the General Staff of the Army of the Republic of Vietnam in I Corps was now bivouacked in the ruins of the Buddhist temple outside the gate. They had indicated that they would unleash heavy small arms fire and perhaps automatic weapons and light artillery on any more Marines seeking to cart away truckloads of rocks. Upon learning this, the motor pool, in true Teamster fashion, and the working parties, in true laborer fashion, declared a wildcat strike, and construction of the OM club screeched to a halt. Colonel Creed could not persuade any of the grunt commanders to counterattack, because they had been fighting side by side with these men for over a year, at least on those occasions when the ARVN showed up and did not leave early, and the grunts had been indoctrinated not to engage in hostilities with their allies unless provoked, or at the very least until they had received orders from some higher command. Besides, they had their hands full with the bad gooks without taking on the good gooks. The motor pool and the working parties refused any attempt to retake the ruins, stating that that sort of work was out of their MOS and that special training was required for it.

The army was the Buddhist-dominated wing of the Vietnamese militia and had some obscure attachment to that fallen-down temple. It looked like they were there to stay. Colonel Creed could not frag an air attack on the temple unless it were suspected to be occupied by the enemy and, unfortunately, the occupiers were *bona fide* friendly forces who would scream all the way to Saigon and cause real trouble if he bombed them. He thought of trying to disguise his airplanes as MiGs, but the ARVN were too used to seeing the Phantoms come and save their ass to be fooled. Nguyen Van Dan was already running out of stone and the critical path method dictated that the walls had to go up before the roof went on, and if they didn't have the roof up before the monsoon came, there would be no club until next year. He had to find a way to drive the dinks out of his personal rock quarry, but for the moment the colonel's hands were tied.

He needn't have worried. All the fuss was over Premier Ky's announcement that he was postponing the long-promised elections for another year, which wasn't a major development in view of the years they had already been postponed, but the ARVN command got miffed and declared a state of sedition. Ky was a Catholic, and as the *ipso facto* dictator, was the figurehead of the Christian minority, which controlled, some said oppressed, the great unwashed, who happened to be of the Buddhist persuasion. Ky said that a civilian government could not be functional for at least a year, which was probably true, so he would just stay in office and keep a handle on things until it got straightened out. To back him up he had the Vietnamese Marines and the Air Force who were all good loyal Catholics, and, being guided by superhuman wisdom, knew that Ky was absolutely right. This idea chafed on the Buddhist Army Command some, and they kept talking insurrection. *That* idea rankled Ky, so what he did while most of the Army was in the field was move the loyal Marines in and take over the I Corps Army Headquarters, which is why the Buddhist Army was camped out in Colonel Creed's temple.

When Ky, who was also the commander of the Air Force, brought his crack squadron of ADs, looking like a swarm of Spads from the Great War, into Da Nang, the Buddhist Army knew what to do. They set up their four-deuce mortars and began to indiscriminately lob rounds toward the flight line where the Spads sat, in retaliation for the Marines' adverse possession of their headquarters. This irked the VNAF no end and they knew what to do, too. They launched a bevy of Spads and began to indiscriminately fire rockets and 20 mike-mike into the temple ruins and the surrounding city. The only real loser in the mortar attack was not the VNAF, but the U.S. Air Force. None of the rounds came within three hundred yards of the Spads, but one scored a direct hit on a USAF C-123 that was loading up on Agent Orange to go water the jungle. The plane was destroyed, two troopers were killed outright, and a half dozen more were sloshed with the defoliant, which took the hide off. Actually, that was the least of it. It would be fifteen years before Agent Orange would be unmasked as a killer carcinogen and four of the splattered airmen would sue the government for $30 million and collect, claiming service-connected cancers, impotence, and hair and earning-power loss.

Colonel Creed rubbed his hands together with glee as he observed the rocketing and strafing of the temple. He sensed, with his keen military intuition, that this was the beginning of the repatriation of his stone yard. He couldn't know it yet, but this was to be the shot heard round the hobo camp, because it would lead to the allies being certified as also being the enemy, at least temporarily, and would allow him to frag a couple of missions to the ruins to help put down the insurgency and regain his precious building materials. It would also allow Moon Dog to establish the all-time unchallenged TPQ record of just under seven minutes, chock to chock. The night, radar-controlled, random bomb drops called TPQs were usually short because there were suspected VC all around the base, and the radar people often chose to harass positions quite nearby. The record had stood for some months at eighteen minutes, but when Moon Dog checked in with Night Owl Three while he was still in a burner climb, got his heading, altitude, and airspeed directions, did an Immelman, came out of burner, rolled out on the money, dumping fuel, rippled his bombs on the downwind leg, popped the speed brakes, and called for landing, the old mark was shattered forever. The thing that wasted so much time, Moon complained, was taxiing. The sound and the shock waves of the thousand-pounders detonating in the nave of the old Buddhist sanctuary nearly deafened Colonel Creed, who was sitting on a folding chair on the porch of his hootch observing through night-vision binoculars. He loved every minute of it.

Lance Major Slocum weighed over two hundred pounds. He had played guard in high school and he was pretty good; he was tough. In college he got cut because he was too slow. He could never pull and get to the hole before the running back was gone. If the coach could have seen Slocum move when the first mortar round exploded outside his tent and sent searing, rough-edged fragments of metal zapping through the tattered, furiously flapping, snapping canvas, roaring and forcing the concussive waves and the smell of cordite into the ears and nostrils—if the coach could have seen Slocum cross the five-man tent floor in two strides and dive through the mosquito netting at the side, carrying it away, dive headlong into the entrance to the sandbagged bunker outside—Slocum would have made the team. He was sound asleep on his folding cot, sweating peacefully, when the first angry, buzzing, hissing shrapnel whizzed by above his face and the concussion rocked the wooden floor of the tent. A few milliseconds later, he was en route to the bunker like a terrified buffalo, crushing anything that stood in his way. And Slocum was not alone. The hobo camp was set up along no particular lines. A jumble of five-man tents on wooden decks, pitched randomly, it had grown much as the war zone had, in various directions, by differing increments, as the effort mounted. It housed all the officers of Marine Air Group-22. There had once been an official sign saying:

MAG-22
OFFICERS QUARTERS

The sign had disappeared, and no one knew where it was except Hang Dog, who had needed lumber for the desk he was building, and the sign was now part of it. Someone had substituted one that said, simply, in a scrawl:

HOBO CAMP

There was a clearing at the general center of the tents where a bunch of the boys had been catching some rays in the altogether. That was before decency came to Da Nang in the form of a group order that forbade nude sunbathing.

When the first round went off, there was a spectacle that would have warmed the hearts of the distaff members of every culture, had any been present. There were assholes and elbows and swinging dicks with varying shades of suntan going to all points of the compass.

Lance Major Slocum crashed into the bunker like a wounded elephant, and nearly crushed Rawlins, who had beat him there by a step. Slocum's cheek was bleeding. He spat out a tiny piece of shrapnel and said: "God, what if that would've been my eye."

"Fuck your eyes," said Rawlins. "Get off me, you horse's ass." Slocum didn't move, but began searching in the soft dirt for the frag that had pierced his cheek. Rawlins struggled, rolled him aside, and started to rise. Another round hit nearby and he hunkered right back down again.

"What the fuck's going on here, Rawlins?"

"We're being mortared by the ARVN."

"I thought they were on our side."

"That was yesterday."

"What the fuck are they mortaring us for?"

"They're not. They're mortaring the VNAF, but they're so far off target that they're hitting us by mistake." The crash of another round blew a wall of thick, choking dust and smoke into the mouth of the bunker, and the men shrunk inside themselves as they lay stuck to the soft dirt of the deck.

"Fuckers never could shoot straight."

Slocum squirmed tighter into a corner. "Well, if they're not mortaring us, what the fuck are they mortaring the VNAF for?"

"Because Ky is the head of the VNAF and he won't let them hold elections for another year."

"Tell me this. What the hell are we doing in this good-deal war anyway?"

"We have to drive the Communists back out of here so the masses of South Vietnam will continue to have the freedom of choice."

"But the ARVN is mortaring the VNAF because they *already* don't have the freedom of choice, right?"

"You got it, Slocum."

"Then why bother to drive out the Communists?"

"They don't believe in democracy."

"Then the North Vietnamese Army is trying to give them the same thing they don't have now, wouldn't you say?"

"Well, in a way, yes."

"Then what the fuck is wrong with the NVA? They're the same as what they got."

"They're Communists."

Small arms fire began to crackle along the perimeter of the base. Scared Marines who didn't have anything real to shoot at blazed away at imagined movement in the elephant grass. It was contagious. One would fire a burst and three or four others just couldn't hold back any longer. There was lead flying all around the place and Rawlins and Slocum gripped their useless little .38s and hugged the ground.

"I don't care if they are Communists or Republicans. If both sides are offering the same thing to the people, what's the point of having the goddamn war?"

"You just don't get it, Slocum." Of course Rawlins didn't get it either, nobody got it, but also nobody admitted that he didn't get it.

Moon Dog, Hang Dog, Cavendish, and Captain America were in another bunker. Hang Dog was mimicking a U-boat captain, fooling with an imaginary periscope and quoting all the lines he could remember from World War II movies. "Up periscope! Fire one! Fire two! Down scope! Dive, dive, dive!" A mortar round shook the ground, and Hang said, "Oooh, doggie! Rig for silent running. They're walking in with the depth charges."

Every time the ground shook and the heat and dust blasted over, Cavendish, rolled up in a ball, languorous face buried in his hands, stifled a squeal. Moon Dog was cleaning his finger nails with his K bar. Captain America was popping up with his camera during each lull, trying to snap a picture of an explosion. He found all this downright interesting and wanted some good shots. Moon nudged the Horst Buchholz figure as he manipulated his periscope. "That crazy Captain America's gonna get his ass blowed off one of these days, Skipper." Hang Dog switched to another character.

"Ugh. Big boom come from father sky. Kill many pony soldier."

Colonel Creed was furious. The ADs rocketing the ruins had at first been encouraging, but this was getting out of hand. If those meddlesome fucking indigenous personnel dropped so much as one round into the stone revetment of the OM club, they would have a real war on their hands. He had already alerted all the hot pads, and they were standing by to scramble on the Buddhist temple if matters deteriorated. That night he would frag some TPQs over the place with thousand-pounders and run the bastards out. One of those missions would be Moon Dog's record-setting sortie.

As if controlled by whim, the mortaring stopped. Gradually the ecdysiasts went back to their sunbathing. Slocum went to sick bay and got a Band-Aid on his cheek. They signed him up for his Purple Heart while he was there. Rawlins had to go fly a hop. Cavendish busied himself with a letter to the editor of his hometown newspaper, telling the folks how they had nearly been overrun by hordes of crack troops. How they would, indeed, have been overrun and routed, but for the intrepid leadership of certain young officers, whose names it would serve no purpose to mention here. Suffice it to say that the writer was in the thick of the fray and he could personally testify that the Marines acquitted themselves with no small measure of glory. And so on.

Casualties were light. A C-47 was hit in a main fuel cell and burned to the ground. Lance Major Slocum suffered a small hole in his cheek. Two airmen and a mama-san were found dead, partially clothed, in a clearing in some brush near a shit ditch along the base perimeter. It was wondered what they were doing there with their clothes off, but according to the letters to the airmen's next of kin, they were bravely defending the perimeter. There was no letter to the mama-san's next of kin.

Things really picked up in town, though. Patrols of Vietnamese Marines and ARVN soldiers started to ambush each other in the streets of the city, spraying small arms fire all over town. The Spad drivers were madder than ever. They began buzzing around the city in random racetrack patterns, diving at intervals to squeeze off 2.75-inch rockets or strafe capriciously.

Small children, born and nurtured in war, ran and played in the streets, shrieking and laughing, following the patrols, often only ten paces behind the skirmish lines in the nasty little firefights. Some of them fell.

So General Jefferson not only inherited a war he didn't want, he inherited a war he didn't want and hadn't even known about, *within* a war he didn't want. He reported to higher command what was going on and they told him he was crazy. He looked off at the clouds of black smoke billowing up over the city and the specks of ADs droning around them. He half-expected to see a great ape with Fay Wray in one hand emerge. Maybe he *was* crazy, he thought. He didn't know whose side he was on. He hoped they would straighten it out by tomorrow. They wouldn't, though. If he had known Rawlins's LAW, he would have known that things would get a lot worse before they got better.

9

California, 1970s

As the seventies and all the attendant trauma, violence, and division got underway, Rawlins didn't think about the war much. He did not have a television set, didn't subscribe to a paper, and largely didn't give a shit. It may have been that he was subconsciously avoiding thoughts of the war. Oh, a few more acquaintances were killed over the years, but no close friends. Rawlins would not have suspected it, but the truth was that he had no close friends. This was, at least in part, because of his years in the fighter-pilot community. If you got too close to someone, he might suddenly be plucked away and that was painful, unsettling, and confusing. He discovered this early on in the training command, when one day his roommate did not return from a routine hop, having buried himself, an instructor, and an F-9 Cougar in the desert sands of east Texas. Better to have casual acquaintances, to the memory of whom, when they killed themselves, you could drink a flaming hooker, say "There but for the grace of God go I," and continue the party.

But this idea went much deeper with Rawlins. He thought of himself as being hard and fairly invulnerable to "weakness," but in truth he was by nature very sensitive. This sensitivity had left him open to pain at a tender age and his mind had then set about protecting itself. He had unknowingly constructed a tortuous network of mental defenses. After his first *bona fide* broken heart, administered by a teenaged vamp whose name he tried for years to forget, but couldn't, his mind said to itself, "Never again."

So Rawlins never let women or anybody else get close to him. They were fine for dancing, sleeping, and sharing his secret and rudimentary attempts at poetry with, but that was as far as it went.

A battery of graduate students in psychology, or chimpanzees with typewriters, could probably have posited, devolved, and extrapolated that Rawlins's motivations were much the same as the Commandant's had been when he put General Jefferson in charge of the war. All he wanted was a quiet, peaceful life of war, undisturbed by the complaint or other annoyance of the occasional civilian. They just didn't want to have to deal with distress and disharmony. No waves.

If Rawlins didn't often think of the war and the deteriorating situation in Vietnam and, *ergo*, the unraveling of the American society, he *never* thought of his own situation or the unraveling that was surely taking place in that quarter. His flying career was temporarily reprieved by Valium. The little yellow pills were truly magic. He could swallow one and go fly his airplane just like in the old days. The dread was gone. The monkey was off his back. On a bad day he could swallow two.

The first time it happened outside the airplane it really scared him. There was no excuse, nothing to blame it on. There was no bad oxygen, no pressure differential. Something was wrong with his body and he assumed that of course it must be a heart attack. It struck him one hungover morning in a coffee shop. He was having breakfast with a friend, speaking very carefully, tentatively, about the funny little problems he was experiencing, when it hit him. The fear. The dread. The chest pains, or were they imagined chest pains? The tightness, the numbness of the fingers, the shortness of breath. But mostly just the fear. He absolutely *knew* that he was dying.

Rawlins persuaded his friend to drive him straight to a doctor's office. He hoped, with the desperation of a dying man, that they would be in time. They were.

"Hypertension," said the MD, a spare, lanky man with gold-rimmed glasses. The air hissed out of the cuff that embraced Rawlins's arm. "There's nothing wrong with your heart." He dropped the stethoscope from ears to neck. "In fact, it has to be working pretty well to get your pressure up to two-twenty over one-thirty." He began to write on a prescription pad. "Take one of these four times a day," he said.

And thus did Rawlins discover Valium. He followed the instructions faithfully for a week, finding that five milligrams of Valium four times a day thoroughly neutralized his short-term memory. He would promise with great enthusiasm to meet someone for lunch and then forget to go. He was so zonked out that Friday or Saturday, he couldn't remember which, he seemed to recall having had a close brush with life. Four a day seemed not the ideal dosage for Rawlins, so he countermanded the doctor's orders and took the pills only when he felt he needed them.

One morning, while flying for the Reserves, he took two. He was hungover, had very little sleep, and felt the demons raging inside him, so he dropped two of the yellow tablets down his throat. He taxied out to the end of the runway and had to wait for his clearance. Sitting there in the bright morning sun, feet on the brakes, the airplane idling smoothly, he dozed off. He did not know how long he was out, but awoke to the tower's fairly agitated radio chatter.

"Marine five lima zero seven, Los Alamitos tower, how do you read? Over.

"Marine five lima zero seven, do you read the tower? Repeat, five lima zero seven, do you read me?"

"Oh, tower? Five lima zero seven. Uh, I seem to be having some radio problems, but you're five-square now. How me?"

"Five lima zero seven, loud and clear. I have your clearance. Ready to copy?"

"Five lima zero seven, go."

So he fell asleep for a minute. It was kind of funny, sitting there in the airplane ready to take off and falling asleep. But it was only for a moment. No big deal.

When the body that Rawlins abused, the physical plant he ravaged and ignored, when that fell into deterioration and weakness, he needed the infusion of false serenity and the semblance of strength that came from the little yellow pills. And once in a while, when he happened to read or see something about Vietnam, it was usually a disclosure that that bothersome little nation was being administered a new dose of salts by Dr. Nixon. Guns and money. It occurred to Rawlins that the therapy was bound to fail. But those wretched buggers clung to their fabulae, took their pills, and assured each other that things would indeed, get better. So did Rawlins.

10

California, 1960s

When Barbi Belheur met Polly Esther Proudbird, who was one thirty-second pure-blooded Cherokee, it was a marriage made in heaven. Barbi was in Sacramento to chain herself to the governor's desk in protest of the new ROTC unit that was being given offices and class-rooms at Cal State Fullerton. As Barbi approached the capitol, sagging under the weight of the tote bag filled with locks and chains, she saw the tall Native American, with the purposeful stride, carrying a picket sign that said:

CEDE SISKIYOU COUNTY TO ITS RIGHTFUL HEIRS

Those turned out to be the unmarried heads of households having Indian blood of any tribe. Barbi inquired of Polly Esther, or P.E. as she was known, whether there had been any reaction to her vigil: storm troopers, tear gas, napalm, or the like? P.E. replied that she had been there for hours and, sadly, there had been no confrontation whatsoever. This, they learned from a young clerk who passed by, was because the governor was not using his Sacramento office. He had never even been to his Sacramento office. This was in protest of his predecessor, who had spent $83 million to refurbish the state capitol building. The governor felt that this was shameless squandering of public funds and that these monies should have been divided among migrant workers, welfare moth-ers, gang members who did counseling, and presidential campaign funds. He vowed never to enter the garish, ostentatious seat of state government until reparations had been made to those unfortunates. His temporary offices were located in an air-conditioned semi-trailer in a bean field just north of Bakersfield. He commuted weekly to New York and Washington,

D.C., to press his bid for the presidency of the United States and had not been to Sacramento for months.

Barbi pressed on undaunted. She marched up the stairs and straight for the governor's office, determined to storm the gates if necessary. No one questioned her. A state policeman at the reception desk in the upper hall covered his yawn with a copy of *The Sacramento Bee* as she approached.

"Which way to the governor's office, please?"

"Through the door on your left, Miss, but he's not here."

"Where is he?"

"Uh. He's in the field." The guard laid his paper down and returned his attention to the crossword puzzle.

"Well, when *will* he be here?"

The guard looked up and tapped his pencil on his false teeth. "He won't, Miss. He doesn't use this office."

"How does he get anything done?"

"Oh, he has a courier come by for his mail every morning. The governor works out of his Bakersfield office."

"Well, I'm going in there and I won't be thwarted."

The guard yawned again. "Help yourself, Miss. Hey, that's it!"

"What's it?"

"Thwart. You've got it. A six-letter word for 'foil.' " The guard filled in the squares of his puzzle.

Barbi thought this all might be a subterfuge to protect the governor from his constituents, so she entered the executive offices bristling with assertiveness.

"I would like to see the governor," she demanded with a baleful eye.

"So would I," said the receptionist. "I've been working here four months and I haven't seen him yet."

When she finally reached the plush inner sanctum, Barbi noticed that every flat surface was piled with stacks of papers. Paper was everywhere, most of it unsigned bills from the legislature and requests from special interest groups. The polished mahogany desk fairly creaked under its load. "So that's where all the redwoods are going," thought Barbi. Suddenly it seemed futile to chain herself to the desk. She might be buried alive in paperwork, and it was unlikely that she would get an audience with the governor, or even call attention to her cause in that manner. Barbi retreated from the field of honor.

In the hall she encountered State Senator Rexford Sneed, brigadier general in the California National Guard, and past president of the NRA, the VFW, and the American Legion, although he had never been in combat. She began to upbraid him for his stance on fascist military brainwashing, at taxpayer's expense, in the state colleges, but he ducked into the men's room and disarmed her. Her first impulse was to follow him, but she saw the guard eyeing her and thought better of it.

Barbi left the building gnashing her teeth in impotence. Still, she knew that Rome was neither built nor destroyed in a day, and she would fight on other fronts. As she descended the steps in front, she caught her breath. Barbi was struck by the tall, staunch, steadfast figure of P. E. Proudbird, still at her post, undaunted and unwavering. She marveled at P.E.'s dedication. They powwowed, and it was decided to abandon that battle for that day, because it is damned frustrating to be a protester when no one pays any attention.

They adjourned to P.E.'s pad for politics and strategy. Barbi bought two bottles of imported wine; she honored the boycott of domestic agri-business. Had she known anything about the Rothschild family and other oenocrats of Europe she might have selected Red Mountain, but she didn't. It was good wine. P.E.'s pad was decorated entirely in pillows and Navajo blankets. It was a warm, intimate, womblike place. P.E. lit candles, incense, and the hookah, in that order. They kicked off shoes and snuggled back into the mounds of pillows, sipping their wine, hitting on the pipe, the Doors playing, not too loud, and they entered into that incredible state of ESP that good dope produces. They smiled, grinned even, and several expressions like "ohhh, man" and "dig it," followed by soft chuckles, could be heard. There was a profound sense of camaraderie, sharing, and omniscience. As they lounged there, facing each other, P.E. smiled intensely and extended a lithe, tan foot, resplendent with pink toenails, to tickle Barbi's midriff. Barbi giggled softly and settled herself lower, against the electric foot that felt so good on her skin. The foot disappeared beneath her sweater and worked its way slowly upward. Barbi giggled softly and took another toke. She lay back and surrendered to the moment completely. As P.E.'s foot encountered her breast, Barbi felt a pang of pleasure swell through her. She had always known this would happen. P.E. moved her foot gently and, like a coursing river, the cosmic bond swept over the two women and linked them, inexorably, with Susan B. Anthony, Madame Blavatsky, Eleanor Roosevelt, Sappho, and all their sisters throughout the ages. It was Barbi's first conscious contemplation of feminism, and sisterhood was, in a manner of speaking, the nuts. Barbi felt at last that she knew God, and that She was unfailingly sweet.

Afterward they talked long into the night about the need for a sweeping, grass-roots movement that would serve the needs of the people, the downtrodden. A radical political arm of steel that would clash with any windmill, would scale any height, would lay siege to any fortress of oppression.

Thus was born Socialized Labor's Unrelenting Revolt. A lot would be heard from SLUR in the next few years.

11

Southeast Asia, 1960s

Stateside, Rawlins had been wont to volunteer for any detail that would get him into the war faster. He was praised by his superior officers for high patriotic ideals and admirable *esprit de corps*, neither of which, of course, had anything to do with his volunteering. Rawlins wanted to get to the war as soon as he could for one reason: The sooner he got in it, the sooner he would get out of it. He knew, ineluctably, the war would get a lot worse before it got any better, and he would be happy to serve his tour before it got worse. It was bad enough already.

And it did get worse right along. Even the war within a war got worse. Oh, there were bright spots, like the night that Moon Dog set the all-time TPQ record, or the time Major Poltroun did the impossible; when they moved the war to Thailand, now that was a bright spot. When they could fly back from bombing, hop in a rickshaw, go straight to town, get drunk, and get in bed with girls, real beds at that, ah yes, that was bright. But it only lasted a week, and for the most part the war and the war within a war just got gradually worse.

Not that the air-wing pogues knew what bad was. No, the grunts didn't have it nearly so lovely. They frolicked by day with jungle and insects and humping and getting their asses shot off, and by night with foxholes and mud and things that bit and slithered and sapped and went boom and getting their asses shot off. And always *anticipation*. Maybe that was the worst. Because they could never find the goddamn enemy. The enemy could find them any time he wanted to, but they could never find *him*. They humped up and down hills and through the brush and across the paddies and rivers and through the villes, and never saw this alleged Vietcong or NVA or whatever the intelligence report called for that day. Every so often the point man would stroll through a trip wire or step on a land mine and they would have to elect a new point man. Or an ambush would open up and wound a few people and those who still could would take cover and cut loose with a very devastation of automatic fire that manicured the bush and threshed the elephant grass, but then, when they advanced, cautiously, they never found anything except maybe a twelve-year-old dead boy in black pajamas with a rifle and a few grenades, or a faint trail of blood that led nowhere. But usually they found nothing. Where was this fucking army that hundreds of thousands of them had come to fight? It was goddamn frustrating. It was maddening and it was exasperating.

One hard-charging captain, known as Brass Balls Obradovitch, who enjoyed a measure of fleeting local fame, decided to do something about it. He assembled a volunteer group of crack recon troops and began a special training program. His idea was to out-gook the gooks. To so emulate the enemy that you became him, and thus he would lose any shred of advantage that he had gained by being himself. To that end Brass Balls sent a detail into town and had them buy black pajamas and conical straw hats for everybody. He took away their boots and all their gear except rifles, grenades, and canteens. They donned their new get-ups, darkened exposed skin (within the dictates of ethnicity), and began snooping and pooping through the terrain just like the other guys did. They thought native. They spoke a rudimentary version of the language, ate rice with *nuoc mam* sauce, and practiced their squatting. They *became* Vietcong. Brass Balls Obradovitch figured he would show the dinks a thing or two about being dinks. Anything they could do, he and his troopers could do better.

No, the grunts didn't have it so lovely. They were stuck out there in that eerie wilderness of rain and mist and heat and danger for thirteen months, if they lived that long, and didn't know why. Their boots, socks, and feet rotted. Their crotches rotted. Especially their spirits rotted. The germs of chronic decay were already beginning to thrive in this steamy tropic medium, only nobody much realized it yet. The disease was to infect not only the armed forces in Vietnam, but the entire society on the home front.

In much the same manner, the microscopic bacilli of botulism were multiplying and spreading through the tub of red death that DeVille Hoggins muscled over to the door of the reefer, set down, and forgot about. Hoggins had been promoted back to lance corporal and promptly assigned to mess duty. It was a damnable billet, not only because it was ferociously hot and sweaty work in that galley, but because the one saving grace of mess duty, that you could kype all the chow you wanted, was nullified by the fact that there was nothing to kype except red death. Hoggins thought the Marine Corps sucked. He would not work on the flight line under O'Flynn, thank you, and he didn't dig this mess-hall shit either. Lance Corporal DeVille Hoggins wanted to be an office pinky at Wing Headquarters, but he couldn't type.

Nor was Colonel Creed having all that lovely a time of it, either. The goddamn intransigent Buddhists were holed up in his temple ruins and they simply wouldn't leave. It galled him no end that a bunch of second-rate lackies playing soldier could defy the will of a full colonel in the United States Marine Corps. Whose blasted war was this, anyway? Colonel Creed would not tolerate insubordination, especially when it was bollixing the progress of his master project, but his hands were tied, and so he seethed. It was frustrating, maddening, and exasperating because the ragtag Army of the Republic of Vietnam would not obey his orders, and he could not talk any of the grunt battalions into recapturing his temple. In fact, though, some of the grunt commanders were seriously considering it, because they could never find the real enemy to have a regular battle with, and here was a made-to-order scenario. Circle the fort. If only higher authority would declare the allies to be the enemy, just for a short time, they could have a bang-up battle with live ammunition while taking that fortified sanctuary. If it accomplished nothing for the war, still it would be excellent for training purposes.

Except for an occasional dash to the bunkers when the friendly mortar fire from the temple strayed their way, things were humdrum as ever for the pilots. Colonel Creed envisioned his OM club as a shining example of American ingenuity and enterprise, one to stand through the ages. Rawlins envisioned going home in a few months and never hearing of Southeast Asia again.

"Oh, shit, Moon," said Rawlins one evening, pointing at the flight schedule tacked up in the ready room. "Look at this."

"Ohhh, I see." Moon Dog rubbed his chin and gave Rawlins a slow wink. "That's a goddamn dirty shame, ain't it? To send him out into a thing like that. And on Friday the thirteenth."

"Yeah, it doesn't seem fair. In number thirteen too. I mean, I ain't superstitious or anything, but there's no sense in pushing your luck."

Cavendish, who was stuffing his short, plump body into a torso harness, narrowed his eyes and looked past his left shoulder at the two, who seemed unaware of his presence.

"I flew thirteen the other day and that damn oil pressure in the right engine was a-fluctuating again. Just a skosh, you know, not so as you could hardly notice it, but still it was wavering a little. Probably just the gauge."

Rawlins wrinkled his brow and looked thoughtful. "I think that was the airplane where Ludlow had to shut one down the other day. Probably the same engine."

"Well, you know. It doesn't seem like those maintenance people can ever fix anything right."

"I'll tell you, Doggie, I wouldn't want to fly that son of a bitch tonight, not into no thunderstorm. . . . " Rawlins managed just a hint of a shudder.

Moon Dog looked up at him. "Thunderstorms, huh?"

"Yep. Cumulonimbus in all quadrants. Foul shit."

Cavendish started to say something, then busied himself with his helmet bag. Moon Dog and Rawlins continued their conversation, unmindful that it was being closely monitored.

"The TPQ boys will put you right in the middle of that shit, too," Moon said.

"Oh, yeah. They like about sixteen thousand feet, three hundred and fifty knots. Right in the worst of the turbulence."

"There'll be wind shear, too, I s'pose."

"Hell, Moon, you ever hear of a thunderstorm that wasn't full of convective currents and down drafts and all that shit?"

"Yeah, I know it. And they get you about half low and slow, with a heavy load, IFR, in all that turbulence and wind shifts and everything, and then you have a little engine trouble or something. No sir. It's not for me." Moon Dog made a sound somewhere between a grunt and a sigh.

Rawlins became more animated. "Ain't it a bitch, man. Say you have to shut that engine down. That's bad enough, but then you throw the entire electrical load on the other generator and if they're out of phase the bus tie opens up. Sometimes those suckers will kick off the line from the overload. Oh, you can reset them, but you have to wait forty-five seconds and by then it's too late. You're out of lights and instruments and by the time you get things turned back on and the gyros start to re-erect and come up to speed, it's too late. You're in an inverted spin falling straight toward the jungle, and not far to go." He chuckled ironically.

"Well," said Moon, "and that ain't even the worst of it. If you have to punch out, you know you'll get captured because these radar pogues have vectored you right over the Cong, to drop. You'll probably land in their camp."

"Man, I don't even want to think about what happens then."

"Tell me about it. You hear about that grunt they captured a couple of weeks ago?"

"What happened?"

"They found him with his hands and feet tied. They had put two rats in a gunny sack and tied it over his head. His face and ears and throat were just gnawed away. Well. Let's go get a beer and talk about pussy or something."

"Yeah." Rawlins followed Moon Dog through the door. "I'm just glad it's not me going out in weather like this. Not in thirteen. Not at night."

"Well, as the poet said, 'It's day all day in the daytime and there is no night in Creede.' "

"What poet said that?"

"I don't know, but one did."

"Where the hell is Creede?"

"Just north of South Fork."

"Where the hell is South Fork?"

"I don't know. South of Creede." They wandered off toward the club.

Cavendish was checking flashlight batteries, pencil flares, and his beeper radio. His pudgy face seemed to have lost some of its pinkness in the poor light of the hootch, and there were tiny beads of sweat on his smooth forehead. But then most everybody sweated most of the time in that neighborhood. Especially in summer.

It could not have been apprehended by anyone, possibly excepting a Grampaw Pettibone or a Murphy, them having supernatural powers of perception, but that was a strangely propitious evening, that Friday the 13th. Propitious, that is, for the enemy, whoever the enemy was. For that was hardly clear. The germs and seeds that were that night inauspiciously engendering devastations both large and small were surely propitious for the VC and the North Vietnamese Army. And yet they were also propitious, in a different way, for their avowed enemies, the Army of the Republic of Vietnam. They augured well for Barbi and P.E. and the burgeoning membership of SLUR; they augured well for numerous senators and congressmen, yet not for others; certainly they boded evil for General Jefferson, Colonel Creed, and Brass Balls Obradovitch.

The germs, both literal and figurative, were multifold and multifarious. There were those in the tub of red death that DeVille Hoggins had left out of the cooler. As the hot, tropical night wore on, they bubbled microscopically and proliferated into a thriving colony of botulism within this happy stainless steel tub of warm nutrients.

At the same time the operations team was putting together the flight schedule for the following twenty-four hours, one that would result in Major Poltroun doing the impossible, Al "Shaky" Morgenkrank doing the irredeemable, and the squadron becoming the laughingstock of Naval Aviation. It would provide an entire column for Grampaw Pettibone in a future issue of *Naval Aviation News*. Ambrose Bierce defined an accident as "an inevitable occurrence due to the action of immutable natural laws." The flight surgeons described it as the result of arguing with your wife or not eating three nutritious, well-balanced meals each day. There being no wives present to argue with, Goldfinger, the OB/GYN flight surgeon, would ascribe those events to mild cases of food poisoning from the red death. In truth, the operations people were as guilty as anyone else, because did they not, like master chess players, place Major Poltroun and Al "Shaky" Morgenkrank on those fateful squares of the board at precisely the times of the occurrences? Still, Poltroun and Morgenkrank would have to shoulder a little blame themselves.

And the ARVN garrison that was holed up in Creed's brickyard was hatching a nuisance of its own. Their efforts to destroy the Catholic VNAF had been ineffectual, at least partly because the VNAF parked their ADs in revetments in an area of the sprawling air base that was beyond the effective range of the ARVN mortars. The fucking VNAF was strafing and rocketing them at will. It had to be stopped. A new strategy was called for. They feared that they hadn't the strength, nor the effectiveness, to take the base. With Ky, the premier of the nation, general and commandant of the VNAF, sitting inside the perimeter and dictating policy, it was not likely that they would be invited in to destroy his airplanes. Even if they were able to take the base, they would be hesitant to do so, because the multibillion-dollar American air effort was of some value when fighting the real war. They sent word to the big ARVN base and Buddhist sympathy center at Hue for more troops, but they knew that in itself was not the answer. No, a new strategy was called for. If they couldn't hit the VNAF planes, there were, indeed, squadrons of American planes, parked closer to the fence, that even *their* gunners could almost certainly destroy.

It was determined that the expeditious thing to do, in the circumstances, was to inadvertently blow up a few American planes (which had already been done on a small scale, in true inadvertence) by inept gunnery. This could be easily explained away at the diplomatic table, but would also send a clear, unstated message that, by God, the Americans had better do something to cause the VNAF to take steps to cease the intramural squabbling. It may or may not have been a sound decision, as would be seen later. For one thing, the troops from Hue did not arrive as soon as requested, causing the ARVN to wonder about its own zen solidarity. What did arrive, posthaste, was a company of monks trained in self-immolation. They were determined to iron this thing out. At first this power was not properly harnessed and directed, and resulted in only a few flickering funeral pyres here and there about town. The thing about those monks, though, was that they were careful never to light the match until a *Life* photographer was set up and ready. God knew they deserved that much for their efforts. It was rumored that some of the more eager photojournalists requested that they touch off a small can of kerosene before the first take, for light meters, silhouette angles, and such.

So, the ARVN, having nothing stronger in the way of reinforcements to throw against their brothers of the VNAF and Vietnamese Marines than a gaggle of human torches, decided to blow up American planes and get their message across. Also, the fuel farm for the entire base was within range. Surely that would get someone's attention if it went up. These actions would seem, on the surface at least, to bode well for the ARVN, because they might get the VNAF off their backs. They would bode well for the VC and the NVA, in one way, by reducing the number of American airplanes available to harass them. In another way, though, they would also bode ill for the Cong and the NVA because, if they worked, they would free up the ARVN to more assiduously pursue their real war. So that was a push.

The action of the ARVN against the Americans would surely not enhance the careers of General Jefferson, who didn't need enhancement but would take it, and Colonel Creed, who did. On the other hand, the actions would be serendipitous for Rawlins, Moon Dog, Hang Dog, C. Ross Culpepper, Captain America, Lance Major Slocum, Second Lieutenant DeWayne Ludlow, who had two years of college, and the others, because they would cause the war to be moved to Thailand for a week, where they could immerse their feet of clay in the ooze of debauchery, wiggle their toes in the flesh pots of human gratification, and become happier soldiers. They would not affect Lance Corporal Hoggins, who worked in the mess hall, or Sergeant O'Flynn, who worked on the flight line, significantly. They would piss Buck Sergeant Parton off because of the increased message traffic.

Brass Balls Obradovitch, concurrently, was cultivating the seed of his own plot, to out-gook the gooks. He was, at that moment, assigning areas of responsibility for his ersatz VC patrols for the next twenty-four hours. His pajama-clad raiders would be slinking through selected sectors of the boondocks that next day, visible at times from the air, if not from the ground, and indistinguishable, of course, from the real VC, who would also presumably be sneaking around the area in their own pajamas. The Obradovitch irregulars meant to be reckoned with in this skirmish. Their presence would indeed prove pivotal in one of the small dramas of the larger social tapestry.

And the VNAF was, meanwhile, concocting its viscid cup of broth, which would sweeten the general pot. Premier Ky and his planners, all trained in the U.S., recognized the buttery side of the toast and reckoned that it might behoove them to mollify the Americans some. It was more embarrassment than anything; bad show to allow the guests to wage the entire war for *their* country, without at least token participation by the hosts.

"What we will do," they said, "is keep up the combat air patrols against our brothers in arms, the despised Buddhist insurgents, but also extend each sortie to include one half hour of checking out the boondock hinterlands, where Cong is King. We'll do our part in this bloody fracas."

Minuscule bricks were being laid, too, in a tortuous line of self-defense for Candyass Cavendish, self-proclaimed future Commandant, who was at that moment inspecting the yellow sheets on squadron airplane number 13. He didn't like what he was reading. The yellow sheets showed a history of fluctuating oil pressure and vibrating sounds from the right engine. They also showed the maintenance measures that had been taken to correct these complaints.

Gripe	Response
A/C down—fluctuating oil pressure, right engine	Replaced oil press. transmitter R/engine checks ok
A/C down—press. still fluctuating R/eng. + vibration sounds	Replaced oil pressure indicator right engine checks good on runup
A/C down. Shut down R/engine. Pressure fluctuating, too low—grinding sounds	Replaced wiring bet. O/Press. TX and Rcvr. O/P ok on runup

And so on. The last two hops had similar gripes. Why was it that pilots, on dark and stormy nights, heard noises clearly and distinctly that maintenance people absolutely could not detect while running the engines up on the ramp? Cavendish signed for the airplane. Thunder cracked and rolled across the airfield. It began to sprinkle. The real rain wasn't there quite yet. He walked out to the airplane and it was very dark on the flight line. He tried to do a thorough preflight with his flashlight, but the red lens afforded poor illumination.

Cavendish had one overwhelming fear at that point of his exemplary, phony young life. He was afraid that he would be killed on his last hop in Vietnam.

Rawlins and Moon Dog were afraid that they would be killed on their last hops in Vietnam too, but it was academic, because if they got killed on any hop, that would indeed be the last. They were more acutely afraid that the interim club, a half a hootch, would run out of beer before they were ready for bed. Cot, that is. They had already run out of ice. DeWayne Ludlow, disconsolate, sat at the other end of the bar sipping a warm Seven-Up. He did not wish to be in the interim group officers club with his fellow flyers in their grubby flight suits, pistols, and cartridge belts, most around one shoulder with the holster under an arm, some around the waist, each with a chamois around his neck to soak up the sweat, all of them with eyes a little too bright. DeWayne Ludlow would have preferred to be in his tent, but he couldn't sleep this early, and the overtaxed generator of the hobo camp, together with the high-resistance, makeshift wiring, would not start his fluorescent lamp, so he could not read, write, or build model airplanes. He sipped his warm Seven-Up.

"You reckon Candy is out bouncing around in them thunder bumpers about now?" Moon inquired in his best drawl. He and Rawlins cracked up. They laughed until they fell on the table. It was so funny because there was nothing else to laugh at.

"Well, I'll tell you what," Rawlins sputtered through his guffaws, "I'll bet he's monitoring the shit out of that right engine."

Cavendish was at that moment taxiing back from his aborted TPQ. He had downed the airplane for fluctuating oil pressure in the right engine. He would not even attempt to describe the sounds he heard that dark and rainy night. Just taxiing and running up the engines.

The thing that he did not realize, nor did anyone else—well, maybe Murphy and Pettibone did—was that it had been so easy. So easy to transition from the guise of an unbridled warrior to the reality of a timorous, deliberate, self-preserving human who could never persevere in the political arena and become Commandant, or whatever, if he was dead.

And it was so easy. Surely the foundation was in place for Cavendish's non-flying career as an aviator.

So, many sub-growths were in the larval stages that evening, and the burgeoning of all those geneses would surely enliven the days to come.

12

California, 1970s

More and more, Rawlins began to sense that it was all slipping away. In idle moments he tried to puzzle it out. There was a sickness within him that he had not perceived before. It became harder to deny that it was getting worse. As surely as botulism thrived in the medium of red death, something debilitating was spreading through Rawlins's psyche. In earlier times he had never known depression, but now it seemed always to be hovering around and he could not fathom why. He examined his motives and priorities. Nothing had changed. He would admit to being a hedonist, motivated primarily by gratification, but saw no inherent evil in that, so long as he did not harm or take unfair advantage of others. It may have been one of Rawlins's major barriers to adjustment that he never accepted the concept of evil, per se, nor that of universal responsibility, and hence guilt. In his youth, Rawlins had not experienced the gnawing pain of guilt or the ideas of blame, self-loathing, or even self-doubt. He had been taught, or had determined for himself, he didn't know which, that intent was everything. If one had acted out of admirable motives, nearly any result was justifiable, or at least forgivable.

And Rawlins had always meant well. He had never intentionally abused or exploited anyone, at least in his own view. For that reason, he had seldom felt himself to be culpably at fault and therefore had never worried much about the consequences of his actions, so long as he had tried to do the right thing, or at least the socially acceptable thing.

And it had always seemed to work fine. He had thought of himself as an honorable, if unorthodox, fellow, living out the destiny that was manifestly his. If things were somewhat dark from time to time, there was little that he could do about it anyway, and they would improve. But of late, this feeling that he could only categorize as depression abraded the fringe of his generally sunny consciousness. He felt somehow tainted as if, perhaps, he did *not* ultimately and unquestionably *deserve* to be happy. Maybe, he began to fear, things would *not* improve this time, but would continue to worsen.

Rawlins had of course recognized that there was evil in the world at large, but had never admitted, nay even suspected, its presence in himself—as an inextricable part of that world. His innocence of the notion of *schadenfreude* had so protected him from critical self-examination that he never questioned his own worth, merit, or prospects. He knew that there were individuals, *forces* maybe, that derived enjoyment, sustenance even, from the suffering and misery of others, but the idea was so genuinely foreign to him that he had never conceived of evil as being, possibly, universal and therefore inherent in him as a member of an imperfect race. Heretofore. But here of late Rawlins had grudgingly, and fearfully, entertained the suspicion that maybe the nation, or the whole world, perhaps, was infected with a—what?—an impurity. A nescient epidemic of unwholesomeness. Something neither perceived nor comprehensible. And that the world was being punished. Or punishing itself. As if some sort of mystical, divine retribution were at work, inexorable and certain. As if he were being made to pay, to atone for something that he did not understand, something the existence of which he had not reckoned on.

So Rawlins's innocence was slowly being stripped away. It was the blissful innocence of a whole generation of golden boys of the fifties, with crewcuts and crooked smiles, who had nothing to fear and nothing to regret, and who had gone forth to adventure and to prosper, and, probably, to make the world a better place in the bargain.

It was mortality, partly, and perhaps original sin, but even more, it might have been viewed as the hangover from the excesses of the sixties. Healing was needed and a Valium wouldn't do it. Only time, tolerance and temperance, and the natural rehabilitation of the endless pendulum of human fortune would cure such wounds.

He was getting older, but not wiser. He was losing his enthusiasm for life.

If he was losing his enthusiasm, certainly he was losing his grasp. It seemed he could no longer make things happen to suit himself. Girls were becoming scarcer and less amenable to his desires. In truth, he was usually so drunk he drove them away, but that notion hadn't occurred to Rawlins, though it had been obliquely suggested on occasion. At least he didn't consciously give it credence. It was because he saw himself as being basically as witty and charming as ever. It confounded him that they seemed to have changed the game without explaining the new rules to him. In a sense he was right; he had not changed his attitude or approach, but the world viewed him differently. In another sense, the opposite was true; he was aging in body, mind, and habit, but the world at large was much as it had always been. Whatever the case, he was confused, frustrated, often angry. These emotions made him less attractive. And things just didn't seem to be as enjoyable anymore. Aside from infrequent sexual encounters, his moments of solace and joy grew more and more to be chemically induced. Consequently he was drawn more and more toward those chemicals, which rendered him less vibrant and natural, and so the cycle went. The less pleasant life became, the more he sought, unconsciously, to escape it. The more he immersed himself in unnatural escape, the more distorted and less natural and viable he became, and the less happy. But the irony was lost on Rawlins. He did not see himself as running away from life, but rather running toward it, as if having to try harder to regain the gratification and tranquillity that he had always known.

The separate and independent nation of South Vietnam, during that period, was also in a state of decline. The age of opulence was fast burning itself out. Those heady years of unbridled optimism, with victory certain, thanks in large part to the undivided commitment of an indomitable and inexhaustible America, the years of limitless promise and sure prosperity for all, those years were winding down. A sense of dread was beginning to fester throughout the land. The Communists had steadfastly refused to give up and go home. The Americans continued to pound the North with hundreds of warplanes every day, but it seemed to no avail. The Vietcong and the NVA pushed on implacably, not yet winning the land outright, but winning its inhabitants. Inexorably they were capturing the hearts and minds and balls of more and more of the people. And they would not stop. It seemed nothing could deter the march. They won by bits and pieces, by attrition, by erosion, and by relentless pressure. Saigon was becoming an enclave of fear and dread and discomfiture. Oh, the politicians still promised the moon, victory was still within their grasp, but the politicians came and went and deposed and displaced each other, and they all said the same things, yet still there was no tangible sign that the Communists were being beaten back. Or would ever be. The middle class, the entrepreneurs, the capitalists, the white-collar thieves, had come to feel a sense of foreboding. Maybe this time things would *not* get better. After a years-long binge of excesses, of relative luxury and self-indulgence, life was no longer so enjoyable. The picture was not so rosy as before. To counter this unhappy condition they gravitated more and more toward artificial stimulants. The black market soared. The saloon girls' skirts inched up higher. Inflation ran wild. They clamored for more and larger infusions of American largesse. As a nation they craved false elixirs. They gulped any drug that promised to make things okay. Mostly they refused to acknowledge reality.

Nor was America undivided anymore, if ever it had been. Anything but. Barbi Belheur and P. E. Proudbird had propelled their Socialized Labor's Unrelenting Revolt into a national movement. SLUR had chapters in twenty-three states and was spreading like wildfire. Barbi was putting on concerts and giving lectures, P.E. was doing television spots, and they were throwing fund-raisers right and left. Dulcie and Mrs. Staff Sergeant O'Flynn were catering up a storm at fashionable guilt parties, and antiwar sentiment was snowballing. Suddenly millions of American lads were finding out, *Yes! It is highly immoral, unethical, and inhumane for us to go over there and get our asses shot off*, and, *Hell no, we won't go*. And the entire fabric of domestic society was rent. Ripped, twisted, wrinkled, and soiled. The parents of dead boys were saying, *Wait a minute. I won't have had my son die in vain. We must support this noble cause*. Others were insisting with equal vehemence that, *By God, enough is enough and we must end this idiocy*. Numbers of draft-age folks, often traditional, conservative, hardy young men, felt that their country was calling and, like it or not, they must answer. Numbers of others, sometimes more extensively educated, perceived the war as being unconscionable and refused *on pure intellectual principle* to sully their high ideals by participating in such a moral outrage. It was of passing interest to anthropologists that alarming numbers of those who *went* did so in terror, scared shitless, but went nonetheless, and yet equally vast numbers of those who elected not to go did it not out of any professed fear, but only from strong-willed dedication to an ethical code.

Barbi Belheur and her people from SLUR had laid the bed and rails of an underground railroad to Canada and were conducting draft-evasion clinics in all the major cities. They had cram courses in how to feign neurosis, homosexuality, flat feet, trick knee, and sundry other maladies that would exempt one from conscription.

Every time Barbi threw a concert, the VFW or the American Legion would put on a march with a drove of pot-bellied, bifocaled patriots wearing navy blue piss-cutters and tarnished Bronze Stars pinned to their short-sleeved shirts. They exhorted whomever would listen, with some stridence, to support their country, right or wrong. But that was the question. They all thought they were supporting the country, but differed widely on just what true support amounted to when it came to the war.

Half the politicians were for it, half the politicians were against it, and all the politicians, in an election year, were furiously testing their elective waters to find out just what the hell they should be. No matter what your position, things were bad. Life had become less enjoyable for everybody and there was no tranquillity in any camp. It looked to everyone that this time things might *not* get better, at least not for a long time. Rawlins found himself in spiritual and physical disrepair; the rest of the world did too.

13

California, 1970s

It had been a long and difficult road. As in any worthwhile cause, there had been many obstacles, and countless more remained. The work was never done, but they were fighting the good fight and they drew strength from the sure knowledge that they were right. But the subversion of a nation of 200 million people is no easy task and they knew they had only begun. They had won the college constituency, but there remained the rest of the country.

The rhetoric played well in the radical community, and the pseudointellectuals of the nation, indeed the world, were solidly behind them, but they had to gain credibility with the Establishment. This fact was not lost on Barbi, and she had a plan.

"My plan, P.E., is to address the Democratic National Convention," she beamed. "What do you think of that?"

P. E. Proudbird sat on an enormous pillow, painting her toenails pink. "Great, Barbi! You can straighten those assholes out." P.E. had seen the birth and phenomenal growth of SLUR and had come to believe in the power of Barbi's elocution. "Why don't you do that, man, you'll be great."

"Well, sure, P.E. Listen, it's not that easy. I mean, shiiit, man, to be invited to speak at a national political convention is a big honor. Very few people get a chance like that."

"What do you mean? I watched the last one on TV for a while and it seemed like everybody got a chance like that. Did they ever speak! It went on and on forever. Everybody in the place had something to say. And mostly it was the same shit over and over. And it was dumb, y'know? Like they all talked about how they could win the election and how they could turn the country around and all. But like very little about the poor and the hungry and the oppressed, y'know?"

"P.E., the Democrats?"

"I'm not sure which one it was. It doesn't matter, though. They're all the same."

"Well, they won't be when I get the fuck through." Barbi's eyes flashed. "But seriously, it will take a major effort to get on that agenda. It will take organization, regimented support from the downtrodden, more committees."

"Amen, baby. You can't have too many committees."

Barbi swept P.E.'s feet into her lap and blew on her freshly painted toenails. "It's going to take a lot of love and a lot of work, is what it's going to take."

"You can do it, babe." P.E. felt that there was no limit to what Barbi could accomplish. Had she not, through her connections, gotten P.E. a high-paying television commercial? It was the greatest piece of business P.E. had ever done. She was paid scale for the job and every time it ran she got a residual.

In the spot, P.E. walked onto a set that was crammed with random trees and cornstalks, smoking fires, flat rocks, and "Indian" women pressing out "venison." A deer, not yet skinned, hung from a tree. Another's carcass was suspended on a spit over the fire. P.E., tall and darkly made up, was resplendent in an ankle-length buckskin skirt, a colorful shawl, and lots of silver concha jewelry. Her long, lank, black hair was gathered in a single braid. She wore a very authentic-looking headband with one feather in it. She held up a piece of beef jerky.

"You may call this beef jerky," she intoned. "But my people call it pemmican." She did not point out that she wasn't a Cree, whose word pemmican was, but rather a Cherokee, if only one thirty-second. Wearing Navajo jewelry at that. But it did not hurt the integrity of the piece, because, as P.E. forged on through her dialogue, the viewer could have little doubt that she was of the cigar store tribe. Calija would have been done proud.

"This age-old Indian food-preservation method sustained our hunters through their long and arduous treks. . . . " She went on to assure those members of the audience who hadn't slipped off to their refrigerators for some more dip and a beer that Pemmican brand was the only one that used methods derived from the original Indian recipe and, therefore, offered more protein, food value, natural taste, and what have you.

The director did three takes and then ordered the crew to cut, print, and wrap, because he saw that they had as fine a product as they were likely to get.

P.E. was tickled pink because it only took a few hours, and she got all that money. She enjoyed seeing herself on the tube, too. She secretly thought she looked rather statuesque. And she did.

"We have to put together a coalition of all the people who are not represented at those conventions," Barbi mused. A seraphic look came over her and she gazed beyond the walls of the room into every corner of this great nation. "We must use the power of the masses to force those assholes to address this issue. We must bring the machine to its knees and make it act. We must twist arms and bust heads if necessary and *compel* them to stop this war."

P.E. thought it was quite a speech. "What are you going to tell them, Barbi?"

Barbi's jaw muscles flexed. "I'm going to tell them that our boys are being killed. That men, women, and children are being slaughtered. And all for nothing." That part was right. "I'm going to tell them that if the people of Southeast Asia choose to have a socialist government, they are entitled." There would perhaps be some question about the choice factor. "I'm going to tell them that we must stop this senseless killing." No one would argue that point. . . . "I'm going to tell them that they absolutely *must* pull every American killer out of Vietnam tomorrow. That we must walk away, unilaterally and unequivocably, without question or delay, and stop the bloodshed immediately, regardless of any other consideration. We must admit we are wrong and give up *now*." She would get some foot dragging on that one.

"We must beam that message forth, from the Democratic Convention, over national TV, so that every citizen of this land knows what's going on. So that every voter knows that they are personally guilty of cold-blooded murder as long as this administration and its policies are still in effect. We must bring the message to every American that they are a criminal and a murderer until we end this genocide." Barbi was pretty worked up.

"Hear, hear, Sister," P.E. said softly.

That evening they attended a fund-raiser at the swosh Beverly Hills estate of some alleged independent film producer, Dulcie and O'Flynn catering. Barbi, approaching one of the linen-covered, silver-laden tables in the lawn garden, came upon Mrs. Staff Sergeant O'Flynn conferring with Ismael, the Mexican waiter, and Mustafa, a member of RABIES (Rent an Authoritarian Badass for Internal and External Security), the official enforcement arm of the Panthers. Mustafa was cadging a bottle of scotch whiskey and a tray of canapés for the refreshment of the brothers.

"Perfect," said Barbi with a winning smile. "You can be my coalition." It was the ideal mixture. She had here a downtrodden anti-Establishment black, an undocumented worker from Mexico, and a middle-aged woman. These were just the elements that she needed to force the hand of the Democratic Party. She began to speak in earnest to the three. They were cynical and skeptical, but blandishments would be offered, and Barbi was very persuasive.

14

Southeast Asia, 1960s

When Major Poltroun did the impossible, it is safe to say that no one expected it of him. It was often in doubt that Poltroun could accomplish the simple, indeed even the picayune; odds would generally be given against the wildly difficult; and no one but no one expected the impossible out of him. Except that nobody else was stupid enough to get himself into the situation required for this particular stunt, and Murphy's LAW stated immutably that if it could be done somebody would, so maybe Grampaw Pettibone and the other omniscients would have known that Poltroun was the man for the job. But nobody else did. Poltroun sure as *hell* didn't suspect that he was to make history or he would never have taxied that night.

He had acquired the knack from Captain Cavendish of downing airplanes before they left the ground, and had he anticipated the feat that would render his name opprobrious, but nonetheless immortal in the annals of Naval Aviation, he would have shut that sucker down right in the chocks and written up a masterful yellow sheet, spilling over onto the back of the page, detailing at least a dozen reasons why the airplane was unsafe to fly. But he didn't know, and he taxied out.

In truth, Major Poltroun was not feeling well. As Goldfinger, the flight surgeon, would write in the accident report, food poisoning would be a strong contributing factor. The previous day, after DeVille Hoggins had set the tub of red death by the door of the reefer and forgotten about it, no one else had noticed it. Hoggins was the regular man in charge of dispensing red death and nobody else much cared about it. The regular cooks were all taking correspondence courses in how to be salad and pastry chefs, hoping to catch on with one of the gourmet chains when they got out, and would not demean themselves by handling red death.

Nor would they eat it, having secreted preferable rations for themselves. The upshot was that the tub sat out in the warm, fecund, tropical air all night and nobody paid any attention to it until Hoggins reported for work in the morning, late, and discovered that he had neglected to refrigerate the staple of all three meals for that day. He quickly muscled it into the cooler and no one was the wiser. But the damage was done. The bacteria had thrived and were well established throughout the tub.

Most people just had watery powdered eggs and stale blackened toast for breakfast; they couldn't face red death that early in the morning. Nothing much seemed out of the ordinary until after lunch, and then it took several hours before the bellyache began to appear epidemic. Major Poltroun lunched on crackers and a can of deviled ham that his wife had sent him, so he had no red death until evening chow. Even as he taxied for his TPQ hop, the rumbling in his guts that would only get worse and then worse was just beginning.

But Poltroun was not a well man and he mused on the sacrifices he so willingly made to prosecute this moral campaign. If they only knew, all the generals and colonels who controlled his fate! If they but sensed what a selfless and dedicated officer he was, surely his name would be on the next promotion list. But at the same time he knew that he must suffer quietly and patiently, that in time his excellence would be acknowledged and he would take his rightful place in the pantheon of national heroes, the quiet professional who gets the job done. Not that Poltroun was especially self-effacing, but still, he was a realist. Deification would not come overnight.

Nothing, it seemed, would come overnight. Years had elapsed, centuries perhaps, in the evolution of these affairs of men to where they stood now. It had all happened so many times before. The Vietnamese peasant armies had first whipped and ousted the overwhelmingly superior strength of the Chinese in the tenth century, and they did it the same way they would successfully defend themselves for the next thousand years, by boxing instead of punching, by jabbing and ducking, with footwork—the strategy of allowing the enemy to beat himself. The most important tactic would be to use natural phenomena to your own advantage.

In the thirteenth century they repelled the Mongol hordes of Kublai Khan, a little chore that several others found most damnably vexatious, in pretty much the same way. The Viets lured the invaders deep into the confines of their own peculiar turf and let nature take its course, albeit aiding at every turn. They mired them in the mud of the monsoon rains and picked them off. They cut the supply lines and harassed and interdicted. They watched them die from the tropical heat and starvation and thirst and insects. And disease! Malaria was the greatest secret weapon the Vietnamese had, from the uprising of the Trung Sisters to the Vietminh and Vietcong. The locals were immune, thanks to countless generations of coexistence with the anopheles mosquito and its attendant protozoa, but shame on the interloper from less taxing climes. You can't fight very effectively with a fever of 105, puking, sweating, and shitting. But those early combatants were Mongols and Chinese and Chams and Khmers, tough customers who had marched and lived through months or years of the hardest conditions just to get there—not well-scrubbed towheads from the temperate plains of North America, fresh off a Continental champagne flight. And still they got zapped. They bogged down in an unfriendly, unhealthy place, got sick, got ambushed, seldom saw the enemy, never captured anything worth having, and finally died or went home.

And the amazing thing was that nobody seemed to know it, except Barbi Belheur. Oh, Barbi didn't know the *facts*, of course, her two-year higher education having been perforce somewhat limited in the classical sense, but she had a "gut feeling" as she described it to P.E. She just knew that it was wrong and that we shouldn't be in that place. And everyone *should* have known. It had been going on like this since the time of Christ, for Christ's sake. But none of the principals seemed to get it. They thought like the Portuguese, who put their Jesuits ashore with instructions to convert the populace. They had some luck in that for a while, and even slapped together a Roman-style alphabet so they could get a handle on the sometimes incomprehensibly inflectional murmurings of the local lingo. The Portuguese opened up a trade center in central Annam and settled back to monopolize the trade routes to the Orient. And then got kicked out. Books burned, missionaries expelled, trade center closed down, and that was it. For some reason, these Vietnamese swine just didn't want a bunch of foreigners telling them how to run things.

The Dutch gave it a half-hearted effort for a few years, but then they too left, scratching their little haircuts that looked, maybe, like the boy on the paint sign, or a By God whole generation of half-pint American preadolescents with that hairstyle who are referred to as cute. But leave they did.

Then came the French. They were more persistent and luckier than their predecessors. They hung on for a hundred years. Colonized the place, raped it, exploited it, starved it, and infected it with the multifarious diseases of the civilized world. To their lasting credit, the Frogs introduced perhaps the second most devastating natural enemy of man that the Vietnamese ever saw: refined opiates. They produced opium and heroin, got the population hooked, sold and controlled the drugs under government monopoly, and then charged the addicted peasants an arm and a leg for what was already theirs. Of course the full effect of that development was not demonstrated until many years later when all those healthy, ignorant, naive, all-American saps came to town and discovered that, Wow! not only could they get drunk, fondled, caressed, and laid between booby traps, ambushes, and malaria attacks; screwed, blued, and tattooed; but for a couple of bucks they could score a blast of smack that would make that whole miserable time and place go away, man, that "terrible war" fucking dematerialize, cease to be for a while. And everything else too.

Everybody should have known. Barbi knew. Grampaw Pettibone almost certainly knew. Grampaw could have filled a year's issues of *Naval Aviation News* with one column on the dangers of the situation we were getting ourselves into, the "inevitable occurrence" that would surely happen, "due to the action of immutable natural laws."

"Jumpin' gee whillikers," he might have begun, "only a durn fool would get himself into a spot like that. . . ."

Yes, there were things to be learned from the local excursions of the Asians and the Europeans. Old Doug MacArthur had warned about land wars in Asia. But they didn't seem to get it. Even Chiang Kai-shek, no dove exactly, turned down a chance to govern Vietnam after World War II. He remembered what had happened to would-be governors of that place for the last couple of thousand years. The French were the last to learn. They were slow to catch on. After the war the Frogs just couldn't wait to get back in there and collect some more. Nobody was going to pluck the jewel of their empire, boy. They came with lots of troops, lots of arms, and lots of arrogance. Came and started snapping their fingers again, usurping the land and the wealth. And they brought lots of modern equipment and thought they could push the Vietminh around. That adventure lasted nearly ten years, and then one rainy day in 1954 they found themselves and all their fancy gear stuck in the monsoon mud. They couldn't get around very well. And Vo Nguyen Giap stood there, maybe on the same hilltop where one of his old ancestors had stood and watched the Chinese die nine hundred years before. And Giap watched the French die. Of malaria, of gangrene and bullet wounds and a thousand

things. And he saw their machinery fail, rusted, flooded, and wallowing
in mud, their air supply lines cut by the weather and AA fire, their
bunkers destroyed by flooding. A modern Occidental army, helpless, im-
potent. Giap and his boys further deluged them with shot and shell for
enough days and then walked down the hill and accepted their surrender.
That's all.

Our generals and politicians and whiz-kid managers might have
learned some about the weather and the terrain and the determination
of the age-old independence movement, but nobody paid much attention.
They thought like all those who had gone before: "Hell, that skinny little
underdeveloped backward country? We'll march right in there and
straighten things out."

Even as Major Poltroun was preparing himself to become infamous,
Rawlins was learning more about the weather and the natural adversity
of Vietnam. All the bomb loaders were down, their high pressure hydraulic hoses rotted and burst, pistons rusted, belts snapped, clutches
slipped, and so forth. Water and sand got into everything. The humidity,
the putrefactive, malignant ethers of that particular section of the globe
went through man-made materials like salts through a widow woman.

"Bring your end up just a cunt hair, Lieutenant."

"Right." Rawlins set his feet, then heaved up on the pipe across his
shoulder. He heard the metallic snap of the spring-loaded locking mechanism as it closed around the bomb lug.

"That's got the fucker." Staff Sergeant Sam, the NCOIC of the ordnance shop, was overseeing the loading (by hand) of this bomb, while
Rawlins and the corporal lifted it with steel pipes stuck into fuse holes
at either end of the bomb. They traded off. There were hundreds of
bombs to go.

"Well, that takes care of old seventeen," said Sam, stepping out from
under the wing and straightening. "Jimmy, run them sway braces down
snug."

"Right, Sarge." Jimmy, a tall, lanky, red-haired PFC ducked under
the wing and went to turning his wrench. The underside of number 13
bristled with the blunt, green 250-pounders with yellow rings around
their noses.

Sam grinned and wiped sweat off his forehead. "C'mon, Lieutenant.
Let's smoke a cigarette." They walked away from the airplanes, lighting
up. Rawlins looked at his watch. He had a hop in a couple of hours.

In addition to flying, Rawlins was the ordnance officer. He had been
helping his "staff"—a staff sergeant, a corporal, and a PFC—load bombs

since he got off the air-to-air hot pad at 1630. That was it. The entire ordnance crew consisted of three men. The TO called for twelve. They were able to borrow troops from the other shops and the flight line to load bombs when absolutely necessary, like now, but these guys had been muscling 250-pounders around since six o'clock that morning and they looked it. Of course these three were responsible for keeping all the armament systems on all the airplanes combat-ready, too. Rawlins was tired just from helping a couple of hours, but his troops were bone-weary. Jimmy, the PFC, was nineteen. The corporal, Torres, was twenty-two. Sam was in his early thirties, but the hollow eyes, the premature wrinkles, the mirthless, resigned expressions made them all look the same age. Rawlins reflected that these people got no recognition, but they contributed as much as anybody. He would see if he could do something about that.

"Sam, when are you going to get those damn loaders fixed? A guy could get tired doing this shit."

The crow's feet in the corners of the staff sergeant's eyes contracted, as close to an expression of humor as he was capable of at the moment. "Oh, we're a-waiting on parts, Lieutenant. I expect they'll come in on the one-thirty tomorrow. Them damn things are down more than they're up." He exhaled a thin line of smoke through pursed lips.

In fact, Colonel Creed had caused the parts to be off-loaded from the C-130 that would arrive in the morning, to make room for window and door casings, and plush velvet booths for the OM club.

"You guys been humping these around all day, have you?" It was obvious, but Rawlins had spent the day in the little ready room trailer for the air-to-air pad, which was curious in a way, in that no MiG had ever been seen within two or three hundred miles of Da Nang. Indeed, without an in-flight refueling capacity they could not come that far south and expect to get home again, and wouldn't anyway, because it would be suicide to venture into such a hotbed of American air superiority. No, the MiGs weren't coming and everybody knew that, but still, in the guise of prudence, twenty-four hours of every day of every year some squadron had to have two birds and two crews sitting around on alert. And then Captain Cavendish, when he had the duty, liked to stage mock scrambles in the middle of the night, just to harass the people on the pad. He called it a "high state of readiness." It made him feel powerful. General Jefferson, of course, had been a Boy Scout as a lad. He had never forgotten the motto. He would, by God, "Be Prepared."

"Yeah, Lieutenant, we been jumping." Sam didn't like to call his juniors sir, so he always called Rawlins Lieutenant. "This morning the Skipper said we was going to break the all-time record for ordnance delivered, so we been loading everything that would run. We got a full schedule for tonight too, so I expect we'll be here a while."

In fact, the Navy had finally got a barge full of bombs unloaded, so there were plenty for everybody. Colonel Creed was not one to wait and want. No sir, he believed in making hay while the sun shone, striking while the iron was hot. So he told Al "Shaky" Morgenkrank and the other squadron commanders to put on a max effort. His outfit was going to drop more fucking bombs this month than any Marine Air Group in Vietnam had ever thought about before. Of course there was no corresponding increase in targets to go with their new wealth of explosives; things were pretty much as they had been last week, with no additional threatening hordes, no newly discovered high-priority objectives to speak of. No matter. They would merely drop twice as many on the targets at hand, whether they warranted the attention or not, and dump the rest, with random precision, in premeditated stochastic patterns, over the free-drop zones, which included most of rural South Vietnam. In the North, the enemy's country, the rules were very strict. You could only hit preselected, verified military targets. That was it. Period. But in the South, the friendly territory, hell, go ahead. Deliver that shit anywhere except downtown. Chances are you'll hit some Cong. Get some.

Someone like Pettibone might have remarked that it was damned expensive, not to say dangerous, to fly all those stores out into the trackless jungle to make splinters. If one bomb utterly destroyed a hootch, left nothing there but a crater, why drop another one on it? Wouldn't a small percentage of those illustrious young heavy-handed, head-up-and-locked drivers be likely to run into trees, mountains, each other? Get hit by SAMs, AA, small arms? Would not an over-worked, ill-tempered DeVille Hoggins, conscripted for manual bomb loading, after a full shift in the mess hall, straining and swearing in the night, be apt to let his sweaty hands slip off the pipe and drop a Mark-81 on Staff Sergeant Sam's left foot, thereby reducing the manning level of the ordnance shop by one third, if not two thirds, because Sam was the NCOIC and the only one who really understood fire control systems, and so on? What, in reality, was to be gained by this whim of the colonel's, and mightn't it be somewhat costly?

Well, that was war. After all, there were records to be set, reputations to be made. Careers to be enhanced.

They continued to hand load. When it came time for Rawlins's hop, he was positively thrilled to sit down, even in an ejection seat. And in an air-conditioned airplane yet! "Sam, after you get those last two loaded, you guys secure, okay?"

"You won't get no argument there, Lieutenant. I think me and the boys has had about enough for today." They had been going more than fourteen hours. "But they got TPQs scheduled all night and I reckon they'll be wanting somebody to load 'em."

"Well, they got a fucking night crew, Sarge. You guys have to sleep a little sometime, so when you finish these last two, you and the boys hit the rack. And I don't give a shit what anyone says."

"Aye, aye, Lieutenant." And so it went.

Rawlins had known to a certainty three days before when he heard the gauche and ill-chosen doggerel over the radio. It could be no one else. A voice that somehow managed to sound cocky and bemused at the same time came up on button three. "Hellooo, tower. This is the ace of the base with three in place for a parking space, over."

It was R^2 Jones. It could have been no other. Who else possessed the crassitude to so embarrass himself? Such talk on the radio was so utterly, abjectly tasteless that it caused a twinge of involuntary shame in every pilot who overheard it. Rawlins had not heard a word of the continuing exploits of R^2 Jones since his notorious performance while entering the break approaching Mach 1.3 back in the States. That was because they had stuck Jones, who with that one hot break (which somehow he managed to survive) had either distinguished or destroyed himself, depending on how you looked at it, but who was officially a pariah of the most scurrilous rank because of the repercussions of his shock waves, they had stuck him immediately, overnight, almost, into the deepest primordial slime of the jungles of Vietnam, with a hundred pounds of radio gear strapped permanently to his back, as a forward air controller with the grunts. He was advised, in fairly convincing terms, not to go near the air wing. Not to even *phone* the air wing until his FAC tour was over. So they hadn't heard much of him. But R^2 Jones had continued his vaunted proclivity for fuckuposity while with the grunts. He had mistakenly called in strikes on a friendly river boat, his own company (inflicting only minor casualties, thanks to the ineptitude of the F-100 drivers), and a convent, which was destroyed. He had lost two radios and three weapons. The kicker came when he got separated from his unit during a firefight one dark and gloomy night, couldn't find them again, and felt very much alone in that foreign, pitch-black geography. For a while. Then he began hearing sounds, but they were most definitely not heartening: occasional twigs snapping, muffled shouts in a language so unintelligible and eerie as to make the skin crawl, the metallic clinks of weapons, bandoliers, canteens, and the like. He was no longer alone, but R² Jones was far from content. In fact, he felt downright unstable. Then, just when things seemed about as dreary as they could get, Deliverance! A wandering medevac helicopter whop-whop-whopped its way overhead. R² reacted as any bright, intuitive young tactician would. He called up the helicopter and asked for a ride. Called that sucker up, found a clearing, popped a flare, and climbed on board. No sir, not much use in threshing around that inky abyss looking for the friendlies. Not tonight.

R² took his radio and went back to the base for the night. He would come out first thing in the morning and fight, when he could tell the white hats from the black. Only his company got overrun that night and took more than 50 percent casualties. There wasn't anybody much to rejoin the next morning. And when the battalion commander found out that his rifle company was out there getting their nose severely bloodied and couldn't call in air support because Jones and his radio were back in camp, he was sore perturbed. He was, in fact, so sore perturbed that he checked the clip in his .45 and decided to convene a summary court-martial for desertion in the face of the enemy right then and there.

But, again, Deliverance! Jones had not known it, not having tucked a calendar into his field marching pack, but that fateful night in the quagmire of the boondocks had been the last official day of his FAC tour. The company clerk, combat office pinky, some faceless counterpart of Buck Sergeant Parton, had arrived early at his typewriter, in fresh utilities, and cut orders sending Jones back to the air wing. The LAW said that once you had served six months as a FAC, you had to be returned to duty within your primary military occupational specialty. For Jones that meant fighter pilot (although this was by no means a unanimous assessment). Nope, even as Mother Six (the battalion commander's radio call sign out in the sylvan fields of his professional endeavors) was checking his sidearm, R² Jones was lifting off in a supply chopper on the first leg of his journey back to the flight line.

When Rawlins had heard the mortifying R² gaffe of the "ace of the base" his eyes rolled skyward. He had one thought: "Great God, one request. Don't let him be assigned to our squadron." But of course he was.

Rawlins finished his poststart checks and watched until his wingman's exterior lights came on. Shortly thereafter, that singular voice came up. "Condone five five dash two up." The voice wore a grin. Jones grinned a good part of the time. It was his subconscious defense against any situation of which he was unsure. There were many. It might be described as what is widely known as a stupid grin. In only two or three words the voice would manage to take on just a hint of insolence.

"Five five, button two." The headphones hissed and popped as the radio tuned itself to the preset frequency of Channel 2. "Da Nang ground, Condone five five, taxi two."

"Condone five five, taxi runway three five, wind is zero three zero at ten. Altimeter two niner niner six."

Rawlins had Hang Dog in the back seat, which boded for an amusing couple of hours. Hang Dog's patter combined with having R² Jones on your wing almost guaranteed that you would be amused. The dog had run through his BIT checks while they were taxiing and determined that the radar was down as usual, so he had little to do except improvise. And Hang Dog could improvise. He was a running entertainment concern.

They checked in and out with a host of agencies and controllers and C³ folks, blathering away over the radio at various bureaucrats both airborne and ground-bound; Jones, first acute, then sucked in his angle off, eventually came aboard, a few hundred pounds of fuel lighter for all his flailing about, but so what? This night they were on a Steel Tiger mission, which meant Laos. That was good because Rawlins would get to hear Hang Dog's latest off-the-cuff rendition of the hit tune of his own composition, "Oh, Souvanna." Souvanna Phouma was the prime minister of Laos at that time. He was a wily politician who kept surfacing every time the smoke cleared. He was content to serve as prince, prime minister, or probably most any other title (after all, his half-brother Prince Souphanouvang headed up the Communist enemy) depending on which way the wind was blowing. Right now there was an ill wind blowing from the northeast—Vietnam. Souvanna had his own brand of Vietcong to deal with, including his brother, calling themselves the Pathet Lao. They controlled the north end of his country, a mountainous, rocky, nearly impenetrable stronghold, and looked to take over the rest of it. This would put Souvanna out of a job, and he liked his work enough to oppose the idea. The problem was that, like certain of his neighbors, he couldn't hold those dogs at bay without a little help. Guns and money. That was it.

Now it happened that the Ho Chi Minh Trail ran right down the eastern panhandle of Laos. The Americans were righteously pissed off that their enemies the North Vietnamese could march down the trail with troops, weapons, and political science instructors, with total impunity, to invade the South, and America couldn't do a damn thing about it.

Because Laos was neutral. Declared so by the Geneva accords. No Vietnamese and no Americans allowed. By world LAW. The North Vietnamese liked things fine because they were using Laos as a safe highway and nobody much knew it or cared. Souvanna didn't care, those armies weren't bothering him. They were merely passing through a little of his largely uninhabitable real estate on their way to wreak havoc somewhere else. But that wasn't his problem. He could not afford to provoke North Vietnam by openly siding with the West. He was officially neutral. What *was* his problem was the goddamn Pathet Lao. They kept encroaching on the government-held territory of his country, slipping down of a Saturday night into the Plain of Jars and knocking off an army outpost, that sort of thing. And he needed American aid to stop the bastards. Only the Americans knew that the NVA was using Laos as a safe highway, and they didn't like it one little bit. So they kind of had Souvanna over a barrel. Officially he ruled from Vientiane, but his office may in fact have been in the Ionian Sea. He sat somewhere between Scylla and Charybdis.

"Okay, pal," they said, "we'd be glad to help. Only there's one minor obstacle. Those pesky Communists are strolling down the trail night after night, fetching powder and shot, which they use to blow off our arms and legs and worse, and we don't like that. So you let us slip in there with our airplanes and drop some surprises on those assholes and we'll send all the guns, butter, T-28s, and crisp greenbacks you need. Deal? Without the infiltration we'll get things sorted out here in the South and bring an end to this, umm, police action."

As has been suggested, Souvanna Phouma had not just recently fallen off the *trái xòai* truck. The North Vietnamese were holding forth to the world that the uprising in the South was strictly a domestic insurrection and that there was no invasion and no Ho Chi Minh Trail, so how could they complain very loudly about the Americans bombing something that wasn't there? Oh, he wasn't foolish enough to go public and openly support the American position; that might piss the NVA off enough to cause them to sick their puppet Pathet Lao on him with greater zeal, and he didn't need that. But, he reasoned, if he were to tacitly imply by omission in his diplomatic discourse that, sure, go ahead, if you find invaders repel them, but don't hit any of my subjects—I don't want any uproar—and don't tell me about it, I don't want to know, what could the NVA say? They weren't supposed to be there anyway. On this issue Souvanna was of a mind with General Jefferson and the Commandant of the Marine

Corps—he felt that military operations should be conducted in such a way as not to engender a lot of carping and civilian complaints.

So there it was. With Souvanna forced to look the other way, he couldn't condemn the incursions into his country because he didn't know about them, and he had to look the other way to keep the American aid coming. The Americans could not cry out to the world in righteous indignation that the NVA were using a neutral country (no fair) to illegally import the engines of warfare, because they were right over there in that neutral country (no fair) bombing the shit out of the place every night. The North Vietnamese, for their part, could hardly complain about having their asses blown off along some mythical trail through a sovereign neighboring nation when they weren't there.

Of course Grampaw Pettibone, Ho Chi Minh, Souvanna Phouma, MacGeorge Bundy, *everyone*, probably Major Poltroun and R^2 Jones, maybe even Barbi Belheur, knew that without a steady infusion of troops and supplies, the South might not crumble for years, maybe never. So the NVA had to keep coming, the U.S. had to keep knocking them back, and the Royal Laotian Army had to ignore both of them and concentrate on the Pathet Lao. They were all over the same barrel. And so on.

As they passed, in a moonless sky, over the rocky escarpment of the Laotian border, Hang Dog broke forth in a clear melodious voice—so much as it could be heard over the hum and whine and clanks of the airplane, and his breathing of pressurized oxygen:

> Oh, Souvanna, oh don't you cry for me,
> For I come from Lackawanna,
> In a bad-assed F-4B.

> Oh, it rained all night in old Da Nang,
> We feared we could not fly.
> But here we are in Laos land,
> To rain death from the sky.

> Oh, Souvanna, oh don't you cry for me, . . .

Of course they weren't really in Laos, because the government said they weren't. And the tracers they would be seeing were just optical illusions, because there was no one down there to shoot them. Humming along there, in a period of inactivity, Rawlins had plenty of time to wonder about just what was below him. There were no lights, but he knew there were countless people in the hills and the jungles and the paddies. Some, he knew, were decidedly hostile. Most were probably either guardedly friendly or ambivalent. Maybe that was the fundamental thing, Rawlins mused. No American could begin to understand the peasant. He worked from morning to night every day just to subsist; there was no concept of getting ahead or improving his lot; no vacations, no retirement. For the peasants there were no economic or political theories, no communist or democratic ideologies; that stuff was of no practical use to them. The only real difference they perceived between the Vietcong and the ARVN turned on who happened to be maiming them that day. No, the only reality was the struggle to inhabit this planet for another day or another year. It had been like that for a thousand generations and would continue to be. That was why the Americans could never hope to win their hearts and minds. It was a matter of concepts. The rhetoric of democracy was claptrap to the peasants. They didn't care who sat in power. He would tax them, it had always been so, and then leave them to their struggle with the earth. The only ideology they understood was being left alone. Left alone by all these goddamn armies and politicians so they could grow their rice and catch their fish and beget their next generation and not have to think of napalm as a natural hardship. It didn't matter who was torching their hootches, they didn't like it. They wanted to be left alone— and fuck Hanoi and Saigon and the Americans and the Koreans and anybody else who wanted to complicate their incredibly hard but simple lives. So Rawlins couldn't see his side ever really winning. They could bomb them into submission, but so what? No easy solution appeared.

Lance Major Slocum's solution was to seal off the DMZ and the Laotian and Cambodian borders with nuclear land mines, a kiloton every hundred yards. They would then buy, condemn, or commandeer every seagoing vessel in the free world that was needed, every moth-balled Navy ship, every barge and tug and shrimp boat, pleasure yachts if required (more could be built), ferries, tramp steamers, etc., and marshall them in the South China Sea. The combined military forces would conduct a sweep from the DMZ south and load every single living breathing human animal, regardless (or as Lance Major Slocum would say, "irregardless") of his political affiliation, onto those ships, which would then be taken out to the twelve-mile limit. They would then muster the Seabees, the Army Corps of Engineers, Brown and Root, RMK, and every other construction concern available and move in there with their Barber-Greene machines and pave the son of a bitch. Border to border, sea to shining sea. Make a parking lot out of South Vietnam. And then sink the ships.

And it could be done. American know-how could accomplish anything—everyone knew that. Pyrrhic victory.

> Oh, Souvanna, oh don't you cry for me,
> For I've come to bomb your peasants,
> With a load of TNT.

Rawlins reduced power and began to let down. He knew more or less where they were going, having been there fifty times before.

"Coon Dog one four, Condone five five, two fox-fours with delta-ones for your control. We're, ah, two five seven at forty-seven off Dong Ha, descending to seven thousand, over."

"Roger, Condone. Coon Dog one four . . . I'm about ten miles southeast of the crossroads at three thousand. Smokey's overhead. I'll have him drop a flare." In a minute the sky lit up with an eerie kind of orange glow. Strange, spooky shadows appeared on the ground in the half-light, great for disorientation. The scene seemed not of this world, a small pale of dim, unnatural light surrounded by the endless black maw of the night. The sphere of partial illumination was constantly changing as the parachute flares descended, burned down, and new ones were dropped. Oh, those shadows, the misperception of the landscape. More than a few intrepid dive bombers had pulled off the target into lumber or granite in these conditions—or never pulled up at all.

The crossroads that the FAC referred to was at Tchepone, the major cargo hub on the Plain of Jars, where several segments of the Ho Chi Minh Trail came together. Of course Hang Dog had a ditty for this oft-visited spot:

> Tchepone, Tchepone, ya ta da
> da da da da da da da da Tchepone.
>
> Oh, life could be a scream,
> If I could blow your ass
> To paradise up above. Tchepone.
> If I could blast the trucks you're so
> protective of. Tchepone.
> Life could be a scream, Sweetheart.
>
> Hello, hello again, Tchepone,
> and hopin' we'll meet again . . .

Rawlins keyed the mike. "Coon, Condone fifty-five. I'm about three klicks at your five o'clock. What have you got for us?"

"Roger your posit, Condone. Ah, I've got a suspected truck park under the canopy. I'll mark with willie peter." The O-1 banked sharply and fired a white phosphorus rocket into a clump of high trees off the road. "Got my smoke, Condone?"

"Affirm."

"Roger, cleared hot." By now they were on a real intimate basis and dispensed with most of the ID business.

"One's in hot."

Rawlins did indeed have a tallyho on the Coon Dog FAC, and had seen his smoke. R² Jones, on the other hand, on his first mission under the flares, was disoriented, had some vertigo, and was faking it. He was looking furiously around at the ground, had lost sight of the leader, and passed the run-in heading, still not sure where he was going. Then he saw the smoke. "Two's in."

"One's off."

"Coon Dog fourteen. Good hit, One. Break, break, Dash two, break it off. NO DROP, NO DROP. That's not my smoke!"

By the time that message worked its way from the large ears, well adapted to sensing the sound, through the data transmission system of Jones's head to the executive branch, not so well adapted to processing it, got a decision, and moved on out through the available channels to tell the thumbs, the right thumb had just pressed the bomb release button. Oh, Jones had seen smoke all right, it was just that he had never seen the FAC and had also not seen *his* smoke, which marked the target. Jones had seen smoke coming from a spot a half-mile away. It was about five hundred yards off the road, and everybody knew that Lyndon's national security and foreign policy and defense people had decreed that even though they weren't bombing in Laos, if they should just happen to *be* bombing in Laos, they were not to bomb anything more than two hundred yards from the Ho Chi Minh Trail. Souvanna did not want his civilians getting irate. So Jones had fucked up.

"Goddamn it, you idiot, that's an unauthorized zone. Get off the target and hold high and dry. Dash one, abort this run and let me mark again."

There was a silence. A profound silence.

"Wait a minute, Dash two, you've got a secondary."

The transportation gooners knew as well as anybody what LBJ's rules were, so they had tunneled back under the canopy five hundred yards or so to a nice little settlement and established a truck stop. It was much like any American truck stop, plenty of rice and bread and beer and tea and fuel and lubricants. But with fish in *nuoc mam* sauce, which perhaps distinguished it. Also, many of the trucks were started with cranks. At any rate, R^2 had tracked the pipper right down to the wrong smoke, and his bomb had hit square in the middle of a truck full of artillery shells. And it made a dandy secondary explosion.

"Jesus, what a secondary. There's another one!" Pause. "Nice hit, Dash two. One, put your next one right on Two's hit."

Tracers began to hose up from the neutral peasant village.

"Hold it, Dash one, drop two hundred meters east on the driveway. I've got movers headed for the trail. We'll try to box them in. Crater that road before they get away."

They each dropped a pair of 250-pounders on the path leading to the truck stop. Hang Dog rolled his eyes back for his own amusement and said over the intercom, "That ices it, Smilin' Jack. The man upstairs really does guide the drunks and the idiots of this globe."

Though they could not see it, that popular theory was further manifested with a touch of irony; Rawlins's bombs cratered the trail nicely, but there was still a clear space, covered by the jungle roof, where the trucks could get by. Jones missed the road entirely, but, by a combination of happenstance, divine guidance, shit-house luck, and so forth, his bombs felled half a dozen hundred-foot-plus timbers in a tangled breastwork that trapped the trucks.

"Outstanding, Condone flight," said Coon Dog 14. "We've got 'em nailed."

As Rawlins pulled off he noticed again the stream of tracers sluicing up toward him from the truck stop. This time they were too close. He wrapped it away and loaded the airplane up. "Dash two, that gunner's got our pattern down. Jink off the target and we'll come twenty left on run-in."

But as Rawlins reestablished himself in the pattern, he observed a longer, rolling secondary explosion in the village. There had to be some heartburn in the area of those ammo trucks, with fire and steel and shit flying *every* goddamn where.

The young forward air controller was having multiple orgasms. It was far and away his finest hour. "Shit hot, boys. We got a dandy here. Get some."

And the tracers stopped, the gunner hoist precisely with his own petard. It was like fish in a barrel or rats in a cage. They expended the rest of their ordnance, demolishing the rest stop and all of its customers.

Pulling off the target, Rawlins, as prebriefed, took up a heading of 145 degrees and climbed to twenty thousand feet, maintaining three hundred knots to allow his wingman to get aboard. Now clear of ground fire, Rawlins reached a finger to turn on the exterior lights to expedite the rendezvous, but saw that he was too late. The evasive R^2 Jones had lost him again. Rawlins saw the twin tongues of flame of an F-4 in burner hurtling past his left shoulder toward the stratosphere.

Hang Dog laughed. "Smilin' Jack, Doggie. I do believe that fucking R^2 Jones is going to the moon."

"Well, at least he missed us." Rawlins keyed the mike button. "Coon Dog, Condone fifty-five is off high and dry, break, fifty-five Dash one is heading one four five, three hundred knots, angels twenty. *Wings level.* Come back, little Sherpa."

R^2 Jones rolled inverted passing 25,000 feet, looked to the southeast and sure enough, there about a mile below him were the flashing red, green, and white lights of his leader.

"Condone, fifty-five, Coon Dog. Your bravo delta alpha: I give you six trucks, three hootches, and three automatic weapons destroyed." R^2 was going through phases of vertigo and general disorientation. He had accepted a combination of Venus and a twinkling star or two as the perfect aspect of an F-4, and had been initiating his join-up. Venus was a long ways away, though. After Jones had looked down and found the real leader, as he and his terrified RIO were describing diversified octoflu-gerons and other imprecise aerodynamic maneuvers to get aboard, Coon Dog came up again.

"And ten KBA." Killed By Air. *Semper Fidelis.*

As the turbines were winding down in the chocks, Rawlins felt dead-tired. So Jones had blundered into a good target. So the so-called war went on. Had Rawlins still been up in the neutral nation whose name they dared not speak, where, officially he had not just come from—had he still been there on Coon Dog 14's frequency, he would have heard that *arbiter elegantiarum* giving the identical battle damage assessment to a flight of A-4s that he had given to Rawlins: six trucks, three hootches, three weapons, and ten KBA.

So that would get reported at least twice (more likely three or four times), and the scorekeepers who told everybody how we were winning the war could say "Boy, we really kicked their ass last night. At this rate this thing will be over in a matter of months." And it wasn't even an authorized target.

But Grampaw Pettibone knew. A lot of people, among them Rawlins, knew that surely things would get a lot worse before they got better.

So as Rawlins debriefed, Major Poltroun taxied out for his TPQ. So did Al "Shaky" Morgenkrank. Imagine that. So covetous was Colonel Creed of the most-ordnance-delivered record that he had both the CO and the XO flying night TPQs, the least popular of all hops, excepting maybe helo escorts.

And Major Poltroun could already feel the tension and sharp pains associated with the rising pressures in his gut. And the sick bay was already beginning to fill with officers and men who had those same complaints. And the common denominator was red death. They had all eaten it because there was nothing else. So they knew the culprit, but it was too late. Chow was over.

And the VNAF was posting their flight schedule for the next day, which would cause the grunts grief on two fronts, both in their renewed zeal to crush their hated enemies and brothers the Buddhist ARVN and in their generous decision to also keep an eye toward harassing the Cong.

And the ARVN were setting up their mortars to look at a different part of the base, which would cause Colonel Creed and General Jefferson considerable gastric distress for different reasons, but would indirectly cause near elation in the squadron pilots because it would cause the war to be moved to Thailand for a week.

And in a very few hours Brass Balls Obradovitch would be awakened by the clock in his brain, to lead his company of irregulars on a search-and-destroy patrol. One member of that patrol, a young second lieutenant fresh out from basic school, was so excited he couldn't sleep. As he sat recleaning his weapon a third time in anticipation of combat, he spoke to a hardened veteran of the same age who had been there six months. "How did Captain Obradovitch get this handle 'Brass Balls,' anyway?"

"You haven't heard *that* story yet?" Almost in disbelief. "Son, that is hard evidence of a highly developed state of bootness. How long you been here?"

"All day, and I like it."

"Well, let me tell you the legend of Brass Balls Obradovitch. It seems there was this ville right in the middle of a hotly contested sector. We would pound the shit out of it during the day and then at night the Cong would slip in and conscript young men, bother their women, torture selected people, and commandeer all their provisions and stuff. Some of the locals decided this was less than the ideal life-style, and when it had gone on for a few weeks they asked to be relocated. That was fine because we had decided to level the fucking place anyway. It was right in the middle of our AO, and we hadn't been able to get rid of the bastards. It was a spot on our brass, y'know? So we went out and began to escort these refugees away before we blew the place up. And got ambushed, man, I mean lit up. Charlie was in a tree line and he caught us out in the paddy. And the ballgame was on. You saw nothing but assholes and elbows for a minute."

"They shot at the civilians too?"

"Shit, man, they weren't really shooting at anything. They were just hosing us down. Anyway, Obradovitch grabbed the nearest two gooks and dragged them down behind a dike. His radioman was right behind him. So there's the two of them down behind this paddy dike with the two refugees who turned out to be girls, one about eighteen, the other one maybe fourteen. O.B. fell on top of them to kind of protect them with his body 'cause he ain't afraid of *shit* and he's always doing that kind of bullshit. He takes his war pretty serious. So we all opened up on the tree line, and Charlie, as he sometimes does, quieted down and started to fall back. We had three or four WIAs, and if the Cong is outnumbered they'll take that and fade away. Or pretend to. So pretty quick our fire died down too, but nobody showed himself. It was a waiting game there for a spell, with only sporadic rounds from someone on either side who thought he saw something.

"Well, Obradovitch weighs two hundred pounds and he is one hard, bony son of a bitch. The girl he was lying on began to squirm around some. He rolled back, half off of her, but still keeping his head down. He looked at her for the first time and she was absolutely terrified. I guess there was hot brass flying around, maybe some burning her a little, bullets whizzing overhead, and she figured this might be her last trail. The younger one scooted out from under the various arms and legs and lay apart, not quite shaking, but scared too. The girl still partly under O.B. squirmed around some more trying to get comfortable and then he said the strangest thing happened. He felt his dick starting to get hard. He grinned at her and I guess she gave him kind of a frozen smile back. The firing had died off. He checked the tree line and then ran his hand over her rump. She didn't move. A lot of these assholes claim she was a lady of loose morals, but I say bullshit. I think she was scared so shitless she *couldn't* have done anything. Anyway, Obradovitch slipped his hand under those black pajamas and began to work them down. She didn't say a thing, just kept that smile frozen on her face."

"You mean he started undressing her while they were under fire, for Christ's sake?"

"Well, there wasn't much fire right then. Man, we were all layin' chilly." The lieutenant paused and chuckled. "Layin' chilly, motherfucker, listening to the blood pound. And there's old O.B. gettin' it on with this slope broad right out there in front of her sister, his radioman, us, the Cong, God, and every fuckin' body. Ohhh, that motherfucker's got some balls. He said he couldn't believe what he was doing, but he reached down, got his dick out, and slipped it in. She never made a move or a peep. O.B. said he was so horny, so fucking compelled at that minute, he didn't think he could have stopped if he caught one between the horns."

"Did you see it?"

"Me? Shit no. I was sucked down into the dirt so close I was breathing on credit. So old O.B. just poured it to her right there in the middle of everything, keeping an eye on the tree line."

"So that's how he got the nickname."

"Shit no, man. That's only part of it."

"What's the rest?"

"Well, as O.B. worked up to his passion, so to speak, the radioman, a hard-charging young corporal, started working his way over. The Bronze Star citation says 'to rejoin his commander under fire,' but there are those who claim to have witnessed it who say he was trying to get closer to the fourteen-year-old. Anyway, he stuck his ass up a little above the dike, heh heh, some say it was because he was pole-vaulting across the paddy, but at any rate, some Charlie put a .762 through said ass— both cheeks. He crashed, in some pain, right next to Obradovitch who was getting ready to come, the fourteen-year-old, again, scooting out of the way. O.B. saw the muzzle flash of the dink who got him, and, they say, without missing a stroke, opened up full auto—rock and roll, man— and greased the motherfucker. Loins pumping against a nameless cunt, M-16 bucking against his shoulder. Agents of life, agents of death, you know? There was a lot of emotion there. O.B. told me that it was an orgasm that can have no equal—unless he has one while he is dying, which could add dimensions, maybe."

He was not going to be having one when he died, though only Pettibone and those fellows knew about that as yet.

"To top it off, the story goes, O.B., while still in the saddle, reached calmly over to his wounded radioman, grabbed the handset, got on the horn, and called in a dust-off. If that ain't brass balls, I don't know what is."

That was the story, maybe apocryphal, of Brass Balls Obradovitch, who would be self-awakened in a couple of hours to lead his stalwarts into the fray.

As Rawlins walked, dragged more like, to the personnel carrier that would take him back to his tent on the other side of the field, he encountered a line of thirty or forty men outside the hangar bay. Somewhere in the middle stood Sam and Jimmy and Torres, the ordnance crew.

"What the fuck are you guys doing here? I told you to go to bed."

Their eyes were sunken, their faces showed no expression. They were zombies. They held canteen cups of cold coffee, not drinking it. "Major Poltroun countermanded your order, Lieutenant," said Staff Sergeant Sam.

"What the hell are you talking about? He doesn't have anything to do with maintenance."

"He said every man in the squadron has to get a haircut before they secure. That's what we're waiting for. There's only one barber."

"Well, I'm countermanding *his* fucking order. You can get a haircut tomorrow. You are required to obey the most current lawful order you have received. That is: Get your ass on that pickup with me and SECURE. Understood?"

"Aye, aye, Lieutenant. Lead the way." Somehow Sam managed to get a twinkle in his eye. He would get his ass chewed tomorrow, but they couldn't do anything, because he was acting under a lawful order from a commissioned officer—his OIC, at that. Rawlins would also get his ass chewed, but they couldn't do anything about that either, because, under the circumstances, Poltroun's order would not be considered lawful, because everyone knew he was an asshole of the largest caliber and didn't care what he ordered anyway, and besides, he would have some tall explaining to do himself by morning. And Al "Shaky" Morgenkrank, the CO, would also have a little explaining to do, and wouldn't be much concerned whether the ordnance crew, who had done yeoman service, got a haircut or not, or whether Rawlins had defied his flaky XO. And so on.

15

California, 1970s

Around '69 some intrepid warrior of the sky was doing loops in an airway somewhere and not looking out the window like all good aviators always do—they tell you and tell you—when he smartly and fatally struck, in midair, a commercial jet climbing out from Umptyfratz International Airport. The repercussions were considerable. This event stood out in Rawlins's mind as the symbol for a number of strictures and limitations that heralded the decline of military flying as the ultimate sport, the one really fun thing left to do.

After that incident the Reserves could no longer either launch or recover under visual flight rules. For their little bomb/strafe/hassle hops on the weekends they had to file instrument departures, cancel out at altitude, go do their scheduled thing, then climb up, and refile for an instrument approach and recovery. The FAA, meanwhile, passed a LAW that said no one was to exceed 250 knots below the altitude of ten thousand feet while over land, anywhere. And no aerobatics except in restricted areas. No more hot breaks. No more breaks at all. No more sight-seeing, no more buzzing the yachts at Twin Harbors, scaring the buffalo on Catalina or the goats on San Clemente Island. An end to road and river recces. No flat-hatting, no more booming the Sandpiper or following the railroad tracks to Yuma, pulling up for the power lines. They were taking all the fun out of it. The politicians ruined everything. The boys used to fly up the Colorado River at four hundred knots, twisting and turning in tail chase, each attempting to keep his airplane over the water at all times, or losing face. That river can seem pretty narrow when you're snaking along just above it, pulling three or four gs, in and out of buffet. Entering the Grand Canyon they would smoke along below the rim, unseen and as yet unheard, looking for groups of tourists at observation points along the way, whose hats they would try to blow off and whom they would startle no end as they screamed up from below, unexpected, and roared over their heads at fifty feet rolling inverted. Lots of the pilots liked to buzz the girlfriend's house or the family farm if they had either.

Moon Dog was once reconnoitering the ranch where he grew up in southern Wyoming. It was roundup time and from Moon's vantage point he could see that the cowboys had missed an old bull who was holed up in thick brush way up on the side of a mountain. Well, old Moon just popped over to the nearest air base, which was in Denver, and called home and told them where to find the bull. Then he picked up some fuel and smoked on west. Perfect cooperation between the military and civilian establishments. It didn't cost Moon Dog more than an hour of his time, either. Ah, but leave it to the bureaucrats, they would put an end to such friendly relations.

At the same time, the Congress was finally putting some fiscal restraints on their military. The doves, who seemed to have started a thriving business by this time, thanks in no small part to the efforts of Barbi Belheur, P. E. Proudbird, Mrs. O'Flynn, and SLUR, thought they could force the president and his army to stop this immoral war, or at least cut it down in size and scope. But of course the military establishment, showing, it may be said, something of a killer instinct, just sent all their money and supplies and ammo to Vietnam, not wishing to diminish the only good thing they had going at the time. There were all those careers to be enhanced! This left relatively little for the Reserves to play with, who, it was felt, didn't need career enhancement anyway, and they were running out of gas money. So the official announcement came down: no more cross-countries. Well, that did it. No more escaping wife, kids, lawn-mowing, Little League, and that shit to meet the golden stewardess in Las Vegas. No more trysting with the Navy captain's daughter in Jacksonville, whose husband was a POW and who was faithful to a point, but still, who had certain biological needs that couldn't be denied. He would come home completely mind-blown, get on the booze, and divorce her anyway. No more parties in New Orleans, Chicago, San Francisco. No sir. Civilian military flying had deteriorated to the point where it sucked. And talk about the Reserves not needing career enhancement! The next program they started was a reduction in force. RIF. They just started sending letters to thousands of people saying they had two choices: Either you resign or we'll discharge you. That's all. Cutting right and left, indiscriminately. That's when the colonel came to

Rawlins with his ingenious plan for keeping him in the active Reserve and in the air wing.

"What are you getting at?" Rawlins was just a tad suspicious of anything the Marine Corps wanted to do for him.

"We send you to the grunts for a couple of years."

"Uh, negative on that, Colonel. I tried the grunts and I don't like it." Just one more good deal, he could not help but think, one good deal after another from the Corps.

"Look, Jack, you're only a captain. They do this RIFing by rank, higher-ups first. You'll be pretty safe for a while. This grunt outfit has a billet for a FAC. I already talked to the colonel over there and I can get it for you. You'll be safe in that assignment because there's nobody else around to fill it. In a year or two, when this blows over, we'll get you reassigned to the squadron and you'll be covered."

"Where do they drill?"

"Pendleton, Twentynine Palms. But it's just a boondoggle one weekend a month."

"And two weeks every summer." Another good deal. "No sir, Bob, I'm not going to spend the next two years riding around the Mohave Desert in a jeep, or worse yet *walking* through that sumbitch. And even if I did get back, the flying around here sucks. No cross-countries, no VFR. Radar-controlled everything. It ain't no fun anymore."

"Oh, things'll get better. They always do." The field-grade optimist.

"Well, I'm not going to wait around. With all due respect for your trying to help, just draw up my walking papers, Colonel. I'll try my luck as a real civilian." Rawlins knew that things would get a lot worse before they got better. One more good deal.

So his military flying career was over. In a way he was relieved. Sometimes the Valium didn't work quite as advertised. Then the fear would come back, the cold dread of—what? He couldn't say exactly, but it was very real, the icy fingers of the fiend clutching the organs inside his chest, sending the ominous alarms to his brain that made him feel debilitatingly, well, *sick*. In mortal danger. Sometimes, probably when he had inundated his brain and nervous system with just a little too much caustic alcohol, deprived it of a couple too many hours of healing sleep, pushed too far, the pill he had taken wouldn't be enough. The angst would creep up on him in midflight. Those were bad times; he could only suffer, *pray* in his own agnostic way. He used to carry a pill loose in his pocket for emergencies. In Rawlins's troubled mind, those little tablets took on the awesome status of the ultimate fetish; they warded off the most iniquitous evil; they were his only salvation besides booze, and you can't always order three quick doubles. Like just before you step into an airplane. Such a fetishism had he developed, that even when he was feeling fine, which was still most of the time, and he sallied forth into the joyous world on some errand or other, and then discovered that the pill was not in the pocket, he began to worry. The symptoms would subtly begin to manifest themselves. If he was distracted it usually passed; if he had nothing else to occupy his mind, and brooded on it, it got worse.

One weekend he had flown to San Francisco to see his most highly rated girl of the time. They had what would later come to be known as an upscale dinner at a joint that saw fit to take a single-column, one-inch ad in the back of *The New Yorker* from time to time. A slew of cocktails, wines, and postprandial conflations came along with the spread. They danced and later rollicked back to her apartment. They promised, and pretended, and partied into the night. The girl lived high on one of the fabled hills and drove a Porsche 912. She had, and seemingly could not rid herself of, the unfortunate habit of riding the clutch. Up those endless city hills, in all the traffic, at every signal and intersection, she rode the clutch. And burned one out every couple of weeks, it seemed. She finally had to get rid of her fancy car because she couldn't afford to keep it in clutches. Porsche clutches aren't cheap. She traded it for a Chevy power glide.

Rawlins had, in a somewhat attenuated sense of relativity perhaps, a similar flaw. He refused to learn how to properly operate his body, the physical vehicle of his earthly existence, and things were starting to slip— to spin loose and fail to mesh and harmonize just so. Here and there within the intricate channels and circuits of his machine, from time to time, a tiny gyro would tumble, a capacitor would discharge to ground, a servo encounter excessive friction. People had suggested that he was leaning on it too hard, but he paid no heed; like his current love, he kept riding that clutch. The difference, of course, was that he could not trade his in for an automatic.

Late in the morning she took him to the Alameda Naval Air Station, where he'd left his airplane. It was kind of goddamn glamorous, really, to be driven to your jet on a leisurely Sunday morning by a gorgeous blonde in a red Porsche (no one noticed that the clutch was slipping), except that his neurological condition was something akin to a luffing jib in a stiff breeze. But it was okay. He had the magic tablet. He kissed her good-bye at the transient line shack, went in, got a drink of water, and took his pill. He got the ground crew and start cart and headed out to his airplane. Everything looked good and he suited up, strapped in, and lit it off. And the fucking generator wouldn't come on the line. He cycled the emergency bypass switch, kicked a side panel in frustration, and summoned the crew chief up the ladder to confer. The crew checked some things in the nose wheel well, looked in a couple of engine and accessories section access doors, and signaled him to shut down. They would have to change the generator, it looked like. They would call the duty electrician right away, but they would also have to check on the availability of the parts. It being Sunday and all, they couldn't promise him the airplane before tomorrow.

She had waited, leaning against the fender of the Porsche, to watch him take off. He had been feeling expansive in a way, in his element, and he was proud of that element; he was showing off a little (mustn't he seem dashing, careless, competent—ready, with a terse nod, to commit himself in the tiny, screaming jet to whatever nature had to offer— the raw edge of adventure, all in the day's work) and now his act had been sabotaged. There was nothing to do but shut down and send a message to homeplate that he would have to RON another night. Fortunately the girl was still there.

They went to Fisherman's Wharf for lunch and then had a really fine afternoon strolling around hand in hand, sight-seeing, browsing at Ghirardelli Square, stopping for a drink. Rawlins was in a great mood, enjoying himself and now glad the generator had died. Except he had to cool it because he had no Valium for tomorrow. They touristed, saw a performance of *The Fantasticks*. "Try to Remember." The song would haunt Rawlins years later. ". . . and if you remember then follow." They bought wine and cheese, and returned to her apartment.

It was a much quieter evening than the one before, and more enjoyable. They shared little domestic discoveries and surprises and got pretty comfortable around each other. They promised and pretended some more, but less so than the night before—they were genuinely drawn to each other and the things were becoming truer. Rawlins thought maybe he was falling in love. He pondered that idea sometimes. What might this fabled state be like in reality? He was fairly sure he had never been in love in the conventional sense. On occasion an old song, a movie, a passage in a book, or some such mnemonicon would trigger in him an intense, a momentarily overwhelming recollection of the combined ecstasy and torment of his adolescent concept of the condition. Passion, ardor, lament, and melancholia; supposed eternal commitment and dedication (only eternity didn't seem to last so long in those days)—he achingly recalled those emotions from time to time. There had been a girl once, when he was first in college, who was already pinned, engaged really, when he met her. They were forced together on a ski weekend in the mountains because her sorority and his fraternity had planned the trip together with joint functions and much merriment. These two innocents were so strongly drawn to each other that it just happened. They gazed long into each other's eyes, drank a little too much beer, embraced furtively. She was neither coy nor dissembling, but perhaps they let the emotions run too free; she let him believe, or Rawlins let himself believe, that there was hope for this most perfect, if ill-fated, romance. A week later she dispelled that notion in a letter praising his sensitivity, honor, and magnetism, but imploring him not to love her, for her fidelity was a *fait accompli*, and she could only cause him pain. From a ten-year perspective, that idea was amusing, because her bittersweet note, at such a precarious moment in his life, caused the smitten Rawlins more pain than he had thought the world might contain. To expand on the words of the song, he was a walking, talking, crying, soundly beaten but barely beating broken heart. But he reckoned, now, rightly, that his wisdom and sophistication during that period were roughly the same as those of Tom Sawyer, lying under Becky's window, wishing he were "drownded" because, boy, that would cause her to care.

Since the inevitable disappointments of youth, Rawlins had not seen monogamy as a desirable condition. No, he assured himself, the idea is to love everybody a little bit and no one person to the exclusion of others. That way nobody gets hurt. One is merely fair and open and humanistic about these matters; the idea of monogamy is only a Judeo-Christian perversion, chiseled into this particular society by the Puritans, neither natural nor sensible. It is born of weakness and fear and confusion, which, in an extended perversion, foster the absurd concept of the proprietary interest in another person. That notion should have been stamped out along with slavery, but it persists. And it produces jealousy, which, along with guilt, may be the most self-defeating aspect of human thought. And leads inevitably to pain. Don't husbands and wives go around with the idea that they own one another, with the consequence that they are forever shooting and stabbing and maiming each other? They immerse themselves in endless bitterness and litigation (as if that particular form of socially condoned vengeance could in any way improve the quality of life), permanently injure themselves and their children, and perpetuate the misery. Now would anybody in his right mind visit that sort of distress upon himself? No thank you, I'll pass. No, this love stuff has its draw-backs. And what will it get you? Kids? A broken heart? An alimony payment? And what is the brightest side? You share intimately for life, that is to say, statistically, for that period of life during which the marriage will predictably endure, *everything*. All your likes and dislikes, prejudices and conceits, your beliefs in common and your antipathies—*everything*. Maybe not so rosy a prospect. And you have someone to depend on for "ever." And someone to be dependent on you for that same eternity. Only you couldn't really depend on it.

Rawlins's parents were divorced when he was young and he remem-bered that mess. Marriage, he thought, may be a little like the war. If you get to believing too much in things they have a way of burning you. Didn't Captain America, the perfect Marine, get his red, white, and blue patriotic ass blown to kingdom come by a SAM that he never saw? What about Brass Balls Obradovitch? You have to watch things closely. Don't commit too quickly or too deeply. Don't invite disappointment; you get enough as it is. Deal with everything at arm's length. Safer in an imperfect world. Isn't there always another girl, another cause, for the clever cynic?

"I think I might be falling in love with you, Rawlins," she said. She lay with an arm draped across his chest, warm and fragrant.

"I'm afraid it might be reciprocal." He squeezed her. They lay there, into the night, and drew inexorably closer, more attached.

Early in the morning, before work, she dropped him at the base. Rawlins had not had enough sleep, had given his liver too little time to detoxify the hydraulic system, not allowed the old neurons to completely realign at their synapses, suffered a touch of circadian desynchronosis, again had the foresail rattling in the breeze. But she departed, taking with her the aura of romance, the celebrative air of yesterday. Rawlins was left in the gray light of Monday morning on a military air base, getting ready to launch. Without a pill. It was a less than festive occasion because the anticipation was already there, and that was nearly as bad as the angst itself.

He was, nonetheless, a fighter pilot. He lit it off and smoked on out to whatever destiny awaited him. He filed a VFR flight plan so that he could fly at low altitude, which, for some reason, was a little more com-fortable when the demon came. And he did.

It was the worst of flights. In a cold sweat Rawlins hung in there, feeling that death was imminent, not fearing death itself so much, a sometime companion throughout his career, but fearing the *fear*. The anticipation, the symptoms. He suffered silently the tingling of the extremities, the shortness of breath, the pressure in his chest. Or were they all tricks of the mind, the nervous system? Still, every fiber of his being told him this was the onset of heart attack, that the fainting spell was touching him with a cold finger. Intellectually, rationally, he knew he was imagining all this, but he had never known such numbing, enervating terror. He toughed it out, gritting his teeth, belching, hyperventilating, sweating, often with a hand on the face curtain ready to blow himself out of there if he felt his systems actually start to fail.

Hurtling along the rocky California coast at five hundred miles an hour, crammed into the tiny cockpit of the A-4, it was just the three of them: Rawlins, the demon, and mortality.

But, somehow, he made it home, as he always did. One time it had been soaked in Da Nang river water, in the back of a rescue helicopter, but he always made it. Only this time he was a bundle of rags inside. His soul shook. In the rush of relief at being back on the ground, it had occurred to him that maybe he should stay there. Valium or no. So he said to the colonel, "It ain't no fun anymore."

"Oh, things'll get better. They always do."

"Well, I'm not going to wait around. With all due respect for your trying to help, just draw up my walking papers, Colonel. I'll try my luck as a real civilian."

So your days as a jet driver are at an end. No more flying hops. What does that mean? Well, for one thing, you'll never be locked in that cockpit alone with the monkey, seeing your own death flying formation on the shadow that streaks along beneath you on the granite of earth. No more fear of the unknown, exacerbated, intensified, accelerated by the proximity to instant destruction of your imperiled place in a fragile man-made capsule rocketing through the air in defiance of natural laws. Yes, that.

Ah, but no more rush of cockpit air as the throttle goes forward, the exhilarating acceleration of the afterburner pressing you against the seat, tires thumping on the joints of the runway ever faster, slight shimmy as you rotate, release from earthly friction and limitation, bounding into the air, freedom in many axes, the soaring burner climb, earth receding, but even as it does, revealing more and more of itself, showing its continuity, the unity of its very diversity, the sun glinting and coruscating off the canopy, tangibly bluer sky contrasted to the pure whiteness of cumulus clouds, the feel of the structural integrity of the airplane as it answers the touch, bounces through unseen turbulent pockets, powers toward the sky, rolling inverted at twenty thousand feet to gauge the earth, stretching off to far horizons in balanced tessellation of fields and section lines, roads, rivers and ridges, a mosaic of green, brown, and gold, the ocean verging from cobalt to turquoise as it shallows, vivid green of forest or jungle, the sudden, profound silence as you pull it back to idle and execute slow aileron rolls as the nose falls through, once, twice, three times, earth, sky, earth, sky, earth, sky. No, no more of that. No more the g-suit squeezing your lower body reassuringly as you pull into a high-g barrel roll or bend it starboard hard as possible, nor the sense of precision and accomplishment when you track the pipper right up to the target, relax a little g and squeeze, or fly a tight wing, tucked right in there, an extension of the leader, bounding through light turbulence, wingtips two feet apart, dropping on the turns into you, rotating with him on the turns away, executing perfectly, or when you feel the wheels clunk down on the concrete, right on the money, as the meatball slides off the side of the mirror. No more waxing some group major's ass—turn in from a couple of miles abeam at angels twenty, three or four claw-scraping turns down to twelve, "Dash two, say your posit."

"Five-thirty and tracking"—then have *him* debrief *you*. Gone the society of the ready room and the club at happy hour. You're no longer a member of the lodge.

Yes, that was all gone, but so was the monkey, so was the fiend. He figured maybe it was all for the best. Only the monkey wasn't really gone. He hadn't even begun to know the monkey yet.

It eventuated that Rawlins would likely have to get a grown-up job of some sort and play the games that normal people play in order to sustain life. This was not an entirely attractive prospect but was hastened, yea, rendered inevitable by the vagaries of the Chicago Board of Trade. For more than a year, Rawlins had managed to purloin fairly regular stipends from the commodity futures market. It worked like this. He had met Rodney, a broker from the august house of Cragle, Gerschenson, and Habib who subscribed to a very expensive technical service out of Texas. He was a touch wary of the little fellow, who wore leisure suits and neither smoked nor drank, but constantly beamed and chewed Juicy Fruit. But, he came highly recommended; what the hell. The Texas outfit dumped bushels of data concerning selected commodities into a computer. The program was based on a complex formula that, essentially, as explained to Rawlins (upon whom any more comprehensive an exposition would have been wasted), said that if, under certain circumstances, any given issue moved a certain number of points in either direction, within a certain period, then it would invariably move further before reversing. All this was predictable by a closely guarded theory of technical momentum stating that if so many contracts of March soybean oil moved a certain amount within a given time, a mathematical law of the market would cause them to move so many points more before they could stop and turn around. And it worked, or seemed to, for quite a spell. Rawlins was raking it in. Especially when he got into a rising silver market. He started with one contract and rode. Every time it went up enough to cover his margin, he bought another one. After a couple of months of this, he was getting so terrified of losing his paper pile that when the service recommended getting out, oddly enough he did. And pulled a nice piece of change. Hoo boy! This was the way to do it.

Except Rodney, the broker, who was a convert to the Mormon Church strictly for business purposes, but a fulfilled member, in good standing, had been doing a little charting of his own. He developed his own formula, which seemed to work just as well as the Texans' did. So why pay them all that money for the service? He canceled. Rawlins had given him permission to trade the account whenever it was indicated; the thing was working pretty well and Smilin' Jack didn't want to be bothered with all that shit every morning. Lots of mornings he didn't even get up. No sir, that was Rod's business, let him take care of it. Rodney somehow forgot to mention in his frequent updating phone calls that he didn't need those piddling Texans any more. That outfit was, as a prominent transplanted Texas politician would later remark about another group, all hat and no cattle. Not to worry. Rodney could predict that sucker his own self.

The upshot was that ol' Rod consulted his crystal ball one day and saw the big kill coming. There it was, as plain as the nose on your face. Figures didn't lie. His charts told him incontrovertibly that hogs were being slaughtered at an unassimilable rate and that there would be a glut on that summer's market. Correspondingly, with fewer pigs left to stick, there had to be a shortage in the fall. Rod got right on the hook and put Rawlins into a couple trainloads of pork bellies. One trainload was to be delivered in June. That was when the market would be flooded, and the price was way too high, so he went short on that train. The other would not come chug, chugging out of the Chicago packinghouse spur until October, when bacon would be scarce. Everybody eats more bacon in cold weather, don't they? The price for October futures was relatively low, so old Rod went long on that one. Wow, the commission on this little piece of business could be a ton if things went the way the numbers indicated!

Only somebody was betting the other way. H. L. Hunt, maybe. Or maybe the farmers hadn't read the charts, but for some inexplicable reason those pesky June bellies started to inch up. Not to worry, a short-term aberration. October futures stayed the same. For a while. Then they unaccountably started to fall off little by little. Rawlins was straddling the two like a Roman rider on Trigger and Champion with Roy on one side of the corral and Gene on the other, both whistling.

Very soon Smilin' Jack began gettng up *every* morning. That was because the accounts section for Messrs. Cragle, Gerschenson, and Habib would give him a margin call each day about eight.

"Rodney? What the fuck is going on? Your people have called me for money every day this week."

"I'm not worried. It's just a little deviation. A technical adjustment. It's the institutional investors. They don't understand the fundamentals. The market will straighten itself out."

"Well, *I'm* worried. I can't write a check for a thousand dollars a day for very many days. Get me the fuck out of this thing."

"Jack, if you sell out now, you lose. My advice is to hang in there another week or so. When this thing turns around, and it *has* to, we could make some real money."

Well, Rawlins was greedy. And Rodney *had* made him money. He hung in. Too long. By the time he escaped, without most of the gains of previous deals, not to say his shirt, he was well on his way to becoming an Orthodox Jew. He didn't even want to hear the word "pork." Excluding a few ladies dragged out of the Sandpiper at late hours, he would never go near another pig in his life. That he didn't garrote Rod, throttle him with his polyester tie, was surprising. He guessed he wasn't capable of murder except in an airplane. But Smilin' Jack's very minor fortune had dwindled. Short of bank robbery, it looked like legitimate work was the only thing.

Rawlins took stock of his options. First of all, he reckoned that sitting at a desk beat standing in a ditch. The pen might well be mightier than the sword, but more importantly, it was easier to operate than the shovel. He did not want to be a goddamn salesman of any sort. He was not a business major, an engineer, or an accountant. He had studied English and flown airplanes. That was it. He decided that the burgeoning field of aerospace publications was the spot for him. Actually, that was as far from legitimate work as you could get and still collect a pay check, but he didn't know about all that yet.

So Rawlins came, approaching the ebb of his still youngish life, to the

Vulcan V-belt and Avionic Pilotage System Corporation, for an interview with a Mr. Malcolm Xavier "Bud" Malison, manager of the proposals group at Vulcan.

The interview was interesting. He showed Malison a résumé and some samples that he misrepresented as his own work. Malison flipped through the stuff, paying no attention to anything except paper weight, type font, and the size and line weight of the illustrations. He found two similar pictures that had not been drawn to exactly the same scale and leaped on that as an example of something that would be totally unacceptable at Vulcan. Then he began telling Rawlins his troubles. Here was a man with personnel problems, budget problems, organizational problems, and communications problems. Nothing about the proposals they supposedly produced. No, it was all real estate and manning levels and furniture. Management concerns. The stuff of empire. Rawlins emerged feeling that he had learned a great deal more about Bud Malison than he would ever want to know, and that Malison knew almost nothing about him. The parting assurance was that an ex-fighter pilot and English major in the same body was a rare find and that he would be hearing from them.

Rawlins had set an arbitrary bottom line on salary, which was really merely how much he thought he could get. He was convinced that his number was realistic and was coaching himself to stubbornly insist that he could accept no less. Ah, little did the innocent know of aerospace. The personnel office called in two days and offered him half again as much as the rock bottom figure that was in reality his fond hope. He could have bargained and almost certainly upped the ante a little, but again, he didn't yet know that the value system of the defense industry is based upon obscure writings of Lewis Carroll and Franz Kafka that were too bizarre to be published. It seemed like so much money to him that he was afraid to kill the goose, so, being a touch more discreet than valorous in these matters, he jumped at it. And became, for better or for worse, for richer or for poorer, in sickness and in health, an employee of the Vulcan V-belt and Avionic Pilotage System Corporation. He was assigned to the Advanced Programs and Prognostications Division, which, he was assured by Malcom "Bud" Malison, was a very hotbed of proposal activity.

Rawlins arrived having little idea of what a proposal was, or should be. After five years at VVAPS he still didn't. Well, he had garnered some pretty strong impressions of what a proposal should *not* be, but he had yet to see a positive example of what one *should* be like. Aside from being paid to read newspapers and do the crossword puzzles most of the time, the most palliative antidote to the boredom and intellectual folly of proposal work was lunch. Officially it was from noon to 12:42. In fact it went anywhere from eleven up until as late as three on a slow day. That was good.

That was also bad. A lot of martinis or Rob Roys can slide down your throat between eleven and three. And if you straggle back to the office, even at 2:15, spewing a breath that would pollute Munich in October, red-faced, eyes glazed, and fuck around at your desk, laughing much too loudly at the inane remarks of your cellmate and half-pretending to work, if you do that, where do you rush at 4:42? Yes! To the bar of the Mexican restaurant right down the street from your office to have just two or three more to boost you back up onto the step and set you there solidly, with great calm and that sense of well-being. And then you roll on home in fine fettle and even if the cops don't intercept you and turn every goddamn thing into misery for the next eighteen hours or so, and more in weeks to come, even if they don't, your evening's scenario is already written.

And even if you haven't yet been forced to seriously consider the source of your depression, the debilitation of your C^3I apparatus, haven't seized the *taurian cornua* as it were, still all those cocktails are likely to have long-term effects as well as the short. But some things are learned, no, accepted so slowly, so bitterly—if at all.

So Rawlins was plunged into the commercial phase of his midlife, the nine-to-five shit that everyone seems so to lament. He phased into the satisfactionless ennui of the great white-collar bureaucracy of paper, and the monkey wasn't far behind.

16

California, 1970s

Barbi and P.E. had decided to sponsor a peace conference. They got down with Dulcie and Mrs. O'Flynn and began planning the workshops. They had to have plenty of workshops, that was *de rigueur*. Dulcie was going to limit herself to food workshops for the starving masses, but Mrs. O'Flynn would get in on the intellectual side of this conclave. She would offer a testimonial to the evils of the military machine. Had they not sent her husband, against her will (though perhaps not against his) to some godforsaken place to fight in an awful, immoral war against innocent civilians? (She had learned, rote, from Barbi that the war was indeed awful and immoral, that it was fought exclusively against civilians, and that they were, to a manjack, woman, and child, from Dan to Beersheba, immaculately innocent.) Had they not allowed their despoiling, undisciplined, inept pilots to fly supersonic over the PX, causing the shattering of numerous glass shelves and the subsequent plummeting of her most treasured Hummel figurine to the concrete deck? Of even greater concern, did they not inhumanely continue, *persist*, in demoting her husband and thus diminishing her allotment check? Ah, there was perversity for you. The Marine Corps was evil itself. A Mephistophelian force that created Faustian regiments out of hand and promulgated policies wholesale that were beyond even the imagination of a poor, innocent, godly bingo player. Because, Mrs. O'Flynn had come to truly believe, this war was human folly of such colossal proportions that something had to be done. Mankind was demonstrating a tendency, born of greed and politics, to destroy itself. By God, she could tell them a thing or two about the military establishment.

Barbi saw the conference as a stepping stone to her avowed appearance at the Democrats' convention. She had big plans. Under the auspices of SLUR, they would mobilize a very corps of antimilitary consultants to fan out through the land. They would have an office on every block in the nation where there was an Armed Forces recruiting substation. Next door, if possible. They would organize all the elements of the peace movement into one indivisible power. They would refine and tune it to run efficiently and effectively. They would *militarize* it. Barbi's strategy was to have the most highly trained, most capable persons in just the required places at precisely the times they were needed. By regimenting the antimilitary militant Left she was sure she could defuse the military establishment and the military-industrial complex of the militant Right. Still, it would take a great deal of concentrated effort to get these legions of peacemongers deployed into the field. To that end, she was planning her conference carefully.

In addition to Mrs. O'Flynn's seminar, Irene Arena, Barbi's voice coach from the People's Republic of Santa Monica, would give a workshop on lisping. The fascist pigs thought that all homosexuals lisped, so that skill might go a long way toward a 4F classification. Barbi was trying to get the governor to give a short talk on eclectic administrative policies within a cause-oriented coalition of diverse elements of society. Not to say special interest groups. But he was a busy man. Barbi had finally met the governor by chaining herself to his trailer in Bakersfield. He was cute. That was her first impression; it wasn't until later, over a cup of souchong tea inside the trailer that she began to plumb the depths of this man, to understand how truly brilliant and revolutionary he was.

As for the boy governor, he had been astounded when he arrived at work one morning in his '59 Plymouth, with the fins, to find a bright, energetic, cause-oriented, *white* girl, woman that is, chained to the outside dual of the second axle of his office. Normally there would be a Chicano or two chained there (not field hands, they had to work—usually students or members of federally funded counseling programs), maybe a black welfare mother, an Indian, some dissident Russian Jews. But this was amazing. Here was this petite brunette—well, WASP, maybe—in designer jeans. She was a child-woman, at once both profound and innocent. He was drawn to her. Then he recognized her as Barbi Belheur. He had attended one of her concerts, unannounced, and been captivated. He immediately summoned security personnel with bolt cutters to unchain her, which action she would have resisted, but she was chained up and could not fight very well. The governor then invited Barbi in for the tea. She was perplexed. She had seen this campaign as one of confrontational politics, had intended to refuse to leave or be released until the news cameras were rolling and she could make her statement to the media. But here she was, loose already, not a reporter in sight, and the man was cordially inviting her in. Well, after all, one of the objects of her demonstration *had* been to gain an audience with him. And he *was* cute. Besides, he might well be the next president of the United States, and, who knows, a stint as first lady wouldn't hurt her cause any. Barbi, in an instinctive tactical flash, saw that the cause was better served here by cooperation. They became fast friends.

Meeting the governor was the most important thing that had ever happened to Barbi Belheur. She had never known anyone with real political power before, and any number of possibilities floated into her mind. Maybe she could wangle a seat on the Civil Rights Commission. Maybe she could persuade him to put a peace initiative on the state ballot. Maybe he would put in a plug for her at the Democratic Convention. Maybe . . .

As for the governor, he had never met a rock star before and was equally impressed. Maybe he could get her to sing at his next fund-raiser. Maybe she would endorse his campaign and solidify the support of the radical Left. Maybe . . .

When she told him about her peace conference he was most enthusiastic. He was sure that a hall could be arranged for at either UCLA or Berkeley, whichever was preferred. He was sure that the Speaker of the State House of Representatives could be persuaded to address the convention. He was not, alas, sure he could address it himself. Primaries were coming up, he had many commitments around the country, several in California, even a couple in Sacramento. He would see what he could do.

And that was where things stood. Barbi and the governor were not dating steadily, he was too busy for that, but they saw each other when they could. She couldn't decide between UCLA and Cal. The very fount of the radical Left movement was in Berkeley to be sure, but she was an L.A. girl, woman that is, and she felt more at home at home.

The workshops were shaping up nicely. She had on the agenda the Relevance of Marxism to Freedom, Handicapped Homosexual Weight Lifters in Christ for Disarmament, Strategizing to Combat the Anti-Communist Hysteria of the Fascist Right, Benevolent Activism in the Area of Militant Dissent, Poster Art as Weaponry, The Politicization of Poverty, and Media Techniques to Promote Civil Disobedience and Insurrection. Shaping up nicely.

Barbi found herself musing on the triumphs that might lie before her. Perhaps, with the governor's clout, she could finagle an appointment as the keynote speaker at the Convention. She certainly knew as well as anyone the crises facing the Democratic Party and where it should be going. The first two planks of Barbi's platform would be to end this obscene war unilaterally and immediately, with unlimited aid for the new Communist government of Vietnam, and to legislate, in the absolute, equal pay and allowances for all women, minorities, and social ecology majors. What kind of government would allow a fat-cat Republican who owns his own business and lives off the sweat of others less fortunate to make more money than a completely selfless Marxist mime who dedicates her life and art, three days a week, to the enlightenment of the valiant pickers in the lettuce fields? Barbi knew what had to be done. It was just a matter of getting hold of that microphone.

And her most consuming secret desire, that nearest to her peace-loving heart, was to dismantle the Pentagon. They would, she had decided, turn it into the largest public marketplace in the world. There, for all the masses to partake of, would be the bountiful produce from the farms of this great nation, the arts and crafts of the gentle people, the products of organized labor. There would be music and poetry and theater. Throngs, multitudes of beautiful, peaceful people would come to this serene and happy place daily to barter and trade, to buy and sell, to sing and dance and rejoice in the brotherhood of man. The Pentagon would be vacant because she would by then have disbanded the military, except for a skeleton crew to disassemble and destroy all the weapons that were stockpiled. Once we had eliminated our nuclear arsenal, the Russians would fall all over themselves getting rid of theirs. What would they need it for? Why incur the expense and danger of maintaining a fleet of hydrogen bombs and missiles when there was nobody left to attack you?

No, peace would reign throughout the world. With the billions saved from the so-called defense budget, they would build federal soup kitchens, mess halls in every city in the country to feed the oppressed, so that no American would ever go hungry again. The vast land holdings of the military would be converted into communal farms and public wilderness areas. All the homeless would be housed in the thousands of barracks and BOQs across the land. Unemployed performers would entertain for the standard wage in all the former enlisted mens and officers clubs on all the bases. All the parts and metal and systems of the airplanes would be converted into fabulous tractors with air-conditioned cockpits, UHF radios, TACAN, and titanium plowshares. The uniforms would clothe the poor until the economy had so burgeoned under the massive infusion of dollars that all were comfortable and could procure the vibrant, colorful clothing of the age of Aquarius. Those dollars would be turned from the very anal, paranoid use of the so-called Defense Department, warmongers really, to joyous, productive support of the *people*. Discrimination would be eliminated, as would violence and hate; there would be no robbery or mugging—you would get everything you needed for free. All the people would learn to live in contentment and harmony and then the police could be disbanded as well, leaving more millions to be transfused into the socialist economy. The huge, blood-sucking corporations would devolve to the workers or else they would be boycotted and put out of business. Classes and groups and jealousy and dissension would disappear and all humans would live together in perfect tranquillity. When the rest of the world saw the success of the experiment, they would be close behind. Barbi knew what she wanted; she need only persevere and prevail. Barbi would get things straightened out.

P.E. had landed a commercial for Top Kick, the pantyhose that "comes all the way up and stays there." So viewers got to see those great long curvy Native American legs, that went all the way up too, from several sexy angles, kicking, skipping, and clattering around. P.E. was a born clotheshorse and she really enjoyed the modeling game. It was so different from work. P.E. had debuted as a waitress at Roseanne's Blue Bell Café in Eulala, Oklahoma, and it wasn't easy. Slinging hash may be the back-drop for all American success stories, but it's not real pleasant when you're actually engaged in it. P.E. remembered wiping those endless countertops and pie cases at Rosie's. The jibe of the occasional less-than-cosmopolitan truck driver was not forgotten. Lining up three chicken-fried steaks on one arm, all the plates hot, and juggling the tray of simultaneously served wilted salads in the other hand, running the gaunt-let of pinches and pats and other personal gestures, just between the two of you, only played out in a crowded coffee shop with everybody aware of the interplay—no, that was not an easy way to make a living. Not at Roseanne's Blue Bell, not anywhere else. And at the end of the shift your heels hurt, even in the spongy, foam rubber–soled shoes, and your tips total up to three dollars and thirty-seven cents and the sweat stains have pushed out around the armpits of your uniform and the ballpoint pen stains splotch the area around the pocket of your apron, all must be laundered, and there is a bad run in your nylons and the dry goods is out of your size, and will the goddamn Ford start and get you back to your trailer house where the air conditioner is on the fritz? No, P.E. appre-ciated this modeling stuff and she was going to stick with Barbi come what may.

As for Mrs. O'Flynn, she was working her job and becoming a genuine, dedicated peace missionary. Barbi had, without knowing it, planted the seed of inductive reasoning, and O'Flynn had begun to ponder the larger picture. She hadn't won anything at bingo in over two weeks and was in exactly the right frame of mind for protesting. Who better to disseminate the hardships and vagaries of war? Mrs. O'Flynn had begun to explore the teleological significance of burning her bra.

P.E. was rubbing some lotion on Barbi's back. Her smooth, firm fingers manipulated the skin and moved Barbi to a state of heightened awareness.

"I'm going to do it, P.E." Barbi was practically purring. "Between the governor and I, we're going to turn this country around."

"I believe it, babe. You have the power and you have the dedication." P.E. was working on the small of her back.

"Can't you envision a world of gentle people with no war or other crimes? Where people have plenty to eat and everyone has a job and can openly and freely practice the philosophy of loving their neighbors? I rilly feel that we are approaching such a society."

Recalling Roseanne's Blue Bell, P.E. wasn't all that sure she wanted a regular grown-up job. Modeling would do fine. And some of those truck drivers and grease monkeys that frequented the Blue Bell one could find a mite tough to just plain *love* unconditionally. Still, Barbi had the right idea and P.E. did not wish to appear the naysayer. Barbi's skin was taut and firm beneath her touch.

"Just think of it, P.E. All our sisters will be free, our black brothers will have broken the chains of oppression once and for all. We will all be equal and live in concordancy and affirmation." P.E. wasn't quite as comfortable with the terms concordancy and affirmation as, say, an old pair of shoes, but it sounded pretty good to her. Things would work out.

"Roll over, babe." P.E. slathered some oil on Barbi's front side and began working it in. Barbi gave herself over to those marvelous fingers, and politics was forgotten for the nonce.

17

Southeast Asia, 1960s

Since Cavendish didn't fly anymore they had to find something for him to do. Serendipity! General Jefferson was much distressed with the orange-clad gang of self-immolating monks that were hanging around. They needed to be organized and regimented. He needed a hard-charging young spit-and-polish officer to take command and work some uniformity into that bunch. Cavendish was his man. He loved to strut and fret and hand out orders. He was put in charge and told to indoctrinate those fucking monks and drill them up to something resembling a military unit. Having had no real mission with the ARVN and getting a shabby welcome there at best, because rations were short, the monks had come to the air base hoping to drum up a little support for the cause in that quarter. The general said any protesting, demonstrating, or creating of martyrs and the like had to be military and by the book if it were to take place on his base, or the participants would be shot for sedition; so the elders decided to go along with this secular tomfoolery, as it seemed the most effective way to advance their concerns.

Cavendish had them coming along nicely. He was a swell training officer; it was all he ever did. He was mesmeric. He could put an entire amphitheater either to sleep or to reading *Stars and Stripes* inside of a minute, which was the primary function and contribution of training officers. He gave them plenty of lectures. Oh, did Cavendish savor his lecturing. He had arranged for an interpreter to be assigned to him full-time. He assembled his monks every morning after prayers and seated them on wooden benches in the movie yard for lectures. The wooden benches were a bit luxurious for the monks, they being used to shorter shrift, and they were somewhat self-conscious, but the lectures made up for it. It is true that Cavendish's lectures may have gained something in translation, but still it was no bed of roses. Any listener to the Cavendish rhetoric was guaranteed to be uncomfortable, notwithstanding the language in which it was delivered, so the self-sacrificial monks endured it happily.

"Gentlemen," Cavendish declaimed, "you will never attain your goals if you go about this martyrdom business in a slipshod manner. Now I won't gainsay the merits of self-immolation. No sir, it can be one damned effective tool for social change, and mighty noble I might add, but only if executed in the correct fashion. Men, you have to be organized and do this thing in an orderly and efficacious manner. No sir. I submit that you can burn yourselves up all day long and accomplish absolutely nothing— zip, zero—unless it's done right. We're talking theater—the dynamic of communication. You may have seen commercials on television that were truly motivational, that really moved you to some desired action. Those are relatively few and far between. And you may have seen others that, well, heh heh, just fell flat on their you know what."

They hadn't.

"Now forgive me, gentlemen, I don't mean to be vulgar, I respect the fact that you are religious men, but I think you take my point. There is a right way and a wrong way to express any message. We will study several successful advertising campaigns to see if we can't nail down the essence, the quiddity of the effective commercial message.

"And gentlemen, I cannot stress too much the importance of doing it properly the first time. Self-immolation is a singular form of expression— there are no rehearsals. You only go around once, as they say. It's no 'three strikes and you're out' in this game, gents. You only get one cut at the old ball, and we're going to ensure that we hit some home runs on first pitches." And so on.

The traffic was getting so fierce around Da Nang that there had recently been two incidents of taxiing airplanes clipping each other's wings. Colonel Creed would not abide this abuse of his vehicles, so he changed the policy. From now on everyone would taxi with his wings folded, which Major Poltroun was dutifully doing. The good major's guts were beginning to rumble in a most uncomfortable and unsettling fashion. He was involved at the moment in an intensive debate with himself as to whether or not he should scrub this mission and run for the twelve-holer. The human, or animal, side of him said, "You are queasy and a little green behind the gills, not to say in increasing internal pain, your sphincter is starting to cycle out of control, you are salivating excessively, and those little nerve centers under the back corners of your tongue are commencing to send warning signals—in short, you do not belong in this airplane."

The military, that is to say the *major* side of him, replied that "The show must go on—when the going gets tough, the tough get going—another *x* on the board, another entry in the log book, another point toward the next Air Medal."

He had already taxied, TPQs were always short hops, what the hell, he could make it. Poltroun decided to press on, and was downright gratified because he admired himself so much for his exemplary dedication to duty. But he was not paying much attention to the airplane, and that is one of those little transgressions that can come back to haunt you.

Some other irregularities that can haunt you are to dress up like the enemy, lest you be mistaken for him; Brass Balls Obradovitch would find out about that one. Also, if you bomb your allies in their Buddhist temple, they may become less friendly and turn their guns on you. That remained to be observed by Colonel Creed as he watched a bunch of his airplanes burn. And then, as Al "Shaky" Morgenkrank would determine, if you got too excited and intent upon Major Shithead Poltroun's airplane and how he was operating it, you might fail to make certain adjustments to your own bird that are requisite to routine flight. There are several others.

At that moment, only three things stood between Major Poltroun and infamy. He must first fail to go through the takeoff checklist. Then he must ignore two indications on the warning-lights panel. Finally he must not look out the window. Also, the disgruntled C. Ross Culpepper must do the same. Culpepper, however, was assigned to fly with Poltroun against his will, because nobody wanted to, and they drew lots in Operations, so he refused to pay any attention to anything. It may be wondered how the major might overlook three such seemingly clear and necessary, not to say routine, steps in his prosecution of the mission, but Poltroun's ineptitude is not to be gainsaid. In addition, there were certain malefic forces in play that would encourage his misfeasance. Not the least of these was his increasing discomfort from that vexatious ptomaine poisoning—collywobbles *in extremis*, as it were. Furthermore, as he moved from the arming area to the runway, they began to hurry him. And he couldn't get Culpepper to talk to him.

Culpepper was doubly sore because not only did he loathe and despise Poltroun and not want to entrust his body to those sometimes questionable hands, but John Wayne was playing in the movie yard. C. Ross Culpepper would vouchsafe no conversation unless directly and forcefully queried. Lieutenant Colonel Al "Shaky" Morgenkrank was just ahead of them, also up on tower frequency, and Major Poltroun was worried about saying something stupid, causing a delay, or doing anything else unprofessional in the presence of his CO, who was probably going to write him a bad fitness report anyway. Poltroun was worried about those things. He was distracted, and as he approached the runway a billowing pain swept through his nether regions.

"Da Nang tower, Condone seventy-six, takeoff one."

"Seven six position and hold, break, Condone seven one you're cleared number one, traffic is a fox-four in takeoff position."

"Seven one, roger." That was Moon Dog returning from his all-time record TPQ of just under seven minutes. He was elated. He knew he had the record and he wanted to land fast, turn off early, and taxi back at thirty knots to put it out of reach. He also wanted to get to the club to celebrate this feat.

Colonel Creed was elated too. As he watched Moon's thousand-pounders blistering the Buddhist temple, the bright orange flashes casting eerie shadows through the roofless old compound, walls tumbling down (building blocks for the OM club, as he saw it), he set down his night-vision glasses and rubbed his hands together in solipsistic glee. His elation would soon ebb, however, when the ARVN put their retaliatory plan into operation.

And the ARVN were definitely not elated. They had just absorbed six tons of general-purpose bombs in their camp, courtesy of their American brothers and protectors, and they were madder than a wet hen. Considerably madder. Madder, in point of fact, than the combined population of the Egg City chicken ranch in Moorpark, California, after the passage of a classic fast-moving cold front and its attendant squall line. The first thing those of them still hale and hearty did was start pointing their mortars at the American flight line.

The VNAF, of course, were highly elated. They didn't operate at night, so they were lined up on top of the revetments watching the Marines pound their hated brothers.

Other than Moon Dog, with his new record, the squadron pilots were not yet elated about anything, most of them being in sick bay with food poisoning. Every bed was taken, and nearly all the floor space. Corpsmen were stepping over bodies to minister to more bodies. They were all moaning and writhing and expelling the toxic red death by way of nature's intricate system of emergency procedures. And the corpsmen couldn't do much for them. They could administer emetics, but this bunch was not in particular need of those; they hadn't enough pumps or hands to pump all the stomachs, but then that was not required overmuch either. These boys were figuring it out for themselves. Had Major Poltroun elected, as the better part of valor, to go to sick bay, he would have found that he couldn't get in. DeVille Hoggins had accomplished, single-handed, what the entire NVA and Popular Front, or whatever the Cong were calling themselves these days, could not: He had effectively demobilized MAG-22, taking the air-harassment monkey off the local soldiers' back for a day or two and giving them respite until the boys got well. Had he conceived of this development, he would have been proud.

Poor Major Poltroun. He was harried, rushed, distracted, in the beginning of a major short-term illness, and way behind the mental power curve in the Mach 2 lane.

"Condone seven six, cleared for takeoff. Can you expedite, sir? I have an F-four off the one-eighty."

"Seventy-six, roger expedite." Major Poltroun should never have been asked to expedite anything. It wasn't in his nature. As he pulled onto the runway, Al "Shaky" Morgenkrank's burners lit and the two tongues of flame moved off down the runway. Poltroun had adopted an unfortunate mind-set. He was not a well man. He did not like to fly at night anyway. Now the tower was pressuring him to hurry up and the skipper was listening. All his self-serving career-enhancement instincts said "Go! Let's get this machine airborne and get this thing over with and no fuss." As he was a career officer, he allowed those instincts to outweigh the less excited civilian ones that called for a calm, rational assessment of things in the interest of self-preservation. He ran up the engines quickly, skimming the instruments, and glanced at the takeoff checklist. CON-TROLS, check . . .

"Condone seven six, Da Nang tower. Request you expedite. Traffic is turning final, over."

Moon Dog was furious. If this hand-job didn't get the fuck off the runway they would wave him off, and a go-around might cost him the TPQ record.

"Seventy-six on the roll." Poltroun released the brakes and rolled into history. He was still reading the checklist, but like a robot. The airplane had started to move and his mind was beyond the cockpit, somewhere out in the darkness. WINGS, check. TRIM, check. FLAPS, check. HOOK, HARNESS . . . He went through these items in a trice, but he was not really paying attention. Another pain was spreading through his bowels. The runway markers were sliding by and he was gaining speed. He looked straight ahead, in a trancelike state, where he could still see the skipper's burners. He had not actually checked any of the items he mentally rattled off. A little null circuit in his brain said "check" each time, but the thought processes were elsewhere.

WARNING LTS . . . There were in fact two lights illuminated on the panel. One said L WING PIN UNLOCKED. The other said R WING PIN UNLOCKED. But those lights had been on the whole time he was taxiing. He was used to them. They had become a friendly part of the panoply of tiny lights around him that were supposed to be on. Also, Poltroun was not accustomed to taxiing with his wings folded. Normally the wings were spread and locked in the chocks and visually checked by the plane captain. You didn't have to worry about them at the end of the runway. And still he stared straight ahead.

Through whatever combination of intestinal grief, extraordinary procedures, post–field-grade-lobotomy ineptitude, haste making waste, and so forth, Poltroun was rolling down the runway with his wings tucked up in the folded position. Grampaw Pettibone would have loved it. It was just the sort of blockheaded failure to go by the book and to anticipate the dangers inherent in driving airplanes that inspired Pettibone's most incisive journalistic sorties. When Moon Dog, who was on final approach, saw the red and green lights on the wingtips, way too close together, of the aircraft that was in its takeoff roll, he thought something was very wrong. He was right.

So Poltroun, head up and locked, wings folded for storage, rolled. And did he roll! He rolled and rolled and fucking rolled. C. Ross Culpepper was pouting and intentionally not paying attention, or he would probably have punched out around the eight thousand foot marker. Poltroun was sorely perplexed. They had flying speed, but they were not flying. There was not enough runway left to abort. What the deuce was going on? Well, he had a heavy bomb load. So what? They always had a heavy bomb load. Well, everybody knew there was less lift in the air at night. Poltroun hardly ever flew at night and maybe it just required a little longer takeoff roll. Not *this* long! He was running out of runway, airspeed was a hundred and eighty knots, he had the stick back in his lap, and he was still hitting bumps. Something was grievously wrong and Poltroun idly wondered if his life were going to start flashing before his eyes. As he was mentally corroborating his impression that it was just about time to instruct Culpepper to step over the side, through some incredible quirk of physics, some dark forces that defied the laws of aerodynamic design, the Phantom became airborne. Not entirely controllable, mind you, not smooth and straight and level—ballistic actually—but airborne nonetheless. At first,

Poltroun—wiping out the cockpit with the stick, slapping it from stop to stop, furiously kicking rudder pedals, bellyache forgotten—could only say "OH . . . MY . . . GOD." The airplane was going its own way, hurtling happily through the night in heavy buffet, with shudders, wing drops, and a pronounced Dutch roll. He got the gear up, selected full flaps, and hit the fuel dump switch.

"Da Nang tower, Condone seventy-six—I've got an emergency—control problems—requesting downwind—repeat SEVERE control problems." It all came out in a rush, without a pause or a breath—and then Poltroun went to aspirating like a Chicago Pneumatic 105 air compressor trying to inflate the Hindenburg. He was hyperventilating, gulping, swallowing, and his great heart was pitter-pattering in the manner of an impact wrench on a frozen nut.

"Condone seven six, Da Nang tower. Cleared downwind number one. Understand you have control problems. Crash and rescue is being alerted."

"Roger. Seventy-six is requesting a wide downwind with a modified straight-in, over."

"Roger, seven six. Cleared for straight-in approach. I'll keep the pattern clear."

When Moon Dog, who had just rolled out after landing, heard Poltroun's bleating about control problems, he suddenly understood what he had just seen. He keyed the mike. "Check your wing-fold, seventy-six."

"What you talking about, Doggie?" Hang Dog, too, had recognized the XO's terrified squeal, but didn't know what was going on.

"I reckon your buddy Poltroun is flailing around up there with a half a set of wings, Doggie." Hang Dog convulsed in gleeful laughter.

As soon as Al "Shaky" Morgenkrank heard his executive officer's lament, he pulled the power back and headed for the field. It was his goddamn airplane that Poltroun was about to wreck and, by God, he was going to be there to see what transpired. If this was a Poltroun fuck-up, the skipper would have his ass in a New York minute. Morgenkrank entered the landing pattern, dropped the flaps, and began motoring around listening to Poltroun's misfortunes and offering his own two cents' worth. He wanted to join on the unfortunate major and, by force of will, bring that fucking aircraft home intact.

So Poltroun and Culpepper went hurtling through the ebon sky, night air short on lift, an unguided missile essentially, to their destiny. "What the fuck's wrong with this fuckin' fucker?" asked Culpepper suavely. He was by now keenly interested in the conduct of the flight.

"I don't fucking *know* what's wrong with this fuckin' fucker," blathered Poltroun, who tried generally not to use profanity; but then to paraphrase Mr. Twain, profanity, in some situations, has a power denied even to prayer.

When Colonel Creed altered the group policy to require that everyone taxi with his wings folded, it was not envisioned that this operating concept would be carried over into the flight regime. In fact it was not generally held by the hoboes that the airplane *would* fly with the wings folded, so that was not an eventuality that was considered at any length. Ah, but Grampaw Pettibone could have told them, Murphy, indeed, could have told them (if not Barbi Belheur and P. E. Proudbird), that if the aircraft were designed so that the wings *could* be folded, then eventually someone would attempt to fly it that way. If those sages could not have singled out Poltroun, he at least would have been in the running to be the one who demonstrated it. At the moment he was so preoccupied, struggling to get the shuddering, wallowing, bucking machine under some kind of control, that it didn't even occur to him to jettison his bomb load— he was fighting for his life and career. But as more and more fuel was dumped it became somewhat more manageable and he began to have a glimmer of hope.

As Poltroun and Culpepper sped through the thin, black, night air, battling the beast, Brass Balls Obradovitch was preparing to lead his hand-painted, black-pajamaed irregulars out to set up an ambush on a trail that the Cong were thought to frequent. While he and his men were saddling up, the VNAF night crew was methodically loading rockets and ammunition into the Spads for the first launch. The sick bay was over-flowing with otherwise healthy young jarheads who were so polluted with nature's poisons that they either thought they were dying or wished they would, compliments of the Lance Corporal Hoggins refrigeration unit. The Buddhist temple was still aflame here and there, and in the flickering shadows the ARVN gunners could be seen realigning their mortar batteries. The field was closed for Poltroun's emergency, and returning airplanes were starting to stack up, wanting to land. Cavendish had his monks bivouacked downwind of the hobo camp where they would be available for special assignment on a few minutes notice.

The Vietcong and the NVA were, frankly, a bit puzzled. The war was going on spectacularly, with explosions all over the place, flashes, con-cussions, the rattling of machine guns, airplanes zooming around, but they didn't know precisely who was doing what to whom. Because they weren't doing it to *them*. With all the battling in progress, none of their units was in contact. They were all sitting around wondering who was getting their ass kicked and who was doing the kicking. A lot of people were beginning to wonder about that. It was becoming more and more difficult to establish just who the enemy was.

To Barbi Belheur, the enemy was us. To us, it had been the Cong and the NVA, but as the mortar rounds from the Buddhist temple walked up to the flight line, it became unavoidably apparent that it was now the ARVN. To them it had been the Cong and the NVA, then it became the VNAF, and now it was obviously the Americans, who were bombing the shit out of their temporary headquarters. To the VNAF it had been the Cong and the NVA, then it was the ARVN, and it was soon to become the Americans, after they mistakenly strafed Obradovitch's patrol and the Americans started firing sidewinders and 20 mike-mike at their Spads. To the Obradovitch irregulars it had been the Cong and NVA, then it became themselves because they had *set out* to become the enemy, so as to beat him at his own game. It was shortly to be the VNAF, who would mistake them indeed for Cong and start delivering rockets and bullets. Then it would be the Marine pilots, who would also mistake them for Cong and deliver more of the same. Then, of course, the air wing would abruptly switch back to being friendlies when they found out what the VNAF had done and began shooting their planes down. To DeVille Hoggins it was the Marine Corps, pure and simple. Mrs. O'Flynn would have agreed vehemently on that. To the conservatives it was the liberals and vice versa. To the Buddhists it was the Christians and vice versa. To Goldfinger, the OB/GYN flight surgeon, it was red death. To the Sky Pilot it was the devil. And so on.

The only people who didn't seem to have any active enemies at the moment were the Cong and the NVA, but they were considering some intramural squabbling just to keep a fine edge on their animosities.

C. Ross Culpepper despised everyone as a rule, but if he had a true enemy at the moment, it was the imbecile Poltroun, for his inconceivably blunderheaded idiocy in thus exposing Culpepper's life and limb to imminent termination. Culpepper, for one, did not aim to get killed on his last hop in Vietnam, or any other one, especially the despicable TPQ. But it appeared that the preeminent field-grade plumber of Naval Aviation was doing his best to see that indeed happen. In truth, Poltroun was, almost imperceptibly, beginning to win the battle. Sort of. He had kept his airspeed up, dumped his wing tanks and established token, if precarious, control of the lurching, swaying, galloping steed on which they rode.

"Seventy-six, this is Condone seventy-five. Say your airspeed." It was Morgenkrank, following Poltroun around the pattern, giving advice. While he thought he was being helpful, this only served to unsettle the major.

"Two-twenty."

"Roger. How's your control situation?"

"Better. I can make gentle turns without excessive buffet."

"Okay, when you get set up on final, hold two hundred knots till you have the field made. You can take the arresting gear at the far end if you need to." As things evolved, he would not need to.

"Roger." This business of the skipper meddling and nagging at him further addled Poltroun. That condition would, at least in some measure, incline Poltroun toward the neglect of one more fairly weighty procedure. He was frustrated, he was scared, panicked really, and very self-conscious. Al "Shaky" Morgenkrank's patronizing advice, for all the world to hear, only upset him the more. Oddly enough, Al "Shaky" Morgenkrank's overzealous attention to Poltroun's situation would also, in some measure, support his own failure to perform a routine task. They thundered on through the night.

Barbi Belheur would have had a grudging admiration for Major Poltroun. He was really on her side. She had hired a bitter, unsteadily employed veteran, a former Army aviation mechanic and door gunner who had returned from the Nam a junky and found that the price structure for white powder was some different back in the world. His name was O'Malley and he needed the shit, man. He had bad memories and nightmares and flashbacks and he had to be drunk or stoned or both—well wasted—before he could sleep. You can't do that every night and arrive at work (if you can find any) each morning trustworthy, loyal, helpful, friendly, courteous, kind, obedient, cheerful, thrifty, brave, clean, reverent, and on time. Not to touch on physically strong, mentally awake, and morally straight. A week's unemployment check would get him about one day's smack ration, and, as Willie Nelson was later to intone, "one night of love don't make up for six nights alone."

So O'Malley's life was not an abundance of joy. To pick up some needed change he had signed on with Barbi to give a workshop on the sabotage of friendly weapons of war. He would touch upon foreign object damage, disabling electrical systems, and the uses of plastic explosives and armor-piercing projectiles, among other things. Scrawny and petulant, he appeared to be composed mostly of hair and tattoos, although it would later be revealed that he had an abnormally large dick. Mustafa, the Panther enforcer, greeted him.

"Say, bro. Where the fuck you *been*, mothahfuckah? Look like you had to done some seerious crawlin' to crawl out from under whatever it was you was beneath, man, is what."

O'Malley was one of those unfortunate children of war who likely would not have amounted to much in excess of the "hill of beans" so favored in folklore, but now he had something to blame his wretched condition on, and a growing anathema at that. It was fast becoming chic and sagacious to lambast and vilify that immoral fucking war. It was seen in many and increasing quarters as the root cause of every problem of society. It was said to bring unemployment, recession, inflation, stagnation, imbalance of trade, genocide, apostasy, antinomianism, nihilism, bankruptcy (both moral and fiscal), epidemic psychodamage, Detroit lemons, falling grain prices, generic trade goods, and the dissolution of the nuclear family unit, just to name a few. While it should by no means be inferred that former Corporal O'Malley was other than ill-used and ill-affected by the Vietnam flap, as was the rest of society, both here and there—still it may be arguable that had he not elected to assuage the horror of his particular war with ever-increasing doses of alcohol, had he not stuck needles into his arms and smoked everything that would burn, had he shaved his face, cut his hair, washed his clothes, and himself, and arrived on time talking civil language—it seems within the realm of possibility that personnel recruiters, foremen, supervisors, policemen, judges, elderly ladies, merchants, and society in general would have held him in less disfavor, not to say contempt.

But O'Malley was a bitter man, and not much concerned with how he fit into society or what those fucking civilian swine thought of him. They owed him, man. And he discovered that there were millions more just like him—disaffected, unemployed, aimless, of wounded psyche, and most of all, bitter. Naturally, they banded together. It has been said that misery loves company. And the general populace did not want to talk about it. Period. They did not want to be reminded of this national embarrassment. The man in the street was only just able to cover up, avoid acknowledging, the guilt and shame and anguish and hurt that he surely shared in this categorical atrocity, so that he could comfortably get on with the business of bettering himself in this world and assuring his ascension to them golden streets in the sky. The last thing he needed was a shaggy, bearded veteran with no legs, a specter in old army fatigues (or, in later years, a good facsimile sold in surplus and sporting goods stores) to point out in terms unrefined, but not uncertain, that, indeed, no man is an island. No, they didn't want to hear about it, pure and simple. Society wanted it all to go away, much as the combat troops had when they were surrounded by mines and booby traps and concertina and ambushes and sappers and leeches and malaria and jungle rot and friendly fire and so forth. It is even possible that, had narcotics been available at the corner pharmacy, over the counter, at a frugal price, as they had been at the turn of the century, and had there been no moral proscription of their use, as had not been discovered until around 1920—it is entirely possible that the Presbyterians would have started using them to make the veterans go away just as the troops had used them to make the war go away.

No one wanted to recognize the existence of their predicament, nay, even the existence of *themselves* as such, so the veterans banded together. They formed clubs and councils and therapy groups and began to demonstrate, and held endless rap sessions. It remained only for Barbi Belheur and her cadre of SLUR radicals to embrace the vets as abject victims of the new holocaust brought on by a fascist administration (elected), to encourage and succor them, to shape and rally the counterculture, and recruit millions of adolescents and pseudointellectuals to the cause. Lance Major Slocum called them the Brainy Chickenshit Brigade. Moon Dog sometimes wondered why Kennedy was still their hero, since he had started the whole thing. The antiwar movement would loom so ominous as to preclude the average old-line Democrat, Republican, or appliance salesman from even conceiving of the threat it would pose to "society."

Major Poltroun and C. Ross Culpepper were most painfully aware of the threat that an F-4B, in flight, with its wings folded, posed to their little society. They alternated between perplexity, prayer, and profanity, their smallish brains riffling through banks of memory circuits in global search of something comforting to hang on to. The airplane shook and shuddered and swayed. It rattled and bounced and veered. And the *noises* it made. There is a category of sound called night noises. It covers the entire aural spectrum from squeaks and grinds to hums and clanks to scrapes and whines. Airplanes magically produce these sounds on dark nights when you are far from home and a warm and cheery, well-lighted place like the club, especially when you've had a radio failure or your TACAN needle is idly rotating, with no distance indication. Poltroun's and Culpepper's airplane was a sure enough cacophony, grating and rasping, screeching, thumping, lurching through the night. They were sore afraid. So terrified was Poltroun that he was just not rational. Procedures had gone out the window. Routines were forgotten. The one thing in his mind was to somehow, against great odds, get this thing on the runway.

"Da Nang tower, Condone seventy-six on a two-mile final."

"Roger, seven six, cleared to land number one. Crash and rescue are standing by." That was comforting.

And Poltroun did get it on the runway. Fighting it all the way, running on adrenaline and egotism, scrapping, tugging, jerking, and wrestling, he dragged that outlaw right down to the concrete. And made a reasonably good landing, all things considered, with one major exception. When Poltroun had become airborne, he had, as is usually done, raised the landing gear. It was still up. If it was thought that the airplane was protesting in wings-folded flight, it really threw a fit when it was slapped on the deck *sans* rolling stock. With a great shrieking, rending and rasping, in a shower of sparks, fifty thousand pounds of airplane, fuel, and armaments went skidding down the concrete on its fuel tanks and bomb racks, at two hundred miles an hour, yawing crazily, bombs and rockets coming loose, bouncing, rolling, flying like tenpins, crash trucks racing back from midway down the runway, Poltroun and Culpepper just along for the ride, the tower operators stuttering and stammering. It was bedlam. It was out of control. Everybody was just mainly waiting for the explosion that must come. Including Al "Shaky" Morgenkrank who was certain that when the explosion came he would lose a three-million-dollar aircraft. That saddened him greatly. He took only minor comfort in the sure knowledge that when said explosion came he would also lose the boob, the incompetent buffoon, who had caused the whole mess. So all the troops at the air field were just kind of standing around with their hands over their ears, waiting for the big boom.

Only it didn't come. God knows Poltroun and Culpepper were expecting it. Poltroun was making his peace with the Lord and Culpepper was beseeching Him. They were all set to ride a fireball to glory. And everybody else was waiting in prurient, shameful, vicarious anticipation for the big flash. But it wouldn't come. It was teasing everyone, this conflagration. Al "Shaky" Morgenkrank was reduced to secretly, unconsciously maybe, wishing it would go ahead and blow. God knew he didn't want to lose his airplane, but goddamnit, this dynamic was in play, he was an observer, it had to happen, fate was tempting him, so let's *"Get on with it,"* his subconscious was saying. Let's get what must be done done.

The airplane skidded off the runway, the sparks stopped, most of the ordnance was gone, and almost gently, as it plowed the soft dirt, it slowed and came to a shuddering stop, both engines still running, swallowing foreign object damage by the fistful, true, but running, lights blinking merrily, Poltroun and Culpepper miraculously delivered, alive to fight another day. It came to rest in a cloud of soft, shimmering dust, lights ablink, systems humming, wings folded, restored to terra firma, human cargo intact except for combat-damaged flight suits and lesser garments. Poltroun shut her down and climbed out amidst a light show of converging fire trucks and ambulances, overflowing with gratitude, in a state of profound benediction, ready to fall to his knees in thanks to all deities for sparing his life and breath, but sorely perplexed about how he was going to explain this fuck-up, careerwise. C. Ross Culpepper emerged from the chaos shaken, scared shitless more like, aquiver with the adrenaline that his glands had been dumping on the system in recent minutes, and most egregiously perturbed. And without a word, with only a discernible grunt, knocked Major Poltroun flat on his ass. Threw a haymaker, a roundhouse, a looping Sunday punch, and cold-cocked the son of a bitch. Knocked him plumb galley-west. Would have stomped him flat, but the crash crew pulled him off. C. Ross Culpepper did not take it lightly when people endangered him and, major, executive officer be damned, he would make his displeasure known. Major Poltroun would write him up for forty-three counts of various sedition, mutiny, insubordination, assault, conduct unbecoming, and so forth, but few of them would stick.

Al "Shaky" Morgenkrank was another one who would make his displeasure known. He was furious, he was discolored with rage that the asshole of his professional life had not been toasted in a flaming fireball. Oh, he was thankful enough that his aircraft had been spared, but that was scarce compensation for the fact that Poltroun had not been incinerated. Well, he was going to see the comeuppance of that shit-for-brains major, and that right away. As Morgenkrank called for landing, with gear and flaps down, he lied. He was in such a state of fury, so intent on retribution, that Goldfinger, the OB/GYN flight surgeon, would later report that Lieutenant Colonel Morgenkrank may possibly have temporarily lost some of his faculties. The skipper had not eaten any red death, so there was no exoneration there. At any rate, he was sufficiently concerned with the Poltroun issue, and he didn't even know that the poor major lay at that moment stunned, semiconscious, due to a C. Ross Culpepper sucker-punch, but had he known he would personally have recommended Culpepper for a decoration, but he didn't, and he was so intent on disciplining the culprit that there was nothing else in his mind. Procedures had gone out the window. Routines were forgotten. Grampaw Pettibone would have savored the moment.

To join on Poltroun, so as to aid in his time of need, the skipper had dropped his flaps and slowed to landing-pattern speed. To retain maneuvering flexibility, to move around and look him over, he left the gear up. As he flew around the pattern again, after observing his XO's folly, dumping fuel to get to landing weight, he was so filled with anger and the sense of betrayal, so determined to "straighten" Poltroun out, so single-minded and obsessive, that it became one of those little transgressions that can come back to haunt you. As he turned final, so wroth was Morgenkrank that he forgot to lower *his* landing gear.

So Al "Shaky" Morgenkrank, commanding officer of a fighter squadron, pranged *his* bird onto the numbers, almost in Poltroun's skid marks, and slid off the other side of the runway. There was scraping and rending and showering of sparks, then Morgenkrank, too, plowed into the dirt. As the realization swept over him, he was so sick with anger and impotence that he might as well have had red death for chow. He couldn't have felt much worse. It was bad enough for a CO to make a gear-up landing, but to do this in the midst of his holy crusade to flay the dunderhead Poltroun, to strip the flesh from his bones for being so colossally dumb as to do the same thing, was too cruel to be believed. He had stolen his own thunder. As he slid, powerless, through the dirt, he realized that he had completely nullified his own rage, derailed his own rampage. What could he say to Poltroun about landing with the wheels up, except to compare techniques?

So Al "Shaky" Morgenkrank was demoralized to the point of being ill. The only significant difference between his slide through the rich loam at the side of the runway and that of his XO was that one of Morgenkrank's triple-ejection bomb racks, acting as a sure-enough plowshare, was making a furrow deep and true. Right through all the subterranean wires and cables that powered the entire runway lighting system. With fire trucks, follow-me trucks, staff cars, tractors, and ambulances roaring to and fro, with troops running helter-skelter to disarm the bombs and rockets that were scattered everywhere, with angry pilots who were running out of fuel demanding to land, not only was the field in chaos, now it was also in the dark.

This was a semi-serious situation, so General Jefferson was summoned to command. Poltroun's and Morgenkrank's airplanes had cleared the runway nicely, but now there was no light. The Air Force pilots and

Marine pilots and Navy pilots who couldn't make it back to the ship could not see to land. "Light the flare pots," went out the command.

"Someone has drained the fuel out of them," came the reply. "They won't light." Although the subsequent investigation would never identify the culprit, Pettibone knew that it was Lance Corporal DeVille Hoggins who had drained the flare pots. He did it on the orders of Captain Cavendish, who needed the kerosene for emergency fuel supplies for his monks. He felt that his unit should be in a high state of readiness— prepared for any eventuality. It was a good judgment.

Something had to be done, and quick. Then General Jefferson had perhaps the most expeditious and innovative brainstorm of his lengthy and illustrious career. He knew a way to light his runways. "Get me Cavendish," he screamed at his aide. When that was done, he bellowed into the field telephone handset.

"Cavendish, get those fucking missionaries over here on the double."

"Sir?" Cavendish was not sure what the general was demanding.

"Those gooks that burn themselves up. Get their ass down to the end of the runway ASAP."

18

California, 1980s

Not unlike former Corporal, now saboteur, O'Malley's existence, life at Vulcan V-belt and Avionic Pilotage System Corporation was less than an abundance of joy for Rawlins. In the Marine Corps the watchword had been, regardless of the difficulty of the task, insurmountability even, We Can Do It. At VVAPS the drill was, notwithstanding the simplicity of the request, to have at least three convincing if obscure explanations why it simply couldn't be done. People made entire careers, and exemplary ones at that, out of rationalizing why the publications department could not give the customer, usually an engineering manager, what he wanted. To be completely fair, however, it should be noted that most of the engineers demanded the impossible most of the time. The typical engineer would come to Rawlins or one of the other editors with two hundred pages of incoherent ravings, a hand-scribbled lucubration that would make any doctor's prescription look like calligraphy, interspersed with the author's sketches, without a hint of scale, magnitude, relative size, etc.—a week after the mutually agreed upon deadline—and want it back in the morning. Formatted, typed, spelling corrected, art built, laid out, and photocopied. "And gimme six copies, will ya?" They seemed to think it all got done by elves, overnight, while deserving engineers were home in their beds.

At first Rawlins tried to comply. He stayed late, begged the production shops to give his jobs priority, to finish for him overnight, wheedled others into helping him, ran himself ragged, and still failed. Very soon he came to understand the GREAT TRUTH of aerospace, and began stockpiling excuses why it absolutely could not be done. And the engineers, used to the system, usually accepted those pretexts, having expected them anyway. He found that one of the slickest and easiest ways to buy some time was just to say, "Well, it might be possible. Of course we'd be talking overtime." When the boys heard that word "overtime" they recoiled as if stung. Every program, project, or proposal manager, invariably, has already run over his budget long before his masterpiece is ready to print. He is already going to have to beg for more money, and Rawlins found that if he so much as mentioned overtime, they got real easy to deal with, deadline-wise. Harley Cadavery, his cubiclemate, who had been in the business a long, long time, had a standard reply for the engineer, eyes a little too bright, flushed, exhibiting a sort of *spes phthisica*, glowing, having finally finished his project, late to be sure, but finished nonetheless, or so he thought, even though it was usually already in the throes of death, still he felt he had finished, and he was euphoric. When one of those fellows would come to Harley Cadavery's desk and ask for the impossible he would fool with his pipe for what seemed like a full minute. Then he would snug his rimless glasses up a little higher on his nose, and fix the overeager customer with a baleful stare. "Sure," he would say. "We can do anything you want. All it takes is time and money."

The engineer cares not a whit for grammar, syntax, organization, order, continuity, or whether it makes any sense to anybody else. He is bound by two ironclad and inviolable principles. The first is that only *he* fully understands the subject matter, however simple or simplistic any given paragraph may be. Though he scrawls unintelligibly on a yellow pad, the words may be considered as chiseled in stone, and for that reason, should a presumptuous mortal, schooled only in the English language and the written communication of ideas, insert or delete a comma, change a word, or break a twelve-line sentence down into two or three, he is "changing the meaning." This cannot be tolerated. The second is that the engineer must, above all things, sound smart. Never mind that no one understands the piece; so long as he feels he has imparted the notion that he is smarter than the reader, then everything is swell. In a case where three words might all fit reasonably into a place in a sentence, Rawlins found that the engineer would almost invariably choose the longest one, or, failing that, the least satisfactory of the three. If there were another word that did *not* quite fit, but was longer, less well known, or more obscure, he would seize upon that one. The obscure, the arcane translated to smart. That led Harley to remark, "When you walk into an aerospace office, you can instantly tell which desk is the engineer's and which the secretary's. On the engineer's desk will be a thesaurus, so he can choose the wrong word. On the secretary's desk will be a dictionary, so she can spell it right."

Rawlins's particular nemesis was a certain Doctor Lieutenant Colonel McKinley Mortadella. Mort, he insisted upon being called. He was a double-dipper, retired from the Air Force. VVAPS hired every officer who retired from any service if the other companies didn't get him first. The ex-military pogues were not engineers. They were not anything very identifiable. Some had majored in history, some business, some political science, some engineering, even. Some had not gone to college at all. But for the last twenty or thirty years, none of them had practiced any sort of trade except being pilots and then military staff officers, a mutant discipline that requires little or no cerebral participation. The dumbest of them eventually found their way into an incondite and confounding pseudo-science known as ILS. This stood for "integrated logistics support." These boys were not, for the most part, even pilots. They had been supply officers and maintenance people, many of them former warrant officers and enlisted men. To protect their territory and lend a sense of legitimacy to their scam, which was, put simply, merely a schedule of how many gallons of gas and quarts of oil and numbers of armaments and spare parts must be delivered to each airplane, and how many people were required to install the stuff; to obfuscate this task and render it arcane and unintelligible to the average Joe with his average I.Q., they made up their own language.

Everything was acronyms and abbreviations. They discoursed about MOBs and FOBs (main operating bases and forward operating bases), they talked of FEBAs (forward edge of battle area), FLOTs (forward line of troops), POL (petroleum, oil, and lubricants), and C³I (C cubed I = command, control, communication, and identification). They had mean flight time between failures (MFTBF), mean man-hours to repair (MMHTR), maintenance man-hours per flight hour (MMHFH), maintenance actions per flight hour (MAFH), and an endless bunch of other "means." And then there were the "ilities." They rambled on at great lengths about reliability, maintainability, survivability, repairability, sustainability, vulnerability, replaceability, producibility, supportability, and surgeability. They had depot maintenance, organizational maintenance, and field maintenance. They sketched out great realms of graphs and charts to measure and display all these things. And not one in the bunch could write a simple declarative sentence. They were fun to play editor with. It is possible that Theodore Bernstein had the ILS boys in mind when he created his acronym "APPALLING." It stood for: "acronym production, particularly at lavish level, is no good."

As for Doctor Lieutenant Colonel McKinley Mortadella, Mort had at one time been a pilot. Back in the F-86 days, it seemed. Despite the plethora of plaques, certificates, citations, models, and photos with famous generals and such in his office, there was no evidence that he had ever flown a modern, supersonic airplane, and even less indication that he knew anything about them, their characteristics, their performance, or their tactics. It seemed likely to Rawlins that he had been given an endless succession of staff jobs, probably to conserve operational airplanes, and that his florid manner and debonair demeanor had served him well. Mort, in truth, thought of himself as, well, maybe not dashing, but certainly a colorful and impressive figure. He was in fact a fop, in at least one sense of that word. True, he always had some sort of generic handkerchief in his jacket pocket, but God only knew what color or pattern it would be. Usually, this seemed to be governed by calculated disharmony with the gaudy tie he would have on. And the blue blazer was always buttoned, although it had not originally been cut to serve the paunch that it now embraced. Oh, the tight, wavy gray hair was becoming, but it was a little too long. The trousers were always an unoffending gray; maybe there was only one pair, because the seat was always worn slick, Rawlins didn't know. But the shoes were the downfall of the man. Every day of his life he wore plain, black, plastic oxfords, which Rawlins had known by the brand-name Corfam. They were shoes composed of some man-made, patent-leather substance that never had to be shined. It looked as if it had an eternal light coat of oil, and sparkled and shone all over the place without ever having tasted Kiwi. Only when the heels are worn off on a cant and there is several days' dust congregated around the soles and welts, these shoes are reminiscent of a Mexican policeman. The Marines are very big on shining their own shoes, and Rawlins had not entirely lost that proclivity. All in all, Mort seemed not to have received his fair slice of the right stuff. He reminded Rawlins of an aging Candyass Cavendish.

But mainly, above and beyond all other demands of decorum, Doctor Lieutenant Colonel McKinley Mortadella, who had received a Ph.D. in it wasn't clear exactly what, but some sort of cross-discipline having to do with engineering management, geographics, demographics, psychographics, sociographics, and military ecology, from Gaston College in connection with the Armed Forces Postgraduate Institute, considered himself to be a sure-enough world-class linguist. To the extent that he often made up his own words. If he couldn't find one that was nebulous and recondite enough, he would just make one up. The first one Rawlins came across was "obtusivity."

"For years," Mortadella wrote, "the less saliential pretenders to aerospace design, in total obtusivity of the apposite functions of supersonic flight . . ." Rawlins flipped an imaginary coin and, in that state of mental weariness or apathy fostered by knowing that you will have to argue every point with an angry adversary, but still goaded by the notion of doing right, he decided not to challenge "saliential." "Obtusivity," though, was a little much. He looked in his *Webster's Collegiate*. No such word. He looked in the unabridged third edition. Nothing. He even double-checked the *Oxford English Dictionary*. It seemed the authorities just would not recognize "obtusivity." Rawlins changed "in total obtusivity of" to "ignoring."

When Mort saw what had been done on his return copy, he yelped like one of Hemingway's gut-shot hyenas, surely the closest connection between Mortadella and Hemingway that could ever be made, and charged off toward Rawlins's cubicle at high port.

"You've changed the total complexion of this sentence," he hissed, flushed.

"No, I didn't. I made it mean what seems, if not obvious, at least likely that you intended it to. 'Obtusivity' is not a word."

Mort drew himself up to full stature like an airplane with the nose strut extended for takeoff, and his cheeks reddened. "On what authority, sir, do you consider yourself qualified to pronounce judgment on what is a word and what is not?"

The implication here was how dare you presume to question my superlative vocabulary, you insignificant, servile publications menial.

"It's not in the dictionary." Rawlins gave him a big smile.

Mort's usually puffy, protruding eyeballs narrowed somewhat. "Just because it doesn't happen to be in your piddling desktop dictionary doesn't mean it's not legitimate."

"It's not in any of our recognized reference books. I checked them." Again the sunny smile.

"That doesn't prove a thing." Mort was getting frustrated and angrier.

"Oh, that's a constraint we observe pretty regularly in this business. As a kind of general rule of thumb we tend to think that if a word doesn't appear in the dictionary, its authenticity *might* be questionable. We generally try to substitute one that *is* in the book. That way it's a little easier for your reader to look it up if, God forbid, he gets confused by the piece. It's just a conceit we have." Rawlins was sanguine.

Mort was becoming furious. "Don't patronize *me*, mister. I happen to have a rather large and versatile vocabulary and I have been known to utilize it to advantage. Once I was briefing the commander of the Tactical Air Command. The general had been an English major and he thought he was quite a wordsmith. Well, he questioned me on a couple of points and quibbled with my word effectuation, trying to assert his superiority over me. I fixed him. I simply shifted my elocutionary powers to a higher gear and pulled away from him. And the general didn't even *know* I had shifted gears. I used words that general had never even heard before. When the briefing was over, he just sat there numb. Totally confused. That's the kind of thing I can do."

Rawlins did not point out that the purpose of the briefing had likely not been to baffle and bewilder the general. "Yes," he said. "I reckon it's pretty easy to confuse people when you make up your own words."

Mort was turning purplish. His parting shot, as he blustered out of the cubicle in a major huff, was: "Just put that sentence back the way it was. And don't change any of my words unless you check with me first!"

Mortadella was paid sixty or seventy thousand dollars a year for his expertise, Rawlins something over thirty-five. He let the sentence stand, as emended, just to needle Mort. But these encounters extracted a toll from Rawlins. Outwardly, he handled it smoothly and appeared unruffled, but inside, he boiled. He suffered fools for money, but his nervous system paid a price for each such collision. Stress. It was the old, loathed monkey, just like it used to be in the airplane. And in the chemical process of defusing the nerve bomb, he did further damage to his physical plant. And, in the seemingly unbreakable cycle, additional harm to that frail and failing agglomeration of nerves, imagination, anticipation, depression, and dread. Plain old fear. Yes, the monkey was back, the heart attack, the seizure, the unknown. Right there at his desk at VVAPS. He was driving himself, in the vehicle of this job among other things, toward Forest Lawn, and it looked like a one-way street. And it was getting on towards eleven-thirty. He gazed over at Harley Cadavery, who, in a fog of rancid pipe smoke, was reading his latest volume of the Berkeley series of Mark Twain's journals.

"Luncheon?"

"Chez Ray?"

"I'll make the call."

Chez Ramon was as unlike its grand title as a meat-and-potatoes restaurant in a semisleazy, blue-collar neighborhood could get. If a soufflé or quiche had ventured through those doors, it would have received around the same welcome the Blob got from Steve McQueen. Oh, sure, it was a notch or so above Mom's Chicken, Ribs, Links, and Tapes, over on Figueroa, but only a notch. The front side of Chez Ramon, on one of those wide California thoroughfares with gray grass, struggling underbrush, a blizzard of junk food wrappers, once the right-of-way for the long-lamented big red electric cars, was a coffee shop. A sure enough red-boothed coffee shop, with leatherette and tarnished chrome stools hard by a gray floral-patterned plastic counter. A six-tier, once-clear plastic dome at its northern end, next to the register, frustrated the occasional fly from getting at the banana cream pie of yesterday's oven. The waitresses, mature, in black nylon short-skirted outfits, with ruffled white aprons, would certainly have called anyone, white or black, "honey," even though it wasn't a deli. Ah, but, strategically perhaps, one or two teenagers had been slipped onto the staff. For reasons more critical than bread alone. They were slow, inept, and saw this as a job, not a career. They smiled bemusedly, great white teeth exposed, only a foot or so above youthful, independent breasts thrusting at the nylon. Their tips were bigger even though their service was lesser, but the old broads accepted it, because that was the way it was. Besides, they had been there. Harley used to say that the true test of a Ray's waitress was her aplomb at transiting a noon-hour dining room, with a purposeful and serviceable demeanor, while avoiding the eye of every patron who might need a drink. If Rawlins was a cynic, Harley was a doomsayer, all in good humor, however.

But if you parked in the lot in back, and came through that door, or pushed through the louvered fir bat-wing doors from the coffee shop, you transcended to the real Chez Ramon. It was dark. The walls were covered with hardwood parquet tiles. The booths were a rich, red Naugahyde, here and there cigarette-burned, with the occasional two-by-four framing member having worked its way through the kapok to make for hard seating. The walls were wondrous, out of plumb, festooned with ersatz tapestry-work portraits of deer, elk, and the Kennedy boys. Where tapestries didn't hang, gilded platters and bas-relief crusaders' helms with crossed maces and battle axes beneath them did. Ray's was to the hoi polloi of Hawthorne what the Polo Lounge was to the independent film producer. It was a place for lunch and drinks and talking shop. Although few deals were made here, still commerce was carried on in a sense.

Rumor and company gossip and inside information flowed continuously, but of course employees of the defense industry are paranoid about secrecy, and you never know when the guy on the next stool is snooping for the FBI, DISCO, the KGB, or even SLUR, so little of substance passed between strangers. Each company had an array of identifying badges that were to be worn at all times at work, but not displayed in public. A typical conversation at the bar might go:

"Oh, you work for TRW. Are you in El Segundo?"

"No, I'm in a building over this way, but I can't tell you where it is. You in aerospace?"

"Yeah, Lockheed program, but that's about all I can say."

"I heard about that crash you guys had out at Edwards. Do they know what happened?"

"Shit, they tell the newspapers more than they tell us. They forbid us to even mention the name of our project when we're locked in our own goddamn office, but I read all about it in the *Times*."

"I know how that goes. We're not even supposed to tell each other what program we're working on. I went over to one building on temporary assignment, and you have to have an escort to go to the mens room, for Christ's sake. Think the Dodgers'll do it this year?"

"Well, you know. If they can stay healthy. . . ." And so on.

At 5:30, Chez Ramon filled with senior citizens on fixed incomes queuing up for the early-bird special. The place was always busy. Waitresses and bartenders, once they got on at Ray's, never left. It was hard work, but the money was good and business was steady, day in and day out, year-round. And mostly from the same people, who tended to tip better after they got to know the staff. Harley knew everyone by name, including the busboys, who had worked there in the last fifteen years. And there was a certain kind of threadbare elegance about the place. The yellow napkins and tablecloths were linen, the china was heavy, and the glasses big enough to hold something. And real value. The drinks were cheap and substantial and that peculiarly American denomination of cuisine that embraces the pork chop, the chicken-fried steak, the mashed potato, and the canned string bean, was out of this world.

At lunchtime, Harley drank gin on the rocks, Rawlins martinis up. They would have two or three before lunch, to take the edge off, another with their liver and onions or tomato stuffed with tuna fish, and frequently two afterward. By that time Rawlins would be half drunk, eyes too bright, flushed, a couple of decibels louder, happier than he really was. But Harley had a hollow leg. His expression never changed, nor did his deportment. The only effect gin had on him was to awaken the slumbering stand-up comic within, which he (and he alone) saw as the symbol of his true calling. Some of his favorite stories should have been declared controlled substances, so narcotic was their effect, when dragged out properly.

And Rawlins would drift back to the office around 1:30, in a pseudo-pleasant haze, back to the people he loved. Back to those who never made a deadline, but required you never to miss one, those who not only capitalized proper nouns, but insisted upon capitalizing *all* nouns, who did not consider personal pronouns or the active voice to be legitimate components of the English language, who could never "do" anything, but always must "achieve" it or "accomplish" it, might not "use" anything, but had to "utilize" it. Yes, those gifted lads (and here and there a lass, now) who had mastered their calculus and aerodynamics at Purdue, but never learned to make the verbs agree with the nouns, or the difference between "which" and "that." (And they had never operated so much as a Cessna 150, or ridden in one.) And there were those patriots who were paid—for what?—commensurate with the number of imbeciles they knew who had not opted to cash in on the aerospace swindle, but still prowled the echoing, endless halls of the Pentagon for colonel's and general's pay, and put in the orders for arms that kept the old pyramid game going.

And, of course, the lowly. The support personnel. The clerks, the typists, the contract illegal-alien janitors, and the contract (because it was cheaper) sub-Neanderthal rent-a-cop guards with all their uniforms and radios and absolutely unintelligible "security" policies. They had, by their own LAW, to touch your badge every time you entered your work facility. They never looked at the picture to see if it was you, asked where you worked, where you were going, or if you spoke English (many of the engineers did not, because Pakistani engineers are cheaper than Purdue engineers—and none of the guards did, adequately) but, boy, if you were one of those harried, gray men with identical faces, with fifteen ballpoint pens in the plastic holder in the pocket of your polyester shirt, with your meat-loaf sandwich ensconced in a brown paper bag, they would scope that sucker out every morning for *goddamn* sure. You could walk out the gate, looking official, with boxes of top-secret documents all day long and throw them into the trunk of your car and drive off without being even questioned, but, by God, at 4:42 no briefcase or woman's purse would pass those portals without proper scrutiny. And, of course, it was because they had not even the vaguest idea what it was that they were looking for. Typewriters, maybe. Cathode-ray tubes. But how do you get those in your purse?

Everybody was always getting exercised about the wrong things. The publications managers cared, and knew, little if anything about the quality, accuracy, or honesty of the documents their people produced. They thought only of square and linear feet, staff, desks, staff, desks, and where all the telephones would plug in. And staff and desks. It was difficult to get a dictionary. You could not obtain, through the company, a *G.P.O. Style Manual*, the handbook of defense-industry writing, which cost $1.50 from the Government Printing Office, because such things were not considered necessary for publications personnel. You could not get Pilot Razor Point pens, which were preferred by many, because they cost thirteen cents a box more than the competing brand they had found, which leaked, blotted, smeared, and went dry weeks or months earlier, but of course the Productivity Utilization Development (PUD) Division was authorized to pay $687.00 for a simple open-end wrench.

But to the managers, especially in publications, all was empire. And oh! Did they have managers! It seemed that the validity of a solution varied inversely with the number of experts doing the solving, because in spite of the swarms of physicists, plane and spherical trigonometry buffs, pure mathematicians, and other categories of "smart" folks who got their inflated checks there, the Chief-to-Indian ratio was completely out of whack. At one point Rawlins was reporting to three separate managers *on the same job.* In his group one summer, there were three managers assigned and only five workers. And managers did not work—all they did was manage.

This all came about because the way to get more money was to become a manager. But the way for *managers* to get more money was to have more junior managers working under them. This pushed them up the manager scale and made them more important and richer managers. So all the big-shot and middle-shot managers couldn't wait to promote their favorites, thereby shoving their own careers up the line, and consequently nearly everybody was some sort of a manager. This situation was nearly fatal to production because the only thing that managers do is have meetings. If they would all just go to each other's meetings and leave the workers to do the work, this would be fine, but they won't do that. No, they all feel that they have crucial managerial erudition that, by way of managing, they simply must pass along to the troops. Also they feel that an essential function of managing is to pretend to know each day from each worker what he or she is working on, how he or she is working on it, and what problems he or she has encountered that can be "managed" away. Instead of observing this in the field, so to speak, they preferred to do it by recitation in mass meetings. And when you finally got out of one of those interminable group therapy sessions and thought you could get back to work and maybe avoid overtime that night, along would come some other manager and suggest that you and she have a "one-on-one" for counseling and career planning.

Rawlins hated these the worst. Or you would be summoned by Upper management to a Political Action Committee meeting where big shots would exhort you to give, give, give, so that they could contribute the money to the campaigns of known hawks who, when they got back to Washington, would ensure the purchase of more instruments and systems of death. And so on. Rawlins drew the line here. No threat, from any manager, however high up the ladder, would get him to a PAC meeting. If he were going to contribute his money to any politician's war chest, he would damn sure select the beneficiary himself.

Then they would march everyone ("roll will be taken for both sessions") to a hot, overcrowded room where you couldn't smoke, to sit on folding chairs for eight hours and listen to some charlatan of a self-styled industrial psychologist drone on about his mystical theories for overcoming stress, becoming more assertive in the workplace, and planning and scheduling your time so as to be more productive. At the end, when they passed out the chits for comments on the presentation, Rawlins noted that he had not "planned" to attend this boring meeting, but would, according to his own "schedule," have done eight hours of work and would thus feel considerably less "stressed," knowing he would not have to stay at his desk until midnight. The breakdown here, Rawlins opined, was that first-line management lacked sufficient "assertiveness" to excuse people who had work to do from these endless goddamn meetings.

So nobody ever got anything done during business hours. They did all their "accomplishing" at night and on weekends. And, for Rawlins, stuck in this veritable Sargasso Sea of inactivity, it was the smugness and self-importance of these poseurs that rankled the most. They all acted like they had real jobs, of great moment to society and the conduct of the world; weighty, sacrosanct trusts that must be recognized and respected. And they were a pack of incompetent fools, most of whom did next to nothing and were grossly overpaid. It may be said that Rawlins did not like his job. But, of course, he too was grossly overpaid, so he kept going to it. And hating it and the thousands of sinecured loafers and

idiots, whose sole mission seemed to be to canonize the mundane, to
glorify the defective.

Rawlins sat at his desk day after day, killing time, going through the
motions, pretending. He knew he was pretending, and was ashamed of
it. He was becoming more and more a part of this thing that he despised.
But he was too scared or too lazy to get up and leave. So he sat there.
And he kept drinking more at lunch to make the whole fucking thing go
away. After five cocktails at lunch and more irritations throughout the
afternoon, when 4:42 rolled around, Rawlins found himself headed
straight for that next one, wherever he was going to pour it down.

He had had to move up to the city to make this job work; his already
wobbly nerves could in no way handle a long rush-hour freeway commute.
And he found a reasonably comfortable apartment in a 1950s complex of
flagstone and stucco, built around a central pool, which was ten feet from
his door. It was only four blocks to the beach; there were a good Irish
pub, an Italian restaurant, and a rib joint within three blocks; and across
the street a liquor store, a fine, eclectic little French restaurant, and an
okay family place for breakfast. Once home, he could park his car and
walk to any kind of place he would want to go. He could walk a few blocks
farther, to the pier, and go to a club that had jazz music every night. On
the pier itself were more bars and restaurants and tourist attractions,
and, always, people. There were grocery stores, drugstores, hardware
stores, clothing stores, all within a block or two. The location was perfect.
Rawlins did not need any more drunk-driving arrests. He'd had three or
four over the years and never gave them a second thought, just paid the
fine and pressed on. But now they were getting *serious* about that shit.
Since those MADD mothers had got into the fray, the legislative and
judicial communities were applying more zeal to the prosecution of the
drinking driver than they were to the premeditated murderer.

Which was probably a good thing, because, owing to sheer numbers,
the drunks probably posed more of a threat to society. The thing Rawlins
objected to was the arbitrariness of the process. In their eagerness to
contain this menace, they had decided that a blood-alcohol content of 0.1
percent was a legal presumption of intoxication. Three drinks. That's all,
baby. You're guilty and you're going to jail and it's going to cost you
thousands and you may lose your license for a while. Rawlins reckoned
that over the last twenty years, after dark at least, he had probably
averaged 0.1 and never had a wreck or hurt anyone. And he thought it
possible, probable even, that he was a better driver with three drinks in
him than 90 percent of the other people on the road whose lips had touched

no liquor. That might even include himself. But all that was moot. They were, in fact, getting *serious*, and he didn't need the hassle.

So his fondness for the location of his digs. He could walk wherever he wanted to go. But there was one drawback. He had formerly lived in that other beach town for twenty years and he knew half the people. Most of his old pals from the Marines had settled there. He had been surrounded by friends, had a support network, was happy and secure in that familiar habitat.

Here, he knew no one. Oh, he had met a few bartenders and cocktail waitresses, but that only caused him to spend more time and money in their establishments, to kill off more brain and nerve cells in that pursuit. He just was not very happy. The great love in San Francisco had become inaccessible, geographically unsatisfactory. He was too old and too drunk and showing the wear too much to make friends easily in the young, frolicsome crowd that he encountered in the bars. He despised most of the people whom he had to "interface" with during the day, and there were no sympathetic old friends, acquaintances even, to wind down with at night. So more and more he palliated that despair with whiskey. And it seemed it must go on forever this way. Where had he to go? What would he do? He was probably too old to get a flying job, and anyway there was the demon. Even if he could find some spot as a copilot with a second-rate carrier in goddamn Africa or Arabia or some such place, he figured he would have to quit drinking to control the monkey. Cold-ass turkey, man. Forever. He couldn't even contemplate that yet; it was the only thing he had left. And would he be any happier? No, not likely.

No, Rawlins was locked in. He was en route to Forest Lawn and he didn't know how to cancel his flight plan. He poured himself some scotch, half-watched the old movie on an independent channel, clinging to those alpha waves that kept the reality of his predicament away for a while. His life was not an abundance of joy.

19

California, 1970s

Former Corporal, now saboteur, O'Malley knew a good thing when he saw it, and Barbi Belheur, the mother of SLUR, was the best thing he had seen in quite a spell. She was perfect. A glamorous pop star, she was rich beyond measure, anti-Establishment, antimilitary, becoming more and more influential in both the counterculture and the loyal opposition, and endless doors were opening up to her. No sir, O'Malley was not going to let this slip away. And Barbi found a certain magnetism in the ex-warrior. His wild red curls and panther tattoo excited her. And there was further propitious chemistry there. God knew they both hated war and also they liked to sing. O'Malley had a pleasant tenor voice and could play the guitar at least as well as Barbi; in the technical sense, better, except no one would pay to hear him do it. They smoked joints and strummed guitars and sang protest songs and talked strategy together and became fast friends. Then lovers. At first P.E. was somewhat jealous, but then one night, in front of the fire and behind a little wine and a little dope, O'Malley fucked her too, and after that everything was all right. The dynamic duo became a terrific trio and the three were seldom apart.

As for O'Malley, it was Valhalla. Here he had two dynamite women who were physically and politically attracted to him, for whom he was a kind of hero, having lived through that terrible war, seen it firsthand, and now doing his level best to end it. He had only to conjure up scenes of death and deprivation, to invent ever more brutal and horrifying war stories, and to decry the barbarity of the American military machine for them to love him the more. All this and Barbi picked up the tab for everything. If it wasn't heaven on earth, it was close enough for O'Malley.

So the abject misery of his life was becoming, indeed, an abundance of joy.

Of course Barbi still dated the boy governor, but he had taken vows of poverty, celibacy, and vegetarianism, if not silence, until the last American boy was removed from the soil of Vietnam. Live one, that is. So their relationship was mostly a social and political one, and Barbi and P.E. and O'Malley started all sleeping together in one big bed. The governor was also quite taken with O'Malley, partly because he had played football in high school and the governor had not been allowed to, and partly because he had seen that horrible war firsthand and had a panther tattoo. Also, he sang nicely in duets with Barbi. O'Malley always needed money, so the governor gave him special staff rank and put him on the payroll as a veteran's affairs coordinator for the Los Angeles region, in which capacity O'Malley chaired the thrice-weekly rap sessions at the local state-subsidized rap facility. Of course he didn't give him a budget or trust him to get any sort of a hand in any cookie jar, as it were, but O'Malley didn't really care, because now he got a salary for doing what he used to do for free, and that was bullshit with his buddies.

If O'Malley thought he had died and gone to heaven, the boys over in MAG-22 in Da Nang were shortly in for a similar transcendence. As the ARVN mortar rounds walked up to the flight line, to vie there for precedence with the VC rockets and the occasional sniper, who zipped the occasional hole through the skin of the occasional airplane or trooper, Colonel Creed had to think more and more about moving the war to Thailand, to preserve his airplanes. Why, even his maintenance personnel were in short supply! And Rawlins and the boys were going to love it. To come happily home from a bombing raid, shower and put on civilian clothes and ride rickshaws to town to drink that abundant cheap whiskey with genuine ice, and get into those real beds with those real, full-breasted Thai girls, and fuck them as adequately as was common in those climes for five bucks, and then roll off and crash, absolutely dead, until four in the morning, when you snapped awake and rickshawed back to the base to see if you were on the O-dark-thirty launch. Rawlins was a fine physical specimen then; they all were. Able to crash beside that girl, dead drunk and dead to the world, sleep those three or five hours, and automatically spring awake, fully awake and functioning, when the mental time clock said so. And rickshaw to the base, or take the personnel carrier-pickup to the flight line, strap on the airplane, and go for it. He lost all that in the later years. Those later years were a time of accounting; they began to call in the physical and mental markers and it grew more and more obvious how much he had overspent during the good times.

He would remember the Australians fondly. They had their own section of the Air Force Base, their own club, their own gate. The Aussies were flying aged and relatively ineffective F-86s. They had less than half the speed, power, payload, or sophisticated systems of the Phantom. They dated from the early '50s, the Korean War. Still they were game old birds, and the Aussies knew how to drive them. And the Aussies had spirit. They had more gamesmanship, more of that competitive fine edge, as a group, than anybody he had been around before. The Marines in their Phantoms, no slouches exactly at the macho contest, were constantly being jumped by those F-86 Sabres. They might be on GCA final, with the gear and flaps down ready to land, for Christ's sake, and here would come a pair of Aussies making a five-hundred-knot pass on them, saying "Rat-a-tat-tat, yowa dead, Yank," on GCA frequency. They were irreverent, they were feisty, they played hard and constantly. They were the consummate pub games players, from dice and darts to their own made-up events. The epitome of the Australian game was perhaps "Dead Bug," played throughout Southeast Asia. It was a progressive game, assumed to have started somewhere, at some time, in some Aussie club, but ongoing, endless. It had to do with the lads sitting around at the bar of the club (happy hour was its best time slot). They would be draped on their high bar stools, above a concrete deck more often than not, regaling each other with flying stories, told with both hands imitating combat-maneuvering airplanes. Then, at any random time, the one who was "it," from an hour before or a day before, meaning the one who had lost the last game, the identity of whom some of the unknowing participants (everyone at the bar was required to play, knowing or unknowing) might not be aware, could shout out "Dead Bug" and begin the next chukker. The object was that the last man to be flat on his back with arms and legs sprawling in the air, resembling a dead bug, was "it." He had then to buy the bar a round of drinks and could initiate the next game. You can imagine the spectacle of thirty hard-charging, fearless, drunk aviators trying to beat each other to the deck, amid flying drinks, toppling chairs, and breaking glass. It was heartwarming. Hang Dog and some of his cohorts were shortly to plagiarize the theme and bring forth the game "Cocksuckers Can't Dance," which was also quite lively, and used much the same format. In this game, the participants had only to fly off their stools and into some sort of wild, gyrating hornpipe to be exempt. Velos and Yolanda they weren't, but those non-cocksuckers could sure dance. Again, the last one observed to be tripping the light fantastic was adjudged "it," required to buy the drinks, and allowed to start the next game by yelling, "Cocksuckers Can't Dance."

The Aussies were paid only a fraction of what the Americans got. If you took a rickshaw from the Air Force gate, it cost you the equivalent of two bucks for the leisurely ride to town. If you left from the Aussie gate, it cost only a buck, and the rickshaw boys were made to race all the way, with pari-mutuel wagering, of course. The same was true of the girls and the merchants. Everyone charged the Americans more, and seemed to like the Australians better.

The daily message traffic indicated that back in Da Nang the war within a war was heating up nicely, and that pleased the boys no end, because it portended a longer stay in Thailand. It most noticeably did not please Colonel Creed no end. The accursed Buddhist ARVN were still holed up in his temple, intractable and intransigent. Not only had they closed the valve on his building-materials pipeline, but their infernal stochastic mortaring and sniping were coming uncomfortably close to the half-erected OM club, as well as the airplanes he still had left on the base. Something had to be done. One night Colonel Creed met the commander of the local Navy Construction Battalion at the somewhat posher officers club at Wing Headquarters. While they were both lamenting the slipshod supply system and enumerating the things that they really needed to get on with this war, it was disclosed that the Seabee had an Underwater Demolition Team assigned to him to help clear bridge abutments, dock pilings, and such. Those UDT boys could be the answer to Creed's prayer. By strategically placing charges of C-4 explosive at stress and bearing points, keystones and the like, they could drop that old temple into neat rows of stones with one push of the plunger.

The Seabees' problem was that they had badly needed supplies and materials in the Philippines, but they couldn't arrange for airplanes to bring the stuff to them. The Cong had sabotaged the docks and channel in Da Nang so the ships couldn't bring the stuff in, but they had to have the stuff in order to clear the channel and rebuild the docks so the Navy *could* bring the stuff in. They needed cargo planes and Creed was the man who had them. So the deal was struck. C-130s for a UDT team. Oh, maybe the troops would have to live a little longer on red death, which somehow always got delivered, but *c'est la guerre.* One dark night those UDT boys would slither up there with their C-4 and just *flatten* that goddamn temple. Then the ARVN, exposed, with their fucking pants *all* the way down, would have to regroup and dig in somewhere farther back to protect their asses from their brothers the VNAF. This would also serve to protect Colonel Creed's club and airplanes, because the mortars would be farther away. So synergistic did this solution appear to be that Colonel Creed could not help licking his chops a little on the way back to his hootch. Two birds with one stone.

"What we've got to do," Barbi said to O'Malley, "is make those cock-suckers dance."

"I don't get your drift, sweet warrior." His teachings in true feminism were only just rudimentary.

"We've got to do something so big it will shock every fucking member of the Establishment, get their full attention, convince them that the antiwar movement is so strong and so determined that we will stop at absolutely nothing. Scare the shit out of them, plain and simple. We've got to jerk every politician in the country around to our point of view, the *people's* point of view, and make that cocksucker *dance*. To our music."

"Boy, you're one wild lady. What did you have in mind?"

"You know how to blow things up, right?"

"Hey, tell me, baby. I'm one of the slickest saboteurs working this country, and learning more all the time." This wasn't quite true, but he had given Barbi a rather expanded résumé to get the job at the peace conference. And he *was* studying up on explosives.

"Well, we're going to blow something up, O'Malley." Barbi had that gleam in her eye; she was serious.

"Like what?"

"Like the Air Force Station right here in L.A. The Space and Missile Systems Office, SAMSO."

"Woweee. That's a big order, honey. I don't know if we could pull that one off. Place'd be crawling with guards. Gates, fences, alarms, everything."

"Well, there's got to be a way. And your assignment, my rampant revolutionary bull, is to start studying the problem and see how it can be done." She gave him a wet, fervent, revolutionary kiss and held him long and hard. He began to get an erection, so disengaged himself to think a little. Damn but that girl, woman, that is (he *had* learned that much), could manipulate him.

"Yeah, babe, I'll scope it out. Let's see. I guess C-4 would be our explosive of choice. Of course we would have to place it at strategic architectural positions. Stress and bearing points, keystones, that kind of thing. Hmmm. Tell you what, I've got a buddy down at the rap facility.

He was a Navy SEAL. They get UDT training. Let me sound him out about it."

"Well, don't tell him the real story, at least not yet. I'm serious about this and I don't want anybody blowing it. Feel him out real slow and if you think you can recruit him, bring him to talk to me."

"No sweat. I'll be real vague. Tell him I'm thinking of a Bank of America or a draft board or something. He's cool, though. I don't think we have to worry too much about this dude. He's one bitter sumbitch."

"And another thing, stud. Move as fast as you can on this. My idea is to blow that sucker on the last day of the peace conference. *That* ought to open some eyes, get some attention, demand some loyalty to Socialized Labor's Unrelenting Revolt. What we'll do is let on at the conference that through our nationwide intelligence network we have been informed of a *major* antigovernment gesture which will occur on that last day. Of course they won't be able to connect *us* with it, but the *people* will know."

P. E. Proudbird was engrossed in the preparation of her seminar for the conference. It was to be on the parallel perils of the indigenous American on his native soil and the Vietnamese on *his* own turf a couple of centuries later. And striking parallels there were indeed. Both of these societies were simple hunters, fishers, and farmers; rural, pastoral chaps who had ancient cultures and religions that suited them fine. They did a little fighting among themselves, between tribes and factions, but by and large they were pretty happy. But one fine day, in both instances, in marched a horde of weird-looking white men in strange getups, from God knew where, with advanced weapons and firepower that was not to be believed. And they set out to change everything, which had been pretty much the same for centuries, millennia for Christ's sake, around. They brought with them the notion that they could *own* certain of the natives' lands and rivers and harbors and such. They just built fences around these places and said, "You can't go there anymore." And as often as not, some families' hootches were right in the middle of one of these areas. Already built. There before the paleface ever stepped his brass-buckled shoe or tractor tread–soled combat boot on the shore. But now there was a fence around your hootch or teepee, and, by God, Thomas Clayton Wolfe must have had something there: They *couldn't* go home again. Never having seen a fence before, and having no real concept of man owning the land except, perhaps, in the family or tribal sense of traditional use, these societies took exception to the shenanigans of the milky complexioned land developers and their high-handed notions of real property law and riparian rights. When they protested, they were shot. When they protested being shot, they were shot some more. And the whites always fetched missionaries along. That was almost worse.

It wasn't long before they began to cast about for ways of ridding themselves of these interlopers. And boy, did they find some ways. Any GI impaled on a pit full of punji stakes, or settler staked to an anthill, or missionary burned at the stake would think twice before he interloped again. As P.E. pondered these phenomena, she became more and more convinced that *any* action, anything whatsoever, was justified in stopping the white man's aggression.

She thought Barbi's idea of blowing up the Air Force Station was marvelous and volunteered any service she could provide.

O'Malley recruited his buddy the ex-SEAL, also a doper and bitter, and they began casing the Space and Missile Systems Office (SAMSO) at the Air Force Station. They took notes on SAMSO, made sketches of SAMSO, observed the gates and the guards, procedures for admittance, kinds of commercial vehicles allowed in, and so forth. It began to appear that it might be easier than he had first thought. Security was really pretty lax. All manner of civilians came and went (mainly to the plush officers club, where the drinks were cheap and everybody was welcome); the huge structure was nothing more than an office building where the Air Force managed, negotiated, and oversaw the thousands of contracts they had with southern California defense companies. Telephone trucks went in and out all day, sandwich trucks, deliveries from everywhere, Federal Express, UPS, you name it. The place could be infiltrated. O'Malley was getting excited about this caper. Maybe he could just pull it off. Give the motherfucking government a taste of its own medicine.

Barbi had buried herself in the planning and organization of the peace conference. It was a major undertaking and her raw management skills were taxed to the limit. She was as dithered as some of the managers at Vulcan V-belt and Avionic Pilotage System Corporation. And it was mostly about the same issues, real estate and furniture. The governor had got Royce Hall for her at UCLA, but there were endless details. Some of her group leaders were a little . . . not flaky, but, well, remiss. They hadn't got their course materials to her. All that stuff had to be printed, handouts for every participant in every workshop, leaflets, flyers, schedules. She had to arrange for the rooms and tables and chairs for each session, transportation and lodging for the important speakers she hoped to attract. There were coffee and doughnuts and posters and lunches and her speeches and her paramilitary outfits and a thousand things. The master schedule was her first concern. She was not yet precisely sure who was going to show up or exactly what would be offered. Yet, as many a professional manager will tell you, the most important part of any project, at least in the beginning, is the schedule. Nobody pays any attention to it *after* the beginning, but to start off with, it's top priority. So she had to print something up that accounted for every hour of every day, detailing what would be done, where, and by whom. She *would* have a schedule (Barbi pronounced it *shedjool* because she thought it sounded more cultured). Of course she couldn't do all those things herself; she must delegate many of the responsibilities to loyal members of SLUR. The first thing she decided to delegate was the schedule. It would be difficult to say, categorically, whether Barbi was a disciple of the X school of management, or the Y school. She could be, however, rather demanding and, oh, assertive in the workplace, not to say aggressive. It's lonely at the top, they say.

P.E. had amassed a slew of *Life* magazines, A.I.M. literature, and history texts (to point out their fallacies) and was doing research.

O'Malley was researching too. He had stolen an explosives text from the library and was studying the variants and derivatives of trinitrotoluene and their qualities and effects. He was thinking big demolition, man.

So things lurched along toward the great American Peace-In and the destruction of the Air Force Station, from the rubble of which would emerge an unmistakable lesson, an omen, a portent. Of course nobody would learn from it, they never did. Nobody but a few Arabs. But it would get people's attention. Barbi would eventually go to the Democratic Convention. Of course she could not have dreamed at that point that she would one day be invited to Vietnam to entertain the troops. North Vietnam, that is; enemy troops, whomever that might really be. And so on.

20

Southeast Asia, 1960s

While it may be that Major Poltroun bore the opprobrium of his, shall we say, less than professional airmanship on that infamous night TPQ mission with some discomfort, it was really only to the extent that he felt his career amelioration juice had been diluted. In the case of Lieutenant Colonel Morgenkrank, the pill was more bitter. It galled him, vexed him grievously to have been guilty of such deplorable amateurism as to land with the gear up. The difference was that Poltroun had never been a good enough pilot to take real pride in this professionalism; Morgenkrank had.

The visible evidence gave mute testimony to the night's misadventures. Pilots entering the landing pattern at Da Nang could observe at the approach end of the runway, just beyond the threshold, a jagged rent, a scar in the soft earth curving off to either side for a hundred yards or so. The runway, long and straight, together with these uneven, skidding slashes through the dirt, took on the appearance of an arrow drawn by a child. Pointed south. Added to this image, bracketing the runway's end, spaced militarily every thirty paces or so, was a series of black, scorched spots in the sand. If these were inspected closely, overlooked bits of charred debris could be seen scattered about the site of each pyre, fragments of bone and prayer wheels, remnants of the stuff that had burned there. The headline in *Stars and Stripes* a week or so later trumpeted:

SELFLESS BUDDHIST CLERICS GIVE LIVES
IN SUPPORT OF AMERICAN AIR WAR

Cavendish was recommended for the Bronze Star for his intrepid and exemplary leadership of the paramilitary brigade. And so forth.

Al "Shaky" Morgenkrank and Major Poltroun were maintaining low profiles. Neither wanted to talk to anybody about anything. Al "Shaky" Morgenkrank was awash in mortal chagrin because he could not convene a pilot disposition board and yank Poltroun's wings. He could not do that without dealing himself the same card, so there it was. He couldn't even *chew his ass,* for Christ's sake. Oh, it was frustrating and exasperating. The two airplanes sat side by side outside the hangar, up on jacks, getting new wing tanks and bomb racks and antennas and random sections of skin, an engine or two, etc., more mute testimony to folly.

Moon Dog and Hang Dog had still been in the ready room when Poltroun was fetched, in disgrace, on his shield in a sense, back from the scene of his infamy, shuddering uncontrollably, pale, sweating, legs wobbling, red welt and Band-Aid on his jaw from Culpepper's haymaker, unable at first even to fill out the accident report, his hands shook so.

Moon nudged Hang Dog. "Doggie, your old buddy Poltroun looks like he's been ate by a bear and shit on a anthill."

By morning the troops had the two airplanes up in seemingly strategic positions in front of the hangar. The squadron's call letters were "sierra hotel," painted boldly on the vertical stabilizer of each aircraft. On one bird this was left intact, but on the other, before light, someone had sprayed out the "sierra hotel" and painted in "india tango." From the aspect of the flight line, they were aligned perfectly and the silent message was displayed to their little world: SHIT.

That was bad enough. But before a sharp-eyed maintenance officer spotted the jape and had it rectified, a dutiful *Stars and Stripes* staffer, having inquired about the planes and been assured by some wag or awe-struck patriot, likely the former, that they were shot up on one of the terrifying missions that their pilots regularly flew, set up his camera and took the picture. He never noticed the counterfeit call sign, but every aviator in the Pacific theater did. The picture sailed through the editorial process and ran on the front page under the banner:

INTREPID MARINE AVIATORS BRING
BATTLE-DAMAGED AIRCRAFT HOME

That timeless record of two well-ruptured ducks spelling out SHIT, slapped into thousands of scrapbooks, clinched for the squadron its distinction as the laughingstock of Naval Aviation. As the story spread, the legend of the incredible back-to-back landings grew. The no-wings take-off. The emergency runway lighting system. And so on.

Colonel Creed's empire was already tottering on supports just as wobbly as Poltroun's knees after they ran the smelling salts under his nose, applied a styptic pencil to the cut on his jaw, restrained C. Ross Culpepper, and sent them back to the ready room in separate ambulances. Only Colonel Creed did not yet realize just how shaky his ground was. He would have to live with the *Stars and Stripes* cover shot for the rest of his career; though he was not directly involved, it *was* his Group. He had not yet been able to dislodge the despised ARVN from the temple, and construction of the OM club would soon be suspended; when next he heard from said temple it would be in the form of a bombardment of his flight line. He could send most of his airplanes to Thailand and roll the rest into hangars and revetments to hide them, but not the two up on jacks. They could not be moved quickly enough, and would sit there like turkeys at a turkey shoot and soak up mortar rounds until they flamed into an inferno and then collapsed together into what, as adumbrated by their erstwhile tail numbers, was no more than a huge pile of shit.

These aircraft would cost from two and a half to four million apiece, depending on your understanding of the then-year–dollar enigma. That was a fiscal scam wherein the Pentagon tried to represent the cost of future weapons systems in current-year–dollar value, showing that the taxpayer was getting a steal on his weapons at any price because those future, inflation-hammered dollars wouldn't be worth much. Congress, using the converse approach, saw the purchasing in future-year dollars, failing to factor in inflation, and bleating in indignation at the seemingly astronomical sums the Armed Forces were always requesting for new toys. There was perhaps a little more to it than that, but no one really understood it, so all the aerospace companies, including Vulcan V-belt and Avionic Pilotage System Corporation, had at least one insignificant jack-straw who did nothing but sit in his modestly lavish office, on his worn-shiny backside, study *Aviation Week*, *Aerospace Daily*, and other esoteric trade publications, and write two or three eleven-page white papers a year purporting to decipher the then-year–dollar enigma. They were paid fifty or sixty thousand a year for this and the papers were universally ignored because no one could understand them, or gave a shit anyway.

At whatever rate, the planes represented several million dollars' worth of Creed's assigned materiel, and he was sorely vexed as he stood helplessly by and watched them blaze. Colonel Creed's feeling was not unlike that of Major Poltroun as he went careening down the concrete at two hundred miles an hour, atop fifty thousand pounds of potentially explosive materials, utterly out of control. Creed was riding a vastly larger and more explosive (both figuratively and literally) conglomeration of things, attitudes, policies, people, and consequences—above all consequences—and, like Poltroun, he was in the driver's seat, but he was not driving. He couldn't know yet that first the VNAF and then his own pilots would begin shooting at the wrong Cong, and then, by order of higher command, begin shooting at each other. This eventuality would move his tactical situation from the relatively comfortable one of having been allied with the VNAF and the ARVN against only the Cong and the NVA to one of having all four of them against him. Then, when the American grunts began shooting at his planes, it was everyone against his Air Group. It would be a little lonely. And he couldn't know that one of his troops, an officer, would shoot the right man for the wrong reason, and that another, a staff NCO, would shoot the wrong man for the right reason, and that those little transgressions would come back to haunt him in the form of protests from everybody from the Commander in Chief of the Army of the Republic of Vietnam to the Red Cross. No, the augury was not bright, career-enhancement-wise.

Gunnery Sergeant O'Flynn was also pretty disturbed. The metal shop, like all the other ones, was undermanned and overworked. They spent hours and hours each day cutting and drilling new skin-plates to replace the duct tape with which they had patched all the bullet holes so the planes could keep flying until they got around to the cutting and drilling. It was an endless cycle of patching and repatching, and for some reason this particular aspect of a generally frustrating job irked O'Flynn more than other things. The story of Major Poltroun's preternatural and ever-reliable hostile fire had spread throughout the squadron. The uncanny thing about it was that it followed Poltroun around. He hadn't made it up, others would see the tracers too, but it seemed to manifest itself only when Poltroun was in the neighborhood. The Poltroun ground fire was always observed in the same general area, close in on the VFR approach course to the landing pattern, where the aircraft were down to one thousand feet and pilots could see the flashes if they looked carefully. The spot was well within the perimeter of ARVN control, but somehow this bothersome fucking Congster slipped in there every blessed day to shoot at Poltroun. Only Poltroun. Even shot him down once. But never anyone else. It was a puzzle and O'Flynn didn't like puzzles.

He also didn't like wasting thousands of maintenance man-hours patching the holes that this fucking mystery marksman was putting in his airplanes. Enough was enough. Since no one else seemed to be able to,

O'Flynn vowed to track down the phantom fire team his own damn self. To that end he took Staff Sergeant Hebblethwaite, and armed with M-16s and plenty of clips, they drove the maintenance jeep off the base. They had checked with several pilots and pinpointed the spot on a map. A small road ran near the wooded area from whence came the spectral Poltroun ground fire.

The XO was out leading a helicopter escort, which would probably last a couple of hours. O'Flynn was going to be ready when he returned. He and Hebblethwaite found the dirt road and headed for the encounter that would temporarily stanch the flow of Air Medals to Major Poltroun, disenhance O'Flynn's career further (and in some measure Colonel Creed's), piss off the Commander in Chief of the Army of the Republic of Vietnam, among others, and ultimately lead to the further reduction of Mrs. O'Flynn's allotment checks. As they approached the infamous wooded area, they were somewhat surprised to find an ARVN jeep parked in a clearing beside the road. That being the most suitable parking place in sight, they parked beside the other jeep, and set out.

The Daily Harassment Detail from the Vietcong, out snooping and pooping through the fruitful plain, observed from hiding the jeeps and those crazy-looking Americans slinking off through the brush. The scene was more interesting than anything else going on that day, so they elected to follow, watch, and maybe ambush the dogs if it looked safe.

Rawlins had dwelled on the lot of his ordnance crew. These guys, the skeletal three of them, were giving their all. They were doing backbreaking labor sixteen and twenty hours a day, day after endless day, and there was little he could do for them. He could try for meritorious promotions, and would, but that would take time and a lot of politicking because all the troops worked their asses off and they couldn't promote everybody or pretty soon they wouldn't have any Indians left. He couldn't get them R and R unless some more ordnancemen checked in; they were too much needed. Well, he would get them a medal. Napoleon, faced with dwindling coffers and insufficient cash flow to pay his army, is said to have started handing out bright shiny pins and gaily colored ribbons that signified service and bravery. What a ticket! Ever since then a soldier of any stripe had loved medals as much as he does tattoos. They mean saltiness, balls, experience; they mean, I've been there and came back and I'm a *BAD* motherfucker. Rawlins put his boys in for Bronze Stars. Well, that is he tried to. When he brought the recommendations to the awards office he was turned away.

"Sorry, Smilin' Jack, my orders are not to submit any more commendations, UFN."

"What?"

"Until further fucking notice."

"Who the fuck said so?"

"XO."

"What for? This is a war, isn't it? Don't boys get medals when they play good in the war?"

"Well, this is a special case. Kind of extraordinary circumstances, like Candyass would say."

"Like what?"

"Well, like Candy might say again, I'm not at liberty to disclose that information."

"Liberty my ass. What the fuck's the deal here? C'mon, what's Poltroun up to now?"

"Nothing. Much."

"All right, asshole, tell me or it will prey on my mind. I'll get distracted. Routines will be forgotten. Procedures will go out the window. I might turn the wrong way on a missed approach in the goop and fly into Monkey Mountain. And take my wingman right along with me. You owe him better than that."

He laughed. "You won't mention it to anybody?"

"Nobody but Moon Dog, Hang Dog, and Private Hoggins or Corporal Hoggins or whatever he is this week. Now what is ass-eyes up to?"

"Oh, nothing, really."

"Tahk or I shuet jou vis my sahty ayaht." He pulled out said .38 and waved it menacingly.

"Well, you remember when the A Shau Valley was all hot a month or so ago?"

"Yeah."

"Well, Poltroun flew one of those hops up there with Colonel Creed in the clag."

"So? Everybody went up there and it was socked in tighter than Boston Harbor when the eighteenth-century hippies were smoking all that tea."

"Well, Poltroun and Creed reportedly found a hole in the overcast and got in to drop. They said it was terrible weather and all kinds of AA fire and everything. Max hazardous."

"In a pig's rimfire. I'll give odds they dropped right through the overcast. So?"

"So they wrote each other up for a DFC."

"Hah! Any BDA?"

"Pilot observed. Knocked out AA batteries, and, well, you know."

"So what? I've got three good men and true who've been busting their well-known asses lo these many months, and I want to get them a little Bronze Star to slap on their chests. What's that got to do with two idiots dropping their bombs through the clouds and probably hitting the friendlies, if they hit anything?"

Well, it emerged that Poltroun, not one to roll the stone of Sisyphus exactly, seeking to grease the skids of career enhancement, and not wishing to overburden the market, had instructed the awards officer not to submit any more recommendations until he got his. Why render the waters murky? Why glut the Venturi tube of the indrawn effluvia of pseudo-supereminence? No, there would be no further entrants just now. So for the time being the militocracy had frustrated Rawlins in his quest to get even a symbolic reward for his troopers. War sucked. At least the conduct of this one by its Pecksniffian perpetrators did.

Someone who could not have identified more completely with Rawlins's sentiments was Lance Major Slocum, who was on club duty that day. He and Hang Dog were washing what was left of the stones from the Buddhist temple and handing them up to Nguyen Van Dan who was laying up the final course on one wall of the OM club. It was ninety-two in the shade if you could find any, and the aviators were less than serenely happy with their lot as hod carriers for a captured gook. The sweat rolled off of them, and they were flushed from the exertion. The only thing cold about the scene was Slocum's eyes. They were narrowed and icy. He had been brooding silently about their state of affairs, and he seethed inside. It was inglorious, it was unglamorous, it was hard work, and it was hot. Slocum had come here to fight a war, to die if necessary, but with guns blazing and burners lit, not of heat prostration in the dust; to kill gooks, not to truckle to them. It was embarrassing for a fighter pilot, a warrior, to be doing day labor. It was frustrating, maddening, and exasperating. And Slocum had had about enough.

Nguyen Van Dan had escaped from the Cong and allowed himself to be captured because it was too fucking hard out there in the boonies, constantly on the run, *hounded* by the goddamn Americans and Koreans, if not the ARVN, sleeping in tunnels, short of food, short of *every* damn thing. No, it was not so lovely out there in the field, and his life had not been an abundance of joy. So he let himself be captured and things improved right after his interrogation period. Now he had three squares and a cot and didn't have to hump it through the jungle anymore, but only work middling hard for eight hours a day on the OM club. That, he could handle. And no more getting his ass shot off. Or so he thought.

But Dan was a budding bureaucrat, something of an entrepreneur even. He had a taste for ease in life, if not luxury. Dan saw himself as having decided executive abilities, and was not one to shun the limelight. He was a take-charge guy. Had Dan emerged from another culture, with all its privileges of mediocre education and white-collar elitism, he might have gone far at the Vulcan V-belt and Avionic Pilotage System Corporation. He fancied he had the knack for managing personnel and resources. In that spirit, and because he was the one who was there every day, *all day*, he came to think of himself as the *de facto* foreman of the OM club project; from that elevated position he was wont to affect a somewhat, well, imperious air from time to time. After all he *was* building the goddamn thing, and these American pilots who showed up for two hours once in a while couldn't find their ass with both hands and a view-finder when it came to brick-laying. And *lazy?* Why, getting a day's work out of those white boys was like pulling teeth from a brass monkey. But Dan was not a military man. His induction into the Cong might have been amusing to the disinterested observer, though it was decidedly not so to Dan. He had left a lucrative situation as a *mercanti noir* dealing in adaptable women and boys, jeweled watches, and what have you in Da Nang, to return to his small, native, rice-growing village. He did this to avoid being pressed into service with the ARVN and forced to carry an M-1 or M-14 through the forests and paddies of central Vietnam. When he'd been home a few days and was beginning to adjust to the idea of work, the Cong moved in one night looking for recruits. They explained that the unrelenting struggle of the people required sacrifice by everyone for the common good. They said that what was needed at that time was 20 percent of the village's rice harvest, a two-year hitch from all able-bodied males between fifteen and forty, and the collusion and cooperation of the village chief. They said they didn't want to be unreasonable or overly abrupt, so they would give the villagers a week to think it over. But when they returned, if their demands were not met, unfortunately for all concerned, punitive measures would have to be taken.

And return they did, in a week's time. First they asked the village chief, the *Huong Chu*, if he was ready to join the glorious cause and support the National Liberation Front. He had just that day been visited by a Saigon government emissary, who had paid the chief bribe money as usual and exhorted him to be absolutely true to his lawful government, because they were now winning by a convincing margin, and in a few months, after the hostilities, loyalists such as himself would be looked upon in a most favorable light. And, what the hell, had the Cong ever slipped him any money? Not piaster one. And he was fiesty. And yes, he had allowed himself a taste of *ruou nep* to take the edge off. So he said no, he thought it wiser for his village to remain neutral for the time being, so as not to offend anyone. Okay, they said, and two of them grabbed his wife. A third one clicked the safety off on his AK-47 and loosely covered the villagers. The fourth one held the wife's left hand on the table, separating the little finger from the others, and the fifth one, with a slight flourish of his machete, chopped it off. "Now you think about it for another week," they said. "When we come back, we hope you will have seen the pure, unsullied way." The chief was already beginning to see.

Next they selected a husky thirty-year-old man and inquired if he were ready to join them that night for his period of service to the people. He replied that he had a wife, three children, a water buffalo, a hootch, and a paddy. He worked from dawn until dark to sustain those things, and if the army took him, his family would starve and he would lose his land. So they grabbed him, stuck the AK-47 to his head, and chopped *his* little finger off, more as an incentive to the other young men than because the individual himself needed convincing. They would have taken him anyway.

"Comrades," said Nguyen Van Dan, "*Comrades. . . .*" His revolutionary zeal had been awakened. He could see the pure, unsullied way all right. So Dan, by opting not to carry an M-14 through the jungle all day for the ARVN, put himself in line to carry an AK-47 over the same ground all night for the Cong. War sucked. Dan was not a morning person. He was also not a night person when it came to humping mines and booby traps through the boondocks to blow up a few Americans and maybe piss them off enough to call a B-52 Arc-Light strike the next day that roared and blazed and zapped and so shook the earth that, even in your safe little tunnel, like a rat, you couldn't sleep. So, eventually he *chieu hoied* and turned himself over to the Americans. And it had been a pretty good gig, so far. But the pressure was on him from that blasted colonel to get the job done, and he couldn't get the fucking pilots to *work*. Dan resolved that he would just have to be a little more assertive in the workplace. Yeah, he was a take-charge guy.

And that was what really rankled Slocum. Here was this pissant little slopehead, lording it over him, strutting and barking and occasionally rolling his eyes skyward, throwing up his hands, and making other gestures of dismay. Slocum had had about enough.

"Hey, boy-san," piped Nguyen Van Dan right at that, the least opportune of moments. "You bringey mo' dock." His tone was wrong. The moment was wrong; his position was wrong. Crouched atop the high, shaky bamboo scaffolding he had fashioned, Dan put Slocum in mind of those snarling, snapping, yapping little dogs that thoroughly surprise you through a half-open car window as you walk past, a foot away. And Slocum reacted. He charted the most direct course to the base of the scaffold and began rattling and shaking it with all the fury of his thick-set bulk.

"Come on down here, you slimy, slant-eyed little cocksucker," he bellowed. "I'll give you mo' dock. I'll give you all the fucking dock you can handle, you little Ho Chi motherfucker."

Nguyen Van Dan yelped and babbled in all the most inflective sort of Vietnamese, more than somewhat excited. Clinging as for life itself to the wildly careening bamboo poles, he did not wish to come down, at the moment, under any circumstances, and most particularly disliked the idea of being shaken down, like a coon from a tree. There would be conflicting testimony over exactly what precipitated the fall of the bucket full of mortar that he had just hauled up on a line, but fall it did. Dan would claim that Slocum himself, by the violent shaking of the platform, dislodged the bucket. Hang Dog's version, on the other hand, that of the only disinterested eyewitness, stated that he clearly saw Dan throw the bucket, in a gesture that was unmistakably warlike, bellicose, and inimical, and that was almost certainly the first step in a daring escape attempt. It was pointed out that most anybody, trapped on top of a ten-foot bamboo platform with the raving, cursing, snarling Slocum attempting to tear it down, would have sought an escape route. But alas, POWs are not always allowed all the same rights and privileges as other citizens; most particularly they are not allowed to escape, no matter the circumstances. So that was a serious issue. At any rate, what went up did indeed come down. The bucket of mud plummeted like a slam dunk and rimmed Slocum's head as neatly as if it had been manufactured to fit there. It was at about this time, and here all accounts seemed pretty much to agree, that Nguyen Van Dan decided there was nothing for it but to bail on over the wall and seek safety elsewhere. And at this time the splenetically vindictive Slocum, armed with a .38 Special revolver, was a reasonably dangerous man.

Some other bamboo poles that were shaking and rattling something fierce were the ones of the thicket in which Brass Balls Obradovitch and his handcrafted pseudo-Cong were laid out middling tight to old mother earth. They had just ambushed an NVA unit, which turned out to be company sized, or larger, and the NVA were giving as good as they got. Maybe better. As a blistering fusillade of small arms fire tore through the jungle above their heads, Brass Balls had to consider something along the lines of a strategic withdrawal. Like get the fuck out of there most *ricky-tick* and call in some air. Except that in their trimmed-down, lean and mean guerrilla profile, traveling light, they had not fetched along a PRC-25 radio and they couldn't call in air. They couldn't talk to the air. But get the fuck out of there they could do, and did. But they were already taking casualties, and things were getting a little dicey. To their backs was a steep, rough, jungle-covered ridge. That looked like the best spot for a holding action. Take the high ground. They leap-frogged up the ridge by fire teams, laying down covering rear-guard fire by turns. A couple more were wounded, but eventually they made it up. Along the top of the ridge were scattered clearings and old bomb craters from some forgotten skirmish. They jumped into some holes and kept firing back down the hill at the NVA, feeling pretty secure in their new position. Feeling that way for several seconds only.

Then there commenced quite a racket and those ominous buzzing, zinging, and ricocheting sounds from behind them, *down the other side of the ridge*. There happened into *that* valley, at purely the wrong time, an ARVN patrol, out on one of their standard search-and-avoid missions. When they heard all the shooting, they prudently took cover and watched the ridge line to see what would develop. In good time, they observed black-clad, conical-hatted soldiers crawling over the ridge, dropping into holes, and firing down the other side. The ARVN commander reasoned that the impudent Cong had closed with some friendlies, probably a U.S. Marine patrol, on the other side of the hill. Now they were retreating and would fade away into the valley. But, *hah!* The ARVN anvil had arrived and they were caught between it and whoever was the hammer on the other side of the ridge. They never dreamed that the unseen hammer, moving up the hill in pursuit of a few belligerents, dressed like their brothers the Vietcong, but assuredly not them, was in fact the hated and feared NVA, and that it was their own good buddies the Marines who were caught in the middle and taking shit from both sides.

Obradovitch, not known widely for philosophical pronouncements, could only think to say, "Boys, we are in some very deep, dark, serious shit here. There's troops on both sides of us and they aren't any of them friendly. We need some help, and not this afternoon." To that end he dispatched his two sneakiest troops, who could still sneak, to sky out along the ridge top, get to friendly lines, explain the situation, and get some goddamn assistance up here *mau* fucking *len*.

The problem had been intelligence. Everybody, from Battalion to I Corps to MACV Headquarters, wanted more skinny, more facts, more news. They could never find the goddamn enemy. They didn't know where he was, what he was doing, where his camps were. They couldn't tell how fast the infiltration from the North was building up the enemy forces or what kinds of weapons they were importing. They needed spies and spooks. Hard-core, unconventional reconnaissance people to get out there and find the son of a bitch. Well, Obradovitch had found him. Found a little more than he was after. He had known that the way to catch the elusive bastard was with small, clandestine, irregular units. Thus the charade. O.B. had known that disguised, covert patrols playing the enemy's own game would bring him in contact. Only his little gang, BAD as they were, hadn't figured on jumping what now appeared to be maybe a battalion, because they were on both sides and probably working around to surround their ass at that very moment.

Yeah, Obradovitch liked that covert shit. He had always seen himself as a rather daring and intrepid nonstandard commando. He sometimes chafed under the bonds and strictures of SOP regimentation, and preferred the role of a sort of Scarlet Pimpernel, galloping through the jungles of Vietnam, teasing and stinging the enemy and setting wrongs right. O.B. and his boys would zap the weak spots, nip at their flanks, then deftly elude capture and come back to do the same thing tomorrow.

Only here they were, pinned down, bad guys on all sides of them, bullets whining and whizzing around like a symphony of zithers. O.B. was quite popular with his troopers, largely because of his devil-may-care insouciance in the face of danger. He was given to walking down the middle of the road in disputed country, daring the Cong to shoot at him; he would be the first to run through a very storm of projectiles to drag a wounded comrade back; that sort of thing. This attitude endeared him to the grunts, but right now, as the NVA elected to start whistling a few B-40 rockets up toward the top of the hill, and the ARVN, not a group to hide their light under a bushel (at least when conditions were right, and these seemed ideal) pulled out their M-79s and began to lob grenades in that direction, no one was walking in the middle of the road. Or everyone was, so to speak.

Just as the rockets and grenades walked up toward Obradovitch's bomb craters, the 81mm mortar rounds surely ambled toward Colonel Creed's flight line. Others skipped up to the hobo camp on the other side of the runway, causing a bevy of nude sunbathers to scatter to the winds, dicks whipping and elbows pumping, in search of bunkers, in that most colorful dispersion of aviators previously alluded to, likely a harbinger of Chippendale's all-male nude dance review. Colonel Creed did not give a fuck about the hobo camp; tents were expendable, and pilots certainly were, there being a glut of those—groupies and wingies, staff pogues— who would kill to get a combat mission. He gave a great plenitude of fucks, however, about his airplanes. They were most absolutely *not* expendable, and now these regrettable ARVN upstarts were fixing to blow some up. Get some. He wondered to himself why the American military couldn't just fight this little war in time-honored fashion. Why did the Vietnamese have to be involved? They were unreliable. Well, be that as it may, this was a crisis situation and something must be done. Quick. He called S-3 and told them to send all the F-4s that were airworthy to Thailand and hide the rest. They would keep the squadron of older, cheaper F-8s around, for perimeter defense, harassment, interdiction, et cetera.

Rawlins, Moon Dog, DeWayne Ludlow, who had two years of college, some groupie major sniveling a hop, and their RIOs were briefing a ho-hum Blue Blazer mission when Cavendish rushed in from the Operations Office bubbling with enthusiasm. He told them their flight was to recover in Thailand and stay there and fight the war UFN. They had fifteen minutes to go get money, socks, skivvies, and a spare flight suit. The unfortunate major from Group was bumped because nobody knew when they were coming back yet, and surely he had a most important role to play in some local planning room or materiel office. Cavendish had written himself down in the major's spot. Imagine that, even Cavendish would fly if it was going out of country.

"Well," said Candyass Cavendish, "I guess I had better assume the leadership of this strike."

"Wrong," said Rawlins.

"Right," said Moon Dog, "*wrong.*"

DeWayne Ludlow said nothing, but he was also thinking "Wrong."

"Now, look, Lieutenant," said Cavendish, pained by this rejection of authority.

"I'm not looking, and none of this Lieutenant bullshit," said Rawlins. "The hop is briefed. I'm leading and you're tail-end Charlie. Think of it this way. Only a man of your accomplishments could fill the shoes of a major, a field grade officer, in this lash-up. Now, your RIO will brief you while I go get my checkbook and six cans of raw oysters."

"Right," said Moon, and they walked out.

Everybody walked out except Cavendish's back-seater. Even the group briefing officer walked out. Cavendish gnashed his teeth and muttered under his breath, but what was he to do? Everybody had gone. Well, he would bring this insubordination up, at least obliquely, at the next All Officers Meeting.

So the boys roared off into the cheerful sky, flung a mess of bombs into the primeval forest at "suspected enemy positions," and landed at Ubon, Thailand. And it was purely heaven. They made a run on the PX for civvies, aviator-type wristwatches with many dials and buttons (the definition of a fighter pilot at that time being someone with a great big watch and a little tiny peter), and pearls and sapphires for their female acquaintances. All that stuff was available at twenty-five or fifty cents on the dollar because it was tax-free. All except an adequate selection of civvies. They had not a pair of pants that even approached the dimensions of Moon Dog's concrete-block body (33 x 29). He had to settle for a pair of shorts and what was voted unanimously the ugliest "sport" shirt ever conceived by the international brotherhood of tailors. And high-top black tennis shoes with green socks. Back in Da Nang the only things the Marine PX sold were Lucky Strikes, Barbasol, foot powder, metal mirrors with holes in them to hang on your tent pole, and writing paper.

Next stop was the Australian officers club. After a few games of "Dead Bug" and great drenches of whiskey and beer, Hang Dog introduced his new game, "Cocksuckers Can't Dance," to the Aussies. They thought it was a bully amusement and added it to their official recreation calendar. And the blokes were perceptive. They had the book on Candyass Cavendish inside of three minutes. And handled him masterfully, Rawlins later thought. At first, quite subtly, they drew him out and established themselves as respectful, if not awestruck, listeners to his declamations on how the real war was being waged. They were not at that time participants in the hostilities, but were just showing the flag, as it were. After a few strong ales, Candy warmed to his subject and began to offer reconstructed adventures that, they were quick to agree, were "bloody chilling, mite." And they quietly began another game, some ways off from where Cavendish was holding court. It had to do with hoisting a pitcher of beer up to the ceiling and propping it there with a hand-held broomstick. You had then to close your eyes and see how many times you could walk around the broom without becoming dizzy, staggering, and spilling the beer all over yourself. One fellow did ten revolutions. Another twelve. Then fifteen. The interest gradually increased, wagers were made, shouts of encouragement and challenge were thrown about, and the game became the center of attraction. Someone wondered if the American captain might not like to have a go at their little contest. It was, he was assured, a function of the hard-polished skills of the true fighter pilot to develop his innate grasp of balance and the wherewithal to retain control in the most trying of circumstances; his resistance to vertigo. By all means, he must keep his eyes closed the entire time, or there was no sport in the thing. In one of the older japes of such larrikins, by the time Cavendish worked up to seventeen circumferences, the club had quitely emptied. Bartender and all.

"Good on yer, mite," cheered the last man out the door. "Yohwa the undisputed champ."

The rickshaw race to town sobered them up some, what with the cool breeze created by the sweating Siamese, pedaling their brains out, urged on, exhorted if not actually whipped by their exhilarated Caucasian fares, with money riding on the outcome. But the boys knew there was twenty *baht* in it for the winner, so they tried harder than might have been expected. A dollar was a lot of money to those kids.

First order of business in town, "to get the road dust off one, don't you know," was a stop at the hotsy bath for an all-over sudsing, massaging, manipulating, etc., by those genuine girls. After the communal bath, they repaired with their masseuses to partitioned cubicles for the best part. But then the ball-busting began in earnest. The jeers and gibes, the catcalls. The lean and mean and couthless, climbing over the flimsy partitions into each other's cubicles to shout encouragement, derision, anything that came to mind. Anything for a laugh; there were no boundaries of taste. Rawlins had drawn a girl named Nantena. He shortened it to Antenna. Moon Dog required not one but two girls, paid the extra price, to grope and knead his coarse body. The spirit of the orgy was contagious; everybody joined in, even the girls, to an extent, because there was plenty of money flying around. The banter increased in volume and pace and slipped inexorably further off-color because of desperation and oneupsmanship. The long-deprived prisoners of the base at Da Nang had a lot of steam to blow off. They began to chortle and whistle; they gave off imperspicuous yowlings and babblings in salacious imitation of excitement, ecstasy, and surrender; Bronx cheers resounded. They swung from the rafters, emitting Tarzanic yodels, pounded their chests, and manipulated their penises. It was not unlike the monkey cage at any zoo.

They next assembled at the King Star Club for serious drinking. They sat around low tables with varying numbers of bar girls, who would sit and talk and pretend to drink for ten *baht* an hour and who would, of course, be available later for whatever adventures might ensue. And the party went on.

Moon Dog's so-called sport shirt stole all the thunder and lightning from the colored lights that reflected off the lazily rotating mirrored globe suspended from the ceiling. The shirt was the brightest and loudest thing in the club. Among the first to be attracted by that visual clamour were the military police who busted Moon for wearing shorts after sundown. There was, they explained, a U.S. Air Force LAW that military personnel could not wear short pants off the base at night, there being a prevalence of indigenous disease-carrying insects, to wit, mosquitoes.

" 'Old on, mite," said the senior Aussie at the table. "This officer is serving on exchange duty with the Ohstreyelian Aeyha Fowhce and we don't 'ave any such bloody rule."

Moon grinned through his Hitler mustache. " 'At's roight, mite," he said in fairly poor mimicry of down-under lingo.

The young AP, sensing that his position was not overly tenable, elected not to have seen anything, in the interest of untroubled waters for the rest of his shift. Why open a can of worms? He judiciously shook his head slightly and moved away. And the party continued.

There are those who would say that Rawlins over-partied that night, but such a concept had no legitimacy with the boys of that time and place. He remembered only fleeting fragments of the middle-to-late fractions of that particular liberty. He snapped awake at four-thirty, in a narrow bed in a narrow shack, with a warm, sleeping body beside him. He remembered, vaguely, being with the girl, but not where or how he had met her. There was something sinister swimming around there in the backwaters of the brain-housing group. Ah, yes. The rickshaw. Wispy images floated through, of them riding and riding in a rickshaw, like around in circles, maybe. The town wasn't that big. And the girl having words with the cabbie, then arguing, maybe a little drunk herself, but protesting something, apparently the route he insisted on taking, and Rawlins, drunk, not understanding anything, not caring much, only wanting to get wherever the hell it was they were going, and more argument and the buggy finally stopping, the girl saying, "Come on, we walk from here," and then the rickshaw boy, a little pushy out here in some unlighted back street of a little town in Thailand, wanting a hundred *baht*—a *hundred baht*—ten times what it should be to anywhere in this town, and Rawlins, *No fucking way, pal, I'll give you ten*, but then him demanding the hundred, and two more boys materialize, with machetes in their sashes, ominous, and the girl saying, *You better pay*, and yelling at the boys in Siamese that had to be less than polite, Rawlins seeing through the vapors, but clearly for the moment, his survival instincts aroused, that yes, he'd better pay, and paying. But now, awake and somewhere near sober in the small, creaky bed, the girl beside him, still flushed, and he, mindlessly mindful of their recent lust, thinking to rub up against her again, but then, no, back to the base.

The rain was drumming quietly but steadily on the tin roof of the one-room hootch. In the dim predawn he saw an infant sleeping in a makeshift crib. He got into his clothes and tiptoed out the door. Along the front of the hootch, which was on stilts like all the dwellings there, to distance it from mud, water, snakes, leeches, and what have you, ran a narrow porch, roofed, but open on the sides. There, on a cot, slept the husband. With no real idea of where he was, Rawlins set out through the mud, in the warm, soft, steady rain, toward a glow of light against the mist that must be downtown. Judging from the weather, there would be no launch this morning, but something there was within him that rejected, emphatically, the idea of having a cup of tea with his host family. He had to get away from there. He craved a shower and ham and eggs on a stainless-steel tray and people who talked American. How soon we become surfeited with pleasures of the flesh.

And how soon we can become surfeited with the thrill of combat. Obradovitch and his boys, by now nearly all wounded to some degree, were huddled in two bomb craters, firing in all directions. They could not really see anyone to shoot at, but continued to return sporadic fire. It seemed like the bastards were all around them.

From the next ridge over, observing the melee through a pair of antique French opera glasses liberated from a former rubber plantation, were a group of *real* Vietcong, who, not surprisingly, thought a good deal like Obradovitch did. To avoid undue scrutiny from FACs, RECON patrols, and other such pernicious meddlers, they had disguised themselves in ARVN uniforms.

Through their opera glasses, the real Cong saw things this way: An ARVN patrol was hiding in a tree line in the narrow valley below and firing a hail of small arms and grenades up toward the next ridge over, where they saw glimpses of troops in black pajamas, their own wonted uniform of the day. And it also appeared that their supposed brothers, more Cong, on the facing ridge—but in reality ersatz Cong, their bitterest enemies, Marines, though that was unknown to the real Cong, ersatz ARVN—that their brothers were also taking fire from the *other* side of that ridge. The bastards had them surrounded!

"Very interesting," said one of the inscrutable real Cong, peering through the glasses between bamboo shoots. "I didn't know any of our boys were supposed to be up in this sector today."

"Let me have a look," said another comrade. "You know, I'll bet it's a detachment from the Chu Lai Chamber of Commerce. They get up this way once in a while." He lowered the opera glasses and inserted a fresh quid of betel nut between his black teeth. "Whoever it is, they need some help, and not this afternoon."

So the Popular Liberation Front, dressed in ARVN uniforms, set up their tubes and began whistling B-40s down on the ARVN, also dressed in ARVN uniforms.

When Brass Balls Obradovitch and his boys, dressed in Cong uniforms, observed this phenomenon, they cheered. *Someone* was giving them a little hustle, taking some of the heat off. High fives were exchanged all around. The ARVN patrol did not cheer, but silently booed as they dug in under what logs and timber they could find. O.B. couldn't see who was down in the valley shooting at him, but, scanning the opposite ridge with his Zeiss Icon German binoculars, he saw what appeared to be ARVN troops coming to his rescue. He cheered again.

The NVA, meanwhile, had reached the top of O.B.'s ridge, some two or three hundred meters farther along from his position. As they peered through their Russian PSO-1 sniper scopes, it seemed that a bunch of their friends must be down in the valley, because they were shelling those assholes masquerading as Cong, which was good; they cheered silently. But they also observed what appeared to be an ARVN unit, which was really their brothers the Cong in disguise, scattered along a tree line on the facing ridge, who began shelling what appeared to be their friends but was in fact their enemies the real ARVN, unseen in their wooded position in the valley, which was bad. They booed silently and opened up on the other ridge, the Americans forgotten for the moment. Upon discovering that they were under attack from some unknown force in a different position on the opposite ridge, the real VC booed rather spiritedly and turned their weapons in that direction, the unknown force down in the valley forgotten for the moment. Which caused the real ARVN down in the valley to cheer with some gusto, execute high fives, or an Asian derivative, and renew their attack on Obradovitch, who they thought was the Cong. The rest of the NVA unit, still working their way up O.B.'s ridge, continued to pour all kinds of lead at the real Americans, dressed as Cong, in the bomb craters, as did the real ARVN, relieved of pressure from the real Cong, dressed as ARVN, on the other ridge. Obradovitch's position at the moment was still not highly tenable.

Someone looking down on it all, from an airplane high above the battle, might have found this firefight most damnably confusing. In fact, someone did. The two scouts that Obradovitch had sent for the cavalry had made it to friendly lines. One of them had set out guiding a REACT company to fight their way back in. The other trooper had boarded an observation plane with a forward air controller to see if they couldn't direct some air strikes in there to spring O.B. And as they looked down on the tumultuous scrap, it was indeed highly confusing. It was an enigma.

Probably few people were more confused than the Daily Harassment Detail of the Vietcong, a few miles away, near the air base, who were following O'Flynn and Hebblethwaite, who were following Tran Van Ban, only they didn't know that yet.

But as O'Flynn and Hebblethwaite tiptoed through the tules, they came upon an ARVN soldier, in full uniform, perusing a sheet of paper that looked, to O'Flynn, surprisingly much like a copy of the squadron flight schedule, though he couldn't be sure at that range. It was. They had come upon Tran Van Ban, who was in the employ of Major Poltroun at twenty bucks a week, and to whom the major furnished unlimited tracer rounds and a copy of each day's flight schedule. (*Shedjool*, Barbi Belheur would have said.) This arrangement was a sinecure of the most opulent adiposity to Ban, amounting to more than three times his soldier's pay of three-thousand piasters a month. It was also a good deal for Major Poltroun, who was collecting Air Medals even faster than the Air Force generals and colonels, aces all from Korea and/or World War II, who jumped out of a brand-new F-4C a week on average, hanging in there too long, pressing on a little far, striving for the next elusive MiG that would push them closer to the five that would signal ACE again, for the second or third time in a career; but then running out of gas in their zeal and having to jump out; or who, being advised (as prebriefed) by underlings in their wing-fighter-sweep turkey shoot that there was a confirmed bandit somewhere in the hemisphere, headed for its reported position, unleashing missiles from miles away, ever bloodthirsty for that one more kill, some of which missiles, it was rumored, found the wrong targets, further depleting materiel and, almost certainly, the morale of the occasional junior officer who, if he was lucky, rode home in a Jolly Green

Giant–type helicopter. But if you observed hostile fire on any hop, you got two points toward your next Air Medal, and Poltroun was piling them up. On one hectic day, there being no company grade swine handy, Poltroun agreed to taxi a bird to the compass rose down by the end of the runway, to swing, or align, the compass. Tran Van Ban, not having fully mastered the intricacies of the inscrutable American policy regarding service in his country, dutifully gave Poltroun a couple of bursts of tracers, right there on the ground, idling, on the compass rose, with maintenance men on the wing and the turtle back, adjusting the compass system; gave him those bursts, although in some peril of being discovered, but gave them nonetheless, just like he was paid to do. The two points were disallowed by Operations, on the technicality that Poltroun had never left the ground, and for that reason was not deigned to have been on a combat mission. That decision, however, was overturned by a higher court that said, ". . . in an antipathetic atmosphere such as that prevalent in the Vietnam police action, any hostile fire whatsoever shall constitute the qualification." Tran Van Ban, in short, was a good employee. It was a damn shame to lose him. But lose him Poltroun must surely do. The fortunes of war.

As O'Flynn and Hebblethwaite huddled in the brush watching Ban, and the Daily Harassment Detail crouched in some more brush, watching them watch him, the scream of the engines of Poltroun's flight could be heard approaching. The stage was set. Ban tucked the flight schedule, upon close inspection of which, incidentally, one may have remarked Slocum's and Hang Dog's names listed under club duty for the two hours of this launch segment, which fact was concurrently precipitating yet another small tragedy having to do with Slocum's .38 and Nguyen Van Dan's ass, but Ban tucked that schedule into this pocket, chambered a tracer round, and pointed his weapon heavenward.

Even as Ban's rifle was jerked toward the sky, Slocum's pistol was being jerked from its shoulder holster. Nguyen Van Dan, as has been suggested, found his position atop the bamboo scaffolding to be something less than tenable, what with the snarling, bellowing Slocum clamoring after him with the darkest kind of threats and looking, for all the world, as if he were quite sincere. And since the bucket of mortar had dumped itself on his head, old Slocum was becoming downright lively. In a fairly rapid demonstration of logical progression, Dan had formed a compelling thesis. Its premise was that, by all indications, this was not the most propitious kind of society with which he might mingle. In short, there was nothing for it but to bail on over the wall and seek safety elsewhere.

In the split second it took for Slocum to fling the bucket about seventy-five yards, wipe the mud from his eyes with one ham-fist, and jerk out the .38 with the other, Dan had negotiated the top of the wall and was rolling over it. Slocum spluttered a screeching, seething, tremolo oath as the pistol descended. He discharged one round, which entered the posterior extremity of the fleeing Dan, who fell over the wall. Slocum then fired his remaining five bullets into the wall out of pure agitation. This produced such a hail of ricocheting lead and stone fragments that Hang Dog hid behind a wheel barrow until he was sure the cylinder was empty. So one well-placed round, fired in the heat of insane anger and frustration, furnished Nguyen Van Dan with a brand-new, but unneeded and thoroughly unwanted, asshole.

Which landed him in sick bay for a couple of days, where he lay in his bunk, prone, not supine, glowered, and uttered the Vietnamese equivalent of "Fuck this shit, man." Dan vowed that, when ambulatory, his first priority would be to escape and rejoin the Cong. Maybe the food wasn't as good, but by God it was a whole lot safer to be the enemy of these Occidental swine than it was to be their friend.

Of course Slocum had to be tried for "reckless endangerment" of a prisoner, but, on the strength of Hang Dog's testimony that the prisoner was trying to escape, the action was deemed necessary and Slocum skated on the charge.

Who didn't skate on his charges was Gunnery Sergeant O'Flynn, whose M-16 buzzed and spat at the same time Slocum was blasting away at the offending wall of the OM club. That O'Flynn would not skate but would be forced to answer to charges was the result of yet another unforeseen action, one of combat journalism, that would thoroughly befuddle the Daily Harassment Detail and Gunnery Sergeant O'Flynn, and, to a lesser extent, ultimately, Colonel Creed. Hebblethwaite was already fairly befuddled and so was not much affected.

As Poltroun's flight screamed into view, Ban opened up, full auto, all tracers, just waving the barrel, not trying to hit anyone. In fact, being downright certain, if it were known, that, indeed, he did *not* hit anyone. Chiseled into his brain pan, graven there for life, was the memory of the summary, albeit hegemonic ass-chewing he had received from an apoplectic Poltroun the last time he accidentally shot him down. That shit would not be tolerated. The next time he even came *close* to Poltroun's airplane he could kiss his twenty bucks a week good-bye, and his ass too. Although Ban had never fully understood why that crazy Caucasian gave him all that money to shoot at him, shoot and *not* hit anything, mind you,

Ban was not so ingenuous as to gauge too minutely the incisors of the *gratis equine*. Twenty bucks was twenty bucks. So he fired in the general direction of the flight, but aiming carefully, so as not to hit them.

Of course O'Flynn couldn't know that. The way he saw it, he had the drop on the phantom sniper who was forever putting holes in his airplanes. He was in position to eliminate a source of chronic damage to the all-American war efforts of his father-mother-lover, the Marine Corps. It was perhaps the high-water mark of his career. O'Flynn, transported with the zeal of righteousness, jumped out of the bushes, rifle at the ready, and roared, "Drop it or I waste your ass, gooner."

The Daily Harassment Detail thought things were getting curiouser and curiouser. First they observed a member of the Army of the Republic of Vietnam shooting at the American planes. That meant he was on their side. Yay. They cheered silently. They then saw the weird Americans, dressed in grease-stained utilities and without any infantry combat gear, but with guns, throw down on their buddy, the renegade ARVN. Boo. At first they were going to ambush the Americans, but now the friendly ARVN was in the line of fire and they hesitated. They might hurt their buddy. On the other hand, if they didn't take a chance and hurt *somebody* pretty quick, their buddy was most *assuredly* going to get hurt. Then the plot thickened noticeably.

Unbeknownst to any of these combatants, the *Stars and Stripes* staffer had observed O'Flynn and Hebblethwaite loading their weapons and ammo into the jeep and checking their map, and, having a nose for news, decided to tag along and see if there was a story here. Just as everybody was getting ready to shoot everybody else, he popped out of a shrub with a Speed Graphic and started shooting pictures of Tran Van Ban shooting at the airplanes, and O'Flynn, readying himself, in no uncertain gesture, to begin shooting at Tran Van Ban. The staffer had not yet seen the DHD, who were about to commence firing at O'Flynn and Hebblethwaite. When that detail saw the photographer, however, one member grabbed the other by the arm and whispered urgently, "Don't shoot! Think of the propaganda value of an American dog shooting his brother-in-arms dog, an ARVN, in the back. If you fuck up this kind of visual statement, for all the world to see, the Political Cadre will have your ass in a Hanoi minute."

So they, in effect, sacrificed Ban, a picture being worth a thousand words and at least one friendly soldier. Of course Ban was not really friendly toward them, but observing his actions, they couldn't have known that.

When Tran Van Ban heard Gunnery Sergeant O'Flynn grunt "Drop it or I waste your ass, gooner," he became highly agitated. He was both surprised and alarmed. Ban was a fairly excitable sort anyway, and the furthest thing from his mind that summer day was to have an irate and heavily armed Marine spring up behind his back while he was shooting at *their* airplanes. Well, ostensibly, shooting at them. As O'Flynn's guttural command knifed into his consciousness, he was startled out of his combat boots. Ban whirled around with an involuntary jerk to contemplate that which threatened him. He was nonplussed. Routines were forgotten; procedures went out the window. He neglected to release the trigger of his weapon as he whirled. The rattling, bucking piece, spewing tracers, arced down toward O'Flynn. From his point of view, there was only one option. He opened up. As Staff Sergeant Hebblethwaite would testify at his court-martial, O'Flynn had absolutely no choice, no alternative; he must kill the wildly firing Ban or be killed himself.

"Hot damn," squealed O'Flynn, the blood lust at full tide. "I got that sumbitch, Hebb. That's the cocksucker's been shooting all them holes into our aircraft."

And O'Flynn honestly believed, knew to a certainty, that he had fired in self-defense. Only that damn-fool reporter from *Stars and Stripes* stood there snapping pictures the whole time. And when the one of O'Flynn, eyes burning brighter than the muzzle flashes, stitching a seam up Ban's gut, ran on the front page a week late under the headline

TRAGEDY OF CONFUSION HAMPERS WAR EFFORT

O'Flynn's goose was cooked. When the generals and ambassadors and politicians in Saigon saw that, they got right on the hook to General Jefferson. They wanted some fucking redress, General, and not tomorrow afternoon, right now. That shit couldn't be tolerated. The Daily Harassment Detail, lacking direction from higher-up, had decided just to let things run their course, and not meddle. It was a wise decision; they could not have caused their enemy nearly as much trouble by butting in.

So Colonel Creed had to convene a court-martial and bust O'Flynn to Staff Sergeant. He didn't want to, but the LAW was the LAW. And the subsequent reduction in pay and allowances would drive Mrs. O'Flynn into the enemy's camp as a full-blown dove.

Tran Van Ban had sometimes reflected that the twenty bucks a week was too good to be true. It had been. His war was over.

When Brass Balls Obradovitch saw the first Spad roll in and sprinkle its 20 mike-mike across his position, he began seriously wishing that *his* war was over, at least for a while. He need not have worried. All of O.B.'s men were by now either dead or wounded. He himself had a bullet hole in his left thigh, another in his right shoulder, and some shrapnel scattered around one ear and cheek. And now the goddamn gook Air Force was attacking him. People were shooting at them from *every* goddamn where, everything was turning smartly to shit, and he didn't see a way out. He could only hope those two troopers had gotten through and would materialize with a REACT force, and soon. He didn't know it, but they were on their way. For the nonce it looked as if things would surely deteriorate before they improved.

The VNAF, for their part, and according to their resolution, had been ferreting around looking for Cong, thinking to give the Americans a hand with this war when they were not strafing and rocketing their hated brothers the ARVN. Which actions had led them to stumble across this humongous firefight, which seemed from all the fire and smoke to be joined by several groups, most of which they couldn't see clearly from the air. What they *could* see was one bunch of what appeared to be Vietcong, dug in at the top of a ridge line. The VNAF were not in radio contact with anybody on the ground, but obviously these Cong were pinned down by friendly units, most likely American, so they rolled in and pulled their triggers in support of their brothers. The real Cong on the other ridge, upon seeing this development, soundly booed the VNAF for attacking *their* brothers. When the ARVN down in the valley saw it, they were torn between loyalties; it was, after all, their despised brothers-in-arms the VNAF who had taken over their headquarters forcing them to bivouac in the bombed-out Buddhist temple, and who were even now strafing and rocketing their fellow ARVN troops around the air base. On the other hand, they *were* attacking the abominable Cong, or at least they thought they were, so it was a push in the ARVN camp; no cheers were heard, but neither were the airplanes booed. Of course the NVA group, when they saw who the target was, gave ready and unbridled approbation to the air strikes. They thought, rightly, that the stupid VNAF were inadvertently attacking their own allies, whoever they were, the imposters, who had jumped the NVA originally and started this whole fracas.

As the VNAF continued their stafing runs, to the accompaniment of unheard cheers and curses, the grunt who had made it back to friendly lines and boarded the little O-1E Bird Dog with the forward air controller came back on the scene.

"Holy shit," he said to the FAC. "Those Spads are strafing my unit. We've got to get them out of there."

"I don't have their frequencies," said the pilot. "I'll try them on guard channel." He banked sharply and made a low pass over the target, waggling his wings as a sign to the VNAF. On guard he broadcast in the blind, "Vietnamese A-1s, Vietnamese Skyraiders, hold your fire. Pull off the target, you are attacking a friendly position. Repeat, A-1s hold your fire." And so on.

It happened the VNAF were not monitoring guard, which was of little significance, because they didn't speak much English anyway. But one of the pilots was well into his run before he saw the slow moving observation plane in his gunsight. By that time he had punched several twenty-millimeter holes through the aft fuselage and tail of the Bird Dog, which got the full attention of both FAC and passenger. "Holy shit," they said in unison, "we better get the fuck out of here." And they did as fast as their six-cylinder Continental would propel them, just a-shittin' and a-gittin'.

"Watch out for them fucking idiot Yankees," said one VNAF pilot to the other on their squadron common frequency. "I nearly blew that *trau dien* out of the sky."

"Rog," he replied. "Two's in hot." And they continued their runs.

"Lieutenant, we got to get them bastards out of here or they'll wipe out my unit." O.B.'s boy was loyal.

"You're right. I'll call Hayride and see if I can get somebody over here to chase them away."

Hayride was the Tactical Air Control Center for I Corps. When they heard that the VNAF were killing Marines, looked like they meant to continue doing it, and wouldn't talk to anybody on the radio, they didn't know what the fuck to do. So they called General Jefferson. Who called Colonel Creed. "Creed, every time one of those fucking Spads takes off, I want an F-8 boresighted on his ass, understood?"

"Aye, aye, sir. Under what conditions do we shoot?"

"Get every FAC in I Corps airborne ASAP. Monitor the net. Talk to the grunts. If a Spad should even so much as make one of our ground commanders uneasy, blow that son of a bitch out of the sky. Is that clear?"

"Yes, General. The F-8s are on full alert. I'll pass the word along."

Colonel Creed did not really want to shoot down the VNAF planes, because they were helping to harass those contumacious fucking ARVN, and if successful, would drive them out of the Buddhist temple so he could get back to work. But somehow he sensed that this was not the moment to argue that point with the general. He passed the word along.

Next General Jefferson called Nguyen Kao Ky, the Prime Minister of South Vietnam and Commandant of the VNAF. "Listen, buster," he said informally. "Your goddamn Spads have been strafing some of my Marines, and that shit's got to stop. *Comprende?* Now what I want you to do is cease air operations. Just ground those fucking planes until we get this sorted out. Is that clear?" It was the repeat of an old pattern in Jefferson's ingrained command acumen. It had worked before and it would work again. If, for some reason, things turned to shit, just shut down operations. It was his tried-and-true technique.

Ky did not agree. "Not possible, General. We have a mission of utmost gravity that must be pursued. The stability of my country is at stake."

"Oh, that's all well and good, Premier, but as far as I'm concerned, one Marine is worth more to me and my superiors than your entire goddamn government. Now what I have instructed my people to do is this: Every time one of your Spads takes off, there will be an F-8 Crusader behind it, armed with sidewinders and cannons. If one more Marine gets hurt, I'll turn your fucking Air Force into scrap iron. Do you read me?"

Ky, hardly a shrinking violet when it came to matters political, slammed the receiver down. Hung up on his general-officer ass. He next instructed his people to configure a dozen Spads for air-to-air combat. Every time an F-8 took off, he wanted a Spad right behind it.

Back on the ridge top, Obradovitch was in deep shit and getting in deeper. Quickshit, they might have called it in a Tarzan movie. He was being pounded with bullets, rockets, and grenades by what seemed like everybody in the universe, now including airplanes; his troopers were eating it; and he didn't see how he was going to get out of this one.

Nobody else did either. Both the NVA and the ARVN thought they had him nailed. When a Spad would roll in for another run, they would cheer, even though all of them despised the VNAF under quasi-normal circumstances. Even the real Cong, dressed as ARVN, on the other ridge, were afraid Obradovitch (who they thought was their friend, but wasn't) was for it. They didn't see how they could keep him from being overrun.

And the REACT force, working their way cautiously down the ridge toward O.B.'s position, who had held up in a tree line to assess the situation, weren't sure just how they could spring him either. The company commander had to figure out where all this fucking shot and shell was coming from and who was launching it. He was not going to just rush headlong into something he couldn't evaluate.

Overhead in the Bird Dog, the FAC was in radio contact with a couple of A-4 Skyhawks that had been diverted to help out. First he had them make a couple of passes through the VNAF's pattern to chase them away. The Spads pulled off and held in a Luftbery circle, trying to figure out what the Sam Hill was going on here, although it appeared for every practical purpose that the Americans were making bomb runs on the same ridge that they had been strafing.

How true that turned out to be. The second A-4 was piloted by the dexterous manipulations of Calvin Coolidge Jones, younger brother of Lieutenant R^2 Jones, who was on his first combat mission. C^2, they called him. Actually, C. C. Jones was only twelve minutes younger than R. R. Jones—they were identical twins. Identical not only in appearance, but in propensity and proclivity, in demeanor and deportment. Two identical nerds. C^2 had been experiencing some intermittent radio problems, but he didn't realize the extent of them. His receiver was fading in and out, so that he heard some transmissions fine, but at other times people were talking and he didn't know a thing about it. He had missed much of the expository chatter from the FAC, detailing what he wanted them to do and why. He had dutifully followed his leader around on two runs that he understood were to be "cold." But he had not heard who these mock attacks were directed at and why. The next thing C^2 heard, back up in the pattern, was the FAC clearing them in hot on their next pass. What he didn't hear was the FAC explaining that they had "done good," the VNAF had pulled back and no longer threatened the friendlies; now they could get down to work. That the *real* bad guys were down in the valley, dug in at the edge of the jungle; that the FAC was out of willie peter and couldn't mark the target, but to roll in on the same heading as before and drop their first ordnance along the edge of the canopy at the bottom of the valley adjacent to where they had just buzzed the ridge. But all C^2 heard was that they were cleared in hot, and, observing his leader's initial point and general heading, assumed, reasonably, that they could get on with the bombing of this ridge, now that those pesky Spads seemed to have cleared the area.

"Two's in hot," piped C^2 Jones, and it was eerie how much he sounded like his brother. And flew like him. He was well below pattern altitude, overshot the leader's roll-in point, still concentrating on the ridge instead of the valley, and ended up with a long, shallow run. And, though it was hidden by his oxygen mask, it was eerie how much C^2 grinned like R^2 when he saw the leader's hit. He almost giggled when he observed that the leader had missed the whole damn ridge and dropped his bombs clear down in the valley. "Must be a crosswind," he said to himself. What he really meant was "What a Dilbert. I'll show 'em how to hit that little old ridge." That stupid grin, it seemed, was a family trait. Yeah, "I'll show 'em how to hit that little old ridge."

Which was exactly what occurred to Obradovitch and his gang when they saw the A-4 boring down straight at them. "My God, hit the deck! He's going to drop on our little old ridge!" Out of the ultimate frustration and fear and anguish, they fired everything they had at that son of a bitch, their brother. Rounds large and small, smoke grenades, a LAW rocket or two. Now they were even being attacked by Marine Air.

They needn't have bothered. C^2, in his shallow dive, released a little late and overshot the target. The two 250-pound, general-purpose, low-drag bombs sailed past O.B. and up the ridge toward the REACT company who were *in medias res* of effecting the rescue of those unfortunates. The second of the 250-pounders landed close enough to the REACT, hunkered down in the tree line on the top of the ridge, to send angrily buzzing shrapnel and noticeable fire and concussion their way. Whereupon, out of frustration, fear, and anguish, they too fired most of what they had at the son of a bitch. Their own brother Marines, bombing them!

They needn't have bothered either. Calvin Coolidge Jones's dive angle was sufficiently low, and his release sufficiently late, to cause his airplane, a little A-4 Scooter at that, hard for anyone else to hit, to hit itself with fragments of its own bombs, dead perfect in a sort of ineluctable progression of the theories of physics. Or, "an inevitable occurrence due to the action of immutable natural laws." Hit itself at the required critical points to bring about the combinations of fuel, fire, electricity, oxygen, ammunition, and general elements of combustion to enshroud it in a sheet of flame. And as that fireball pulled off the target, POOF! C^2 Jones popped out of the flames atop his ejection seat, probably grinning stupidly because he had beat the system again. Well, not really. He landed amidst the second and third three-man cells of the first element of the NVA who were besieging Obradovitch. His war was effectively over. The rest of it would be spent at *Hao Lo*, the Fiery Furnace, or the Hanoi Hilton, however you wished to call it. Heartbreak Hotel, nonetheless. And that incarceration would surely cause reverberations at *much* higher levels of command; higher by far than any at which Lieutenant C^2 had presumed to present himself. But that would be seen later. No, his war was effectively over.

When the various assembled combatant groups observed the explosion of the American airplane, *everybody* cheered. Even the Real ARVN, pinned down in the valley, cheered politely. Oh, sure, they were generally well-disposed toward the friendly American air presence, and they would have rooted enthusiastically for C^2's attempt to annihilate Obradovitch, but after his leader had just bombed the shit out of *them*, some animosity toward that outfit lingered. So they cheered. Of course Obradovitch and his remaining boys, and of course the Marine REACT company, cheered. The son of a bitch had tried to grease them. The Real VC and the NVA merely applauded out of parochial team support. The FAC and his observer were neutral.

The leader of the A-4 flight set up a holding pattern over his downed wingman, determined to protect that unfortunate until search and rescue got there. He needn't have bothered. Oh, yeah, the Jolly Green Giant would come, but they would find no Calvin Coolidge Jones. He would be on his way to Hanoi, elbows lashed tightly behind his back, and no rod being spared.

At about that stage of events, the next pair of VNAF Spads arrived and began chattering with their squadronmates, who were still on station, on their discreet frequency. The new, freshly armed Spads were followed by the first section of F-8s, orbiting at ten thousand feet, who were followed by the third section of Spads, ACM configured, watching the F-8s watch their brothers, at fifteen thousand feet. They, of course were followed by the second section of F-8s, orbiting at twenty-five thousand feet, watching everybody watch everybody else. The Spads couldn't go any higher, so that was the end of the stack, except for the occasional Air Force or Navy flight returning from their targets, who might stop and loiter a while at thirty or forty thousand feet to watch the fun.

"Yeah," the leader of the original element of Spads was saying to his relief man, "there's VC in those old bomb craters at the top of the ridge. We gave 'em what we had, but we were low on ammo. Then some American A-4s dropped bombs on them, but they shot one of them down. They're still alive and kicking, though. There's friendlies on both sides of the ridge keeping them pinned down, but they can't get at them. It's a nice target, give 'em hell. Get some."

"Ah, roger, old sport," said the section leader, who had gone to flight school in France and then done an exchange tour with the Australian Air Force. "We'll give it a bloody go, mite." And in he rolled.

As the Spads positioned themselves to put the *coup de grace* on Obradovitch, the F-8s positioned themselves to put the same thing on the Spads. "You've got to get those fucking Spads out of there," said the tensely excited FAC to the F-8 drivers, "or the Marines are dead."

The F-8 drivers had their orders. "If one more Marine gets hurt. . . ."

Obradovitch had heard the REACT shooting at the A-4 and figured it might be the cavalry. It now appeared that they had opened up on the dinks on either side of the ridge, and since they were the only bunch in the neighborhood who weren't shooting at *him*, he was sure they were indeed the relief unit, come to his rescue. They might get out of this one yet. As their situation in the bomb craters was reaching a most profound perigee, in terms of tenability, *in extremis*, so to speak, O.B. decided the only thing for it was to try to fight their way up to the REACT. To seek safety elsewhere. He feared, however, that the NVA may have attained the ridgetop and cut him off.

He was right. The NVA now had them surrounded on three sides, and the ARVN were still blasting away from the fourth one. It was going to be a very bloody hundred meters to reach those friendlies. But Obradovitch and his boys left the questionable safety of the holes and set out. This move would probably kill them, but if they waited they were dead for sure; the whole fucking sky seemed to be full of airplanes, and no end in sight; and for some reason everybody was shooting at *them*. So out they set, dragging and carrying each other, crawling, humping, firing randomly, those who still could, and taking hits randomly, groveling, every inch slow and painful and bloody. They had nothing left but the instinct of self-preservation and their duty to each other.

When the REACT advanced toward Obradovitch, they met a determined line of NVA regulars in the trees between them. The FAC hadn't seen this development, so no one had told them the enemy was there. Only with the embattled O.B. moving one way and the fresh rescuers moving the other, the NVA was caught in the middle and things got pretty hot for them. But things were pretty hot for everybody. Various of O.B.'s rounds whizzed through the bush, missing the NVA and hitting the REACT force. And vice versa. Lead flew everywhere. Finally the NVA, finding themselves suddenly in the minority, and outgunned, chose to withdraw, but only as the Spads were rolling in to administer the deathblow.

The first one sluiced the ragged, unprotected little band with cannon fire, killing a couple more. But now they were within yards of the friendlies; they were going to make it. Obradovitch was wounded in so many places that he wasn't even aware of them all, but miraculously, he was still going, driven by heart, by the *absolute* refusal to quit, by the uttermost determination to lead his troops out of this stygian conflagration. He staggered back along the ridge for the last Marine, who was in a shock-induced coma, having lost all of one leg, most of the other, and a good part of his innards to a rocket.

"My God," said the FAC, his voice so filled with emotion that he nearly wept. "It's a bloodbath. You've *got* to get those fucking Spads out of here."

"Fox one," came the laconic reply from the pilot of the lead F-8. And he loosed a Sidewinder that roared, looping off through the too-bright sky, leaving a sizzling, swirling trail of black smoke in its wake, and struck, directly, the exhaust manifold of the lead Spad, fulminating the old war-horse and its pilot into a thousand fragments. His war was over.

Though all parties were more or less aware of the explosion of the Spad, oddly, no one cheered. It had gone beyond that.

Just before Obradovitch reached his fallen comrade, a grenade detonated, nearly severing his left arm at the elbow. He felt almost nothing, but crouched there in the blinding sunlight, as in a period of apprehended time, and studied the flopping, useless limb like it belonged to someone else. But it was still attached by some sinews, and abstractly he knew it to be part of him. He grasped the dangling wrist with his good hand, tucked it up under its stump, and clasped it to his side. Then he gripped the collar of the wounded grunt and began, methodically, to drag him toward the friendlies.

The two pilots comprised in the third section of Spads had by this time brought their guns to bear on the unsuspecting F-8 leader, who had shot down their brother. As the F-8 belched smoke and fire, then an ejection seat and a parachute, then veered crazily off and crashed into the jungle, still no one cheered. All the contestants were, by that time, hurt and scared and miserable. They had lost that certain spirit, that *joie de vivre* that is necessary to a good war. Everybody was stung and whipped and smarting, and keeping a low profile.

As Obradovitch began to drag the trooper, he felt only disdain for the futile lumber of his flesh and the bullets and fragments that stung and sullied and stained and defiled it. The nineteen-year-old kid he dragged was already dead, but Obradovitch didn't know that. Nor would he have acted differently had he known. Obradovitch had very little left to lose, but one thing was paramount: He *would* deny even death itself any sort of victory over his will. And at that moment, the pilot of the second Spad in the second section salvoed a nineteen-shot pod of 2.75-inch rockets at the struggling figure on the ridge, and Obradovitch's war was over.

Three of his men made it back to the friendly lines alive, one of those died in the medevac helicopter, and another at Charlie Med. One survivor.

If Brass Balls Obradovitch had survived the day, they might well have court-martialed him; testimony might have shown that it was his hare-brained idea to dress up like Vietcong that was the proximate cause of the whole disaster. But he didn't survive, so instead they gave him the Congressional Medal of Honor. He probably deserved it as much as anyone else who ever got it. But his war was over.

Rawlins's war was almost over too, but he didn't know it. Captain America and his RIO's war, General Jefferson's; all were nearly over but none of them knew it.

Tran Van Ban's war was over; C² Jones's was effectively over, but his brother R² didn't know it for several days because he was whiskeying and whoring with the rest of the squadron in Thailand and carrying on the war without a war. R²'s was nearly over too, but he didn't know.

As Colonel Creed stood on the flight line and watched the two Phantoms, stuck there on their jacks, burn to rubble, and then gaped, absolutely stunned, as the ARVN mortar rounds found the fuel dump, he knew for a fact that his empire was dangerously close to crumbling. A couple million gallons of jet fuel makes quite a fire. Sometimes it seemed like this blasted war would *never* be over.

The F-8s shot down two more Spads before they wised up and skedaddled, but all the ground units had limped off in different directions to lick their wounds.

So nobody cheered.

21

California, 1980s

Life did go on at Vulcan V-belt and Avionic Pilotage System Corporation. In fact it went on and on and on, in an endless cycle of inactivity interrupted by sieges of intense panic characterized by days of wheedling, pleading, cajoling, exhorting the small army of engineers each to get his subsection finished in some form so that the document could be assembled more or less; then furious forays into the night to edit, spec, mark, label, and explain so typists and artists could make some sense of the jumble. Hand out the fresh, clean copies for reviews and critiques, and wait to do it all over again. Life went on, but it seemed to have lost a great deal of its meaning. Existence for Rawlins had become a gray pall of monotony, a slough of bureaucratic malaise. He no longer had any purpose. He would rise, groggy and hung over, shower and shave zombielike, drive to work, usually late, and pour that first cup of coffee. Often his chair would have a stack of the latest iterations of parts of some proposal or other on it. Those would have been dropped off in his absence, put on the chair to demand his immediate attention, before, even, he could sit down, each being more rattlingly crucial, critical, and important than the next, and so they wouldn't get lost among the other piles that littered his desk and table. Paper everywhere. Somewhat in the fashion of Barbi Belheur as she gazed at the governor's legislation-laden desk, Rawlins had an inkling of the fate of the virgin forests.

He would then engage his benumbed brain in the game of tracing the tortuous train of thought of the blithe scholar at hand. Through the shuffled sentences and paragraphs, the transposed clauses, the inverted structurings, following boxes and circles and arrows, deletions and insertions and notes, he would try to determine what was meant here. Rawlins decided that not only had Eisenhower christened the military-industrial complex, but that notoriously glib-tongued devil had also personally derived the organizational criteria and standard of syntax to be followed therein.

What was probably worse was the frequent day when his desk held no critical mass of verbiage. Nothing at all. Then he sat and slurped that coffee, with a generous jolt of sugar to coax the engines up to speed, and searched, with a care born of desperation, through his brain for something of interest. Something amusing, a pleasant memory, perhaps, or daydream to help him through the gloom of the next eight hours. Rawlins learned more about sports and business and politics than he had ever bothered to know as he scanned every corner of the newspaper on these mornings. He could bury himself in the crossword puzzle for half an hour and make the whole fucking aerospace industry go away.

Another thing that provided a spark of interest and helped preserve sanity was the memos they were forever receiving. The memos themselves were invariably insane, but the sport of trying to figure out what they meant and then correcting them to indeed say what it was surmised that they had been intended to was fun and good mental exercise, and did preserve sanity. A typical one arrived from Malcolm "Bud" Malison, manager and editorial mentor of the proposals group, one day. Bud Malison had long years of practice at concocting memoranda that couldn't be obeyed because they couldn't be understood. It said:

TO: All Proposals Personnel
SUBJECT: Secure Waste Paper Disposal System Procedures

It will have been noted that burn barrels exist throughout the Proposals work areas in strategic positions which provide capability for deposit and subsequent secure removal of suspect sensitive-type unclassified written and Graphics waste materials.

Plant Security has issued Directive no. 1133-80-JLH-013-2677 directing that all non-suspect sensitive-type written and Graphics waste materials (unclassified) other than food, drink, food and drink containers, metal objects, wooden objects, plastic objects, etc. also be provided with deposit and secure removal capability to preclude inadvertent disclosure due to personnel oversight. Directive no. 1133-80-JLH-013-2677 impacts Proposals personnel as per the following:

Sufficient waste bins shall strategically be positioned throughout the Proposals work areas so as to provide deposit/secure removal of waste materials comprised of nonfood, drink, metal, wooden objects, etc. materials. All personnel reporting to the undersigned *shall* support this directive and assure that all materials which compose paper products, typewritten materials, notes, computer-written material, sketches, graphs, Xeroxed material, etc. comprising non-suspect sensitive type (unclassified) written and Graphics materials not disposed of via burn barrels as aforementioned above shall be placed in separate waste bins as cited above from other obvious waste material for deposit/secure removal.

Plant Security shall then hopefully acquire the above-described materials and accomplish removal/disposal of it in like manner as to burn barrel material by destruction by the Division Shredder, in accordance with prioritization of Shredder availability.

M. X. "Bud" Malison
Proposals Manager

Rawlins studied it most of the morning. "Harley," he said at last, "I think it says we're supposed to put the trash in the wastebasket."

Although Malcolm "Bud" Malison was widely known for his deft touch with a memorandum pad, he was not alone in this expertise. His brother Haskell "Hack" Malison was also known to turn out a thoroughbred memo from time to time. Hack was the manager of the graphic arts expediters. Nepotism was a *fait accompli* at VVAPS, starting with the chairman of the board, whose wife owned the travel agency that sold all the tickets for all the generals, colonels, admirals, commodores, and engineers who set out daily in the direction of Dayton, Ohio, Patuxent River, Maryland, and Washington, D.C., in search of contracts. She did a nice piece of business, especially come time for the Paris Air Show every other year, which all vice presidents (eighty-seven of them) attended for two weeks. And of course when Paris popped up on the itinerary it was necessary that those of them who couldn't finagle a way out of it be accompanied by their wives. And in the off-years there was the Farnborough Show. A nice piece of business, and it was of passing interest to legions of Pentagon accountants that all those airplane tickets and hotel bills somehow ended up in the zero-based budget of some already-funded program or other.

But then nearly everyone was related to someone else who either worked directly for, or at least profited from, the VVAPS phenomenon. Harley's second wife was a manager of something or other. He couldn't remember just what. It was several big, happy families. All the blue-collar workers lived in Hawthorne or Gardena, clerks and typists in Torrance, middle bureaucrats in Long Beach and Manhattan Beach, big shots in Palos Verdes. And every once in a while a commuter from West Covina or the San Fernando Valley.

Because of the proclivity for professional incest, Hack Malison was able to arrange employment for his two sons, Zachariah "Zack" Malison, and Mervyn "Mack" Malison. They were both administrative assistants to other middle managers who in turn sent their sons and daughters to Hack and Bud for their jobs. It all worked very nicely, and once you got your foot in the door it was only possible to fire you if you were videotaped, recorded, fingerprinted, and observed by two or more agents of the Defense Industrial Security Clearance Office while engaged in the commerce of ideas with known operatives of the Komitet Gosudarstvennoy Besopasnosti and money was seen to change hands. And there was little danger of that, because VVAPS engineers, with all their "uniquely synergistic aerospace design acumen," were seldom able to come up with anything the Russians were really interested in. And the Russians never had any money anyway. One fellow was successfully terminated, over the protests of the Employee Relations squad, after having come to work only on Friday afternoons for two and a half years, to pick up his paycheck, while operating his own bookstore the rest of the time. He was sacked not for dereliction, but for turpitude. He sold chicken porn under the counter and the postal inspectors got him. But when you had once been blessed (cursed, Moon Dog and perhaps certain others would have said) with the VVAPS sinecure, it was not likely to be withdrawn. That was what troubled Rawlins. Was this for goddamn *ever?*

It was beginning to seem that it might be. Hack and Zack and Mack had been there since they were twelve and would stay as long as they lived. The engineers just died at their desks. Nobody ever left, because they were afraid to. The fears were variegated, but some of the more common ones were that they could not expect as much money for doing as little work at another company, that they would be looked for on-time in the morning and restricted to one-hour lunches, and, worst of all, they would have to learn a new system. Or learn *anything* new. The lifers were terrified of having to do things differently, of working in odd new places with frightening strangers and perhaps not being accepted, pampered, and given a raise every year. At VVAPS everyone had his niche and was tolerated by everyone else. None of them really liked it there, in fact they all hated it, but it was *safe*. And it was easy to rationalize. Wouldn't the work likely be just as maddening and the personalities just as unpleasant at any other company? At least here they knew where they stood. And it was bearable. Aerospace paid more money for clerks, and that is what most of them were, really, though they had grander titles. And they never fired you. And while one defense contractor is generally just as shoddy as the next, something there is within the seasoned bureaucrat that resists change at almost any cost. So nobody ever left.

Even as Rawlins remarked and appraised this phenomenon, he felt himself slipping into it. Part of it was the irrefutable recognition of mortality. Things were gradually coming to an end; he sensed that now, and he couldn't change it. So why make a bunch of waves at this point, when you could just be quiet and, as one of the ever-accelerating generational expressions had it, "go with the flow"? The only thing he had ever done that he really enjoyed was flying airplanes, and that was over. It appeared more and more likely that he would be stuck in some dead-end job or other until he died or somehow scraped enough money together to retire. As he approached fifty, his options diminished. Even if he could find some career course that promised to be rewarding, all of a sudden it seemed a little too late to be starting over. To try to go back to school to learn new tricks. And companies didn't much hire fifty-year-olds for entry-level positions.

No, with mortality and the actuarial tables hanging over him like a mantle it suddenly seemed too late in the game to become an architect or a lawyer. He would be forced to spend his final productive years scratching for a living, attempting to gain a foothold in a whole new endeavor; competing with younger people who had more drive and energy; and he would be running out of time. Even if he could attain some kind of professional success, and the odds of that happening were less than favorable, he might well die before he could really get it established and enjoy it. And anyway, he didn't yet have a great driving motivation in any direction. He hadn't thought much about it when he was younger, content just to let things happen as they happened, to keep on flying hops. So now he was a hack; and maybe, all things considered, it was as good a prospect as he had. After these insights he would usually pour himself a drink and begin to daydream about how good things once were. Then he would pour another drink and continue his descent. "Hesitation increases in relation to risk in equal proportion to age," Hemingway is said to have said.

One Saturday Rawlins and Harley Cadavery were sluicing down some scotch at one of their preferred saloons, which was on the lee shore of a yacht harbor and had a swell view. They liked this particular joint because it was the only one that didn't have a candle in a red glass with plastic netting around it on every table. And happy hour ran all afternoon on Saturday. They watched the boats of the semi-idle semi-rich tacking out past the jetty and drifted into serious solving of the world's problems.

"We're all too fucking worried. The whole country is paranoid." Harley tamped his pipe, wheezed forth a putrid cloud, and set to his task. "That's why there's so much crime and violence and swindling and laziness and provocation and misery and unrest. We're all scared to death.

"The conservatives have simple paranoia; the Russians are going to nuke us. The liberals' paranoia is complex; first we're going to nuke the Russians and *then* they're going to nuke us. Each side is terrified of the other's philosophy, probably with good reason."

Rawlins laughed. "The end is near anyway. Go for it, fuck it, grab it, steal it, withhold it, lie about it, deceive, cheat, take, dissemble. There's no tomorrow."

Harley knocked out his pipe and took a long sip. "They want it their way and they want it now. What the hell, we're doomed. It's a world that we didn't make and don't like and are going to be polluted and poisoned and incinerated out of. Nobody seems to have time to worry much about the other fellow these days."

More drinks came. Rawlins moved his in circles on the bar. "But every individual," he said, "lives in a society. You know, the nuclear family, the fifth grade, city, state, nation, or world. If he doesn't go by the rules, sooner or later he's gonna have to pay."

"Well," said Harley, refilling his pipe, "everybody is scared they might not be around next week. So they better grab what gusto they can get, and fuck the other guy, devil taking the hindmost and all that sort of thing."

A fellow, maybe in his forties, on the hirsute side, with graying temples, clad in a flocculent neon blue jacket that didn't fit well, approached Harley. "Excuse me," he said, "but that pipe smoke is annoying my date."

Harley removed the object under discussion from between his clenched teeth and exhaled another rancid cloud. He regarded the upstart with a withering glance. "I'm glad you mentioned that, sir. I was about to say the same thing to you. That perfume your significant other has on flat makes my eyes water."

The regulars at the bar, knowing Harley, began to laugh. The stranger didn't pursue it. "Well, I'd appreciate it if you'd put it out," he demanded and busied himself looking for the hostess, to request another table.

"See what I mean?" Harley sermonized with a huge grin. "No consideration. No concern for other people's rights. Hah! Fellow won't even let me smoke in peace." He rekindled the pipe.

The months moved into years and nothing really changed. An interesting thing about the concept of mortality was that it had been there forever, had been acknowledged as a concrete idea, yet it seemed so new. In Vietnam, when death was all around, when it showed itself every day and was always hovering somewhere nearby, it was just something you lived with. You could see it, hear it, smell it, sometimes even taste it in the dust swirling around a stack of body bags on the ramp, awaiting transportation. But he never thought about it. It was a rule of the sport. Rawlins wondered if he had just been callous, or had, in subconscious calculation, insulated himself against a weakness that might have been ruinous.

Because now, at middle age, ensconced in his safe cubicle in one of the acres and acres of windowless buildings filled with pencil-pushers, bathed in artificial light, he thought about death more and more. Whereas once, when one of his tentmates did not return from a mission, it scarcely seemed to have an effect on him, now it bothered him to read the obituaries in the newspaper. It was as if he were afraid he might see his own name. It seemed like everybody was dying these days. Movie stars, politicians, business leaders; they were dropping right and left from heart attacks, strokes, and cancer. Now, when perhaps the most dangerous aspect of his existence was the possibility of being hit by a bus as he crossed Crenshaw Boulevard, Rawlins began to fear death as he never had before. As he took the walks that he frequently did when he arrived home sober, he would calculate at thirty or fifty points on his three-mile circuit what the chances were of his being found in time should he suffer a heart attack; which house he could stagger to for aid. He stuck to well-traveled streets. He knew these notions were irrational, psychotic maybe, and fought them with whatever resolve and self-reliance he could summon. But they came and he couldn't shake them. It was absurd to return from a brisk walk along the esplanade, supposedly calmed by the plangent sound of the surf, in a state of near panic, to pour a drink and settle yourself down. But he couldn't vanquish the demon. And on hung-over days, nervous system whipped and poisoned, in an atmosphere pressurized by colorless, odorless stress as undetectable as methane gas, with almost imperceptibly growing frequency, the demon would come to his desk at VVAPS. Stalk right into his safe little cubicle would the fiend, fetching the chest pains and the shortness of breath. And the indeterminate terror. Just like it used to be in the airplane. He would get up from his desk, unable to concentrate or sit still, pale and sweating, heart racing, feeling bloated, and pace to the water fountain and back. On bad days he took a pill or went to lunch early. After the second or third drink he would begin to relax. Other times he would call up all he could muster and, in the most abject, if psychosomatic, pain and fear, he would fight it. Eventually it would pass. But, mentally at least, it was a most taxing ordeal to beat the devil cold. Then he owed himself a drink.

Rawlins had three recurring dreams. In the first, and oldest, he was flying without an airplane. It was magical; simply by concentrated effort he could soar to the heights. But he grew tired and always had to leap again with all his might and put forth every erg in his body, flap his wings harder as it were, to get over the next obstacle. Then it would seem that despite every effort he could not get over the next one. Then he would wake up, or the dream would end.

In the second dream, he would be back in his old squadron, scheduled to fly a hop. Everything was vaguely familiar, but he had been away a long time and didn't remember all the particulars. And he never had all his flight gear; always there were troubling thoughts in the back of his dream-mind. He was not current in the airplane. And he worried in his dream that once he got airborne the demon would come. There was always this reluctance to fly the hop. He didn't savor the idea of flying as he used to do and that was always puzzling in the dream. He felt distanced from that which had once been the norm of his life. Usually the dream ended before he ever got to the airplane, but sometimes he took off. But on those occasions he would always fuck something up: He would get lost or forget what he was suppos'd to say on the radio; he would forget his taxi instructions or land on the wrong runway. Often there would be hundreds of military aircraft in the area, flying in huge, loose formations, and he would have to avoid them; always some of the planes crashed, some of the pilots ejected. Nothing terrible ever happened to Rawlins in the dream, but it always ended on an unsatisfactory note.

In a variation of that dream he would be traveling on a commercial airliner. He always knew the crew and they would have him fly part of the way; but he was never really checked out in the huge transport and he was always having to ask someone how to do things; he could fly all right, but he didn't know the details. The regular pilot would take over for landing. And *he* always fucked that up; he would come perilously close to power lines, tall buildings, or hills. Usually they landed on a runway with high spruce trees on both sides and the wingtips barely missed them. He would get instructions at the counter and then have to run and run, heavy canvas suitcase banging against his knee, to get to the next flight, which would then be much like the first one, only he often sat in the passenger compartment on this leg. The trip was always the same. At some point he would end up driving a car back from these excursions, and would encounter vexing problems in finding the way back. They always got there but it was troublesome.

The third dream was simpler. He was back in the Marine Corps, often as a sergeant, billeted in vast transient barracks at Camp Pendleton. There was always an inspection coming up, and he never had a complete uniform. That dream ended two ways. He never got all the gear he needed, never got all squared away with a complete outfit. But sometimes he would go on liberty, south it seemed, into Mexico, which then became a combination of Mexico and Okinawa. It would end with his showing some less-experienced new acquaintance the old red-light section of the town. They would wander through narrow, crowded lanes until he found his favorite bar. He would recognize the place from years gone by, but all the people would be strangers. The girls would be impersonal prostitutes interested only in money, not the friends he remembered. The prices would be high, the employees cool and businesslike, the fondly remembered saloon not the haven it once had been.

Other times, instead of liberty, the whole outfit would move out through a combat zone in open trucks. They drove right through battles, and sometimes engaged in firefights, but they never left the trucks, and there was no great sense of danger. Then they arrived at some sort of forward base where everything was okay for a while. But invariably they had to escape for some reason. This was done by boat. They floated through hostile harbors and waterways. Finally they would plunge down the side of a mountain in a steep, twisting sort of flume, toward a wide river below, and safety, whipping from side to side, moving ever faster. They never got there. The dream would end.

None of these dreams ever ended conclusively. He was left with a disquieting sense of uncertainty; things were never resolved. The dreams were not terrifying, but neither were they satisfying or altogether comforting.

His dreams were fairly simple and straightforward; anyone having a passing familiarity with Freud and Jung and those boys could have interpreted them well enough, at least to a point. The airplanes, the trucks, the boat, were dream *instruments* that projected the capability of will beyond the limitation of the conscious. If a dream is a distorted representation of a subconscious wish or emotion that is frustrated by natural human restrictions, then the obstacles of the dream—mountains, buildings, etc.—may represent those restrictions, and the instruments may represent the unconsciously willed methods and devices to overcome the restrictions and project the intelligence beyond the limits, whatever they may be. And the frustration, the inability in the dream ever to resolve things satisfactorily, to get where he was going, might be a symbol for, among other things, his own unconscious resistance to the wish or inclination. And that might be a manifestation of a dichotomy in the nature of man—the eternal compulsion on the one hand to emerge into the world and compete in quest of adventure and independence, and the tendency on the other to regress to the womb, to seek protection and sustenance—safety.

Only Rawlins did not take much stock in the analysis of dreams. He would likely have ranked dream interpreters somewhere between the haruspex and the Humm-Wadsworth Temperament scale, significance-wise. But he was beginning, if only *just* beginning, to consider such things.

Might the womb-security symbol touch upon VVAPS? The wide river? Might he have been drifting, regressing toward Fromm's "syndrome of decay"? If all the obstacles and difficulties of the dreams, the frustration and failure to conclude things satisfactorily, were manifestations of his own unconscious resistance to his conscious endeavors, did that imply something more immediate about the war that he hardly ever thought about, that he as yet believed had had no real effect on him? The acquaintances he had lost for no apparent reason, but through some caprice of nature; the hundreds he had burned and maimed and killed from the sterile, air-conditioned cockpit of his airplane? There may have been many questions, had Rawlins bothered to ask them. What about the drinking? Why did he punish himself night after night, driving his tortured mind beyond coherence, knowing full well that it was killing him? Why did he drink to the point where he never remembered going to bed or what had been on the television? Why to such excess that it was driving his few friends away, and his liver would be next? The nervous system was already shot. He never saw snakes or pink elephants, but he had his own delirium tremens—it was the demon. He could no longer get through most days without a touch, and never a night. It was right on through to oblivion, every night. In social situations, from the time he began to mumble and slur, when his brain could no longer hold the pace of conversation and he became the object of at least passive ridicule, when he was in fact embarrassing himself, though he never knew that consciously, his brain shut it out. Erased the tape. The old brain housing group didn't want to preserve those painful, guilty, pitiable scenes; it would, striving in the universal essence of survival to cope, just take itself off the air for a few hours until the alcohol, taking with it whatever brain cells and synapses it had captured, left. Then that ill-used organ would struggle back on line, in the eternally essential, instinctive predisposition, shared even by inanimate growing things, that life would get better. Doesn't even the tiniest sprout of grass, having been frostbitten, snowed on, whipped, and abused, yet open itself in pure innocence to the sun the next morning, in natural certainty that conditions will improve? And the human brain is one whiz-bang, advanced technology VCR, multiprogrammable for fourteen days, fourteen weeks, or fourteen years. It seemed like Rawlins's just clicked itself off every day about sundown. It was getting so that, including sleep, an unconscious state naturally, he remembered less of his life than he forgot.

And might not getting soused time after time and revealing yourself as a drunken fool and then blotting the whole experience out, making it fucking *go away*, be connected through the continuum of the collective unconscious to the repression of memories from the excesses of war? Was there a parallel in function, if not in relative time? Might you repress whole years of unacceptable behavior, and through some tenebrous cryptomnesia, think and act in reaction to experiences you don't remember, didn't even allow yourself to consciously confirm? And did the continuity of the collective unconscious bind Rawlins to all the mistakes, failures, misconceptions, and atrocities of his entire family, his nation, his world—mankind *in toto?* Just what all influenced his self-destructive behavior, the failure to recognize his plight and struggle against the malediction? Was it the war? Was it the acts and occurrences of his entire life, indeed those of the complete history of man? There were authorities aplenty who would say so. Or was he just stupid and lazy? Yes, there were any number of questions that begged to be addressed. It was time for Rawlins to look long in the metaphysical mirror. To explore ". . . the first *whence* and the last *whither* of the whole cosmic procession. . . ."

But he didn't. Not Smilin' Jack, who seldom smiled any more. Who used to drink and party and fuck until three in the morning, sleep three hours, and jump up like a spring-loaded automaton, ready to go fly the hop, let it all hang out; but who now passed out during the ten o'clock news, often with a cigarette in his hand. Thank the saints for fire-resistant carpet. No, he just continued to pour in the wrong fluids, contaminating the system, treating all his anxieties with chemicals; and slipped deeper into the muck of VVAPS, resenting all the fucking functionaries and the work they did, which was at best specious but usually spurious. It finally occurred to Rawlins who the real idiot was. By day his brain exploded in indignation at what he perceived as the injustice of it all. Cronyism and political etiquette were rewarded, innovation was feared; it didn't matter whether you did it right or not, just so you made no waves doing it. And by night he sat in the recliner, drink in hand, nineteen-inch RCA shooting him up with a steady barrage of alpha waves, frequently dozing and dumping the drink in his lap. His blood pressure climbed and his brain cells diminished. Life went on at VVAPS, but it had ceased to be an abundance of joy. And, inexplicably, but perhaps like droves of other workers living out their lives of quiet desperation, he didn't fight it. He was going all too gently into that good night the poet warned against. He should have been consumed with epistemological zeal to find out what the fuck was wrong, but he only anesthetized himself so it didn't hurt so much. The only thing he thought about at any length was mortality. It was as Tennessee Williams wrote: "Time rushes toward us with its hospital tray of infinitely varied narcotics, even while it is preparing us for its inevitably fatal operation."

According to Socrates, the unexamined life is not worth living. Rawlins had heretofore steadfastly refused to examine his, and it seemed that, indeed, it was getting to the point that it was hardly worth living. But he had begun to wonder.

22

California, 1970s

It was wonderful. As the hordes of radical leftist teenagers, cowards, ideologists, socialist sociologists, Democrats against Lyndon Johnson and other Rooseveltian Tories and hawks generally, having donned their gay apparel—headbands, shawls, ponchos, obscene T-shirts, tie-dyed splendor—took to the streets, they were joined by a large contingent from West Hollywood who already had their gay apparel on. There were delegations from every ethnic and liberal political quarter, even a few Hell's Angels counterdemonstrating. Millions of singing, gyrating hippies clutched flowers for stuffing into the barrels of National Guard rifles, should they encounter any. And the overpowering smell! It was as if someone had torpedoed a supertanker full of patchouli oil in the Los Angeles River. This panoply of attitudes, vast spectrum of colors, messages, and hairdos, swaying, shuffling carpet of hadjis, was drawn as if by an electromagnetic field to their own personal Mecca, which was City Hall and the other downtown symbols of the murderous, fascist-pig conspiracy. They linked elbows, raised their husky, drug-dented young voices in protest song and chant, and marched straight up Wilshire Boulevard. And traffic absolutely stopped. Did not budge, did not move for hours. Upwards of a hundred independent film producers cursed under their breath, gnashed their capped teeth, and gunned the engines of their leased Corniches in the most extreme frustration because they could not get to the Polo Lounge for the making of all their daily deals. Independent meant they didn't have a job or any affiliation. The precise meaning of producer was less clear.

The Wilshire corridor was paralyzed. Barbi Belheur felt, for the first time in her life, the sense of real, tangible power. It was awe-inspiring. She had single-handedly shut down Los Angeles. It was closed. Derailed.

And she had made this come to pass. It came to her suddenly, as if in a dream-visitation, that she could control the events of mankind. Barbi gripped the elbow of P. E. Proudbird, who was having a wonderful time at the vanguard of the march, and knew she was all-powerful. That realization was sobering. She even felt a twinge of despair; now that she knew for a certainty that she could halt the immoral war, probably in a few weeks or less with this kind of power, what would she do for an encore? She vowed to read all of John Kennedy's speeches in an attempt to determine what to do with the nation, now that she controlled it. Barbi gazed up, no longer abashed, at the imposing skyscrapers that lined the boulevard—centers of commerce and finance, of the mass media and of government, and knew that she held them in the palm of her smallish, well-manicured hand. Her army of urchins, a Technicolor array of the brightest and the grimiest, of earrings, nose rings, rings on every finger and many a toe, of wild tonsorial confusion, of headbands, war paint, peace signs, and slogans, would bring the Establishment to a grinding halt and force the Philistines to listen. It was exhilarating. Barbi had only to suggest, and this sea of dispossessed rebels would execute. The children could control the world. This swelling cross-section of a new American generation, of Jukeses and Kallikaks, of Hatfields and McCoys, of Grangerfords and Shepherdsons, of Washingtons and Jacksons, of Shermans, Lees, Lincolns, O'Gradys, Kowalskis, Garcias, and Watanabes; of every tint, hue, and stripe from black to white—they had all buried their hatchets and they *would* force peace and gentleness and brotherhood upon this world. And artless naiveté.

P. E. Proudbird moved her gaze around the shoals of shining faces and gave Barbi a hug. "Man," she said, "this is one groovy happening." P.E. was dressed in her Pocahontas outfit; fringed larrigans, sleeveless buckskin dress with pattern of porcupine quills worked into the bodice, long braided hair topped with snood of brightest crimson sateen, little feather, eight pounds of bracelets on each arm, and no underwear. She was a little miffed, though, because she didn't even stand out in the crowd. So outrageously bedizened were the kids swarming around her that poor P.E.'s drapery didn't show well. Later, though, when she and Barbi were interviewed on the steps of City Hall by several six o'clock news groups, she would have her moment. The multitudes sported every imaginable combination of habiliment and livery, or lack thereof, that could be contrived to attract the scorn and outrage of the Hampshire, Yorkshire, and Poland China porkers, with jobs and all, who observed, mostly from safe, upstairs windows. You could not have found a brassiere in six blocks of those demonstrators. One plump offering wore a white T-shirt that was inscribed in four-inch black letters, on front and back, perhaps so that, missing the message on approach, one could turn, apprehend it and follow, with this thought:

HIT ME

KICK ME

BEAT ME

FUCK ME

THEN FORGET ME!

After the parade, she and a few marchers wandered along Fourth Street, offering love, brotherhood, and the remainder of their flowers, when one of a group of young idlers, who had just smoked a joint and were allowing a bottle of Tokay to breathe a bit before passing it around to sample the complex nuances of its flirtatious bouquet, read the message and went into action. He was quite obviously a highly literate and clear-thinking young man, because he dragged her into an alley and complied with all five suggestions, in their stated order. This may not, in itself, seem so remarkable. But had she reported the incident, and pressed charges, it might have been different. Of course she didn't, she determined to "go with the flow," as the expression had it, and did not allow the somewhat negative experience to fuck up her karma. She knew the poor brother had not really meant to rape her; he was just reacting involuntarily to an intolerable social situation. He was seething with hate and frustration and injustice and righteous anger. She hoped she had helped in some small way. She didn't take it personally. But *had* she called a cop and *had* he found the scoundrel and *had* the case come to trial, it might have been quite different. To the hundreds of young lawyers, all clad in shirtsleeves and vests, metal-rimmed aviator glasses and scraggly mustaches, who had watched the march from those high portals of affluence, at a hundred bucks an hour on somebody's tab, the trial might have been remarkable indeed. It may have been the consummate test of the implied-consent defense. But of course she didn't call a cop, and the kids dropped their wilted flora and removed themselves from the unsettling realities of reality.

Oh, but they all had plenty of flowers during the pilgrimage, though. The police, "pigs," as they were called, and their fat, spoiled horses were generously sprinkled with colorful blossoms. The horses seemed to prefer the abundant daisy as fodder, Asian poppies being little in evidence.

Flower power, born in the Haight, was now epidemic. To the Trekkies of Barbi's quest it was indeed contagious on this day. One bold initiate, flushed with zeal, attempted to affix a posy to the tail of a police horse. On duty. Alas, it fell immediately to the ground. Undeterred, he snatched up the fallen blossom, moved the gelding's tail aside, and inserted that long-stemmed carnation into the only niche that presented itself as a secure armory for the floral guidon of the movement. Perhaps recklessly. The horse, neither patriotic nor revolutionary, having no parochial position beyond the equine pursuit of life, liberty, and happiness, unaccustomed as he was to suppositories, floral or otherwise, kicked the hippie three rows back in the procession and, seeking only to dislodge the intrusive standard of peace and love, bestirred himself to several high-kicking jumps in rapid succession. The professional bronc rider would have applauded the display, those bucks being high, showy, and straight, affording spurring opportunities that would be impressive to the judges, assuring a good score. Worse be the luck, the police officer, maybe just a touch plumpish, and maybe ever so slightly spoiled himself, was not a professional bronc rider. He was precipitously unseated, without apparent intentional grandstand gigging or ostentatious wither-to-cantle raking. No, bucked down like a blue sack of shit off a renegade elephant. He lasted about as long as Mortimer Snerd would have on old Midnight. And came to rest rather indecorously in the street with roughly the same force as if the last hod of bricks had fallen from the very top of the Empire State Building. Banged onto the asphalt on his back and shoulders, leaving a shallow depression in the hot pavement, knocking him cold as a mackerel, cracking his plastic riot helmet, and nearly collapsing both lungs. The throng roared with approval and surged forward to see what was happening. The other "peace" officers, confused and afraid, formed a cordon around their fallen comrade, radioed for backup, and began to methodically apply their batons to the towheads of preteen girls and other threatening elements of the counterculture.

It became a study in the metaphysics of the microcosm. The human instincts of fear and distrust and resentment flashed through those humans on both sides, or all sides, of whatever the issue really was, faster than any conscious intent could have communicated them. The chaos and feelings of hate and violence spread. Even as the supposedly organized armies of opposing ideologies battled in the throes of abject dread, scathing rage, smoldering odium, and blazing, senseless hostility in the ooze of Southeast Asia, these erstwhile neighbors and fellow citizens kicked and gouged and fought with bricks, bottles, and nightsticks in the streets of Los Angeles. And nobody really knew clearly what they were fighting for, or against, whichever it was. But fight, retaliate, destroy, impose their own will they all felt they must.

The marchers came to a city bus idling at the curb while its driver dunked crullers in his bland coffee at Winchell's. In a small explosion of bitterness and petulance they turned the bus over and torched it. Seekers into the psychology of man might have wondered, Why the bus? What did it represent? On the surface it would seem to be the kind of thing they were demonstrating *for:* cheap public transportation, government-subsidized and user-friendly. Over it went, and up in flames. That particular bus had been built by a subsidiary of a large aerospace company, using inferior materials. When the salvage crew came to get it, they noticed dangerous cracks in the undercarriage, so it would have had to be taken out of service anyway.

The unfortunate peace officer, who literally occupied a central, causative position in the melee, was whisked off to the emergency room. It was later determined that he had sustained sufficiently severe, if obscure and inexactly diagnosed, whiplash-like injuries to qualify him for 100-percent disability pay for the rest of his life. He was thirty-one. But his determination to recover was enormous. After attending a signing ceremony in his wheelchair and waiting to cash the first check and be sure the scam was going to work, he entered an intensive physical therapy program and a couple of months later was able to establish his own piano and large appliance moving business, which thrived for many years. Although they never knew each other, there was a thin ironic thread connecting him to R^2 Jones. When R^2 ejected over North Vietnam he crushed a couple of vertebrae in his back. As the medical facilities at the Hanoi Hilton were somewhat inferior to, say, Johns Hopkins, it didn't heal properly. Consequently, Jones too, upon his release some years later, was adjudged to be 100-percent disabled and was awarded full pay and allowances for life. But like the cop, R^2 was hell-bent on rehabilitation. After undergoing a marvelous new high-tech surgical procedure and a period of intensive therapy, he managed, under the new physical agility guidelines handed down by the Supreme Court to assure that the enforcement of law be sexually balanced, to qualify for the police academy. R^2 served twenty years on the force and he genuinely enjoyed using badge and gun to "serve and protect," which was mostly just snooping into other people's business and forcing them to do "right." Of course he was always a little envious of his brother C^2, who became a pilot for Continental and made lots more money than R^2, until he got fired. But when R^2 ordered a giant-screen TV set, on which to watch the Super Bowl, it was delivered to his high-rise apartment in Marina del Rey by that same disabled policeman whose spot on the force, at least symbolically, may be said to have been occupied by the disabled Jones. And the dog-assed Jets won the Super Bowl again.

But the rioting at the great peace march developed apace. The spirit of violence was abroad and the kids continued to smash everything they could find, regardless of who it belonged to. The cops continued to smash kids. The horse, having rid himself of the offending floral display, boutonniere, you might say, was still somewhat unnerved, and galloped pell-mell away from the scene of his discontent, scattering hippies, bluesuits, innocent bystanders, pushcarts, and Seeing Eye dogs as he went. The police at first attempted some wild-west wrangling on their motorcycles, but after one skidded under a semitrailer and came out the other side missing its rider, and another fetched up devilishly intertwined with a wrought-iron fence, they gave it up. The horse, forgotten now, ended up in MacArthur Park, where he grazed and observed indigent alien women and children picking the lice out of each other's hair, drug deals going down, and ardent swains in search of the love that had only just begun to speak its name surreptitiously cruising the public rest rooms. He had had enough of protecting and serving for that day. And the people in the park didn't even know there was a peace march. Some of them didn't even know there was a war.

Poor former Corporal, now saboteur, O'Malley didn't get to go to the parade. He was too busy blowing up the Air Force Station. He and his buddy the ex-Navy SEAL, who knew all about explosives, had managed to purloin thirty-six cases of high velocity dynamite from an E. I. DuPont de Nemours truck before the driver, one Bull White, whose kidneys were bothering him and who didn't want to get back in his truck anyway, was able to tear himself away from the intimate banter and double entendres of the duty waitress at the Super Q truck stop up along the grapevine, Lavinia "Del" Delmont. Bull White swallowed a handful of bennies and didn't even check the seal on the back of the trailer. He had miles to go before he slept.

The demolition team, thirty-six cases safe in their Volkswagen bus, bought a six-pack, fired up a number, and headed for the city in jubilation. They next had to determine how best to deliver the ordnance to the target.

"You know, I think we got enough shit here to just park out in the street and blow that whole fucking complex into the Pacific Ocean." O'Malley could see huge pieces of marble and granite flying twenty blocks, clipping down power lines and streetlights, swamping empty yachts from King Harbor to Marina del Rey, just obliterating that symbol of the military-industrial complex, dumping it into the sea. It was heartwarming to a dedicated soldier of the Left. Somehow he didn't envision those rocks cutting down ordinary people, offices, Laundromats, preschools in Manhattan Beach.

"No, man," said the SEAL, who was driving. "You've got to get it right up against that sucker or you'll just break windows. We got to figure a way to get in the gate."

"I hear you, brother," O'Malley toked long and deep, then except for a muffled cough or two, was silent for several seconds as he held in the miasmic ether, drew in a few quick snorts of air, and finally exhaled in a whoosh. "Ahhh. So how do we do that?"

"Well, you notice all those telephone company trucks going in and out of there? I think we ought to swipe us one of those little pickups with the van body and the GTE logo, for starters."

"Hey, man, that's good. Real good. That gets us in the gate. What then?"

"We got enough power here, all we have to do is park that bad boy up against the wall in a good place and detonate. Kabloom. It'll flatten that sumbitch. At least tear a wall off."

"All riiight. I know how we'll get that fucking truck, too. You know how they park them things by a manhole, put them orange cones out, and go down to work on their wires and shit? You see 'em all over town, man. We'll just cruise around and find us one."

As it happened, when they went looking, they didn't have to find a manhole with a repairman in it. The first suitable telephone truck they espied was in the parking lot of a 7-Eleven store. The repairman was grabbing a quick Beef 'n' Cheddar and a Dr Pepper as his vehicle idled near the front of the store. Until he noticed it being driven away. It being lunch hour, he had even picked up his laundry. Fresh uniforms hung in the cab, O'Malley saw as he drove away. It was perfect. It was so easy. They stashed the Courier in the old garage where the dynamite was and began assembling the detonation device and their final assault plan.

The lead elements of the peace march had missed the tumult and confusion of the rioting, having passed on eastward before the policeman fell off his horse, starting the free-for-all. Barbi and P.E., Mustafa the Black Panther enforcer, Mrs. Staff Sergeant O'Flynn, and DeWayne Ludlow's younger brother, Digby, who was an honor student in political science at Vanderbilt, were among others in the front lines as the mob of malcontents snaked its way along Sixth Street and up Broadway toward City Hall. Even Dulcie, the doyenne of political caterers, marched the last few blocks with them, her corns and bunions discouraging greater loyalty to the cause. Ismael, the illegal alien waiter, thought discretion to be the better part of political activism and stayed home. Actually, he didn't give a shit about the war anyway, but only pretended to because it pleased his associates and benefactors. In truth he had no politics— there wasn't much opportunity, amongst the three part-time jobs he worked at to support his family. But P.E. was still somewhat put out, so surrounded was she by colorful freaks. A black girl next to her had bleached hair; a few steps away was a Caucasian, who might just have been either sex, with a carefully tended Afro; there were dozens of ersatz American Indians, some in garb nearly identical to P.E.'s, and not a few ersatz Indian Indians. And several real ones.

As the hell-bent-for-pacification throng thrust along Broadway toward City Hall, the rear echelons spoiling and rioting, cops teargassing them and getting out the fire hoses, O'Malley, with a telephone repairman's uniform over his regular clothes, and also on a mission of peace, was threading a course down the freeway in a telephone company truck chock-full of dynamite, followed by the ex-SEAL in the Volkswagen bus. They would rendezvous in a small shopping center a few blocks from the target for their final briefing.

As the forefront of the new American conscience approached their rally point on the steps of City Hall, the reporters and photographers were shoving and jostling and falling all over each other to line up shots and stick microphones in the face of Barbi Belheur, famous rock star and new *enfant terrible* of the Left. Two of the combatants, who had struggled with each other many times on these fields of dishonor, were Clint Clutcher of Channel 5, and Mindy Van Vorhees-Ballew of Channel 9. They were each a little, it might be said, assertive in the workplace.

Clint Clutcher was a genuine, bona fide licensed private pilot and student helicopter ratee who held, among other honors and citations, the world low-altitude flight record of 1,320 feet below sea level, as certified by the Fédération Aéronautique Internationale. Clint had accomplished this singular feat by cajoling his station into sending him to Israel with a camera crew and his instructor, Courtney Hilldebrandt, a sometime beauty pageant contestant, sometime jockey, and permanent part-time flight instructor. There they hired an excavating company to dig a trench beside the Dead Sea, sixty by a hundred by fifteen feet deep. They then rented a Hughes Jetranger and hovered down in their hole, eight feet below the surface of the Dead Sea, at 1,320 feet below sea level, with cameras rolling and a breathless world public waiting to see this awesome display of intrepid airpersonship on the six o'clock news. Clint was tolerably prideful of his many exploits in the wild blue yonder, or, in the case of the low-altitude record, the wild blue propinquity. He strove in every interview and on-camera assignment to slant the story around toward some aspect of aviation, so that he could make available for the enjoyment and edification of viewers several firsthand, gut-level reactions, from the standpoint of a seasoned flyer. He didn't mind when, after his segment, one of the co-anchors would turn to the other and say: "That's very interesting. Of course Clint is an experienced pilot who holds at least one world record and has, I don't know, I guess *hundreds* of hours of flight experience, isn't that right, B. Steven?"

"Yes, Holly. Clint is quite an enthusiast. I understand that he's flown in several areas around the world. But of course he can often give us a different perspective on things, which those of us, and I include myself, Holly, heh heh, who are petrified to get on a 747, would never appreciate otherwise. Yes, very interesting."

That sort of on-air twaddle was known in the business by the acronym HINT. That stood for "happy idiot news talk."

Mindy Van Vorhees-Ballew had met Barbi briefly once before. The introduction had taken place at the Santa Monica bungalow of Irene Arena, the voice coach. Barbi, no Stentor exactly, was working on her breathing and projection for the increased public speaking duties that she knew must come. Mindy had contracted Irene Arena to help her develop a Barbara Walters–like speech impediment, which she figured might cause her to shine in those impersonal eyes of "the networks." Mindy had the talent for stardom in the news analysis game. She was tallish, statuesque, and could summon the most sincere, trustworthy, and studious looks, as she knitted her brow and gazed openly into the omnipresent cameras with large guileless eyes, the blue of which was augmented by contact lenses. That, she reasoned, and maybe just a touch of that soft, mush-mouth sensibility to accent her toughness and set her apart from the horde of competing clones, was all she needed. She would be no sissy Brokaw or preaching Rather; it was Walter, look out. When Mindy talked on camera, she put a strong accent on every other word. Regardless of what the word might be, or its relationship to the sentence, every second one got *stressed*.

At the side of the Air Force building was a long, low, windowless addition that they were still working on. This ominous-looking squat structure, stone on the outside and who-knew-what within, was known by the happy acronym FUCCERS, which stood for "Facility for Unified Control of Communications—Electromagnetics and Radiation Shielded." This edifice was constructed to meet the requirements of the Department of Defense TEMPEST program. TEMPEST was another acronym or portmanteau word, the origin of which had been inadvertently erased from a floppy disk in a vast complex, with no public address, somewhere in Virginia. So no one knew what it stood for anymore, but the dictates of the program had not been erased, and they had to be complied with. There was a substantial inner chain-link fence around the building that would have been tough to breach, but while the FUCCERS area was still under construction, a section of the fence had been removed to allow the various service vehicles to get to the site. Many of these were telephone trucks, O'Malley had noticed, and that was deemed the best all-around spot available to picket their neo-Trojan horse. Clipboarded trip ticket in hand, the uniformed O'Malley breezed through the gate with hardly a question. He was just too obviously legitimate for the guards to hassle. Just another working stiff doing his job. And that was true if, in the somewhat parochial sense of Ghadaffi or the Hezbollah, you considered a terrorist just another working stiff. O'Malley found the hole in the fence, parked his vessel of portent snugly against the building, set the fifteen-minute delayed detonator, locked the truck, and sauntered back through the gate, with a handset and a few screwdrivers, explaining briefly that he had to tap into a trunk line and call back into the facility to check a circuit. "The time has come," the SEAL said, when he picked him up, "to fish or cut bait." They hauled ass.

Clint Clutcher got to Barbi first, thrusting out a microphone, the cord of which trailed back to his long-suffering soundman. The acoustics business could be a fairly onerous duty when one existed within earshot of Clint Clutcher.

"Miss Belheur, as I was flying back from an assignment a little while ago, I believe I literally felt the impact of this demonstration." If the absolute truth were to be observed, there is little question that the eighteen-year-old social-science major from Long Beach State, whose head was at that moment the terminus of the long arc of a police truncheon, had better claim to literal feeling of the impact of the demonstration, but no matter.

"I put the ship into a hover," said Clint, "and folks, incredibly," (a word that he perhaps used with too little discretion) "it was as if I could actually *feel* a groundswell of energy emanating from the multitudes of this march. The ship seemed to want to soar on the strength of that energy. I actually had to lower the collective a little and adjust the trim to maintain altitude. Would you comment on this phenomena, Miss Belheur?"

"The war is illegal," said Barbi of the metallic eye. "It is immoral, inhumane, and contrite. It is inconsistent to the sensualities of the enlightened peoples of the world. The ratifications of this obscene slaughter are . . ." It was the first time Barbi had talked on TV. She had sung, but never spoken.

By this time, Mindy Van Vorhees-Ballew had, with surprisingly little apparent friction, insinuated herself partially between Barbi and Clint. He was accustomed to this aggressive style of reporting, but he did not suffer it gladly. Two could play at that game. Clint had got his start at KSKY in Montana. In three years of frontier life, he pestered cowboys at every opportunity because he at first envisioned "rodeo hand" as the daring, macho persona that he sensed he must create. (He later found it troublesome to master the sitting of the overpriced, unregistered seven-year-old quarter horse gelding that one of the old boys assured him was descended from the great Three Bars, and sold him, so Clint gave up the horseman's life for aviation.) In those three years he learned only one trick of real value. That was how to throw a half-hitch in a length of rope. In truth he had never anticipated that the trick would serve so well until Mindy Van Vorhees-Ballew stepped over the cord to his microphone, forcing herself into his interview. Without thinking, really, he flipped a half-hitch around her well-turned ankle, jerked ever so deftly on the cable, and put her advance to rout. Mindy fetched up sharply on the stern side of her Oleg Cassini interviewing suit, on the hard stone steps. Though she was not given to pettiness as a rule, Mindy was less than noble in this situation.

"Motherfucker," she spat, not sweetly, "you will live to regret this moment."

Mindy was genuinely disparaging of Clint Clutcher's aptitude with ropes and such. It may be taken as assured that she meant what she said. Her husband, Wally, wielded considerable behind-the-scenes power in broadcast journalism; she would have him ruin the bastard. Alas, it was not to be. Determined though she was, Mindy could not know that the very next day Clint would fall prey to a capricious Pacific wind gust and crash the Channel 5 telecopter into a cliff at Black's Beach, while attempting to film sheriff's deputies attempting to film nude sunbathers so they could arrest them, with evidence, before they could put their suits back on and thumb their noses at the deputies. Pettibone knew. But Mindy couldn't have. She was about to offer a couple of additional hastily selected sentiments to Clint Clutcher, but at that moment the news conference was interrupted by the loudest noise ever heard in Los Angeles. Thirty-six cases.

There wasn't a window remaining south of Slauson or west of the Long Beach Freeway. Dishes were said to have rattled on the shelf in Temecula. Property damage was considerable, but surprisingly few people were killed. Oh, some undocumented janitorial workers, the occasional nonflying Air Force lifer or glacially slow-witted civilian bureaucrat, military police, some innocent bystanders, street thugs, a few children, but no one of any importance. That was largely because of the dreadnought TEMPEST specifications to which the FUCCERS facility was being built. They required that walls, ceiling, and floor be solid steel, surrounded by solid lead, surrounded by solid titanium, surrounded by ten-foot-thick reinforced concrete, and so on. The structure bent, but it did not break. It protected the rest of the complex and deflected the blast out across the parking area and the wide boulevard, into the city, in search of windows, fine china, Hummel figurines, and suchlike. The crater in the parking lot was forty feet deep. Comprehensive claims on automobiles were brisk for a week at Allstate and State Farm. One independent film producer, trying to circumnavigate the traffic and confusion of the peace march and get to the Polo Lounge, got lost somewhere in Culver City. He ended up going the wrong way on Sepulveda, which he didn't discover until he dipped into the tunnel under the runways at LAX. He drove a few more blocks looking for a suitable place to turn around. Unfortunately he chose El Segundo Boulevard. He was crushed by a three-hundred-pound chunk of concrete that fell through the rag top of his Corniche. The car itself was salvageable. Another casualty was the cutest mongrel dog, who yipped and yapped the livelong day in pure happiness. Around his neck he wore a sporty red bandanna as he leaped and frolicked among the sun worshippers, in quest of his master's Frisbee. After one spectacular catch he jumped gleefully into the ocean, rolled over in the sand, and positioned himself in the most friendly manner between four bathers for a vigorous, good-natured shake. The little fellow looked up eagerly amid the game of thrown sandals, books, and sunscreen bottles to see his master's disc come spinning down yet again, and positioned himself for the retrieval. Ah, but the canine cavorter was mistaken. The rotating platter that planed down at him was not a Frisbee at all. It was a 120-pound cast-iron manhole cover launched by O'Malley's SAMSO explosion that got there even before the sound. The little dog gauged its descent, steeled himself, and leaped. Brave lad. Plucky lad.

Within the hour, the Islamic Jihad, the Weather Underground and SDS, the Black Panthers, the PLO, the Jewish Defense League, the Aryan Nations, Yasir Arafat, Moamar Ghadaffi, and two surviving Hitlers phoned in to take credit for the blast. Prosecutors would later try to hang it on Charlie Manson's gang; all conspiracy theories were re-examined; a medium called the Secretary of Defense to say that she had just been talking with Tail Gunner Joe McCarthy, and, sure enough, Russian agents were to blame. Everyone was suspected except Barbi Belheur and SLUR. No one had any idea who really did it, and O'Malley and the SEAL were never caught.

But as has been noted, loss of life and property was limited, all things considered, and no one really paid much attention. Oh, it got everyone's notice for the moment, but life in the busy second half of the twentieth century quickly resumed. A few young Arabs made note of the modus operandi; they would later use the technology on embassies and Marine barracks and things. But no one of real importance paid any attention. They sent more troops to Vietnam, Congress raised taxes, and Bull White ended up paying for the missing dynamite out of his wages. Pettibone and those fellows probably even knew when the Tet offensive was coming, but most people just would not see the writing on the wall.

The policeman's horse, on the other hand, grazing on the underside of life in MacArthur Park, when he heard that terrifying, earsplitting, gut-rending explosion, that deafening roar—that was it. He had had enough of serving and protecting, of war and peace marches, of Homo sapiens and their silly civilization. When he heard the big boom, that distant descendent of the noble Houyhnhnm had still some hereditary gene, some scrap of DNA, that abhorred incivility and violence. He set out for some serious high country. Just chucked it all, police pension and everything, and headed for the hills. Somewhere in the Sierras he managed to rub the bridle off on a tree limb. Within three weeks, sweat and the elements rotted the cinch and he was rid of the saddle. He eventually joined some old relatives in a mustang herd in the mountains and deserts of Nevada. He lived out his days there in relative comfort until some years later, when he died in pain from a rare equine carcinoma that was caused by fallout from the atomic testing in the region.

The blast engendered by Barbi Belheur, in the name of peace, was better understood, and heeded, by one horse than by the entire human population. And so on.

23

Southeast Asia, 1960s

They should have drawn portents from the war within a war, but nobody much did. It might be thought that Bundy and McNamara and Westmoreland would have put their heads a little closer together than usual and said: "Holy shit, man, this is one unstable sumbitch. We better watch our fucking step." But they didn't. As soon as the striped phone rang, the direct overseas line, Nguyen Kao Ky had a pretty good idea who it might be.

"Preemeer Ky, this hyeer's Lyndon Baines Johnson, POTUS." That stood for President of the United States.

"*Chào ông*, Mistah President. What is it that I can do to serve you on this occasion?"

"Ah thank yew know what yew kin do fer me, boy. Either y'all patch up yore little differences, and not tomorrow, *raht now*, or ah'll pull the *in*tire Americun Army out of that little pissant country by next week, heah?"

Ky heard. The war would certainly lose some of its flair and panache without the Americans present. Where would he get airplanes? Bullets, fuel, pearl-handled six-guns, and butter? No, he heard, all right. It just wouldn't do to have Lyndon pull his army out. So they patched up their little differences, and *raht now*. In a Saigon minute.

"*Hét ròi, mon ami*. Consider him done." Ky pulled the loyal Marines out of the ARVN headquarters, fired two Catholics and appointed two Buddhists to his cabinet, promised free elections in a month's time, jumped in his personal Spad with the VIP seat covers and tinted canopy, and hauled ass for Saigon inside of an hour. And the war within a war was over.

The ARVN moved back to their regular HQ, and the Buddhist temple was reopened to Creed's hod carriers. Old Mister Mac in St. Louis whipped and cajoled and bonused his lackeys at the war plant, and soon produced lots of shiny new airplanes to replace those lost to friendly fire. Westmoreland requested additional troops; Lyndon authorized expanded bombing in the North. All was tranquillity with the various camps that were us. The worst aspect of this new solidarity was that Rawlins and Moon Dog and the boys had to come back from the sybaritic delights of Thailand and stay home and tend to war. Their airplanes were safe from the mortars of the brother ARVN now, and they were expected to get serious about naping and strafing and living like dogs in the hobo camp again. Civility was restored amongst all the quarreling brethren and a relative serenity descended upon the war once more. The boys got home to their hobo camp, reaccustomed themselves to red death and the twelve holer and no pussy, and things began to run pretty smoothly, as in the past.

It was war as usual, and one morning Rawlins found himself leading the air-to-ground hot pad. And the hot pad was really hot that memorable day. Business was picking up nicely. It seemed the old NVA Division 324B—who lived in the DMZ most of the time because it was declared a neutral zone, forbidden to combatants from either side, and the ingenuous American saps, of course, honored that proscription, so it was safe— 324B was moving south. Had they walked a few miles farther north, into the sovereign nation of their homeland, they would run some risk of having their asses bombed off, but in the haven of the DMZ, bastion of nonagression, no one would bother them. But now they were headed south en masse. They had some notion in those vaunted, cooler, prevailing heads that they would just decimate the puerile 1st ARVN Division, who were supposed to be defending Quang Tri Province. Just rout the fucking sissies and take the place over, in their own microcosmic version of Ike's domino theory: The rest of the provinces would fall in order and then maybe they could segue right on into the macrocosmic segment, as outlined by the Supreme Allied Commander. Laos, Cambodia, Thailand, Burma, who knew where it would stop?

But they failed to anticipate that instead of the couch-partial ARVN 1st, they would run up against eight thousand American Marines, who among them had logged several millennia of person-hours dedicated to establishing with each other and anyone else who had an interest in such things, or who didn't, for that matter, that they were indeed anything *but* sissies; and who had been looking for the goddamn enemy for a couple of years now, seeking to make that point semi-irrevocably by kicking some *serious* ass and taking damned few prisoners. This would be no walk in the park for General Vang and 324B.

No, the jarheads, suffering under a largely self-imposed veil of ineffectiveness, were ready to kick ass and take names. And they didn't bring a pencil. They had RECON troops and airplanes and sensors and spooks and every damn thing they could get snooping and pooping around the DMZ, and they knew just about exactly what was going on with the southern migration. So the Marine Corps' cooler heads put together Operation Piston Ring. They would run 324B, bleeding and stumbling, right back up Hanoi's ass and give pause to this main force invasion idea. And they mustn't give any hint of their plan to the slopes, because even if they *were* the baddest motherfuckers in the valley, they were still outnumbered. Their plan lacked subtlety. The way they chose to not give any hint of it to the slopes was to hit the south end of the DMZ with Arc-Light strikes for four days, causing a number of North Vietnamese infiltrators to poke their heads out of their bunkers, see the thousands of bombs, containing millions of bomblets, raining down from the swarms of B-52s, and exclaim, "Comrade Major, these *Yanqui* dogs must be up to something about half-way meaningful in terms of aggression here. Perhaps we should rethink our position."

And to further broadcast the plan of action, they set up a staging area on the plain outside of Dong Ha. C-130s and an endless drift of helicopters droned in and out of there and drove the dust hundreds of feet into the air, which made some more of the infiltrators peep out of their tunnels and say, "Gracious, them boys is bringing in a great deal of materiel. They must be planning something." It was only five thousand tons or so; still, it was an indication.

So the troopers of 324B, good men and true, plus smart, were less than astonished when a gaggle of CH-46s came wop-wopping over a ridge, swooped into the Song Ngan Valley, and disgorged elements of the 4th Marines, who were spoiling for a fight. Or tried to. There were some glitches.

Piston Ring had not boded uniformly well from the outset. First it had monsooned a while, postponing the jump-off and giving everyone time to ponder the days ahead. There was no hot chow in the staging area, so it was sit in the rain and spoon those cold Cs. Feed 'em fish. If they don't like it, fuck 'em, chow's over. When the sun finally came out it was blistering hot and the last of the raindrops, as they fell, encountered the first of the dust, already rising. One of the choppers in the first wave crashed after takeoff and hurt some folks. The heat intensified and the humidity rose. They knew that hacking their way through the (for sane people) impassable jungle, without even the suggestion of a breeze, would be devastating. And they knew that an entire NVA Division awaited their relatively puny handful of battalions.

When they got to the LZ the shit hit the fan, so to speak. What really hit the fan was bodies. One helicopter, maneuvering in the tight confines of the landing zone, surrounded by hundred-foot jungle canopy, its pilot perhaps watching more intently for the telltale muzzle flashes than he was watching his leader, overran that leader. They mixed rotor blades and that is a procedure you won't find recommended in the *Naval Air Training and Operations* manual for the safe piloting of rotary-wing aircraft. Debris began to fly and both the huge, ungainly, froglike forms plummeted to earth amid a horrendous thrashing, crashing, and whipping of spinning blades. Some Marines were ejected, some fell, some jumped. Many were diced up by the slashing rotors just like the potato in the culinary appliance display down at your Sears and Roebuck store on the mall. Limbs, trunks, weapons, and web gear flew in every direction. A third helicopter, trying desperately to avoid the first two, banked sharply and hit a tree. It too went down.

The boys of 324B were duly impressed with this demonstration of vertical assault tactics by the air-mobile force. They opened up with everything they had, and before the gore had come to rest or the dust settled, they had brought down two more of the iron birds with their delicate human cargo. And they kept right on blazing away at everything that moved. Brush and lumber and disintegrating hunks of helicopter filled the air, bullets whizzed everywhere, screaming jet engines poured heat and flame onto spilling fuel, grenades and ammo began cooking off as one chopper burned. There were pleasanter places to be. And those grunts who could still move began seeking them, helter-skelter.

The remnants of Zulu Company, walking wounded, scared, confused, hurtin' for certain, began to regroup in the thick underbrush at the edge of the clearing. They had NVA on three sides of them and the carnage and inferno of the fallen choppers on the fourth. Nearly everyone was wounded in at least one or two places. They dug shallow holes and tried to pair up with one of the more seriously hurt and one who could still fight effectively in each position. The NVA smelled blood. They had the numerical advantage, which they usually required absolutely before they would engage. The Americans were stung and stunned and dispirited; the jungle was so dense and the light so poor under the double canopy, one at thirty feet, another at a hundred, that they couldn't see where they were going or who they were fighting. The NVA were already at home in that slice of real estate, emplaced and bristling. They zapped them with mortars and followed up with automatic weapons. They were playing ducks and drakes with those Occidental swine. The forward air controller with Company Z ducked a stream of tumbling 7.62 mm bullets, looked around at the pain and anguish and bedlam, and said, "We need some fucking air."

He could hear the Communists moving and huffing and puffing and grunting. "We need air support right now and right here," he said. "On top of our young ass."

Thus was Rawlins scrambled off the hot pad in support of brave comrades, but troubled ones, in a place already becoming known as Helicopter Valley. From the air it appeared as a gorgeous work of nature, ranging from jade to emerald, almost in the shadow of the ominous Rockpile, an outcropping of sheer rock cliffs soaring nearly a thousand feet straight up from the valley floor. A wide river meandered its way at a leisurely pace. A sylvan glade, the beauty of which, to Rawlins at seven thousand feet, air conditioning turned up comfortably, was almost inspirational. To the lads of Zulu Company, at ground zero, in the fierce heat, fire, explosions, dead and wounded scattered all over, bullets flying everywhere, it was a lot closer to Hades than they had hoped ever to find themselves.

It was one of those days for Rawlins. He had joined a couple of hoboes in the elimination of a rare bottle of Old Grand-Dad 100 proof, which required their efforts for the better part of the preceding night. This was deemed an acceptable mission because he was not scheduled to do anything except go on hot pad alert at 0800. He was leading the B team and probably wouldn't launch till later in the day. He could get some Zs in the air-conditioned trailer. This was all the solidest kind of rationalizing, but of course the major driver of his decision was that 100-proof whiskey was pretty scarce in the hobo camp. One didn't turn it down.

Unbeknownst to Rawlins, Operations had penciled him in late for a 0530 wake-up to fly a test hop before he went on the pad. When informed of this development at the appointed hour, Rawlins was less than enthusiastic. He came not gently into that good dawning, but was a bit more inclined to rage at the duty officer, who was insistent. But it was to no avail and Smilin' Jack duly arrived at the flight line, not smiling at all, but groggy and foggy and in a decidedly bearish mood.

He dragged, scowling, into the ready-room trailer, eyes at half mast.

"Oh, sorry about that, Jack," said the Squadron Duty Officer, just a smidgen too bright and chipper for Rawlins's taste at the moment. "False alarm. Maintenance just called. Test hop's canceled."

Rawlins chose his words carefully but quickly as he stumbled through the half-dark trailer. "You motherfucker. You product of a rabid dog and the maggot-infested great whore of Baghdad. You soulless, brainless fucking zygote. I only got two hours sleep!"

The SDO looked up in exaggerated reproach. He raised his eyebrows to the top notch. "*Bite* your tongue, Rawlins! There are ladies present."

"Oh, right. Some *ladies* just dropped by the fucking war to show their support. Well, pal, any cunt that would show her face around this dump ain't no lad—" His speech ended in a croak as he arrived at the duty desk.

The SDO swept an arm toward the front row of seats, where sat, in the gloom, grinning ear to ear, two Pan Am stewardesses. Rawlins's mouth worked, but he could find no words. He plunged his face into his hands with what he considered the right amount of embarrassed exaggeration and mumbled.

"I . . . oh, no, I . . . it's . . . well I, . . . oh, God. This cannot be."

By this time everyone in the trailer was roaring. The girls had not encountered such an abject, mortified son of a bitch in a while. It occurred to Rawlins that he might disappear. Just put on a Claude Rains flight suit and not be there anymore. Transmogrify.

"Mere words cannot manifest my utter and total chagrin . . . ," he began lamely. And everyone broke up all the more. They hooted and guffawed and sputtered and brayed. The girls were convulsed. Rawlins was blushing like an L.A. sunset, despite the humor of the situation. In a moment of inspiration he grabbed the coffeepot and, with what resolve he could muster, headed straight for the female guests that they were so thoroughly unaccustomed to having; indeed had never once entertained before. Through his humility he projected the most conciliatory, engaging grin he could summon.

"Perhaps, ladies, I can resurrect something from this mess by offering you additional refreshment, such as it is."

But in his frazzled state, Rawlins had neglected as yet to lace up his boots; and yes, he did trip over said laces and come crashing to earth. The sturdy Pyrex did not break, but did spew liberal draughts of coffee on the feet of the visitors. Rawlins retired from the field amid such mirth as is not usually associated with wartime. Did not even rise, but, with head lowered, crawled straight to the door and out of the trailer. He made his way to a water buffalo, stuck his aching head under the tap, and let the tepid water run. But the grin was still there.

It was later revealed that an ex-Marine, then flying for Pan Am, had brought the girls over. They were on an R and R junket, had a couple of hours to kill before they loaded, and came to the hot-pad van to socialize with his old asshole buddies. The only thing that day that was maybe nearly as funny as Smilin' Jack's gaffe occurred when the airline crew got ready to leave. A hundred and fifty or so war-weary grunts, all scrubbed and shined, stood behind a chain-link fence waiting to board for their first look at The World in six months or more. The World meant pussy and clean sheets in air-conditioned hotels and sleeping till noon and wonderful food and unlimited whiskey and maybe dope and maybe television. In a rare case it may have meant music and art and civilized places. It meant everything. But mostly it meant girls.

The pilots were already back in the 707 running through checklists and things. The two girls from the trailer were ambling across the ramp, heels clicking, short skirts swishing, breasts thrusting, hips churning, to rejoin the rest of their crew. The spectacle of these, the first round-eyes the boys had seen in months, and comely specimens at that, caused some churning in the hearts and loins of the eager troopers, too. It was estimated by some onlookers that the mass rushing of blood to certain erectile points of the anatomy in that group was equal to or greater than that of the fully loaded 707 pulling six positive gs.

As the women ambled and the men ogled, the Daily Harassment Detail from the Vietcong made their presence known. They whistled a B-40 rocket over toward yonder 707. It exploded harmlessly about two hundred yards away from the strolling stewardi, but the point was made. There appeared to be some danger associated with their situation, and they acted at once to rectify the matter. While their uniform skirts were cut somewhat above the knee, the girls judged them still to be an impediment to the speed required at that point in time, as politicians and engineers are wont to say. With all dispatch they hiked those skirts up sufficiently to permit free movement of the lower extremities. Absolutely untrammeled and unfettered movement, it may be said. And, in imitation of Chattanooga, the chauffeur in the old Charlie Chan movie, said, "Feets, do yo' stuff!"

They cut out across that airplane parking lot like Affirmed and Alydar, neck and neck, feet flying, clean white underwear, garters, and dynamite legs flashing in the sun. That was to be all of The World the poor troopers would see that day.

Nor had the sense of impending peril been lost on the airline pilots, already in the plane. After all, that plane was worth millions, and they were responsible for it. Plus, their asses were in it. They already had two burning and were cranking number three by the time the girls clambered aboard. They taxied while the door was still coming up, took the runway without touching a brake, and cobbed it. That empty Boeing made a takeoff that would have cleared a five-thousand-foot obstacle at the end of the runway, if they had not turned for the sea before they got there.

The troops were disconsolate; crestfallen. There they were, all decked out in liberty uniform, out of the jungle, out of the mud and the leeches and snakes and scorpions, so close to The World, pockets full of money, and all they could do was watch the big white bird fly away. The big white bird, which symbolized ease and comfort and excess and material want satisfaction for a week, symbolized *everything* worthwhile to those unfortunates, circled out over Tourane Bay. And the dejected warriors could only mill around behind the fence and thank the Marine Corps for "one more good deal."

And all because of one lousy rocket. The Daily Harassment Detail had no inkling of the true and underlying value to the cause of their actions that day. The diminution of morale; the anger of the brass; the embarrassment of the perimeter force who had let them in close enough to fire, and then failed to catch them; the outrage of Al "Shaky" Morgenkrank, who, after a minor delay in the chocks because his RIO, in the back seat, couldn't get his oxygen mask plugged in to the receptacle, and so couldn't talk to anyone or breathe much and had to send for a new one, so Al was already mad and, taxiing a little too fast, distracted, hit the hole the rocket had made and blew a tire; the cost of the aborted R and R flight; the additional delay *and* cost of renegotiating with the contract carriers before they would come back into that airport for *any* damn reason. No, the boys in the DHD didn't know all that, but they should surely have been awarded Bronze Stars, if the VC had such.

Rawlins got less than an hour of air-conditioned sleep before they scrambled the first section. He and his boys then had to get fully suited up and be on five-minute alert for the next launch. They didn't have long to wait; Zulu Company and their cohorts in X-ray and Yankee Companies were taking more lumps in the vicinity of Helicopter Valley. Bad lumps. The NVA were massed and throwing themselves at the Marines in waves, blowing horns and whistles and firing all they had. The Marines hung on doggedly, but they just couldn't kill the bastards fast enough. They had to have air and artillery. FACs on the ground were getting plenty of air time on their PRC-25s. Airborne FACs were spreading out over the jungle in Bird Dogs. Phones were ringing in the Tactical Air Control Center, various S-3 sections, and hot-pad ready rooms. Things were starting to snap, crackle, and pop.

Logistics have always been a problem for armies. Consider the importance that Alley Oop attached to his stone ax. If he lost it, he could not go down to supply and draw a new one. Were Arthur to fuck up the cutting edge of his trusty Excalibur and then requisition a replacement from the Lady of the Lake, she would laugh. Supply personnel laugh a lot. As has been pointed out, the hoboes were not without their shortages. One of the more serious ones was that of Zuni rockets. Oh, there were others; tires, edible chow, and Technicolor movies to name a few, but Zunis were really in short supply. It is a LAW of nature that the good stuff is always scarce. If, by some surreal alchemy, the known deposits of gold and lead were to be transposed, sell those gold futures, brother. Lead will be $400 an ounce by week's end. There are those finicky troopers, with a distaste for the fabaceous legume, who will swear that all boxes of C rations contain ham or franks and beans; that steak and potatoes is just a cruel myth. Everybody loved to shoot Zunis, so, naturally, there weren't enough of them. The Zuni shortage was offset by an oversupply of its lesser relative, the ignominious 2.75-inch rocket. These were largely inaccurate, ineffective, and unreliable. They tended, with some frequency, to fail to go off when so instructed. Worse, perhaps, was their parallel tendency to, once in a while, go off without any such instruction. Onanism. Just make up their own mind. The surest way to get your flight leader's full attention is for a nineteen-shot pod of these wretched little missiles to cook off unbidden and go smoking past his work station in all quadrants. Oddly enough, there were plenty of 2.75s around; they always got delivered one way or another. But precious few Zunis.

Some shortages, of course, are created by a genuine scarcity of the material, like Hope diamonds, hen's teeth, and true loves. Other dearths and deprivations, however, are more closely linked with the distribution of existing assets. With the channels and idiosyncrasies of issuance, disbursement, transportation, and relocation. With the post office, in some cases. Supply systems are imperfect. Take, for example, food. The American government spends billions on grain and other foodstuffs that it doesn't want, while the main of Africa starves. That may seem odd enough, but then the government spends millions more on storage facilities in which to keep these comestibles until it all rots, and then more to get rid of the residue. We could save money by giving this stuff to the Africans, who would be happy to take it off our hands, straightaway; then we wouldn't have to pay to store it or dispose of it. Well, it is curious, isn't it? But then Smith, Marx, Keynes, and Congressman Kemp of New York, among others, have discoursed on this matter at some length.

Moon Dog, while walking through the Headquarters and Maintenance Squadron area one day, found some men with pry bars unpacking a large crate. It was a big enough box to hold maybe thirty aircraft tires or a number of rocket packs. They were hurting for tires that week; taxiing slowly on tires with two or three plies worn off and the steel belts showing, turning gingerly, rolling for takeoff and touching down with held breath. Moon stood in the beating tropical sun, wiped his face with the ever-present chamois scarf, and watched the opening of the box. It contained—was chock-full of—snow shovels. There may well have been a shortage of snow shovels at the Marine Corps Cold Weather Training Facility in Pickle Meadows, California, or even at Camp Fuji, on the side of that well-known mountain in Japan, but it is likely that neither installation lacked for F-4 tires, since they had no airports. One of them may well have gotten the shipment of tires; at any rate Da Nang got the snow shovels. Da Nang, elevation thirty feet, mean temperature about 85 degrees Fahrenheit. They don't even have a word for snow.

Yes, supply systems are imperfect. And the Zuni is a dandy weapon for a variety of targets. It is deadly accurate and packs a wallop. To superimpose your pipper over the body of a fleeing belligerent and squeeze off a five-inch Zuni is the surest kind of impetus for him to obtain title, fee simple, on a tract of agricultural land. The Zuni is fun to shoot; it goes straight where you point it, leaving an admirable trail of smoke and fire, and will do substantial damage to any number of things, from buildings to tanks, when it gets there. And so of course they couldn't get enough of them.

It could be argued that perhaps nowhere is the Freudian phenomenon of anal character better demonstrated than in the military. To go a step further and recognize Abraham's developmental stages, it could be said that combat units tend to fixate at the anal-expulsive stage, leading, classically, to a personality syndrome of conceit, ambition, and aggressiveness.

Supply units, on the other hand, may be said to have reached fixation at the anal-retentive level, resulting in a personality that is parsimonious and obstinate. But from all military sections may be inferred the backbone of anal chracter: stinginess, orderliness, and compulsive behavior. So that was essentially the bunch that was confronted with the Zuni shortage.

It was something of a dilemma. They had to have Zunis because they were the weapon of choice and of most efficacy against certain kinds of targets. Only they couldn't shoot them at those targets, because then they would run out and have nothing to shoot, or not shoot, as it were, at more of those targets, should they present themselves. In the beginning, good sense seemed to rule. They reasoned that since the Zuni was a swell antipersonnel weapon, and since their primary mission here was to kill or disable the enemy, that Zunis could be used in situations where pilots encountered troops in the open. This policy seemed to work okay for a while, but, as is not uncommon in the course of combat operations, it came under more and more liberal interpretation. If the odd mamasan or stray child so much as scampered off down a trail into the bushes to keep from being blown to kingdom come, that constituted "troops in the open." Any ground fire qualified, whether there was an observable troop or not. The boys began asking the FACs if they saw any movement whatsoever around the target. Finally, if even a dog or water buffalo was seen in the area, it was inferred that people, i.e., troops, could not be far away. And so on.

So they kept shooting up all the Zunis, and sterner measures were called for. Finally, the cooler heads arrived at a new policy. All hot-pad airplanes would carry Zunis at all times, so that they would have the proper weapon for the assault of certain select targets; but in *no* case would they be fired, so they would not run out of the proper weapon for the assault of certain select targets. The only time that Zunis could be expended was when so indicated by a fragmentary combat operations order from Group. On the rare occasion when such a FRAG came down, the objective was always a suspected truck park in the jungle, so the few precious Zunis that did get fired were used in the swelling cottage industry of splinter manufacture.

So when Rawlins looked over his wingman for leaks, flaps down, etc., gave him a thumbs-up, and released the brakes, he carried four Zuni packs on the inboard wing stations that he was not, under any circumstances, to use. He also had a dozen five-hundred-pound bombs. "Condone thirty-seven's on the roll."

He lit the burners, and the heavy iron beast began to roll, awkwardly at first, thumping its way over the cracks in the runway, humming, wheezing, and clanking, grabbing increments of speed and momentum, the acceleration pressing him firmly back against the seat. Gauges were all in the green, the nose wheels came off the ground, he established takeoff attitude. As he rotated, the airplane shuddered slightly and swayed from side to side. Amid the hiss of cockpit air, the intense hum of the J-79s, and a myriad of lesser sounds, with a little bounce at 170 knots, the main gear left the earth and the Phantom became a weapon. He slammed the gear handle up and as the wheels clunked firmly into their wells, the barber-pole indicators flopped to UP. Flap speed. Attitude, airspeed, heading. Trim. Clear your climb corridor. Three hundred knots, secure the burners. Power back to 95 percent. Climb schedule, gauges, trim.

"Dash two's airborne. Switching button four." Dash two was none other than Candyass Cavendish, who had lost his arbitration hearing, and grudgingly agreed to fly again only after Disbursing had cut off his flight pay for a couple of months. The grunt officers, who hacked their way through jungles generally held to be impassable and slogged in such mud during the monsoon season that they all had brown eyes, even the Swedes and California surfers, were fairly magnanimous on the subject of flight pay. They did not, from their accustomed lowly positions in the morass, swarming with snakes and spiders, centipedes and snipers, heat and heartbreak, begrudge the airplane drivers, for a minute, their flight pay. It was just that they could not, for another minute, see how those assholes justified receiving their base pay as Marine officers. One small serendipitous happenstance did derive from the withholding of Candy's flight pay. The payroll clerk who was charged to withhold it was also handling Staff Sergeant O'Flynn's allotment check, which had been dwindling of late. He didn't know what to do with the extra money, so he just sent it along to Mrs. O'Flynn, figuring she could use it as much as anyone. She could, and did. At any rate, Cavendish was back in the air, at least once in a while. Rawlins noted, in the UHF remote channel–indicator window, that Hang Dog, who reposed in the rumble seat, had switched the radio to button four.

"Hayride, Hayride, Condone thirty-seven airborne on a scramble. Two fox-fours with twenty-four delta-twos, passing angels eight for fifteen, feet wet."

"Roger, Condone three seven, rendezvous with Esquire one four, channel forty-four, two seven five for fifteen. Cleared to Paraguay."

"Thirty-seven, roger, Hayride. Flight, button five."

"Condone thirty-seven radio check."

"Two's up."

"Roger. Hello Paraguay, Condone three seven, three one zero from Da Nang at twenty-seven, out of angels ten for one five, over."

"Condone three seven, radar contact, negative traffic, remain this frequency."

"Thirty-seven."

They flew north abeam the lush coastal plain with its strip of white sand and turquoise shallows separating the deep blue of the China Sea from the shimmering, vibrant green of the paddies, their intricate network of dikes stretching off to the distant, rugged, rock outcroppings of the Karst along the Laotian border to the west. Fifteen miles above Hue, Rawlins turned inland toward the Quang Tri River.

"Condone three seven, Paraguay. Contact Esquire one four on button violet."

"Thirty-seven switching."

"Two's up."

"Roger, Two, go trail. Esquire one four, Condone thirty-seven, do you read?"

"Condone, Esquire one four on the two seven seven for fourteen, Dong Ha, over."

"Ah, roger, Esquire. Two fox-fours with twenty-four delta-twos for your control. We're about twenty southeast, angels fifteen."

"Roger, Condone. Request you hold to the southeast high and dry. I've got Asp flight on the target and there's been a minor mishap."

"What's the problem?"

"Well, it seems like Asp lead's back-seater jumped out. I've got a chopper inbound to retrieve him."

"Esquire, we'll hold just north of the Cam Lo River at fifteen. What the hell's going on with Asp?"

"I don't know. I guess the RIO didn't like the way the guy was driving."

Rawlins and Hang Dog were again immersed in a degree of mirth that is not generally expected in war zones. "Hoo, doggies," Hang Dog managed to blurt through his risible sputtering. "I would hate like the umpteenth degree of fiery hell to be that poor sad son of a bitch when he walks back into the ready room and tries to explain why he left the duty vehicle. Jumped ship like a drunken sailor with two hard-ons and a full tank of gas. Hoo doggies!"

"Asp flight's off target, Winchester, departing. You've got it, SAR." Asp was so seething with fury and chagrin that he was not even waiting around to see if his RIO got picked up safely. He was not even waiting for his battle damage assessment from Esquire. But Condone three seven flight had to wait for the chopper to find and extract the red-faced back-seat driver who had, in his ingenuousness (having only arrived in-country the day before), known to a certainty on one of the thirty-degree-dive runs that they were going to crash and would surely die, and had panicked and ejected himself out of the screaming airplane without any instruction to do so, and, it was subsequently established beyond argument, without necessity.

Well, that at least was how it appeared at first blush. Things not always being what they seem, however, there was something more to it. The weapon that Asp lead was attempting to employ in this contest was the lowly 2.75-inch rocket. After three passes, only one of these recalcitrant would-be instruments of death had been convinced to ignite and wobble off toward the good earth. Asp lead was becoming downright frustrated in his war effort, and was some miffed, like a beaver in a retirement home. After another dud, he cried out in forlorn exasperation, to no one in particular, "FUCKIN' REJECTS!"

Voice transmission being what it is in a howling, shrieking jet pointed straight at the ground at five hundred miles an hour, with any number of other agents talking simultaneously in gutteral half-statements and grunts, perhaps the terrified RIO did not understand his pilot's statement perfectly. In truth he was perplexed and bewildered. The tumultuous hubbub and hurly-burly events of this, his first combat sortie, had left him as confused and addlepated as a whirling dervish in a Hula-Hoop factory.

He thought the pilot said "FUCK IT, EJECT!" That distinct impression was, at any rate, strong enough for his purposes. He yanked the curtain and blew on out of there. His career-enhancement factor was lower than whale shit as the Huey wop-wopped him back to Da Nang.

So Rawlins and his wingman bored circular holes in the sky and burned up precious fuel. On every mission they set an arbitrary amount of fuel as being the least you could burn down to before heading home. This fuel state was known as "bingo." Bingo fuel was computed a little on the generous side, so that you would have enough gas to get from the target back to Da Nang, and, if for some reason the field were closed or the runway fouled, enough to divert to Ubon, Thailand, 198 miles away, and still land with a thousand pounds or so. Everyone was fond of saying that there was no target in this good-deal war worth the price of an airplane. Colonel Creed was fairly firm in his insistence that the boys not park any of his airplanes out in the jungle just because they got too interested in the war and ran out of gas. There was, in fact, a squadron LAW that said you were never, ever to land with less than a thousand pounds. It further stated that if you were to land with less than *two* thousand there had by God *better* be some extraordinary circumstances, and you could expect a middle-of-the-line ass-chewing and probably Squadron Duty Officer for three or four nights running.

Phantoms costing anywhere from two to five million dollars, again depending on your conversance with the then-year–dollar enigma and other such fiscal shenanigans, just could not be frittered away, so the cooler heads all pretty much agreed that if you ran out of gas you would have a power of explaining to do. Colonel Creed even had Disbursing print out a breakdown showing how a pilot could pay back the blue-book value of his lost airplane out of his wages. Only at the rate of pay for a lieutenant with flight skins in Vietnam, if they withheld his entire check it would take some twenty years to repay the debt. Of course during those twenty years he would have to eat something, buy uniforms, pay his dues to the Marine Corps Association and Navy Relief, and buy savings bonds. So they could realistically only withhold half of his pay, and at that rate it would take forty years. Even Charleston Clifford Creed could not compel a lieutenant to stay in the Marine Corps for forty years. Still, the point was fairly well established that one's career would not be noticeably enhanced by flaming out on the downwind leg. Well, R² Jones *did* plan a rather long leg on a cross-country back in the States, with a flameout approach. Damn near made it, too. Only landed two or three hundred feet short of the threshold. In a chain-link fence. But then Jones was Jones, and by and large everybody took their bingo fuel pretty seriously.

Finally they plucked the tremulous radar intercept officer out of the primal bushes and everybody could get on with the war. The NVA had been getting on with it right along. Poor old Zulu Company was some bruised. The boys lay in shallow trenches, licking their wounds and slapping bandages on each other when they weren't firing. The Commies saw that they had a swell advantage here, and started ganging up to overrun the little beleaguered bunch of miserable fellows. Only then Rawlins and, yeah, even Cavendish came on the scene and altered their schedule some. They commenced hailing five-hundred-pound, low-drag, general-purpose bombs down on the gang from Hanoi, and the sting of the shrapnel caused those idealists to begin fighting over the short supply of logs there was to get under. There was a good deal of noise, fire, smoke, and dust, too. Tin trumpets and whistles and AK-47s and 122mm rockets just couldn't upstage a couple of noisy F-4B Phantom IIs dropping five-hundred-pounders in pairs. The jarheads loved it. Peering out of their mudholes with the eye that didn't yet have a swath of gauze and cotton over it, they were able to fully appreciate the mayhem that was being wrought a hundred meters or so away, where the bad guys lived. And died.

They made six passes apiece, dropping pairs. As he pulled off from his last run, Cavendish dutifully called bingo fuel. Cavendish, the stolid day-in, day-out epitome of anal character, was not one to be caught hitchhiking with gas can in hand.

"Condone thirty-seven, Dash two's bingo." Rawlins glanced at the fuel gauge. Fifty-two hundred pounds. Bingo for this mission was five thousand. While he was formulating his response, a tiny segment of the general policy of conducting this one little sortie within an effort of millions, Esquire got on the horn.

"Condone thirty-seven, I can't get another flight on here for ten minutes, and these guys are hurting. Can you give me a little more?" So he had seen the Zuni packs.

"Condone three seven dash two is off high and dry, bingo minus two, Winchester." Winchester meant no more ordnance to expend. Cavendish was hardly one to risk career deterioration by shooting illegal missiles at mere gooks.

"Condone, Esquire one four. It looks like they're massing up to overrun Zulu Company. Can you give me a few more passes?"

The barrage of intellectual inputs that was impinging on Rawlins's brain at that moment would perhaps have stalled an IBM 370 for a few seconds. Years of training, thought, and habit patterns were called into question. All the safeguards of career and status, the procedures of years of practice, everything had to be reexamined in this fleeting moment of time. They *were* fighting a war here; how important was that compared to all the safety precautions? Zulu Company *was* about to be wiped out; how did that change the parameters of the flight plan? His first duty was always to the wingmen. That was absolute.

"Dash two, say state."

"Fuel state is four six."

"Roger, Dash two. Why don't you bingo on back. I've got a little extra, so I'll hang around here a while. See you at the barn."

"Condone, Esquire. Do you have additional ordnance? Zulu six says they're dead if we don't get something more on the target."

So the decision was made in a second. No, less than a second. It may not seem momentous, indeed it was fleeting and may be seen as insignificant in the context of a ten-year war—the only one we ever lost. But it was significant to a few American boys who huddled, hurt and bleeding, in the mud of a tropical rain forest in a place they had never even heard of, looking at death a whole lot closer-up and sooner-on than they had ever envisioned as they swaggered into the recruiter's office to sign the paper. And it was significant to the military flying career of Smilin' Jack Rawlins, even though he wasn't much into enhancement. He would be breaking two cardinal commandments of his outfit. He was already down to 4,800 pounds, below bingo fuel. After a few more runs he would definitely land low fuel, if he got home at all, and invoke the wrath of the squadron hierarchy. Maybe there was no target in this good-deal war that was worth the price of an airplane, but, not much given to party-line jingoism, Rawlins harbored a fairly firm conviction that the lives of those guys on the floor of picturesque Helicopter Valley were worth more, somehow, than any number of fucking airplanes. That point would, of course, be arguable from the standpoint of budget and materiel. More directly, the decision would require that he refute policy. Renounce the years of gouging, the mouthing of the platitudes of the powers that were. He was going against SOP. Also he would have to fire the forbidden rockets, which would be looked upon with pronounced solemnity by those cooler heads. But then what was the purpose of the engines and missiles of war, but to eliminate those with whom we felt we could not coexist in some degree of brotherhood and peace? Even if we *were* in *their* country, and not by absolutely verifiably valid invitation. What conceivable reason for being could a five-inch Zuni rocket have, except to save American boys by killing Vietnamese boys? And what of this wonderful war they had given, with attendance required (roll would be taken), whether you wanted to go or not? Since all the elements and animosities were in place, mustn't it be fought? Was he here to curry favor by bowing to effete procedural policy, petty proclamations, or to fight the goddamn war? Who was Rawlins? What was Hecuba to him or he to Hecuba?

If you came to this most foreign of places, with the sanction, indeed the mandate, of your "country right or wrong," to kill, and had only Zunis with which to effect this killing, then you used Zunis.

"Affirm, Esquire. I've got sixteen delta-nines for you."

"Outstanding. Just lace them along the ridge line from east to west. There's at least a couple hundred of 'em up there getting ready to pounce on Zulu."

"One's in." So Rawlins made shallow ten-degree runs, tracing the pipper along said ridge and cranking off the big, fire-and-smoke breathing, explosive-filled rockets that went exactly where he pointed them. And put this one small NVA attack to rout. Sent them clambering down the back side of that ridge and running up those jungle paths like the very blazes. It was one of the few times that he could actually see the enemy. And he kept right after them until Zulu Company was the farthest thing from their minds and the boys of 324B Division were seriously looking for some peace and quiet. Finally the choppers got in and pulled what was left of Zulu out. And some of those stalwarts would live to fight another day; maybe to die in some similar stretch of uninhabited jungle, but not in Helicopter Valley.

"Condone thirty-seven is off Winchester." He had less than three thousand pounds of fuel remaining and Smilin' Jack had to grab some altitude and head for home base. And *raht now*, too. And he was definitely Winchester. He didn't even have a lunch box to throw at them.

"Condone, Esquire one four. Top-notch strike. They're going in for the friendlies, and I'm going to give you fifty confirmed KBA, with another twenty-five suspected. Outstanding mission." Fifty Killed By Air. Rawlins had done his job.

"Condone three seven. Roger the BDA. Departing the area." Well, he had done his job, but in so doing had expended sixteen of the precious Zunis. That would fetch an ass-chewing. What was worse was his fuel state. He had stayed too long at the fair, as the song has it, and now it was going to be nip and tuck getting this bird home.

Hang Dog, an Irishman and proud of it, which phenomenon may have reached its zenith in the sixties, was not a great supporter of demythification. He may have been termed a metaphysical agnostic, but was not inclined utterly to disbelieve that coaches turned into pumpkins at midnight, and such. Perhaps for that reason, the implications of their probable fuel state were not lost on him. He did not have his own fuel quantity gauge, because Mr. Mac in St. Louis and any number of scrambled-eggs-on-bill-capped swabbies had decided in their endless meetings that the driving of the bus was not his concern. But he had heard all the radio transmissions, kept track of the time, and been riding around for years in a section of the vehicle that Rosa Parks had deemed unsatisfactory as early as 1955. But even from the back seat he had acquired a feel for the conduct and duration of a flight. He knew that they had been droning around the pattern at low altitude, guzzling gas, for quite a spell now, that their wingman had called bingo ten or fifteen minutes ago, and that their reserve of usable fuel was likely dwindling.

"Doggie," inquired Hang without a trace of emotion in his voice, "what's our kerosene quotient? Are we going to have to walk back from this one?" There was no emotion in his voice for two reasons. The first was that aviation people spend their entire careers trying to eliminate emotion from their voices, lest such a tremor divulge an inkling of the truth at any given moment. The other was that Hang Dog, like everybody else, had always wanted to test drive the Martin-Baker ejection seat in semi-controlled circumstances, and he quietly hoped this might be his chance. Fuck the airplane, it was no skin off his ass. He wasn't responsible.

"Naw, I think we're okay. I'm indicating about twenty-six hundred pounds. It should take about fifteen hundred and thirty-five miles to climb to angels twenty from here. That's close to halfway. We can make an idle descent from about thirty-two miles out. We ought to get there with six or seven hundred. The weather's CAVU, we'll just hope there's nothing wrong at the field. We'll most definitely not be making any go-arounds, though."

So it was just a matter of nursing that buggy home. As they were climbing up to cruise altitude, the FUEL LEVEL LOW warning light on the telelight panel illuminated. This is a device designed primarily to scare the shit out of the pilot. It did. Even though he was fully aware of the situation, nobody likes to see that light come on. And it came on a little too early, at an indicated 2300 pounds. The "Fuel Level Low" light is activated by a thermistor switch located in the engine-feed fuel tank. When that switch becomes surrounded by air instead of fuel, its resistance equals that of a reference thermistor outside the tank, also surrounded by air. This balances a bridge circuit that turns on the light. When the aircraft is accelerating, decelerating, or maneuvering, fuel sloshes wildly around the tank, and the warning light is not very accurate. Straight and level, however, at a moderate power setting and one g, if the warning light came on at an indicated quantity above its highest parameter of accuracy, which was 2160 pounds, it became the primary indicator of fuel state. The difference between the fuel quantity gauge and the warning light told Rawlins that the gauge was not accurate. While it was telling him he had 2300 pounds left, when the light came on he could not, theoretically, have had more than 2160. Most fuel quantity systems become decreasingly reliable as they move toward the low end of the scale, the time when you tend to be most devilishly interested in the true facts. It wasn't a big discrepancy, maybe 150 pounds or so; still it was another little nagging irritant. So he was worried, but there was nothing he could do about it except hope the field was open when and if he got there, and pray for good gas mileage.

When thirty-two miles rolled up into the distance measuring equipment window, he pulled the throttles smoothly back to idle and started down the hill. Even at idle he was burning over a thousand pounds an hour and the gauge had dipped to about a thousand. When the gauge went below 1000 pounds you just never knew about it. When he leveled at pattern altitude and added power he would burn between three and four thousand pounds an hour. They would make the field, it looked like, but if they were waved off for any reason and made to go around, they would likely have to step over the side.

"Da Nang tower, Condone thirty-seven, five miles north, requesting a downwind entry for three five, minimum fuel." "Minimum fuel" meant, in aviation argot, that he was in serious straits, but not quite ready to declare an official emergency. That would be recorded, be investigated, and be most egregiously embarrassing, maybe worse than jumping out. If he trashed the airplane, he could always claim the fuel gauge wasn't working, he had taken a hit and sustained a grown-up leak in the JP-4 locker, and suchlike. Of course if he were killed or captured it would be okay. But if not, it would have to be his fault, one way or another.

"Condone thirty-seven, Da Nang tower. Roger minimum fuel. The runway is closed for a Thud being towed off with battle damage. Can you hold northwest for a minute or so, sir?"

"Tower, how about landing on the taxiway? I'm low state."

"Negative, Condone. The taxiway is in use. I think the runway will clear first. Can you hold for about a minute?"

Rawlins checked the fuel gauge yet again. It indicated just under 700 pounds. It was only accurate to plus or minus 150 pounds, and had already shown itself to be a little squirrelly. Sweat and pucker time.

"Da Nang, Condone thirty-seven. I can give you one turn, but I've got to land."

"Roger, three seven, you'll be cleared number one. I'm expediting the tow."

It was, as has been occasionally suggested by those describing similar situations, perhaps the longest minute or so that Rawlins had ever spent.

"Doggie," he intoned to Hang Dog, who had also cranked up his intensity factor some. "If those assholes don't get this sorted out pretty quick we're in deep shit."

"Well, first holler your fucking head off. EJECT, EJECT, EJECT. Then punch the EJECT light. Third, pound on the canopy. If I ain't gone by then, I've fainted dead away."

So it was a longish minute. Rawlins wanted to wrap the airplane up and bend it around to where it was headed back toward that runway.

But if he did that he would use up less time and more fuel, because he would have to add power to maintain altitude at the increased bank angle. So he kept it in a gentle bank and did a 360-degree turn, monitoring the gas gauge, which was now down to 500 pounds or so. Sweat and pucker.

"Condone three seven, Da Nang tower. Cleared downwind number one. Altimeter three zero zero one, wind is zero one five at one zero. Advise the midfield arresting gear is still down."

Rawlins rolled out of his turn on the downwind leg to landing, reduced power, dropped the gear just before the abeam position, called "Condone thirty-seven at the one-eighty, all down, final," and put the flaps down as he turned toward his final approach heading. He did not look again at the fuel gauge. It had nothing to tell him. Either they made it or they didn't. He was, it might be said, highly alert. For an instant Rawlins thought of those poor bastards of Zulu Company, all hurt and bleeding and dying. He was only facing verbal abuse, or maybe a sprained ankle if he had to eject. Fuck it. He would do the same thing again.

As he rolled wings level on a short final, a little fast, the starboard engine began to spool down. But they had made it. They clunked down onto the friendly concrete, Rawlins radiating some silent jubilation, and Hang Dog piping gleefully, "Hoo, boy, Doggie. We is HOME!"

As they rolled out, the port engine flamed out. With his dwindling electrical power, Rawlins called the tower for a tow.

"Roger, Condone three seven, we'll contact your squadron. Break, this is Da Nang tower broadcasting in the blind, the field is temporarily closed for removal of a disabled aircraft. Repeat, Da Nang is temporarily closed. . . ."

24

California, 1980s

It may have been inferred that Rawlins suspected, feared even, that he was not exactly winning the race. But of course at the Vulcan V-belt and Avionic Pilotage System Corporation nobody was winning the race, because they were all racing in different directions. The legion of white-collar clerks, few of whom wore white collars because polyester seldom comes in white, each fiercely loyal to his particular division, system, or discipline, and disdainful of all others, fanned out to the points of the accomplishment compass and strove each to be seen as competent and productive within the confines of his own area of endeavor, or "expertise," as many of them would likely have put it. Thus did the Fuel System and Tankage Section devise a marvelous external fuel tank that would double the range of the Advanced Tactical Fighter design. Only they super-imposed it on a computer model of the aircraft that had the wheels up and locked, which was of no importance to the tank people. Only when the tank was installed, the wheels wouldn't come down. Boy howdy, the Alighting Carriage Group didn't take too kindly to that shit. No siree. It did, of course, give them an issue to occupy idle time. Somewhere it is written in the Magna Carta of the Bureaucracy that the guiding purpose of this agglomerate shall be to accomplish a great number of deeds and activities that, per se, have no legitimacy and don't need doing. The functionaries of VVAPS resembled a Gordian knot of paradoxes in search of a bottleneck.

The hive instinct prevailed at the war plant and most of the little drones seemed happy enough swarming and fussing around, though not in the Aristotelian sense. If happiness is "an activity in accordance with virtue," there were those who would have balked at describing the ac-tivity of developing sure-fire means for the destruction of people and property as entirely virtuous. And, technically, their ostensible happiness would fail the test on the grounds that their labors were not something they chose "for its own sake and never for the sake of some other thing." Every mother's son (and daughter) in the VVAPS community was toiling strictly and solely for the filthy lucre that came on Friday and fetched them VCRs, limited-partnership interests, and time-sharing vacations in Cabo San Lucas.

But they were far from seditious and, for the most part, gave the appearance at least of being happy in their meaningless jobs. A lot happier than Rawlins was. Well, anyhow they thought they were. Among the happiest of the group was McKinley Mortadella, self-described as "the greatest aerospace design engineer alive today." Though he was an engineer in title only, and had never designed anything, he *was* alive, more or less. "No," he would say, looking down in apparent humility at his reflection in the toes of his plastic shoes, "I'm a total concept man."

His latest total concept was indeed inspired. It was called the Hypersonic Orbital Gliding–Attack Stealth System. It was fondly known by its acronym, HOGASS. By everybody except Mort, that is. The idea was that this omnibus, this Laputan dreadnought, would blast off at Mach 15 or so, loaded to the gunwales with the very latest molecularly recombinant descendents of lyddite, pop into earth orbit, and loiter there, unseen, for weeks at a time. It was to be constructed entirely of advanced, radar-absorbing, composite materials, and would not have a point, angle, or straight-line edge anywhere on its surface. It would be utterly undetectable from the earth, would carry two or three crews to alternate on alert status, and would fairly bristle with passive sensors that could track, map, plot, and home on any square foot of the earth that was selected. The scientists, with their instruments, could monitor any hostile continent, island, or state with a resolution factor of something like one to three million. If the General Secretary of any particular inimical party were to discreetly slip into the sack with a blond show girl, they would know about it. They would even know if she was a real blond or not.

When the Commander in Chief rang the bell, this stealthy, spaceborne destructive complex would slip from orbit and glide silently and invisibly to its target. They would dump the nukes, light the burners, and smoke on home at Mach 12 to reload, change crews, and head back on station. "It is simply invincible," said Mort, at one of the eight-hour meetings he conducted each day and tried to cajole his coworkers into attending. "No conceivable defense system can touch it."

"What about lasers?" asked a yawning middle-aged scientist in a white-on-white short-sleeved shirt and unbuttoned vest, calculator in the pocket. His bulky, rimless glasses sparked reflections of the artificial light.

Doctor Lieutenant Colonel Mortadella flexed his chubby face into a most inscrutable smirk. His eyes danced. "Piffle," said he. "No threat."

"How's that?" asked the engineer, polishing those glasses with a handkerchief that was barely big enough, weak blue eyes drooping.

Mort beamed and hunched forward, placing both hands palms down on the table in a conspiratorial manner. This was one of the small great moments that he staged for himself in all these gatherings. He had learned the technique in the course entitled "The Staff Meeting: Invaluable Management Tool, or Waste of Time?" It was part of his graduate engineering management curriculum. That course was a much-acclaimed, highly technical, comprehensive waste of time offered in VVAPS facilities one night a week, at a hundred dollars a unit, paid by the company, conducted by the extension section of Cal Tech. It was designed to add a title to the résumés of lackluster engineers and boost the sagging endowment of the university. And to ingrain by rote the concepts of the Critical Path Method and the Periodic Evaluation and Review Technique. And to teach the student to be assertive in the workplace.

"Gentlemen," said Mort in modulated tones, as if he were announcing the score of the Air Force–Navy game, "we do it with mirrors." There were three women present, two from the Finance and Budget Section, and one psychologist from the Crew Station, Environmental Control, and Creature Comfort Group, but Mort generously included them in his salutation of "Gentlemen."

"All done with mirrors," he continued. "It operates on the principle of the operculum. We have learned from the gastropods and the glyptodonts. We derive from the latest metallurgical advances, esoteric alloys, and sophisticated applications the capability to equip each and every skin plate of the aircraft with a sort of mirrored eyelid. When the sensors detect laser incursion, the entire ship becomes a multifaceted mirror, reflecting concentrated light beams harmlessly away. The technology is in place, gentlemen."

Maybe the whole world was a stage, but Rawlins, half-asleep at the back of the long conference table, envisioned it as a ballroom. A giant, worldwide Roseland, with flushed, rosy-complexioned couples all over the world doing the mazurka, the hornpipe, the schottische, the gopak, the fandango, the Virginia reel, the hula, and the cotton-eyed Joe as the Russian laser beams glinted and coruscated off of Mortadella's mirrored instrument of devastation in the evening sky. What a happy thought.

At any rate, the brightest lights in the Pentagon were intrigued enough that they managed to scrape up a trillion or so dollars and allocate it to Mort's super-secret black-hole design group at VVAPS. It was the largest exploratory design contract ever let, dollarwise, so when they won it, the company spent twenty thousand dollars on a victory celebration, to which six of the most politically astute engineers, two proposals people, the contract administrator, one middle manager from manufacturing and fabrication, and all eighty-seven vice presidents were invited. When they heard the dollar amounts involved, sixty of the vice presidents formed an in-house cartel, set about making the HOGASS project a separate division of the company, and pledged that they would, to a man, all sixty of them, see that it was judiciously and efficiently managed. There remained only the trivial detail that Mort had never designed anything before and didn't know how. To that end, he aligned himself with two of the most renowned, visionary scientists that happened to be available.

The first was Sir Cecil Mullet-Smithpher, a doddering Englishman who derived enough American taxpayers' money, through the auspices of VVAPS, to hang on to all his hereditary lands, titles, peerages, and so forth back home in Jolly Old, where he visited for a month each year. Mullet-Smithpher had been a group captain during the big war, but had, alas, been confined to hospital with aggravated bunions during most of the battle of Britain. He only just got up in time to be shot down over London on the last day, Halloween, but he remembered those times fondly and often. His design experience was formidable, dating nearly to the inception of flight itself. The name Mullet-Smithpher was said to appear on the patent for the Gypsy Moth. He had not, of course, conceived of a prototype since the dawn of the jet age; still his basis in aeronautical design was unassailable. No one knew how old Sir Cecil was.

The other member of the team was a most baffling Chinaman by the name of Gung Hay Wong. Wong had studied extensively in Eastern Europe as a preteen prodigy, until the sibling rivalry between Mao and Nikita turned into a full-blown spat. He then established himself as the foremost theoretical physicist, if not the only one, in China, until the Red Guards effected his transfer from the ivory tower to a rural rice paddy, where he was taught the folly of pure science and exposed to the inspirational tenets of the Cultural Revolution. It was there that Wong, operating a wooden plow propelled through the mud by a water buffalo, had the first inklings of his famous theorem of inverse area–rule drag propagation compensation as related to motive power and energy expended. This fascinating observation, known commonly in the Western world as the Cast Iron Stiletto Hypothesis, boosted Wong to international prominence after his defection, principally because none of his peers would admit to not understanding a word of it.

So the folks at VVAPS were gearing up for a *major* program. There would be lots of overtime, lots of griping, and lots of money in the months to come. Never mind that the HOGASS concept was unwise, unworkable, untenable, and purely impossible. Never mind that this juggernaut and all its attendant crew and cargo could never be built, never reach orbit under its own power, and even if it could it would be absolutely incapable of carrying sufficient fuel to glide down, destroy its target, then fire up the engines and smoke on home, half a world away. Never mind that it defied every law of physics, nature, and common sense—they would cross that *pons asinorum* when they came to it. Mortadella and company would design the sumbitch anyway.

"I wonder what the poor people are doing today," said Harley Cadavery with a grin that overpowered the statement. He and Rawlins were cruising a mile or two off the beach in Harley's immaculate old wood-hulled Coast Rhodes. It was a pleasant, sunny day with good winds and they were lunching on potato salad, Harley's laudable Buffalo-style chicken wings, cheese, apples, and a jug of Gallo wine.

Rawlins drained his plastic cup and refilled it. "Well, I reckon they're sweltering on the freeways and in the ghettos, ingesting the fumes of gasoline, hemp, and glue, hating each other and us, scheming on what they can steal or how to promote a bigger cut from the welfare state."

This was about as close to happy as the two middle-aged bureaucrats got anymore. The soft rush of waves against the hull fostered a pensive, epistemological frame of mind. "The Me generation," Rawlins mused, "the yuppies. Random violence. The so-called survivalists. Kidnapping, terrorism. How'd we get this way, Harley? What's become of our values? What about that old expression the enlightened thinkers used to kick around, 'the dignity of man'? If man ever had any dignity it's long gone now. What poisoned us, Harley?"

"The sixties, pure and simple. Everything became relative all of a sudden. The age-old concept of good and evil disappeared and was replaced with a bastardized idea you might call 'personal ethics.' The notion of a higher virtue or duty that had guided the serious thinkers over the centuries was dismantled and reformed into a hodgepodge of arbitrary, relative values. The test very quickly became if you wanted to do something, like burn down a bank, figurehead of the capitalist conspiracy, that was Purely just; but if there was something you *didn't* particularly want to do, like be drafted into the army and get your ass shot off, that was most egregiously *un*just. Basically, everybody under thirty, those who had never fought for anything, earned or built anything, or paid any dues—students, they called themselves, and some were, many weren't, but bums, dopers, and hippies didn't sound as grand as 'students'—this bunch suddenly came, through pure logic, to the inescapable conclusion that everything ought to be done their way, and they sought to justify that position, to validate it, under the blanket of relative morality."

"What they did," Rawlins forging ahead with this idea, "was tie all these notions to the civil rights movement. That gave 'em validity in spades."

"Damn tootin'. Civil rights is the only genuine plank in the whole Babel of social engineering that has failed so miserably in this country. Nobody is 'entitled' by nature to a damn thing except the purely *equal* opportunity to compete. Constitution says so, and in this country that's the LAW, brother."

"God. And that idea was strong enough to carry all that baggage."

"Sure. The kids, that vast army of children who were rebelling against every policy, rule, proscription, and commandment of their elders, joined together and became politicized. They cast themselves as being vested with all kinds of 'rights' that could claim no legitimate origins, other than that constitutional guarantee of equality; life, liberty, and the pursuit of happiness. But that was enough. If you wanted to support Communist insurgency and Marxist expansionism, you had that solemn right. You could boycott classes, intimidate teachers, avoid the draft, sabotage the Establishment, disrupt meetings, hold hostages, and demand an equal voice in the running of everything from the university to the country, even though you paid no taxes, had no experience, and couldn't even run your own communes without food stamps. And all this in the name of the most immaculate, righteous ideology." Harley began to tamp a new load into his pipe.

"I suspect our little war had a bunch to do with that kind of thinking." Rawlins started on another chicken wing. "Fomenting civil disobedience and that type of shenanigans."

"You bet," Harley blurted between vigorous puffs. "As soon as Johnson sent the troops in and they began getting maimed on the six o'clock news pretty regular, why all our young philosophers, in their dedicated investigation of causes, ethics, and duty, figured out right quick that this was a highly unjust and immoral war, and that their principles just wouldn't let them support it. At least not to the extent of attending."

Rawlins smiled. "Yeah, I guess that was the rallying point, that stupid war. And once they got to demonstrating and protesting and carrying on, they began to discover how much power they really had; how disruptive and formidable an element they could be in an already troubled and weakened society. And they soon found plenty of other aspects of how that society was being tended to, and what it required of them, that they didn't like either. Protesting the war, as an anti-Establishment activity, was getting plenty of ink, more and more support from the moderates, and was becoming pretty successful. So the next step was to just say fuck society in general; anything the society demanded of its citizens that they weren't willing to chip in was adjudged immoral and pernicious. This here organized society, the Establishment, was trying to fuck with their 'rights' that the children had newly adopted for themselves, and they weren't about to stand still for that shit, no sirree Bob."

"Yeah," said Harley, beaming, almost, as he planned his next statement. Never too far from the pulpit, he loved these discussions. "Let's come about." He swung the helm over, and Rawlins saw to the jib sheets.

"Yeah, those holy, inviolable rights turn out to be nothing more than desires. In his infinite unwillingness to face up to the hard truths of a, shall we say less than idyllic existence within nature, a nature that is both hostile and uncontrollable, modern, liberal, humanist, political man, the man of enlightened self-interest, just cast about for a more comfortable set of truths. To reflect that, he fixed up his language, changing the meanings of things around so unpleasantries of old became more bearable. That way an urge, most any old urge—pick one, an appetite, a self-serving course, became a *principle*. Once the vulgar and profane desires of self-determinate man, outside of nature and the gods of old, were elevated to the status of principles, the next step was to install them as 'rights,' having a measure of enfranchised legitimacy. Hah!" Harley grinned. "Pissants make the rules up as they go. Things like 'values' and 'commitment' don't mean what they used to."

He puffed his coals to glowing, the miasmic vapors swept away by a stiffening breeze. "The progressive Left will just legislate everything pleasant and mutually supportive into respectability, and outlaw anything difficult, perceived to be dangerous, or, God forbid, unegalitarian. And if it's something too controversial for the liberal politicians to champion, don't worry; the Warren court will take care of it on the sly, and all of a sudden it will be a 'Constitutional right,' even though you could go through the Constitution with an X-ray machine and not find it there. It's deconstructionism; you get a liberal-enough court, and they'll make the Constitution say anything you want it to."

Rawlins fitted a handle to the winch and hardened up on the weather tack. Quartering seas pounded the solid old hull and salt water sprayed in the wind. It all seemed so clean and forthright and, well, natural. Around their conversation, the silence was profound, broken only by the sounds of air and water, an occasional gull, creaks in the rigging, the plangent snap of canvas. A pair of grinning dolphins leaped and cavorted for a time off the port bow. Catalina Island lay squat and dark on the horizon. The only sign of man was a few distant sails. They had been over much of this before, and agreed on most of the points, but it was a kind of pleasant ritual. As frustrated wordsmiths, who spent their days struggling with the tendentious bombast of aerospacese, and its authors, who were much grander citizens than themselves, the boys enjoyed these talks as a sort of collaborative honing of skills, a communicative test-bed. They tried to use fancy words correctly, make a succinct point, construct aphorisms or short, ironic statements that implied more than they said. Once in a while they would correct each other on some obscure point, and that was fine, too.

"Seems to me," said Rawlins, "that it was set up before my good-deal war came along, though. I mean, what's the difference between South Vietnam and South Korea? North Vietnam and North Korea? China and China? The fundamentals leading to the two wars were almost the same in most ways. After World War Two the countries were partitioned by international conference, Communists in the north, next to China, Democrats in the south. Marxists, of course, are not satisfied for a minute with half a loaf, it being their stated purpose to 'bury' capitalism—they only agree to the terms so as to appear reasonable and nonaggressive to the rest of the world, and to calm the waters, the better to begin their *sub rosa* campaign to have it all and have it their way. When the pro-Western populations don't fall into line quick enough, they invade. China and Russia line up solidly behind them; the U.S., in the guise of the U.N., rushes in to shore up the rightist camp. The war is on."

"Curious, ain't it," Harley mused, "how their side always starts the war, and we are branded as 'imperialist aggressors'?"

Rawlins sloshed the wine around in his cup, then drained it. "Yeah, you know. I mean did Angola send troops to Cuba and East Germany? Did Chad invade Libya? S'pose the Mujahedeen rode their donkeys across the state line and picked a fight with Russia? Did Poland or Hungary or

Czechoslovakia try to expand their borders? Naw, the comrades just keep on stirring up trouble. They cause a big fuss someplace where a lot of folks ain't happy, start the demonstrating and the rioting, the terrorism and the guerrilla warfare, and sit back and wait. We'll come stumbling in there with one foot in our mouth and our thumb up our ass, with egg on our face and shit for brains, prating, posturing, and proselytizing. Arrive in the wake of our 'Agency' spooks and shadows, idealistic bureaucrats who, nine times out of ten, will have already fucked the situation up irretrievably."

"Well, you know why that is. Pour me some more of that swill," said Harley. "It's because official American-policy mongers always appeal to the larcenous segment of any population. Our capitalist ethic is most attractive to the pragmatic element—whatever merchant class there is, the traders, the profiteers. I mean we, and thus our policies, *embody* the fucking middle class of the world. And of course the peasants and the aristocrats have always hated the merchants because neither do they have any lineal legitimacy to wealth or power, nor do they produce anything; but still they cut a profit off of everybody else. The American way, while hardly free of corruption at home, absolutely seems to breed it in any other society."

"Yeah, but blunder in there we will, rattling our humongous collection of high-tech sabers, prattling and preaching, showing the flag, saving the world for democracy. And you know what? Nobody gives a fuck about democracy anymore. At least not about our brand of it. What does democracy mean these days, anyway? Half the Communist dictatorships in the world are called the Democratic Republic of something or other. No, the have-nots are just after a little material-want satisfaction, and they don't much care whether it's handed to 'em by a Wobbly or a Bull Moose."

The wine imparted a certain loquacity to Rawlins. "The Soviet emissaries know that shit. They turn up there and find the disgruntled ones, them sulky sumbitches that ain't got much to lose. 'Look, they say, y'all workers are getting a bum deal and we don't like to see that. Let us help you out and you can have it all *your* way. We'll send you all the machine guns and Cubans and shit you need and help you boot these elitist capitalist-pig aggressors the fuck out of here and then you can run things the way *you* want to.' It's not true, they never let 'em do things their own way, but that's what they tell 'em. And that's what they want to hear.

"We, on the other hand, usually don't arrive until the situation is already hopeless, at the request of the standing government, always corrupt, who has noticed that the natives are restless. The reason they are restless, aside from Marxist foment, is that said government has squeezed them until they resemble so many bloodless turnips. They have nothing left to offer the rulers except bile. And that's who *we* invariably seek out: that most successful native criminal faction, the ruling class. 'No sweat,' we say. 'We'll send you some aid and advisers and help stamp out this brushfire. But listen! You *must* show a little more compassion, and guarantee the human rights of your subjects. The death squads have to go. And you should start thinking about elections and all. Or at least talking about them, okay?'

" '*Certainement, Sahib,*' they always say. 'You betchum, Red Ryder. Consider him done. Look, just send the stuff here to the courthouse. We will be most scrupulous in our efforts to ensure that everybody gets his share.' " Rawlins felt that his mouth was running well. Hell, he was right on the verge of explaining away all the troubles of the world.

"And to the disgruntled ones we say, 'Aw, hey, man. Look, we can settle this thing democratically. There's no need for violence and the destruction of property and all that barbarian stuff. We'll just sit down at the negotiating table as rational men and work it out to everyone's satisfaction. It's a win-win situation.' Which is to say, let's compromise and do what *I* want. So sanctimonious we don't even think to lie. No, it's 'Let us help you out and you can have it all *our* way.' To which they reply, 'Uh, can this be *déjà vu*? We're familiar with the concept. Thanks, but no thanks.' And they can't get out of those homespun peasant rags fast enough, so as to get in bed with the Russians. What the Third World Wretched want is a piece of dirt, the opportunity to grow something on it, and the usurious tax-and-tithe monster off their backs. That's what the Russians promise, but we're a little too naive, a little too honest. Dulles diplomacy and lessons in the art of compromise they don't much need."

"Ya know," said Harley, "I see America in the world today as the kid in school who's just so smug and self-satisfied and holy, you want to take an axe to the son of a bitch. The one with superior information, but who seems to be almost, very nearly, genuinely interested in your point of view—one that, it has somehow been established, magically, is inferior in substance, evidence, and conception to his own. I don't think anybody in the world likes us much anymore."

That image rang true to Rawlins. "Well, they call us the 'Great Satan.' We are whipping boy to the planet, the scapegoat for the unfortunate multitudes, who see themselves as patently better people than we are, though less materially enriched. Some perverse, diabolic quirk of nature has caused her to smile most favorably upon us, the spiritually inferior and undeserving. So we were friendly to the Shah. Why not be? You can't tell me the fucking Shah was any more oppressive than that sweetheart Khomeini."

"Oh, but don't they resent that shit, though. Here, take the tiller. I gotta piss." Harley went below to attend to his business, but raised his voice a couple of notches, and kept right on talking. "The ugly American has reached a state of supreme abomination. And we were champions of the goddamn world when it needed saving. Around 1918 or '44 the citizens were tripping over each other trying to dedicate statues to the doughboys and G.I. Joe. And didn't everybody queue up for their Marshall Plan handouts! Our fucking defeated enemies loved us more then than our friends and allies do today."

"Since these revolutionary peasants of the Third World who, remember, Harley, have nothing to lose, have come into prominence and become the darlings of the progressive Left, which *is* world politics today, we have got ourselves a passle of resentment and acrimony."

Out of nowhere Rawlins was struck with a playful idea. He giggled and, without thinking, acted on it. He threw the helm hard over and jibed the boat in the light wind.

"Tidal wave," he called out in mock alarm, just as the thumping and banging of Harley Cadavery, in mid-piss, careening off a bulkhead, could be heard.

"You cocksucker! You'll pay for this!" could also be heard just a moment later.

Rawlins laughed his ass off as a flushed and flustered but still grinning Harley emerged from the hatchway. "You cocksucker," he said again.

"Couldn't help it, man," said a repentant Rawlins. "Bump in the road. But you were saying, everybody hates us."

"Yeah. Al Capp saw it all," said Harley, silently vowing revenge, but settling in at the helm again. "We have become the Schmoo. Everybody flattens us with brickbats and we bounce right back up, giving forth bread and milk and honey. The funny thing is most of them are so bitter they seem to enjoy knocking us down more than they do collecting the bounty. Hell, modern liberal America in all our guilt-ridden notion of *noblesse oblige* would feed the entire Third World if they'd just do things *our* way. You reckon them poor buggers *like* being miserable?"

"I do think there's some truth in that." Rawlins was in earnest. "Take your average Shi'ite Moslem. He'd pick martyrdom over the bourgeoisie hands down. And there's not a lot of healthy, comfortable, living martyrs running around. I've got a theory on that, too. It has to do with the ranking of sins."

"Ranking of sins?"

"Yeah. Pride, envy, and anger have emerged as the designer sins of choice these days. Gluttony, covetousness, lust, and sloth are out. The savages of most of the impoverished nations have enough touch with reality to have looked around and seen that even under the most immaculate socialism they won't have what we've got. After the 'people' have triumphed and redistributed everything, they still won't have much. That's okay; it has to be, because there ain't no more to pass around. As someone once pointed out, divvying up property won't cure the anguish of the soul. I mean, these terrorists ain't so dumb as to think they're going to *get* anything by murdering innocent people; they just want to hurt somebody. And most of those lovely children don't even understand or want what we've got. But that is by no means any reason that we shouldn't be punished for having too much of whatever it is that we have."

The key idea there may have been punishment. The current terrorism and genocide sometimes appear to be motivated by nothing more than blind retribution. It comes from the masses being so angry they just want to cause somebody pain, and it doesn't much matter who or why. They are so wrathful and sore that they lash out in all directions; they are not trying to secure something better for themselves so much as they are seeking vengeance; just punishing the world and its people, attempting to make others as miserable and sick as they are themselves. Pettibone may well have had an opinion on this phenomenon.

"It's hard to explain, Harley. Why? What kind of satisfaction can be derived from blowing up an airplane full of innocent people? Diplomacy used to be gunboats in Manila Harbor and Rough Riders racing up and down San Juan Hill. However ill-chosen and untoward some of our schemes might have been, at least they were manly. Now it's a car bomb against a synagogue, or machine guns in an ice-cream parlor. What the fuck motivates these people, Harley?"

"Well, for one thing, the degree of guilt or innocence no longer dictates. The disciples of Marx and Lenin have convinced the great bloody unwashed that they are the victims of a worldwide capitalist conspiracy; we're all in it together and the middle-aged housewife or three-year-old child is just as deserving of a bullet or a Molotov cocktail as the next man. If you're an American or a Western European or a Christian or a Jew you're a guilty son of a bitch, that's all."

"Bullshit. They think everybody's guilty. Look what the Vietnamese did to their neighbors after we left. Or take the Iranians. They have public executions once or twice a week just to remind the folks how humane they are."

Indeed, Pettibone could have told them that everybody *is* guilty to some extent. Could have told them things like the fact that Cambodia now has an official "Day of National Hatred" for Pol Pot and the Khmer Rouge. And they weren't even round-eyes. Good, Oriental boys next door. Devout Communists just like everyone else, but they wasted upwards of three million of their friends and neighbors. That's not in Hitler's league, but it's fairly scary for a little country the size of Missouri. The "bureaucracy of death" they call it. As they killed off teenagers, the Khmer Rouge proved most innovative in dealing with the declining school population. Some of our local districts with dwindling student bodies and revenues, beset by mushrooming non-teacher operating expenses, might take note. They just converted the Tuol Sleng High School in Phnom Penh into an abattoir. A regular little shop of horrors, with torture manuals and everything. Then when the "good" Communists from Vietnam marched in and chased the "bad" local Communists back into the jungle, they converted the school again. It is now known as the "Museum of Genocidal Crime." And of course the "good" Communists turned out to be better than the "bad" Communists, but only just. Now instead of being massacred for various unclear reasons, the folks get to work and suffer and starve in a terrifying police state, utterly devoid of hope. And be displaced, separated from family and friends, overworked, abused, constantly indoctrinated, and starve some more. And this by the hand of those lovely, seraphic Vietnamese nationalists who became the darlings of the whole progressive Left of the world when we, the baby-murderers, so brutally invaded "their" country during that immoral war. Ask a Cambodian how he likes Ho Chi Minh's idea of the perfect harmony. You have to be pretty hungry and tired of conditions to get in a rowboat with a bottle of water and no compass, and head for Australia. Oh, Pettibone could have told them many things, but Rawlins and Harley thought they were figuring it all out pretty satisfactorily for themselves.

"Yeah, but when we went to Vietnam, we were the aggressors," Harley said.

"So the world proclaimed. And yet we had no covetous motive. There sure as hell wasn't anything in that shithole country we wanted. I think every one of our so-called leaders truly believed we were helping the people and doing good. They might have been naive; they might have been wrong, but they *thought* they were doing the right thing. Saving democracy for the masses. Guarding against Communist encroachment, Russian expansionism. Why the fuck does everybody hate us so much for trying to do the right thing?"

" 'Cause we do it wrong. The world saw your war as the invasion of a little weak country by a big strong one. They don't like the implications. It's the same thing with Russia in Afghanistan. Somebody invited them in, too, but the world ain't buying it. They don't belong there."

Rawlins mused. "Well, that's true enough, but it brings me back to my original question, why was Korea different from Vietnam? What changed all of a sudden?"

Harley came a point higher into the wind and studied the horizon. "It didn't happen all of a sudden. Maybe what passes for moral thought today started a hundred years or so ago, when Nietzsche announced that God was dead, meaning that modern science had destroyed all our myths, the linchpin of our system of values, by proving that there are no miracles. I don't know."

"Well, if He's not dead, He's a very sick man."

"Yeah. When Zarathustra mouthed the obituary nobody paid much attention, especially Americans, but it was true. I think in a way that was the beginning of all the fear and loathing and instant gratification we're awash in today."

"Why do you think it took a hundred years to sink in?"

"Well, it had to be a gradual process. Suddenly bereft of what had been the basis for all metaphysical thought for three millennia, the scientists and sociologists, the secular humanists and practical egalitarians had to scrounge around pretty sprylike and grasp at a whole bunch of straws trying to replace it. It took 'em a while to put together a scrub team of gods and truths, and get it on the field. Of course America, sometimes referred to as a 'cultural wasteland,' was sucking hind teat. We had no tradition of serious thinking to call upon, no old factories to restart; putting on a graveyard shift wouldn't solve this production problem. About the only concepts we've given the world are the idea of pragmatism and the capitalist work ethic; and somehow, 'good old American know-how' won't fill the spiritual void."

"Well, if the Frenchman was right, and we were a nation that had progressed from savagery to decadence, with no intervening period of civilization, maybe it was time to come up with a substitute for God. That job fell to the social scientists."

Harley leaned back against a cushion, sucked on his pipe, and gazed into the swirling foam of the swells. Rawlins took his shirt off and poured them more wine. The inactivity of his life at VVAPS showed in the gut that hung over his belt.

"And of course we had to import our seed thought from Europe, because we didn't have much to start with," Harley finished.

"Well, we may have grabbed up a few of their ideas, but we only took what we liked, things that seemed to fit with our peculiar idea of absolute equality and universal opportunity. And maybe a few odds and ends of notions to hook them together. We wanted a sure-enough hybrid, a purely *American* God that would provide the foundation of soul, of culture, that was needed for us to reach our potential as humans." Rawlins laughed. "Talk about rose-colored glasses!"

Harley grinned. "Well, sure. America was the perfect nativity setting, the only one, for shirtsleeve utopianism. Because we had the frontier. Everything was possible for *everybody*. The Europeans had been locked in for centuries. Lacking gills, they couldn't pick up and move west when things got dicey. They had long ago begun devising social contracts and systems of thought that would allow them to live in some kind of harmony and safety, at least when they weren't at war, within prescribed geo-graphical and material limitations. They weren't very successful; seems like they spent most of their time at war. But at least they were thinking along those lines. But not us. Boy, we were *free*. If we didn't like the soil in Appalachia or the government in New York, all we had to do was go out yonder and claim some of that rich bottom land. Every man could have as big a farm, as deep a mine, as he could clear or dig."

"Hell, it had to be. The country was founded by people who had nothing, but figured they deserved just as fair a shake as some blueblood. They set it up so no one, including the government and the church, could limit a man's opportunity."

The breeze shifted slightly, and Harley now pointed too high, began to luff, then fell off and sailed again. His mind was much on their con-versation. "This whole society was founded on boundless optimism. That was our only tenet, our only precept: equal opportunity and unlimited potential. Hard work and frugality would get you anything. Any child could grow up to be president, and every man could go as far as he was willing. We were all immigrants and, with the exception of the slaves, all started even, and there was a great, bounteous land out there to be reaped. Raped, it turned out, but they didn't see it that way for a long, long time. The only things our universities concerned themselves with were music, poetry, manifest destiny, and accounting.

"So we blundered into the twentieth century, stomping, scuffing, crashing through the delicate flowers in hobnail boots, a great optimistic bull, fueled by the conviction that nature was ours for the taking, and guided only by the pragmatism of James and Dewey."

Rawlins was amused at the animation engendered in Harley Cadavery, usually stoic and somewhat professorial, by the sail and this line of discourse. The salt breeze was crisp and so fresh it felt better than usual to breathe. The liter or so of wine sloshing around in his gut had given Rawlins that flush of enthusiasm, a sense of well-being and an interest in the world that he used to have with him always, but seldom felt anymore. The jug was empty now, but, ah, they had another one. It was a banner day, and he felt as good as he was likely to during those darkening times.

They wallowed through the wake of a powerboat that had passed. Its stereo shattered the peaceful quiet, and centerfold material lazed on the foredeck. Harley scowled at the noise and exhaust, passed his cup to Rawlins to refill, then settled himself again. "World War One changed our outlook some. Not right away, though. We came out of the first war more enthusiastic and independent than ever. We could whip the world, and at home the sky was the limit. That attitude prevailed on through the twenties."

"Yeah, but the war jerked us out of isolation. I mean, thousands of Americans got a taste of the continent, whether they wanted it or not. The door was open."

And after the war, Pettibone might have observed, we flocked to Europe to study, to write and paint, to party and tour; in search of a culture, really. Even Barbi had learned that. Fitzgerald, Hemingway, Stein, Dos Passos—all our *cognoscenti* were thinking European. And, if not a student or scholar, everyone was something of a dilettante and at least rubbed elbows with the continental thinkers.

"Yeah, but it took a while before the majority began to notice any influence."

"Well, the Depression got everybody's attention, by God. The good old American know-how didn't know enough; limitless, bountiful nature all of a sudden grew her some limits; the American way didn't work any more. Then they started looking for some new ideas." Rawlins chuckled. "People were hungry and nobody was working and *laissez-faire* capitalism wasn't such a hot ticket any more."

"That was right after the Russian revolution." Harley relished this part. "All the knee-jerk liberals were in love with the noble Soviet experiment. They read a smattering of Marx's claptrap and said, 'Gee, won't it be swell when everybody owns equal parts of everything, and has plenty to eat and all the stuff that's needed, and we can all live in peace and happiness and tranquillity for ever after?' So all the intellectuals became Communists for a while. That was likely when the doctrine of nihilism really took root among the literati. At any rate, that insidious notion is still with us, thanks to Kropotkin, but we saw the height of it in the sixties when the kids recognized no authority and figured they had to destroy all institutions, political and economic. 'Burn, baby, burn,' I believe their slogan was. Hah!"

Rawlins showed a kind of rueful smile. "All that rioting and shit. Blowing up banks. Burning draft records. Fighting hordes of armed police with rocks and bottles. I tell you, in the early fifties we just wouldn't have believed such stuff was possible. But then, in a way, I guess those kids were only imitating what we were doing in Vietnam. Violence to effect social change, you know? God, it's ironic, isn't it? Those kids fought their little mock battles, but real enough if you got your head busted, and took their licks to try to keep us from fighting our battles and taking, or giving, our licks. But like I said, in the fifties, patriotism and civil obedience weren't even questioned. Boy, we came a long way in ten years."

Harley came about and headed back toward shore. The wind had slacked. They rigged a finger pole and sailed wing and wing for a time, with no appreciable relative wind, everything suddenly quieter, the sun warmer. "The fifties was a crucial period. To get back to my thumbnail theory of modern man: Marxism spread through the intellectual community during the Depression. And nihilism was there, especially in the radical fringes. We took on other nefarious European baggage like phenomenology and existentialism and the academic stage was set. Or it was set to be set, because the espousal of such doctrines within the institution begets new generations of initiates who tend to be academics because they are comfortable with the teachings and eager to spread the word."

"Then World War Two ended the Depression. That shook things up some. What happened to our national thought process then?"

"Several things. Of course we were more or less allied with Russia against the Nazis. That gave the Soviets added legitimacy in some people's minds. Also, more of our people were exposed to more European ideas, and, because of its scope and malignity, the numbers of Americans involved, and the improvement in communications and news coverage, we were reminded in more graphic detail and with more immediacy than ever before that war is indeed hell. The newsreels brought it right home. And that war is something to be avoided at all costs. Hah. That sentiment is with us more than ever."

"Oh, amen. That's what tore the country apart in the late sixties."

"And there was more, lots more. Huge segments of the population went from being solid, rural groups with deep roots to mobile, urban ones, adrift. As a nation we undertook to save the world, and in doing so lost an innocence we'll never regain. We were on the move, and, for better or for worse, poised to become more closely integrated into the world community. The winds of change, as they say, were whipping up some fresh turbulence."

But perhaps the more important social changes of the period were adjunctive ones. Pettibone knew. The war signaled the destruction of the family in this country. The men were all mobilized. Whether on their bellies through the sand of South Sea atolls, in lumbering troop ships as sitting ducks for the U-boats, or by plane, train, bus, and thumb to every corner of this country, they were all traveling. Traveling, seeing the world, and meeting girls. In some cases girls that another traveler had left behind only the week before. Traveling and fucking everything they could get their dick into, so long as it breathed and maintained a temperature in the neighborhood of 98.6 degrees, because the feeling at large was that there might not be any tomorrow. And most of the girls also abandoned, at least temporarily, prewar decorum. Hell, there might *not* be any tomorrow. Her particular Joe, whether slogging across North Africa or crawling his way up the Marianas, or rotting in a prison camp, might not have been able to write for months; she didn't know if he was dead or alive, but he *was* far, far away. And the boy she met at the USO dance was *so* young, and *so* gentle, and was going overseas in three days. Didn't he deserve at least a memory to take with him?

And all the women went to work. The preschool and the baby-sitting and day-care industries blossomed. Instead of raising the little beggars, mother tripped off to her turret lathe for an eight-hour shift each day. Women began to wear pants! And their men weren't there to influence them, in their not so subtle ways, to "enter ye in at the strait gate." There were lots of strange, interesting males drifting around who would suggest a broader path, but the protective, familial men were all off warring. These women had money and unprecedented freedom. Life, generally, was unfolding at a fever pitch and the temptations were great. Women were handed more liberation in two years of the war than they got in two decades of clamoring for it later on. They bought cars and ran households. They paid the bills, disciplined the children, and devised ways to take eight or ten hours out of each day and still get most of their old-fashioned womanly stuff done. That was the first big step toward the independence that women now have.

And divorce came into its own during that time. So many tenuous unions were formed in the desperation of wartime. A clerk at the dime store would meet a sailor and spend a whirlwind week of her life with him, every free moment, dancing and drinking and clinging, trying to pack a normal multiyear courtship into that week.

In the excitement of those heady times they would fall into profound like. He would beseech her to marry him, because he knew he was going off to die and there was a primeval urge, an instinctive compulsion to leave something of permanence in this world. For her part, she was flushed with patriotism and would take any action to support the war effort. What better way than to comfort and gratify this lonely boy? So after a quick visit to the justice of the peace, he would sail off to Saipan to be scuttled by a torpedo dropped from a Mitsubishi, and she would continue on at the five-and-ten, swept along in the romantic frenzy of the homefront under full mobilization. She would not hear from him for months or years, if she ever did. If he survived, he would go on to subsequent adventures, living day to day, and she would find other sailors in equal need of succor. Yes, Pettibone knew. A great number of these hasty joinings-together must go asunder.

The chicken was all gone. Rawlins ate an apple and they sipped on their wine, the effects of which had by this time so encouraged their natural garrulity that they drew the occasional puzzled glance from the crews of close-passing boats.

Harley rounded the breakwater only to find himself on a collision course with a glass-hulled sloop on a port tack.

"Starboard!" he barked, with more ferocity than was absolutely necessary, sunburned nose glowing pink, eyes bright. They gave way.

"Ease up, Harley." Rawlins laughed.

"Fuck 'em if they don't know the rules." Harley grinned.

"You'll get our ass busted by the Harbor Patrol. But what you were getting at does make some sense," said Rawlins. "The men were all gone, the women were all working, and the kids were being 'looked after' one way or another. And, boy, it wasn't long after the war was over that the babysitting industry, the science of keeping all those children harmlessly occupied while the adults did other things, got the biggest shot in the arm in the history of man. Television, the fucking twenty-four-hour-a-day opiate of the little people, came to us. I'm sure that had as profound an effect on society as any war or plague, and was not nearly so harmless as it must have seemed in the beginning. A whole generation of kids began to spend more time with Howdy Doody and Beanie than they did with their parents. So the war had ended and the boys had come home. Once again we were free of war forever. Forever until the Korean flap. But I guess we were all so noble and righteous that we didn't mind going over to help little South Korea out. That was kind of an embarrassment, but we finally got a truce and preserved the independence of the South. And there was no great division in this country."

"But, like I said, the fifties was a crucial period." Harley steered past the jetty and into the bay. The sun became a huge red ball as it dipped into the haze and smog to the west. Endless rows of pleasure boats rocked at their moorings, tackle clanking against aluminum masts, a testimony to American ostentation, to having so much. Harley loved his old boat, worked hundreds of hours on it each year, and used it; many of the owners seldom saw theirs. It was a symbol, like the Rolex watch and the Mercedes-Benz, of affluence, of American abundance; of why the majority of the world was seized with envy and resentment, why they hated us, pure and simple.

"When the boys came home, they wanted three things, basically." Harley was planning his tack between the two ferries, going and coming across the two or three hundred yards of the channel. Harley planned everything. "They wanted to settle down, produce children, and go to college. In the fifties, for the first time, everybody went to college. There was the GI Bill to pay for most of it, but in addition, the women, when they weren't pregnant, kept working to make ends meet. And all the young people were able to go to college too. School was a real bargain in those days. With a part-time job and a few loans everybody could do it, and everybody did. It was a time of peace and prosperity and great optimism. Everybody was getting ahead in this world."

"Well, then came the Cold War." Rawlins had become fairly cynical at this stage of his life. "That fucked us up some. That was the beginning of all the conspiracy theories, the widespread paranoia. Of course Russia had the bomb by then, so it was the dawn of the nuclear age, too. Enter Joe McCarthy and you have instant chaos."

"That son of a bitch did more harm to this country than anybody since Jefferson Davis. McCarthy couldn't shine a statesman's boots, but he polarized our whole society. He managed, single-handedly, to destroy the mutual respect that Americans of every stripe had historically had for each other. In my view that was the beginning of the internecine squabbling between the Right and the Left that has torn this poor old country apart."

"Bullshit. That ain't necessarily true. We've always had our differences, like the Civil War, for instance. Or some of our labor-management or native-immigrant disagreements. The cowboys and the sheepherders, for Christ's sake. But it *was* a time of major discord. Before the McCarthy hearings even the Republicans, however grudgingly, paid that devil Roosevelt his due. Maybe they didn't like Harry Truman, but they trusted the son of a bitch. He was on our side, and no doubt about that. And the Democrats felt the same about Ike. Then along comes this shithead rhetorician down from Wisconsin and convinces everybody that his friends and neighbors, wife, husband, children, and cousins are closet Communists hard at work plotting your demise and mine. Nobody's been able to trust anybody else since then."

"Well, see, the liberal, progressive Left was in place. The Marxists and the Keynesians and the devotees of Husserl, Heidegger, Sartre, Camus and that bunch had their power base in the university and all the kids were going to college. The beatniks would be abroad to tempt the rest of us. Then up pops Joe McCarthy and the radical Right. That gave rise to the John Birch Society and their ilk. Later the moral majority, the born-again Christian, and even the survivalist Aryan Brotherhood type of screwball. It was ideological warfare, and we haven't got over it yet. The oligarchy versus the classless society. Well, thrust into that kind of polarity, the average American pragmatist is going to lean to the Left. At least they profess kindness. American thought is based on science and reason. We have no myths, no miracles. So of course the typical, semi-intelligent, middle-of-the-road U.S. Yankee is going to find the shit scared out of him by the radical Right. Them rightist fuckers—scripture-guided divine right—get god-awful comfortable telling us, the uninitiated, how things *really* are. Americans don't like that."

"Boy, ain't that the truth. You take any old U. S. of A. citizen who bears the iniquity of some prejudice or other. It hurts him. Maybe he doesn't like Mexicans or New Yorkers or something, but nine times out of ten he doesn't *like* the fact that he doesn't like those folks. He is ashamed of it because it isn't *right*. No sir, this society is founded on indubitable equality and we don't like to see ourselves otherwise. If there is *de facto* inequality, you'll have to scratch some to make an American admit it. Regardless of the truth, we as a nation just refuse to recognize that sort of thing. Of course we would lean to the Left. The far Right is all caught up in fire and brimstone and punishment. Us Americans ain't much into suffering and the paying of pipers and all. You know, manifest destiny, and all men are created equal. Yeah, I reckon we would generally gravitate toward the left hand of God, if forced to choose. And if we had one. Boy, the right wing just can't stand that."

Harley was approaching his mooring. He would come up into the wind with just about the right momentum to float the old boat into its slip. Rawlins would step nimbly ashore and secure a line. At least that was the routine, but Harley had some other stray thoughts. "Yup. The stage was set. The populace was polarized and ready to quarrel. We were coming off a decade of peace and prosperity. There was a generation of kids who had not known adversity and were taught that they didn't have to put up with that shit. Dying in the jungles of Vietnam was not their idea of the American dream. And, of course, if the *real* truth be known, some were more equal than others, and, as a rule, the more equal they were the more they opposed this clearly unjust war."

"Well, there was a bunch of us all-American Sluggos that still figured if the boss told you to go destroy, that's what you did."

"Sure. But you were twenty-five or thirty. You were raised in wartime and still had a notion of patriotism as honor."

A lot of nineteen-year-olds, particularly those of more fortunate circumstances and more liberal education, had learned an important lesson in that fifties mood of pragmatism: You can manufacture truth. You can make it say any goddamn thing you want it to. You don't have to take the bad with the good. Who needs it? So there it was. The politicians presented a nasty war and the more-equal kids refused to fight it. The less-equal kids had to fight it, but they didn't like it much better than their quasi-educated counterparts. So they sought escape from that unpleasant circumstance. They sought it in drugs and refusal and violence and fragging and hatred. Pettibone would have seen it coming. The ones who took the mud and the shrapnel don't realize it, but they may never forgive those who didn't. And then those enlightened, educated worthies who didn't had to justify their position, so they have been coming on ever since as being just a whole lot holier and nobler than the rest. So the society is rent. And it's not the kind of rift that will heal itself soon. Not only does the rest of the world hate us, but Americans tend to hate each other quite a bit these days. They never used to do that so much.

"Here, fill this up, will you?" Harley said.

"Yeah, the opposition to that war brought civil disobedience into flower." Rawlins poured the wine. "And maybe not always all that civil.

That Belheur cunt even went to Hanoi to give aid to the fucking enemy. These days if you don't like something all you have to do is get two other people to agree with you, and you've got instant credibility and a legitimate cause. Me, me, me. Nobody givs a fuck about anybody else anymore. Today's yuppies are still trading on the yippie politics of the sixties. Everything belongs to the people; take all you can get any way you can get it. We will have no wars because all wars are immoral and illegal and not much fun to fight, so we won't be having any. Everyone evinces profound disdain for any law or custom that doesn't please him. The only thing resembling ethics in this society anymore is that fine line that keeps you out of jail. Anything else goes. The aerospace companies cheat the government, the Wall Street traders cheat the stockholders, the televangelists cheat the faithful, and everybody cheats on their income tax. Hell, we can't even pick a presidential candidate because every time a frontrunner gets established some snoopy reporter peeps into his closet and *voila*, wall-to-wall skeletons."

"Yeah. And then their hard-core supporters get plumb nasty with the news people for pointing out the human frailty of those favorite sons, who, invariably, are known to have all the answers for making life in this nation absolutely, utterly *comfortable*, even if they've never had a job or managed any sort of enterprise. And that's all that matters. It's what they want to hear."

"Well, I know it," said Rawlins, visibly agitated. "The supporters don't care if the son of a bitch cheats, steals, philanders, or lies about it afterwards. They blame the fucking newspaper for telling on him. What have we come to? Is there no longer any honor? Any truth?"

"Back when we had our gods and our myths in place, it was recognized that society was composed of classes or subgroups. One man was a mason, another a farmer, a third a senator. And that was okay. We were taught to accept the differences in our lots and live accordingly. Plato saw that a mason making brick walls was just as valuable a citizen as a senator making bodies of law. But he also saw that there were some folks cut out for masoning and others more adaptable to senatoring, and perhaps never the twain should meet. The philosopher-kings, you know? Aristotle expanded on the idea by noting that most any old activity, so long as it was governed by reason, could be seen as the true good of humankind. But they recognized the differences. Plato said God help us if the soldier should aspire to be a politician. Well, Alexander Haig and every junta in South America notwithstanding, that's a pretty fair observation today. Ike was the exception. He was a swell president. He didn't do much, but we didn't need much of anything done during that period. Old Ike just launched his U-2s, expanded the Cold War, played his golf, played footsie with Kay when he got the chance, and accompanied Mamie to teas, ribbon-cuttings, and champagne-bottle bashings. Of course Ike was probably always more of a politician than a soldier. Bradley and Patton and that bunch did the soldiering while Ike sat up in London and massaged the egos of Montgomery and DeGaulle. He graduated first in his class from staff college—that tells you something. But you've got to hand it to him. He came up with two of the most enduring ideas of this half of the century: the domino theory and the danger of the military-industrial complex. VVAPS included."

"But God was dead. Ike didn't know that, did he?"

"No. He had been dead for a hundred years, but we didn't get the word until Kennedy and his fraternity of best-and-brightest Hahvahd-type intellectuals took over the reins. Then it was all science and charisma. Nobody in power had ever had to work or worry about anything. They were idealists, not pragmatists. There was no substance. It was all image. But the outlook was changing. Ain't it a bitch that Nixon, with all his Quaker shit and Checkers speeches, who has probably never stolen a nickel in his life except by lawyering, which is all thievery pure and simple, but legal, who later proved to be the most intellectualy dishonest son of a bitch since Lincoln on racial equality, or maybe Roosevelt on Pearl Harbor, but Nixon, the vice president, riding a wave of anti-Communist sentiment, with the unqualified support of Dwight David Eisenhower, the modern father of our country, was defeated by Kennedy? Kennedy, a Catholic. Protestant God forbid! The elitist, though he would deny it, who had never had a job, got his PT boat sunk through mis-judgment and probably should have been court-martialed but was given a medal instead, whose money came from the sales of whiskey in the same country that produced Carrie Nation and the Eighteenth Amend-ment? I'll tell you, brother, that was a time of transition. There were Sputniks careening around in space, soon to be followed by Gagarins, Shepards, and Gloomy Guses. They were starting to do transplants and implants and reductions and Christine Jorgensens, and the sky was no longer the limit. Haight-Ashbury was warming up. All we lacked was designer jeans and BMWs and personal computers. Science was every-thing. Yes sir, it was a sure-enough time of change."

As presumably Grampaw Pettibone would by then have apprehended, the changing social attitudes were to have profound effects on a gener-ation of citizens. Along came the Vietnam War, and the first generation to say "Hell no, we won't go." The first time in American history that the elite went to college or Canada and the not-so-elite went to war. This became a serious rift and didn't somehow bode so well for that domestic tranquillity that we are so fond of preambling about. The ones most ethically opposed to that immoral war saw to it one way or another that they did not attend. That left the less affluent, the less vociferous, the less righteous to be drafted and sent to the jungle. Only these boys weren't too keen on going either, for the most part. That generation wasn't into wars at all. They couldn't, in good faith, approve of any of them. So the poor drafted boys began to wonder just why it was that they were forced to go, but the other fellows didn't have to. That setup seemed a touch anomalous in a free society based on equality. So, locked into a mode of escaping from that nasty fucking war any way they could, they fried their brains and became adept at everything from mad atrocities to dereliction of duty to sedition to desertion. They became the first solid American generation of hard-core *cynics*. They couldn't win the war; nobody was *trying* to win it. And, try as they might, the antiwar battalions couldn't seem to stop the war, so they became somewhat cynical too—a whole generation of cynics, opposed not only to the Establishment, whatever that had become, but to each other as well.

But the soldiers in opposition to the war probably didn't have quite so immediate a tendency to cynicism as did those within the war. They would be sent out to capture some nondescript rock or other, lose twenty men doing it, sit on it for three days, and then walk away, and hand it back to the Communists. A week later they would be sent out to capture the same rock, lose twenty more men, and walk away from it again. And the fucking rock was never worth anything in the first place. They were zapped by booby traps, picked off by snipers. Teenage girls wore bandoliers instead of brassieres. Harmless mama-sans might have a claymore tucked up under their *ao dais*. It was snakes and leeches and mud and cold C rations and humping. It was sweating blood for no apparent reason. It was dying without a cause. Then when they came back, if they came back, they were soundly criticized, lectured, and preached to about their iniquity and subhuman barbarity by the ones that elected not to go. Somehow or other these boys became estranged. They just couldn't give themselves over in guileless abandon to the embracing of a society that seemed to love them so little. They just kind of said "Fuck it. Don't bug me. I'll do my own thing."

By the time they finished the second jug of wine they had so warmed to their dialectic, voices rising along with their ardor, that they were receiving a wall of curious if not disapproving glances from the other yachtsmen as they tacked up the crowded channel. They paid it no attention. "When they fought Korea, everybody was used to it," said Harley. "Either they had been fighting for the best part of a decade or wishing they could get into it. So they went. Oh, they grumbled a bunch, and said, 'Why me again?' But go they did. Especially the kids who had not been able to distinguish themselves in the big one. They went, ill-equipped, and fought their war, and at least won a standoff and were welcomed home with, if not heart-warming acceptance, at least not acrimony. The population was accustomed to war. That was what young men did, and always for the most admirable causes."

"But Vietnam was different." Rawlins had begun to wonder more and more what it was he had done in that small, impoverished Asian country, and what it implied to his existence as a human being, a citizen of the world.

"Yep. The Vietnam flap came after a decade of peace and prosperity and comfort and acquisition. The Cold War was beginning to thaw some. Kennedy was dead and Lyndon was doing a very poor act of impersonating FDR. Lyndon could get bridges erected where they didn't even have rivers, as Khrushchev once defined the good bureaucrat, and roads built, but he wasn't a statesman. He was a crafty power-politician, but never a statesman. The extent of his political lore was to try to trade Ho Chi Minh a couple of freeways and some low-cost housing for South Vietnam. What worked in hard-scrabble Texas precincts did not fill the international stage. Ho wouldn't buy it, and the war just kept getting nastier right along."

"So we had a generation of peaceniks who didn't see the fighting of senseless wars as the ideal life's work."

"You bet. There hadn't been any war during their majority, and they didn't see any reason why they should try to find some. The kids in college were indoctrinated against rightist foreign intervention by that coterie of liberal professors, who not only vindicated socialism, but abhorred any hint of colonialism. They didn't want any war in the first place and they sure as hell didn't see little old impecunious Vietnam posing any threat to U.S. interests. Socialism was the doctrine of the ever-expanding Left and the people of Vietnam deserved to have any kind of government they wanted, so why the hell go over there and fight? They didn't."

"Then they drafted all the red-blooded American blue-collar boys who hadn't read Sartre and kind of figured 'their country right or wrong' and continued to escalate the war. And that war, at least in one sense, was

just a series of atrocities. Especially the air war." Rawlins remembered
many a thirty-degree bomb run on a village, strafing blindly in the jungle,
kicking off napalm cans straight and level at fifty feet. "I'm sure I killed
three times as many innocent people as Calley ever did. And you could
see it right there on television every night. Everybody knew how bad it
was, so the antiwar movement burgeoned. The kids saw the violence we
were using in the dirty little war, so they became more violent and
dangerous at home. They started burning banks and robbing Brinks
trucks, and pretty soon the National Guard opened season on demonstrators. The homefront was gripped, paralyzed almost, with sit-ins,
teach-ins, love-ins, riots, demonstrations, general disharmony and discontent."

Harley chuckled. "That pretty well sums it up. The wars went on,
both here and abroad, the gap widened, and true civility disappeared,
permanently, I think, from this society."

Once the fissuring began it wouldn't end. Pettibone may have noted
in passing that we have split off into so many special-interest factions
that you can't count them, each one, following the example of the atrocious
war, the soulless CIA, and the anything-goes protesters, willing to get
a little tougher and nastier than the next. And everyone has become so
bitter and desperate. Liberals are incensed that some of their grand social
programs are being scaled back or eliminated while we build a monolithic
war machine. The CIA mines harbors, feeds, clothes, and arms guerrillas
around the world, while people are hungry and homeless in the heartland;
the conservatives, always under the banner of Christianity, are appalled
that their children can't be taught to mouth biblical homilies in school,
and are given books that mention Darwin, so we have to have the monkey
trials again; pro-lifers and pro-choicers battle in the streets and blow up
clinics; the pope rails about the pill and contraception while the arch-
diocese of Miami buys stock in Johnson & Johnson; environmentalists
spike the timber in national forests; the factories pollute the rivers; the
nuclear protesters throw themselves under trains and sabotage power
plants; motorists have taken to shooting each other for the commission
of an abrupt lane change. From the Ku Klux Klan to the Symbionese
Liberation Army to the crack dealers and gangs on the street, everybody
out there is truculent, armed, and dangerous.

As they neared the slip, Rawlins went forward to stow the jib. Harley
bided his time. The wine had taken a degree or two of suppleness out of
Rawlins's sea legs, and he was taking care to step gingerly amidst the
lines and tackle that lay on the deck.

Harley was dwelling on his chagrin after the interrupted urination of an hour or so earlier. "Hey, Jack," he piped, scarcely able to conceal the glee in his voice. "Watch those sheets. Don't get 'em wet."

Rawlins moved nearer the side to collect the lines and Harley caught him in midstride. Heaved the tiller hard to starboard, sending the not quite judgishly sober Rawlins reeling across the deck. He nearly caught his balance, but instead caught his toe on a cleat and it was all over. The jib sheets did get wet, but no wetter than the hapless Rawlins. What goes around comes around.

Harley pulled up into the wind shaking uncontrollably with mirth. "Sorry, Jack," he managed to sputter. "Bump in the road."

"You son of a bitch," came the watery reply.

After Rawlins had been fished out and dried off some, and the boat was tied up, Harley said, with a gleam in his merry eye, "Rawlins, you're a rude son of a bitch. Going off swimming before I finished my speech."

"You asshole," said a tolerably vexed Rawlins.

Harley collapsed in laughter anew. "I was about to conclude with the pronouncement that our society is plumb fucked up. It's a mess, Jack."

"I will try to paraphrase Gertrude Stein," said Rawlins. "We are all a generation in a shambles. And of course the vets are as bitter as anybody because of the short shrift they got from every quarter. Liberals, conservatives, government, and private sector; nobody wants to admit that we have a whole lot of veterans with a whole lot of problems. Maybe that is changing."

"Generation in shambles, huh? That's not bad. You look like it." Even Rawlins laughed. "But anyway, God is dead and society is falling apart. And if not the root cause, your nasty little war was at least the focal point of our crippling."

Rawlins, clear-headed after his swim, thought about that. He would think more about it in the future.

Of course no one at the Vulcan V-belt and Avionic Pilotage System Corporation knew that God was dead, or cared. Their credos ran to three things: the bureaucracy of science, the science of bureaucracy, and their paid vacations. The pusillanimity of their meretricious moral stance was shared and accepted by nearly all. One person, however, who was conspicuous in her dedication to loftier principles was Electra Gunhammer. Educated at Brown University in a combined major of art history, social ecology, and gender studies, Electra worked as a graphic arts expediter. They got lots of overtime because it was infrequent that any engineer would turn loose of anything for typing, copying, or graphics until the end of shift, so the expediters did needlepoint during the day and their expediting after five, which brought in a little extra money. Electra Gunhammer was a staunch vegetarian and was prominent in an animal rights group known as "Embrace Animals, Don't Murder Them." She had two cats, both fixed. One day she was remarking on the inner peace and sense of serenity to be derived from the cuddling of small furry creatures such as baby harp seals, which less noble souls to the north were in the habit of harvesting with baseball bats. Rawlins agreed with her. He said he knew of an aging one-eyed trouser snake that could use some fondling, but she declined.

The HOGASS proposal was soaring, even though the vehicle itself would likely never get off the ground. Hundreds of engineers in several buildings sat at their computer-aided design screens, tapped the keys furiously, ran their mice around like crazy, then pulled thousands of sheets from the printers. Calculators and PCs hummed on hundreds of desks. Lieutenant Colonel McKinley Mortadella, Ph.D., USAF Ret., was in his element, chairing meetings, giving elaborate audio-visual briefings, and lunching in the executive dining room with vice presidents and swarms of colonels and generals from the Pentagon, Wright-Patterson, and every SAC base in the world. His senior staff were also in admirable fettle, and busier than chipmunks in Plains, Georgia, during the goober harvest.

Sir Cecil Mullet-Smithpher had noticed of a morning, as he clipped his gray mustache, that a pinch of color had returned to his cheek, reminiscent of the days when he had played number-one position for the second squad of the Wolvingate and Heathsedge Guards polo club and diligently worked his way from a minus-one to a zero-goal rating in only eight years. Indeed, there was a spring in his step and a spark in his eye of late; he was again busy, and wonderfully involved in the vast HOGASS project. The Hypersonic Orbital Gliding–Attack Stealth System had been a dream of his, ever since Mortadella had stumbled upon the concept of an armed strategic space shuttle. Legions of baby-faced, bespectacled, aeronautical child-prodigies trooped to his office with rolls of computer-generated Mylar drawings under their arms for his approval. Of course Sir Cecil had never mastered the computer—he did all his calculations on an ancient slide rule and an abacus; still, it was remarkable, the data these lads could generate. His telephone console buzzed and blinked merrily all day long, most of which he spent in meetings, but which drove his secretary near the edge; and at the end of each exhilarating day there would be a pile of messages, mostly urgent, but none of which he ever answered. This happy occurrence reminded him daily of his value to the project; indeed to the world at large.

One hectic day Rawlins had been harried constantly by managers, engineers working for managers, footmen, the very young or very old pseudo-engineers working for the engineers, coordinators, expediters, and administrative assistants. The phone had buzzed all day, distracting him from his distractions. Even a mentally healthy man cannot comfortably spend eight hours trying to explain to an irate retired colonel-manager on the telephone why he can't have a corrected, clean copy of his entire volume on his desk at eight o'clock in the morning, while simultaneously dealing with a passive-aggressive retired technical sergeant–engineer-designate who is whining about three of his four pages of input being excised, only because they were Xeroxed from another document and patently did not apply to this project. And such matters of business.

A deadline was looming near and the lemmings were beginning to mill around nervously. He had accomplished next to nothing during the shift and would likely be in that despised cubicle several hours into his accustomed drinking time. Rawlins was still hung over, was nervous, irritated, frustrated, and had already missed lunch, his nerve-calming and rebuilding time. He was about to walk away from all the confusion, hide out in the tech library, and read Grampaw Pettibone columns in the *Naval Aviation News* until the furor all went away, as it did at 4:42 each afternoon. The expression "quitting time" was as weighty today as in the opening lines of *Gone With the Wind*. Then he might get something done. The phone buzzed one more time. He picked it up.

"Hello, this is Jack."

"Can you hold." It was an imperative, not a question, from a harried female voice. Click. Silence.

Rawlins sighed and started to hang up, when she came back on the line. "Mister Mullet-Smithpher's office. May I help you?" Sir Cecil's secretary was no great shakes at video games, or even pinball machines, but by God, she could hold down a phone console. At least under semi-normal conditions. But this was different. She had been dealing all day with a show of buttons lighting up, going out, and blinking, that resembled flying in to LAX at night. She had maybe gone just a little past phone sanity. There were so many people returning calls, asking questions, leaving messages, and on hold that she didn't quite know who she was talking to anymore. Or much care. Rawlins sighed again, audibly.

"You called me, I didn't call you."

Her mind just wasn't up to speed this late in the day. She was exasperated. Maybe a little non-plussed.

"How can I help you?"

"I don't know. I didn't call you for help."

Two other hold lights were blinking angrily at her. She didn't know who she had called. The thing to do was back out quickly and as gracefully as possible, and move on to the other lights.

"Oh," she stammered. "Will there be anything else, then?"

"No," said Rawlins. And trying to inject a note of poetic irony, "Give me surcease."

"I'm sorry, he's on another line."

Due as much as anything to the frustration of the day, Rawlins began to giggle, almost hysterically. She hung up in panicked disbelief. He went to the library.

Gung Hay Wong, the imperspicuous wizard of high science and third member of the triumvirate, on the other hand, almost never got a phone call, and if he did it was usually short. That was because his English was barely intelligible, especially when extenuated through a telephone wire, without benefit of gesturing, rolling eyes, facial expressions, and body language. He mostly talked about quarks and quanta and differential coefficients and stuff anyway, so nobody called. Wong was a walking Asian *quonundrum*, a regular ambulatory *arcanum arcanorum*. But he walked in a very strange way. Or ways, because it varied from step to step. That is to say he generally moved in a rolling, almost stumbling gait, with much side-to-side and fore-and-aft listing, and an unsure attitude, like a top or a toy gyroscope as its rotation begins to slow down. Interspersed with these long, meandering strides, especially when Wong was in a hurry, would come short bursts of stutter steps, and shuffling glides, at irregular intervals. It was said, privately, in the community of aeronautical engineers, that Wong exhibited pronounced dynamic instability. Even his static stability wasn't so good, unless he was sitting down. He would also, not infrequently, latch onto the nearest handhold to steady his progression. The effect of this action on the vast honeycomb of temporary panels made of light, steel-framed fiberboard covered with hopsack, that divided the thousands of cubicles wherein the VVAPS drones buzzed, teetery at best, was sometimes devastating. The domino theory confirmed.

This phenomenon was, however, easily explained, as Gung Hay Wong was also a genuine miracle of modern medical science. While bicycling to his lab one morning in China, he had been involved in a grisly encounter with a train. The damages were extensive. Wong's left ankle and foot were crushed beyond salvation. So were his right midleg and knee. The bicycle was reduced to scrap metal. The train sustained minimal disrepair. He was rushed to the hospital in the hands, as it were, of providence. His good fortune was that a certain Doctor Ying, on the staff of that very hospital, although largely unknown outside China, had in recent years made the most dramatic advances in autoplastic grafting yet accomplished by man. When the civil defense ambulance crew brought Wong in, they fetched along all the parts that they could scrape up. The Chinese are very meticulous that way. It so happened that, from the lower calf down, right ankle and foot were structurally undamaged, though separated from their host. Dr. Ying immediately had that appendage put on ice, and began to plan his strategy. The left foot and the right knee were beyond repair, but the right foot was usable, so there was nothing for it but to attach the right foot to the left leg. Ying quickly assembled a team of surgeons and attendants. After an eleven-hour operation, which was proclaimed a complete success, the right foot was on the left leg. Having been anesthetized only by acupuncture, and not pumped full of noxious chemicals, Wong was cheerful and animated by the next day, though missing his right leg, which was amputated above the knee. When the pain bothered him, instead of shooting him up with morphine, they just stuck a tiny needle in behind his ear or at some other strategic point, wiggled it, and he felt fine.

By a strange coincidence, Wong's identical twin brother, Gung Ho Yang, was struck by the same train three days later. It was the 6:15 from Tientsin. Oddly, his bicycle was barely scratched, but poor Yang did not fare so well. The iron wheels of the 6:15 pulverized his entire right leg to the hip. From that point, the lower trunk was severed on a diagonal line bisecting the cavity where so many vital organs are found. Yang did not survive. Still, the civil defense ambulance crew, as was their wont, scooped up all the pieces they could, and hauled them in, to see what could be done. As it happened, nothing could, but a sharp young resident physician in the trauma center summoned Dr. Ying, thinking he might be able to use some of the remaining components in his experiments. Dr. Ying, having just visited Gung Hay Wong upstairs for a postoperative examination of his right stump and right or left foot, however you might look at it, had lower extremities much on his mind. As he sorted through the odds and ends that were left of Gung Ho Yang, the intact left leg immediately caught his eye. When the identity of the deceased was established, and his relationship to the patient upstairs, Dr. Ying's heart soared. He gave orders to refrigerate Yang and begin the blood and tissue matching and other tests, and headed up to consult with Wong. This was the chance of a lifetime, an opportunity that may have been sent by the gods, had the Chinese been allowed to have any. To his knowledge the operation had never been attempted before, but he had been preparing for it, at least indirectly, for years. Parallel with his investigation of the practical applications of autoplasty, Ying had been a pioneer in developing the still emerging techniques of homologous transplantation. A lot had been done with various organs, but Ying was primarily a limb man. He had never done a leg before. When the idea was put to Wong, he said, "What the hell, if it will give me mobility, let's go for it," so the surgical team was sent home early to get a good night's sleep, and the possible making of history was set for the next morning.

This time the operation took thirteen hours, it being a larger area with more things to be spliced and connected and so on, but again the procedure was deemed an unqualified achievement, and Gung Hay Wong ended up with his own right foot on his left leg, and his dead brother's left foot on his right leg. History was made, even though it didn't get into the Western medical journals right away.

So through Ying and Yang, Wong was made whole again. Well, whole indeed, even though the parts were somewhat irregularly distributed. Sort of like a jigsaw puzzle in which a frustrated child has forced a piece into a slot that was not quite cut out for it, and then ended up having to jam another one into a place where it wasn't really meant to be either. Oh, there were some limitations on his locomotive powers, but then how many people get run over by a train and can get around at all? Two trains, if you consider all his parts. Well, technically one, since it was the same train, but still, the point would seem to be established. And he did make a complete recovery, and went on to become recognized as one of the foremost theoretical physicists in the world. Ambulation is not much required of theoretical physicists. But Wong did walk funny. And some mornings he had trouble getting his shoes on the wrong feet right.

But even though his phone didn't ring much, Wong was happily immersed in the HOGASS project, and was feeling every bit as powerful and self-important as Mullet-Smithpher, though perhaps not quite so much so as Doctor Lieutenant Colonel McKinley Mortadella. Wong did not go to meetings in other buildings or on other floors, nor did he stumble around to the cubicles of his drove of subordinates to inspect their work; he made them come to him.

Everyone, it seemed, was immersed in the HOGASS project as it burgeoned, some not so happily as Wong. Rawlins was chief among the latter. As the tension and pressure of this recklessly prodigal enterprise built, and thus the autogenous stress, his enthusiasm, already low, dwindled apace. Rawlins would get home at nine or ten o'clock at night, pour the first of the drinks that would save him in the short run and murder him in the long, and wonder about what society was becoming. And what he was becoming, and why.

25

Southeast Asia, 1970s

Barbi went overseas to entertain the troops in the grandest sort of style. She had met Irving, the jet-setter and independent film producer, at one of the SLUR rallies. Irving had not only the Midas touch, but the Beatty touch as well. Every material thing he touched turned to gold and every girl he touched turned to a quivering, orgasmic mass of flesh. Irving was absolutely fascinated with Barbi because she was the ultimate, the consummate political activist and also because she gave consciousness-raising head and owned some of the most provocative lingerie that he had ever stretched over his bald head or bristling hairy chest. Irving had stolen upwards of $700 million from various relatives in the studios and the New York mortgage banking establishment, and he lived, not to put too fine a point on it, very well. Barbi saw Irving as her ticket to world dominance and adored him. When she was not in bed with O'Malley or P. E. Proudbird, or both, or the governor, she was usually in bed with Irving. And they were prodigious. Whenever the Lycra spandex began to stretch and snap or the nipple or other appendage to erect, it was a battle of the titans. Irving could cause Barbi's ears to wiggle for hours on end and she could utterly exhaust him, coax every whimper and moan and secretion, every involuntary tremor, every erg from his physical plant. And talk revolutionary politics the whole time.

Irving had produced seventy-five movies, including *Reunion of the Pep Squad Ghouls*, Parts I through VII. He was modestly proud to note that not one of his films had ever gone into profits and that he had never risked a cent of his own money on a project. He was the end-all, be-all of film financiers. He was that rarest of *aves*, the self-described independent film producer who had actually produced some films. His own self. Barbi was the final word in social Erector-set manipulation, so they hit it off beautifully. It was another marriage made in heaven.

One thing that Irving had derived from his nonprofit films *noir* was a decommissioned Navy cruiser, which he had converted into a private yacht and yclept *Simian Negotiation*. He had hired a retired, regular Navy, ring-knocker commander by the name of Davy Jones to drive his boat, and empowered him to sign on an adequate crew. Irving caused the vessel to be outfitted with saunas and Jacuzzis and rebirthing tanks; there were steam rooms, squash courts, mirrored ceilings, hot and cold running masseuses, gurus, holistic practitioners, heads of state, Playboy bunnies, occasionally Dr. Spock or the Berrigans, bisexual actors, Nobel laureates, silk sheets, closed-circuit XXX-rated TV, an Irish pub, and a Jewish delicatessen. There was SCUBA gear, a heliport, a grand salon that would seat forty for dinner. Screening rooms and gymnasia abounded, and there were ship-to-shore phones, wet bars, and VCRs in every stateroom. Irving's pleasure craft was, if we can indulge ourselves in the fancies of apocryphal lexicographers a bit, Port Out, Starboard Home. Not to say red right returning.

When Irving offered up his hedonic ark for the liberal diplomatic mission to Haiphong Harbor, Barbi was transported with gratitude. It was the perfect vehicle for the healing of international strife. She would pack that sucker to the gunwales with cotton balls, Ace bandages, canned milk, penicillin, and other such goods to alleviate the suffering of her beloved Communist comrades in arms. She would load that ship with goodwill and copies of her album, now platinum, *Lovin' You Is Easy, but Polemics Seems to Take the Longest Time.*

The first thing she did was dispatch the hordes of SLUR faithful to the airports throughout the land, where they were to buttonhole the purveyors of cellular telephones, kitty litter, distilled spirits, Gideon Bibles, and Komatsu forklifts. They were to shake down these Willy Lomans for every thin dime, plug nickel, and fast dollar they could cause them to part with, and send the gold to Los Angeles. Barbi would lade that boat with a cache of medical supplies that would palliate even the bloodiest of Richard Nixon's nasty old bomb strikes. She began buying up iron lungs, fluoroscopes, sphygmomanometers, and fiber-optic surgical lighting systems. She had ultrasonic sensors, rabbits for rabbit tests, amniocentesis equipment, artificial hearts, dialysis machines, centrifuges, autoclaves, plasma, and reams of litmus paper. As ship's chandler, Barbi followed the Jurgensen's market lead and tended more toward fancy red sockeye blueback salmon than Spam, and Chambord red raspberry preserves with liqueur instead of Skippy's chunky peanut butter.

Of course all the high-tech medical machinery would not be used by the North Vietnamese because they didn't know how to use it or have the power supplies to drive it, but would be sold to the Russians so they could evaluate our technology, pronounce it inferior, and then copy it.

Barbi knew nothing firsthand of medical equipment, having disdained, in her love of true natural phenomena, even to have the standard nose job or breast expanding process of her peers. But she was doing a *Beau Geste*—a production number. While the Marine Corps followed the prudent line of pacification, which said that if you get 'em by the balls, their hearts and minds will follow, Barbi was going straight for those vaunted, and ultimately just, hearts and minds themselves, with no intervening appendages. She would supply her comrades in glorious socialism with the very latest in medical hardware. To that end she had every spa and salon in Irving's boat piled high with the most sophisticated diagnostic and therapeutic equipment. Barbi the international socialist would fight the good fight and support the struggle of the people in the best way she knew how.

P. E. Proudbird had become disaffected with her penchant for Native American buckskin and suchlike, and had begun to swath herself in silk *ao dais* and black pajama pants. She had taken to twisting her long lank black hair into a single braid and using strategic eye makeup to enhance her somewhat Oriental features. P.E. always dressed the part.

O'Malley affected camouflage dungarees, flight jackets, and fedora hats, what he fancied a well-traveled paramilitary look. He was later to bring suit against Sylvester Stallone and George Lucas for purloining his own true persona for their fictional heroes. O'Malley had a most pronounced capacity for bitterness.

Davy Jones wore his old Navy khakis without insignia and his baseball cap with scrambled eggs on the bill. He had actually commanded the *Simian Negotiation* when it was known as the USS *Hardstem* and had plied the waters of the Mediterranean in '58, when the Lebanese had thrown an intramural spat about whether Mohammed was the true god or whether his son-in-law Ali was the true god, before he got his ass assassinated, or whether *his* son Hussein was the true link to the true god before he got his ass tortured *and* assassinated, as the Shi'ites were wont to claim, or whether God was the true god, as certain Christians and Jews tended to support.

It was, at any stretch of logic, a fairly moot point, because the Sunnis and the Shi'ites didn't get along much better than the Baptists and the Episcopalians, even though they all worshiped pretty much the same basic deity and had no essential differences in ideology except for the parochial ones. Then of course when Iran and Iraq decided to do war, the Iraqis, 60 percent of whom were Shi'ite Muslims, had to decide whether they hated Persians as much as they loved Shi'ites and whether they loved Arab Sunnis as much as they hated Persian Shi'ites, and so on. They never did get that quite figured out, but generally it boiled down to Arabs versus Persians more than Sunnis versus Shi'ites, which may or may not say something about religion and nationalism, but certainly says something about rag-head arbitration and collective bargaining. And something about world oil prices and pleasure cruises through the Strait of Hormuz.

But Barbi and Irving were headed for another spot on the globe and other politics. They were not much enamored of Iran or Iraq either one, those being a touch fundamentalist in nature, somewhat anti-Zionist, and hardly admirable socialist republics. It was also fairly obvious that Islam had two distinct branches, much like Christians and Jews, or Catholics and Protestants, or Republicans and Democrats. The *shahada* was not of great concern to Barbi even though it stated irrevocably that "There is no god but God, and Mohammed is the messenger of God." She worried less about the addition to the *shahada* provided by the Shi'ites that said, "And Ali is the Friend of God." Even less was Barbi occupied with the subsequent torture and assassination of Ali's son Hussein.

No, Barbi and Irving were out to assuage the travail visited upon the glorious Democratic Republic of Vietnam by the fascist-pig, reactionary, American baby-murderers. Besides which, the next round of Mideast wars had not even been thought of yet except by Pettibone, who would have known that they were fated and must therefore one day come to pass.

So they loaded Irving's yacht with expensive medical equipment, which the Vietnamese had no use for, champagne and caviar, and set sail for Haiphong Harbor, on which the Navy and Air Force were raining down thousand-pounders every morning. They were, of course, in violation of the spirit, gist, and intent of every national policy on giving aid to the enemy. Only being as our politicians had never got around to declaring it, technically we were not at war, so technically they were not breaking any laws. Not that Barbi cared much for laws; she felt that they were for barbers and postal employees, not revolutionaries. Oh, there was an official U.S. ban on travel to North Vietnam, but they defied it.

And Barbi knew that God was dead because she had taken a turn at both *The Communist Manifesto* and *Das Kapital* and worked through several pages of both of them. She had spouted the catechisms of dialectical materialism. And she knew that Lenin had once written that "every idea of God . . . is unutterable vileness." That was good enough for her. After all, the master had written it, hadn't he? Barbi loved Russia, although she had never been there.

But anyway, notwithstanding the minor sectarian backbiting and murder and shit, Iraqis trying to decide whether they loved Arabs of a different congregation more than they did Persians of the same one or not, and whether Ali was indeed "the friend of God," those little desert nations were not yet fighting over their oil or whatever it was they were destined to fight over, but likely oil, in the age of the internal combustion engine, but what some sage of an earlier time had suggested they drink, as they didn't have anything else but a limited supply of camel's milk.

That flap had not yet been joined, as had not Afghanistan, Nicaragua, Lebanon, Chad, Cambodia (now known as Kampuchea, for what reason nobody seems to know), Grenada, Sri Lanka, Laos, Punjab, Seoul, and most other places. No, Vietnam was where the action was, and Barbi was drawn there as surely as Mother Teresa was attracted to poor people.

So Barbi set sail, so to speak, for Vietnam, where the action was, the only game in town in a sense, with zeal and rhetoric and Piper-Heidsieck and *pâté de foie gras* and the medical supplies and Irving's support and *petits fours* and things.

But then no one was ever able to determine for sure whether Rawlins's apparent wholesale murder or Barbi's consummate pacifism, both dedicated entirely to the ultimate good of the masses, the people, Rawlins's in support of one bunch, Barbi's in support of the other, the one that prevailed, but that then wrought some fairly egregious woe not only on the losing bunch, but on several additional bunches in neighboring states—which really helped them more, or hurt less. That would be argued for some time.

So they sailed for Haiphong to "open negotiations with the legitimate government of the Democratic Republic of Vietnam."

Ho Chi Minh met them at the dock, Swedish TV cameras rolling, cashing in on that dynamite publicity, and, tugging on his long, scraggly white beard, remarked to Vo Nguyen Giap, who had accompanied him, because, as head of the NVA he wanted to do some serious negotiating with Barbi, that she was a sure enough pretty fetching young heifer for a round-eye. If Ho had been twenty years younger he may have considered some additional negotiations with Barbi his own self. Then he saw P. E. Proudbird with her Oriental cast, and his interest in Barbi flagged. If Barbi was dressed to the nines for this momentous occasion, P.E. was dressed to the tens. As has been amply demonstrated by Fidel for thirty years and by lesser pissants like Yasir Arafat, it is difficult if not impossible to create fashionable revolutionary garb. Still, Barbi and P.E. were about as successful at pulling off this rag-merchant oxymoron as anyone. They had burned their bras years before because such apparel was at the least confining, tainted with the specter of conventional fiat, and certainly not gay or revolutionary. They had recently, however, purchased new supplies of the sheerest, filmiest, laciest, transparentest support garments because Irving thought they were sexy. Panty hose had also come to the fore about that time, but Irving preferred the garter belt and stockings, so the girls stayed with that mode of girding up. O'Malley fancied those garter belts too. Of course his gear was pretty macho, all sorts of flight suits and leather jackets and snap-brim hats. And bandanas tied around his long, greasy hair. It was close to tragic when he began to go bald and had nothing to tie his bandanas around.

Davy Jones had worn khaki uniforms his whole life. Ho Chi Minh had worn sort of modified Nehru or Mao jackets ever since he had changed his name to He Who Enlightens in 1941.

Having been guaranteed safe passage by the imprimatur of no lesser a personage than Uncle Ho himself, Barbi expected seventy-six trombones with a hundred and ten cornets close behind. That ain't what she got. Ho and Vo picked her up in a '53 Citroën that had more miles on it than *Voyager 2*. There were no bands in town because all non-essential workers had been sent out into the country so that Nixon's boys could not rain on their parade so conveniently.

Every time the air-raid siren went off they had to abandon their Citroën and jump into manholes for a while. Manholes tend to already be populated when one jumps in, and one must accustom oneself to one's fellow inhabitants. As these various creatures, spiders, leeches, rodents, lice, etc., might collectively be described as vermin, Barbi and P.E. evinced some reluctance to coexist in complete harmony with them. Uncle Ho explained patiently that all of nature was in coordinated union and that the small furry rats and mice and suchlike were true friends to the people, not infrequently making the ultimate sacrifice by appearing in the communal soup kettle. Barbi and P.E. went on diets.

Irving was flatly terrified by the little beasties and elected to stand up in the street and take his bombs like a sure-enough man.

Davy Jones stayed on board the yacht, painted a red cross on top of it, and prayed that his former comrades in arms would not blow his khaki-clad ass out of the water.

When the wheezing Citroën finally dragged up to the palace, it was not very palatial. The linen was clean but threadbare. There were bunkers in the yard and 85mm antiaircraft guns in the attic. Everything, including the people, was sort of drab and gray. There was rubble everywhere. The people were grimly polite but seemed tired and withdrawn. There were no flowers, no gay apparel. This was not Barbi's idea of a peace convention. The props were all wrong.

Still, it was her finest hour. Those Swedish cameras were rolling and the flashbulbs were popping, and she would make the best of it. This event would propel her to international prominence and eventually into mainstream American politics. And to her address at the Democratic Convention.

After dropping off the shipload of medical supplies she visited a hospital that specialized in maimed children, and a couple of schools with their playgrounds made into little bomb shelters. They went to the crash site of a B-52, which now served as a sort of shrine, with all manner of revolutionary slogans painted on it. The thick, viscous smoke, packed with hydrocarbons and sulphur dioxide, coming from the fuel and oil storage tanks all around the metropolitan area that were under constant bombardment cast a pall over the city. SAM-2 missiles, resembling the by-then famous flying telephone pole, were seen to be launched regularly, sometimes to fall harmfully back into the city. The scream of jet engines combined with the rumble and rattle of antiaircraft artillery to produce a crescendo of background noise while a raid was in progress. The evil black specks of American fighter-bombers streaked through the sky like angry gnats, plummeting suddenly in dive-bombing attacks on some "selected military target." Occasionally one would burst into orange flame or begin to spew ugly black smoke. They would try to head for the sea, and sometimes a white parachute or two would be seen. Sometimes not. Some never pulled up from their dives. Other specks would be seen buzzing wildly, erratically around in crazy circles, firing smaller missiles, flying fence posts perhaps, at each other. Sometimes they too would be suddenly ignited, like a lucifer match, would become roman candles for a while, and then explode or disappear.

From time to time an East German Embassy or a Cultural Center or a Hungarian Commercial Mission would erupt in smoke and dust and crumble to the street in rubble. The light was eerie because of the overcast of black smoke. For years, in addition to the bombing, the Navy had also surreptitiously laid mines in selected strategic waterways.

Barbi and P.E. were revulsed, outraged, and well, uncomfortable. Irving was terrified. O'Malley offered to man one of the 85s, to get his picture taken, but he was scared too. Barbi and P.E. were at least in the relative comfort of the Citroën, but Irving and O'Malley were riding, with a few assorted dignitaries, in an open truck that followed.

When the hosts felt that the American delegation had seen enough of carnage and destruction and war crimes in progress, they conducted them to a prearranged press conference where all the news agencies from Scandinavia, France, and Eastern Europe were gathered. Barbi was the featured speaker. Her invective and vituperation were swell, but there were still some rough edges to the oratory, taken as a whole piece, that betrayed her C-minus in speech class at Pasadena City College. William Jennings Bryan need not have feared her eloquence.

"Comrades," intoned Barbi. "Brothers and sisters." She purposely avoided the standard "Mr. Secretary, distinguished guests, etc., etc." Barbi was a true socialist.

"In my view, and in the world view, in the view of the peace-loving peoples everywhere"—her words were punctuated by the sound of a salvo of SAM missiles being fired at an unarmed reconnaissance plane—"it is absolutely atrocious the way the slavering dogs of the capitalist administration are forcing my people to perpetuate such atrocities on your people."

Something was lost in the translation. The interpreter was only just familiar with rudimentary English, and had to take considerable license in rendering Barbi's impassioned words understandable to the crowd. It was repeated something like this: "Dogs of the American government are responsible for the destruction and they are very very evil for bringing such death and suffering to the peaceful people of Vietnam." They already knew that. There was polite applause only.

"Comrades," Barbi continued, "believe me, it is not my people, but only the veniality of the disassembling curs in the administration which cause such deprecations to transpire on your homeland. We must unite together with all truly humanitarian nations of love and brother and sisterhood so as to insure that in point of fact, and without a shadow of a doubt, we can most assuredly evert the transgression of this most evil reactionary phenomena upon us, and throw off the chains in terms of hunger, poverty, nuclearism, and senseless murder."

The translation became tougher as Barbi warmed up. She rattled on for several more minutes and finished with a nice flourish about the "reactionary fundamentalist butchers."

The next thing on the agenda was for Barbi to interview, on camera, one of the American POWs.

By the time Barbi got to Hanoi, it had come to pass that General Jefferson was again in captivity. Three wars, three internments—a perfect record. Having outgrown his youthful tolerance for fish heads and rice, he was somewhat mollified to discover that the North Vietnamese were more prone to extending the lives of their prisoners, which lives, they shrewdly recognized, carried as yet incalculable political value, with a once- or twice-daily offering of a watery cabbage soup and perhaps a crust of bread. Still, he was not a happy man.

Especially when he lay prone on the fetid concrete deck of Hoa Lo Prison with his elbows and ankles bound up together so tightly that his back arched, and as the guards beat him with rubber hoses he resembled a cross between a gargoyle and a Danish-modern rocking chair. This happened all too frequently. No, General Jefferson was not a happy man. Conditions there were disheartening at best, even for a man with the advantage of having trained extensively in both Japanese and North Korean prison camps. His political aspirations were on hold indefinitely. His wife was probably spending like a sailor, and God only knew what Creed was up to, with no one there to chew his ass regularly and anticipate his fuck-ups. Of course Creed was elated at this turn of events. It gave him a much freer hand on the base and no ass-chewings. But he didn't let on that the general's capture gladdened his heart; he wrung his hands and thrashed his breast and clucked like everyone else. He also made it an absolute LAW that *never* during this tour, for any reason, under any circumstances, would he step into an airplane again, lest he be shot down and, God forbid, rejoin General Jefferson's command yet another time.

When they gave General Jefferson a new issue of prison pajamas and a bar of soap and bade him take an irregular shower, he knew something was afoot, but he had no idea what. When he was all spiffed up, looking as serene and salutary as a POW could, they took him downtown. The general was genuinely puzzled. What could they have in store for him? Then, when he encountered this diminutive Caucasian waif, dressed like

Che Guevara, for Christ's sake, he was really puzzled. What was the equation here? What was the delta?

Barbi loosened up with some standard sloganeering for the folks back home, and then set to her task of eliciting remorse for his crimes and some apologetic concessions from the general.

"Jefferson," she asked, "can you honestly tell us that you feel regret for the atrocity you have perpetuated on these peaceful civilians? Doesn't your consciousness haunt you for the destruction you have brought to the people of Hanoi?"

Actually, he had been shot down at Vinh, a couple hundred miles to the south. This was his first visit to Hanoi, and he didn't feel like he'd brought a lot of destruction along, having been bound in the back of a truck, poked with sticks, and pelted with stones from village to village the whole way.

But the whole thing was taken from *Alice in Wonderland*. Who was this teenage interrogator and what was she doing in Hanoi? And what was she accusing him of, and why, if she was an American? General Jefferson, being well-schooled in these matters, took the prudent, Geneva Convention path, and only muttered his name, rank, and serial number, trying to erase all emotion from his face. But this was enough for the Vietnamese, who had a defector standing by to dub in all the right answers to Barbi's questions. All that was needed was for his lips to move, so they were happy; their message would get out to the world just the way they had written it. Seemingly from the mouth of an American air pirate; a general at that. What a propaganda coup.

But they hadn't reckoned on the general's resourcefulness and natural paranoia. He *knew* they would try to trick him some way, so he began sending Morse code by blinking his eyelids. His first message was this: "Who is this cunt, and which side is she on?"

This multifaceted exchange went on for some minutes, with no real communication being effected at all, but after the tape was dubbed, edited, packaged, and released to the world, it became as successful a press conference as there ever was. The lip-readers could swear that he was only giving his name, rank, and serial number; the code-readers could swear that he was asking who this cunt was and saying that he had been tortured and ill-treated; the liberals, who wanted to hear it, could plainly hear him say, humbly, in the somewhat garbled, subdued voice of a remorseful prisoner, that he was indeed sorry for the terrible crimes he had committed, and deplored all American actions in Vietnam. So, like

Pettibone's Law

most press conferences, anyone could infer from it most anything he wanted to, but there was no real substantive proof of anything, so it was a success. General Jefferson would go far in politics. If he ever got there. Barbi, too, was learning the rudiments. And so on.

But the real centerpiece, the *pièce de résistance* of the outlaw American delegation's visit, was to be a formal luncheon and short sight-seeing cruise aboard Irving's yacht, the *Simian Negotiation*.

Irving had the crew in their dress uniforms, the stewards in starched white jackets; his agents had somewhere located, in that war-torn country, fresh flowers and a string quartet that dated from the French occupation. There was plenty of champagne. This was Irving's main contribution to the war/peace effort. It was to be a real gala.

This august and auspicious gathering was ostensibly convened to celebrate the unqualified support of the entire spectrum of the antiwar American Left for the Democratic Republic of Vietnam. In addition to the generous sponsorship of Socialized Labor's Unrelenting Revolt, they carried pledges, if not representatives, from SNCC, CORE, ADA, the Ad Hoc University Committee, SANE, the Student Mobilizing Committee, SDS, Vietnam Veterans Against the War, and several other concerned groups. As they cast off from the dock into Haiphong Harbor, wine corks popping, the quartet sawing dutifully away at its threadbare strings, bunting aflap in the breeze, TV cameras rolling aboard, ashore, and in a flotilla of small boats, they presented more pomp and circumstance than North Vietnam had seen in a coon's age, so to speak.

It was a heart-warming spectacle there for a minute or two, one that would lift the spirits of true peace-lovers everywhere in the world. Then the ship hit a mine and sank.

That unfortunate happenstance dashed the celebrative airs more than a little bit. One of the mines that the Navy said they hadn't been strategically placing in North Vietnamese waterways, but had been, had slipped its mooring some time before and drifted mysteriously, with the tide and the whims of nature, into Haiphong Harbor. Davy Jones, never seeing it, hit the mine squarely, and it blew a gaping hole in the hull of the *Simian Negotiation*. She went down in minutes.

There were those conservative and reactionary elements, of course, that, on seeing the films, leaped to accuse Barbi of scuttling the ship herself, so as to falsely dramatize the danger of North Vietnamese waters since the U.S. Navy had begun meddling. And who knows but that she did? It was a nice touch, what with close-ups of terrified patriots who couldn't swim clinging to everything from lifesavers to inverted Styrofoam coolers lately emptied of their cargo of champagne bottles and ice, tears in their eyes, begging for salvation. On this festive occasion, with the level of officials aboard, and having just left the dock, there had been no lifeboat drills and no flotation gear assigned. Chaos was everywhere as she went down. Those who could swim were leaping off the fantail, striking out for shore; others clung to the rail, pale with fear, while still others merely ran amok. Some of the lifeboats were successfully launched, but there was no order, no organized loading of them. The term "Chinese fire drill" comes to mind.

At any rate, the vessel of Davy Jones went straight down to the locker that he had reserved there, and quickly, with Davy on the bridge until the last minute, blowing distress and abandon-ship signals, which no one understood, and which only added to the pandemonium. It was no longer in fashion to actually go down with your ship. You were encouraged, after there was no more you could do, to save yourself so as to testify at a maritime board of inquiry.

But down she went, and there were people dog-paddling, people clinging to flotsam, and people going under for the first or second time. Small boats were fishing them out as fast as they could and everybody was trying to scream.

Then, in the midst of the confusion, when the ship ducked under the surface, it generated large waves that added to the bedlam in the surrounding waters. One such wave struck a lifeboat, and Ho Chi Minh, He Who Enlightens, president and premier of the Democratic Republic of Vietnam, was thrown into the sea.

The first person to observe this catastrophe was P. E. Proudbird, a strong swimmer and a game chick by anyone's measure, who had been a lifeguard in her younger, foolish days at the Progress Plunge, a steamy, sulphury, indoor pool in a blue-collar suburb of Denver. Almost without thinking she dived into the frothy brine to save Uncle Ho. Once she had the little old gentleman under tow, P.E. made what turned out to be a momentous decision. Ho had put himself into a trancelike, harmonic, natural state, and bobbed at the surface nearly as handily as a duck. He made himself quite buoyant for a skinny fellow. There was mass confusion around the boats, with people climbing in and falling out at about the same rate. The shore was only a hundred yards or so away, and that through calmer waters. So P.E. just tucked her precious cargo under her arm and stroked for shore, instead of the boats.

Well, didn't the cameras pan and zoom in and cluster around when Polly Esther Proudbird, American Indian and militant antiwar activist, came ashore supporting He Who Enlightens, the octogenarian father of Vietnamese Communism! Oh, it was wonderful stuff. And didn't that P.E., the statuesque one, clad in a silken *ao dai*, soaked through, every square centimeter of the translucent-to-transparent cloth clinging to her gorgeous, tawny hide, didn't she turn a few heads when she stepped out of the water! They couldn't get enough of her. Her hair, still in the long single braid, was perfect, and wet and flushed with exertion, she looked like a sure-enough Greek Oceanid, and the sound of shutters opening and closing drowned out the beating of the gulls' wings. P.E.'s modeling career was made that day, as was her political legend, for having saved Ho Chi Minh from certain death. For a while there, P.E. got more ink and air time than even Barbi.

As for Barbi, who had also swum ashore, she waded out of the drink resembling a Raggedy Ann doll after a stint in an old-time washing machine with no spin cycle. Barbi went almost unnoticed for a few minutes, while P.E., center stage, crackled with purloined thunder.

O'Malley could hardly swim, and, trussed up in all his boots and dungarees and jackets and web belts and pseudocombat gear, he damn near drowned, until a black-toothed fishwife pulled him into her sampan and then seemed reluctant to take him ashore until he had become better acquainted with her black-toothed daughter, the only fat Vietnamese he had ever seen. Must be a gland disorder, he thought.

Irving was the first man in the first lifeboat, and he had to sit idly by and watch his pride and joy slide beneath the waves. Still, he had the old tub insured for more than she was worth, and he called Hollywood that night and commissioned three writers to do scripts on his firsthand Indo-China adventures, so things weren't so bad.

After they got Ho toweled off and into a dry Mao jacket, and some comrade handmaidens had blown-dry his little beard, he praised his brave American friends, cursed the Nixon administration and its insidious mining of neutral harbors (although, in an odd quirk of nature, unbeknownst to any save Pettibone, that particular mine had been sown under the auspices of Lyndon Johnson and had taken all those years, floating in the Gulf of Tonkin, to arrive at its appointment with destiny), and invited everybody over to his bungalow to sit in front of the fire and sip some Chinese brandy, to take the chill off. It was terrible, but they drank it anyway. Concurrently, somewhere down in the harbor, a fishing family was passing around a jug of twenty-year-old Napoleon cognac that floated up from the *Simian Negotiation*. The peace delegation was served cabbage soup, but the fishermen made do with tins of beluga caviar.

For Barbi and P.E. this was just a beginning. There was greater career enhancement in the events of that day than either of them knew. After the TV footage had been seen worldwide and the magazines and newspapers perused by millions, the girls had international fame and identity, and they were off and running. P.E. was to become the toast of the European fashion magazines, gracing the covers of all of them several times. It was a career to which she had long aspired, and when she got it, it was sweet. She became known by every doorman and *maître d'hôtel* in England and on the Continent, not to mention Manhattan and Beverly Hills. The money they pushed at her was almost embarrassing, but she found uses for it. The only bad thing about the deal was that she almost never got to pose dry. For years they kept throwing buckets of water on her, trying to recapture *that look*.

As for Barbi, she had more serious things in mind. She was going to reconstruct the United States. Just rebuild that unfortunate nation, brick by brick; rewrite the laws and customs, the Constitution if necessary, to guarantee *absolute* equality and perfect socialism. Brotherly love, peace, and mellowness would be required by LAW. She would start by going to Congress. She now had international name recognition, a constituency of millions, and a determination that would not flag.

Irving had films to produce and money to steal; he was already working on a deal with one of the studios to finance his sweeping epic on wartime North Vietnam, in which Ho Chi Minh would play himself and have ten points participation. Little did the wily old statesman and politician know what he was getting into here, but Irving made it sound like the money was already in the bank. Well, it was, but as the Gatlin Brothers would later point out, it was "in a bank in the middle of Beverly Hills, in somebody else's name."

O'Malley was destined to forever be a flake, but Barbi or the governor or somebody would always keep him on some staff as a special adviser or assistant of some sort, so his future was assured. Irving had even hinted that he might have the stuff of an assistant producer. O'Malley *was* short on compunction.

But Barbi Belheur was going to straighten Washington out, and It Was Written that that institution was in for some rude awakenings when she got there. And who knows, running in California with the governor's support, she just might be elected.

26

Southeast Asia, 1960s

When Rawlins got fired for doing his job, it came as no surprise. While he and Hang Dog sat there in the middle of the runway, the now *closed* runway, in their airplane, dead after the flameout, in the culinary Annamite sun, he had more than an inkling that there might be, well, repercussions.

And so there were. All the field-grade officers and a suck-ass captain or two were gathering to decide his fate before Rawlins even got back to the flight line.

Not that Smilin' Jack would receive anything less than a fair, full, open hearing, as prescribed by Marine Corps operational orders and the Uniform Code of Military Justice, the LAW. Still, a juridical body composed of springing marsupials from down under suggests itself, as does the specter of Roy Bean out in west Texas.

That panel gathered in the Operations hootch would have voted Socrates double rations of hemlock in an Athens minute. It was like appearing before a tribunal of Draco, Rasputin, Torquemada, and a handful of Borgias, and throwing yourself on the mercy of the court. You did *not* fire Zunis without authorization, and you *never* ran out of gas. So Rawlins packed his bag.

General Jefferson had what *au courant* "I'm okay, you're okay" shrinks would probably call a healthy complement of paranoid personality. Here he was, in his third war, with only two combat missions, having been shot down on his first hop in all preceding wars. He just knew that his asshole buddies and contemporaries back at the Pentagon were laughing their heads off over his combat record. And he couldn't stand it. He fought it for a while, knowing it was folly to go fooling around with airplanes at his age and station in life, but it bothered him constantly; he began to lose sleep and to bite his exquisitely manicured fingernails, and finally he couldn't stand it anymore. He decided to fly one simple, safe little hop and then force the awards officer to write him up for a single-mission Air Medal—that being the only regular decoration he didn't have, not having flown enough hops to get it automatically—which would be approved by his cohorts up the line. That would set the record straight, balance the books, and silence his detractors.

The general called Creed, who called Morgenkrank, who called Poltroun. "What's our best airplane, number two?"

"Yeah, it just came back from overhaul. It's the cleanest one."

"Well, pull it off the flight schedule and get that sumbitch squared away. The general's coming down to fly with us tomorrow."

"Aye, aye, Skipper." Major Poltroun, whose career fortunes of late put him in mind of the crash of '29, saw this as an opportunity to turn the market around. With enhancement stars in his eyes, he loped off to the flight line.

Major Poltroun caused a detachment of snuffies to work all night shining that fucking airplane up to a fare-thee-well. He had the squadron logo, numbers, and call letters repainted. He even had the general's name and rank painted rather pretentiously under the canopy rail of the aft cockpit, and his own under the forward one, although the squadron did not officially affect the conceit of assigning planes to individual pilots. Still, the general could not help noticing as he climbed in, and associating that name with this beautiful airplane, and all the best aspects of the war. Poltroun had already called Operations and instructed them to schedule him with the general. It remained only to polish that bird to a luster challenging that of the stars themselves. After the detailing crew had been given most explicit instructions as to what he wanted done to the airplane, and warned that he would be back to check on them, Poltroun went to his hootch to shine his boots and press his flight suit. Oh, this would be a coup! He also began making notes for his preflight briefing, notes that alluded to the dire consequences of underestimating SAMs and MiGs and radar-controlled AAA, even though they were only scheduled for a local Blue Blazer mission, and would not likely encounter anything more life-threatening than the fragments of their own bombs, should they make a low pullout. Which in Poltroun's case was a distinct possibility. The unique properties of their five-hundred-pound, low-drag, general-purpose bombs would probably be utilized only in the ongoing manufacture of cord upon cord of splinters, in a section of the jungle strongly suspected of being an "enemy base camp," while the gooks sat drinking tea down in their tunnels, out of harm's way.

But Poltroun felt it to be incumbent upon himself, and in the best interests of career planning, to communicate to the general in a lively fashion the whole scope, the real rigors, and the intrepidity of the players in this dangerous war; to that end he would dramatize the process to the maximum, and color in every nuance he could seize upon. He would present himself as one having the highest steely-eyed quotient, effusing self-reliance, efficiency, and dependability. In a word, an above-average career officer doing an above-average job in a difficult situation. Poltroun shined his brass and savored the moment.

The troopers, meanwhile, carping, bitching, and jocularly proposing to inscribe Poltroun's name on a fragmentation grenade, which might then be rolled into his hootch during the wee hours, a new gambit said to be gaining popularity in the Army, shined and polished on old number 2 into the night. They went over that aircraft with sponges, rags, fine-toothed combs, toothbrushes, and pipe cleaners. They scrubbed and waxed and buffed. They washed off the tires and struts and all the oil and hydraulic leaks on the underside of the bird. They cleaned the canopy till it shone, and the glass in the instrument panel. A new, clean parachute, seat pan, and harness were added. They dusted every nook and cranny and crevice. They complained at this wasted effort and cursed and burned elbow grease through the night until number 2 appeared as pristine as the day she rolled off the assembly line.

And, of course, it was all for nought. The general arrived late, with no time for Poltroun's theatrics in the briefing room. But a crestfallen Major Poltroun, never one to give up easily, yet leapt to the fore, determined to salvage all he could from the situation. He could brief the general in the air and still work in some of the better lines he had composed. He saluted smartly and gave Jefferson his most unctuous smile. He had even polished his front teeth with Ajax that morning and they shone like halogen headlamps.

"Good morning, General. It's good to see you, sir. I want you to know it's a real privilege to be selected to conduct the General on a flight which I anticipate will be fairly typical of our day-to-day operations here. But then one can never know," a quick, ingratiating smile, "just what to expect in a combat situation, can one, sir?" He laughed nervously and almost winked.

The general almost retched. Whatever his shortcomings as a commander, General Jefferson was no sucker for the practitioners of this figurative gluteal osculation that he found so much in vogue among his underlings. He had encountered the Pecksniffian sycophant Poltroun on several occasions, in fact on every occasion where Poltroun could see the way clear to insinuate himself into the general's field of attention, and the man turned his stomach, pure and simple.

General Jefferson was not checked out in the F-4, so he was going to ride in the back seat and observe. As they walked out to the flight line, toward airplane number 2, which fairly glowed and sparkled from the ministrations of the night before, Poltroun blathered and babbled non-stop. While he doubted that the general would find this particular hop of major significance to the war effort, in and of itself, still he knew full well that each sortie, though seemingly unimportant when viewed in isolation, was an indispensable segment of a grander scheme; and he, Poltroun, was only too happy to do his small part within the larger plan, conceived by wiser men than he, to rid Southeast Asia of Communism. And he certainly hoped that the general would see fit to instruct him in the theory, practice, and prognosis appertaining to that bigger picture, as he, Poltroun, was every bit as interested in the long-term, strategic goals of this conflict as he was in the immediate, tactical ones, knowing that a career Marine Corps officer must always keep learning and preparing himself for increasing authority and responsibility, if the general knew what he meant.

The general did.

It happened that Captain America and R² Jones were getting ready to launch on a Rolling Thunder mission up to a place called Vinh. Vinh was the main staging area for all the odds and ends that Uncle Ho was sending south to support the liberation effort. The boys would load up at Vinh, have a cup of java, pinch the waitress, and head over the Mu Gia Pass into Laos and on down the "He Who Enlightens" trail to points south. Consequently, the American bombers had been spending a good bit of time up there trying to blow up the trucks before the boys finished their java. Consequently to that, the NVA had put in a brand-new SAM ring south of Vinh that nobody knew about yet.

A photo-recon aircraft had taken an infrared picture the night before of a large, open lot near Vinh just brimming with trucks. Captain America and R² each had six pods of Zuni rockets, which they were instructed to go up and expend on said truck park. This was a FRAGGED Zuni mission, called for by a fragmentary combat operations order. Of course all the trucks had left by then, and the truck park was just a vacant lot, but had Captain America and R^2 arrived as scheduled, they would dutifully have shot all those precious Zunis into the park, creating major dust that would rise high in the still air. Dust was a nice change from splinters, which they usually created. Dust was more visually exciting and looked more warlike. But it seemed like they were always assigned splinters. Of course Captain America and R^2 did not arrive as scheduled; there were some glitches.

As General Jeffferson and Major Poltroun approached the squeaky clean, sparkling number 2, Poltroun was still discoursing on his consuming interest in, and command of, combat tactics, military aviation, and world views. Plus his healthy respect and, it was hardly any secret, he admitted, fondness for the general. Jefferson was desperate.

As they fetched up in front of number 2, which looked for all the world like a virginal debutante, ready to step forth and dance that first waltz, General Jefferson, through an epiphany of sorts, saw a way out of his predicament that would at the same time bolster his self-imagined reputation as a soldier's general, a leader for the troops. He spied R^2 Jones doing a half-assed preflight on one of the old groaning, dirty, grease-stained, bullet-riddled airplanes that were more common to this gaggle of hoboes. The general had never seen R^2 Jones before, and had no idea that he was the confounded idiot who had caused so much trouble back in the States by flying supersonic over the retirement community and into the break. Had he known that, he would probably just have shot him. But he didn't know, and, assuming this lieutenant was the wingman on Poltroun's flight, the general reasoned that he would prefer to spend the next couple of hours in the company of *anyone* other than Poltroun, so why not ride with the lieutenant, sample a junior man's views of the air war? The general did not bother to learn that Jones was going on no little Blue Blazer, but to Vinh, way up in North Vietnam, land of the flying telephone pole, where they did some serious shooting at you. And had he even dreamed of the possibility, R^2 Jones being who he indeed was, that he might spend the next several years in the Hanoi Hilton with that grinning jackanapes for a cellmate, and even worse that they would be joined by Jones's identical twin brother, C^2 Jones, the two of whom bickered and badgered each other constantly; had the general even *conceived* of such a development, well, he would have welcomed Poltroun's society with wide-open arms, and drawn that clever, articulate, sagacious fellow into scintillating conversation for the whole goddamn day—and through the night, if need be. But, alas, we are seldom given to know the events in our future, and General Jefferson had no glimmering of his.

"Poltroun," he said in his most authoritative tone, nearly blinded by the combined twinkling of the immaculate number 2 and the flashing of Poltroun's teeth. "I gave explicit orders that I was to be shown no special treatment. I came down here to observe a sample of day-in and day-out operations by the largely anonymous but dependable and admirable men who are fighting this war. I want a normal, random mission, not some VIP tour in an airplane that's been all gussied up for the general to ride in, and that probably won't even go near the action. No, I want to see firsthand what the boys in my command do in this war. I think I'll ride with the lieutenant here."

Thus are momentous decisions made on the spurs of moments for reasons perhaps less germane to larger pictures than other considerations might have been. Poltroun, seeing his whole scenario for self-promotion coming apart, what remained of his crest now falling too, plummeting, tried to dissuade the general, but to no avail. Jefferson was, By God, going to ride with the lowly lieutenant. He climbed to the back seat of the dirty old airplane and sent the assigned RIO over to the gleaming new airplane, and Poltroun. The assigned RIO was C. Ross Culpepper, who would normally prefer being staked on an anthill to riding with the despised Poltroun. But he didn't quibble. In the first place, it was the commanding general giving the order. Secondly, Culpepper was none too keen on riding up to Vinh (dangerous place) with the frequently less than effectual R^2 Jones. Even though he had not ridden with Poltroun since the son of a bitch had tried to kill him by taking off with the wings folded and landing with the wheels up, at which time he had applied a sockdolager to the buffoon major's jaw and knocked him flat on his ass, and then had his own ass soundly chewed as a result, and stood twelve straight nights of Squadron Duty Officer; still, Culpepper reckoned it might be the lesser of the two evils.

Culpepper had not lost anything in North Vietnam, so he was not eager to go back and look for it. He could endure the opprobrious abuse of Poltroun for a short local deforestation hop, probably draw no fire (Poltroun had not yet found a replacement for Tran Van Ban, the man he had employed to provide hostile fire on his every hop, but who had been greased by Gunnery Sergeant O'Flynn in defense of his airplanes, at which Ban appeared to be shooting, ultimately prompting the demotion of O'Flynn to Staff Sergeant for shooting a friendly ARVN soldier, which the court decreed unacceptable, regardless of the circumstances), and Culpepper could get to the club early and in one piece.

So the switch was made, and capricious fate began another of its tortuous gambits. Culpepper decidedly did not enjoy his hop with the officiously authoritarian major, but after it was all over and he learned what he had missed out on up north, he could almost have kissed old Poltroun, the asshole.

Anyway, they lit 'em off, taxied, armed, tapped their burners, and smoked on out of there, Captain America to glory and the General and R^2 Jones to an extended sojourn in the Hanoi Hilton. Of course those three had no inkling of their respective destinations; it was just a routine hop. Who did have an inkling, though it was only a vague, general idea, a suspicion not uncommon to those on their first combat mission, that just maybe, it was within the realm of possibility, things might not go well—war might prove to be less than an abundance of joy—was Captain America's RIO. He was a boy who looked to be all of eighteen. Thinking it to be the ideal coiffure for combat conditions in the tropical jungle, he had had all his hair shaved off just before embarking on his war junket. For that reason, Hang Dog dubbed him "Slick," and that's what they called him. No one knew his real name, because he had only checked into the squadron the day before.

The Marine Corps had only had the F-4B Phantom II aircraft, with its back-seat work station, for a relatively short time and had not stockpiled a sufficient cadre of radar intercept officers to meet the needs of the service. For that reason they were shoving those boys through the training pipeline like a butcher on piecework jamming meat into the grinder with his wooden pestle—as fast as they could. After an abbreviated classroom stint, and his basic training in the T-39, which was just a little airliner with radar scopes in front of some of the seats so you could practice the basics of setting up an intercept of a fast-moving bogie, Slick arrived in the fleet. His advanced training took four days. The first day was occupied with checking in, paperwork, and indoctrination. The second day he flew familiarization and aerobatics hops in the morning, his first ride in a tactical aircraft. He found pulling four gs and being upside down most of the time somewhat unsettling. In the afternoon he flew intercepts, ground-controlled to the point where he took over the attack. That night he flew his night and actual-weather intercepts. Bright and early the next morning he climbed into a clean airplane with no external tanks or stores, kept that way for this purpose only, and was taken out to the speed corridor at Edwards AFB, where the pilot lit the burners and pushed it momentarily up past Mach 2. This—that he sit there and watch the airspeed indicator gradually climb up and point to Mach 2—was absolutely required for the training of every RIO, though

why was something of a conundrum; there was no sensation of speed at
that altitude and no conceivable benefit from the exercise. Then they
returned to the base, shot a TACAN approach to a GCA touch-and-go,
then came around and trapped in the arresting gear for their final landing.
Multiple Xs were going up on the board for each hop, and they had already
pared the syllabus for RIO training to the minimum. After chow they
launched in section with another crew for a target out in the desert called
"Inkey Barley." There they dropped six practice bombs and shot some
2.75-inch rockets into the sand. Slick got to call out speeds and altitudes,
say "MARK" at the release point, and watch the ground rushing up at
them. Next they climbed up, rendezvoused with a tanker, and took on
fuel. Then they headed out over the ocean in a restricted area, split up,
and got about fifty miles separation. They turned in, and the RIOs got
to look for each other and run modified intercept patterns until visual
contact was established. As soon as somebody got a tallyho the fight was
on. During the ensuing hassle, Slick got his air-combat-maneuvering X
on the board. Thrown into the dogfight milieu on his second day in fight-
ers, old Slick was unable to formulate even the wooziest idea of what the
fuck was going on. He grayed out, blacked out, and redded out by turns;
there seemed always to be some highly unnatural and uncomfortable g
force at work; the airplane described every known and many heretofore
unknown maneuvers: They did high and low yo-yos, barrel rolls, Im-
melmans, Cuban eights, split esses, octoflugerons, whifferdills, and he
didn't know what all, often in and out of a shuddering, gut-wrenching
buffet, throttles going from full burner to idle and back. And never, it
seemed, even for a second or two, could they go in a straight line or right
side up. They did this three separate times, which was more than plenty
for the learning curve of the neophyte radar intercept officer, tail-chased
through more gyrations back to the base, screamed into the break at 450
knots, shot two touch-and-goes, and made another arrested landing.

When Slick finally got his feet on the ground again, he likened himself
to the Shroud of Turin: He had perhaps never been in a holier state of
grace, but his body felt like a very old rag.

After the debriefing they pronounced him fully qualified and ready
for combat. The fourth day was spent checking out and doing more paperwork. They cut him a set of orders and handed him a travel voucher
for a one-way trip to Da Nang. And here he was, three days later,
strapping himself into the back seat of Captain America's airplane to visit
North Vietnam. Slick had not been in the outfit long enough to have
forgotten that Captain America was black. He knew. He had never flown

with a black pilot before; he had never even *seen* one before. The Marine Officer Corps of the time, and particularly the aviators, did not reflect exactly the ethnic makeup of society in general. Maybe Captain America was the only one, Slick didn't know. In point of fact, he didn't know a lot of things. He just wasn't allotted the time to learn the ropes. But in this case, he also didn't care much. Back-seaters perforce develop a strange proclivity for putting their lives unquestioningly in the hands of complete strangers. Pilots are not good at this. But RIOs are a little different. If the cat wears the wings, they trust the training. Also, integration in a combat situation is a little more genuine than in other circles. It's for real. Anyway, Captain America was one of the best pilots in the squadron, and as the flight progressed, Slick became quite comfortable, which was probably just as well, considering how it had to end.

Perhaps at some polished mahogany bar, in some dark O club somewhere in the world, one of the boys will still lift a glass occasionally to the memory of Slick. And Captain America, too, and all the others. But particularly to Slick. He had a thankless job, and did it as well as he could, without complaining, but his advanced training cycle was so radically abbreviated during those times that he never really got the hang of it. And his war was even shorter.

On the day before Gunnery Sergeant O'Flynn was busted to staff sergeant for shooting the wrong man for the right reason, poor old Tran Van Ban, just a below-average soldier doing an above-average job for twenty extra bucks a week—on the very day before those demotion proceedings, Sergeant Parton, the office pinky, had wangled himself another meritorious promotion. One corporal, the only enlisted man in the outfit who had finished college, with a degree in philosophy, called them Parton's "meretricious" promotions. He was a weird dude with thick glasses who smoked this goofy-looking pipe all the time, smiled a lot, and had a footlocker full of big, awesome, formidable books he was always buried in. He also had a modest collection of 8mm stag movies and a projector that he ran three nights a week and charged the troops two dollars a head to come into the darkened tent and watch and fidget and squirm and surreptitiously excite themselves, trying to get off without anybody else noticing. Of course they were all doing the same thing, as many as a dozen of them huddled in that five-man tent. Surprisingly they did not call the college man "Professor" or "Four Eyes"; he was known as "Booger." Booger was also a clerk in S-1, but only a corporal, and Parton was his boss. Booger called him the meretricious sergeant. Nobody knew what that meant exactly, but they were quick to infer that it was derogatory, and the term caught on. Booger was pleased whenever he could expand the vocabularies of those having educational advantages inferior to his own.

At any rate, Parton got himself promoted to staff sergeant the day before O'Flynn was demoted to that same rank. That gave Parton the advantage of time in grade and *de jure* seniority over O'Flynn, who was more than twenty years his dean in the less valid categories of time on earth and time in the Marine Corps.

Staff Sergeant Parton, perhaps overly ambitious, was an adversarial sort. He was highly assertive in the workplace, even though he had not had the benefit of McKinley Mortadella's graduate engineering management course from Cal Tech. Parton could not walk into a room without pissing people off, making them uncomfortable. He saw his position of strength as being solidified by the fear and timidity that he could instill in his underlings. There are really only two ways to manage: through threat and intimidation, or through example and support. Parton was a fear-and-deceit man. When he discovered that ex-Master Gunnery Sergeant O'Flynn was now junior to him, Staff Sergeant Parton began subtly and iniquitously to put the screws to him, to leave no doubt as to what the new pecking order was.

O'Flynn had been doing the pecking for many years, and he did not suffer gladly his return to the ranks of the peckees.

"Parton," he said with some urgency, "I'm gonna give you one piece of advice, once, you simple little shithead. If you *ever* fuck with me, just once, I'll hit you on top of the head so fucking hard it'll break both your ankles." They were in the club. O'Flynn sat at the bar with two or three of his cronies. Six empty beer bottles were in front of him, his Hibernian complexion was aglow, and a dread intensity burned in his slightly wild eyes.

"That's as clear as I can make it. You understand?" In Parton's eyes was the uneasy look of the wary animal who senses danger. He said nothing.

"All right." O'Flynn tapped Parton's chest with a thick finger. "Now shove off, buddy, and stay out of my shit." He turned back to his beer.

Staff Sergeant Parton was nothing if not vindictive, and he controlled the duty roster. Shortly after O'Flynn's third consecutive stint as all-night maintenance Duty Staff NCO, Parton found himself being jerked out of bed and dragged, squealing, from his tent. Words were exchanged. Words forged in the heat of passion.

"O'Flynn, you son of a bitch, if you so much as touch me again I'll have you court-marti—" He never finished the sentence. O'Flynn smashed him on top of the head with a bricklike fist, and although Parton's ankles were not broken as predicted, one *was* sprained. It was never established absolutely in the court proceedings whether the blow on the head was the proximate cause of the sprain or not. But there were other blows, blows causing lumps, a split lip, and a regular Goodyear Double Eagle steel-belted radial blackwall around the left eye. Which swelled shut as tight as the abstract of his perhaps distant cousin Dolly being stuffed into a 32A Cross-Your-Heart.

So Parton got what all his peers agreed was coming to him, but O'Flynn was back in the dock again, and this time they were not hesitant to throw the book at him. He had been too much the troublemaker of late. They broke him down to an ignominious lance corporal, his first time at that rank, since the Marine Corps had not even had such a rating when O'Flynn was on his way up. DeVille Hoggins had time in grade on him there, and shortly after that Hoggins made corporal, so he, too, outranked O'Flynn.

That series of events undermined the poor man's enthusiasm for his job and career. It destroyed his once fierce *esprit de corps*. He took to the bottle, whenever he could find one, vowed to stay drunk at all times possible except when asleep, and announced hourly to anyone who would listen that he patently no longer gave a fuck. The man was dispirited and was destined, through strong drink and resentment, to go down and down until he fetched up at buck private, his wife divorced him, he was transferred stateside, and was forced to attend Alcoholics Anonymous meetings. There he met Chikako, a divorced Japanese war bride who introduced him to the Sokka Gakkai religious sect, which stressed staying off the booze and being assertive in the workplace, to put it mildly. At the same time O'Flynn became acquainted with Chaplain Gaylord, who was both sentient and sententious, and was dedicated to helping his fellow man. The chaplain saw O'Flynn as a project made in heaven for the young priest out to prove himself in the saving-of-souls game.

After his service as chaplain, Gaylord would become widely known as a political activist, and would stand, more than once, on the same podium as Barbi Belheur. After being defrocked, he was destined to become the most outspoken critic of the government's handling of the AIDs epidemic; he would rail and admonish to the end that this evil could not be contained by righteous priestly platitudes urging boys and girls, respectively, to keep their dicks in their pants and their legs crossed until such time as they should fall under divine protection within the sanctity of marriage, monogamy, and the missionary position and frequency of exposure. No! he exhorted the world, billions must be spent on educational and medical measures. AIDS was the most insidious iniquity, the most diabolic blight ever unleashed on man. To prove the point, he died a wretched death of it himself, calling for reform with his last tortured breath.

But that all came much later; when the chaplain first met the bitter, downtrodden, drunken Buck Private O'Flynn, an abject and hopeless soul if ever he had encountered one, and traced his precipitous fall from the truly elite of his chosen society to the very bottom, he figured if he could turn this one around he would be doing real journeyman Shepherd work.

And between the chaplain's maxims and axioms and proverbs, and his positive example that doing good was the best revenge; between that and the militant self-reliance of Chikako's Sokka Gakkai, O'Flynn did get turned around. He sobered up, became offensively polite, smiled benignantly from dawn to dusk, and exhibited that glow of the initiate, the sign of sure salvation, in his now clear eyes. O'Flynn began the long road back. As for Parton, he elected to skip the rest of the paltry NCO ranks and move directly to warrant officer. He thought he would go into PX management, where he could steal himself rich, or at the least be snapped up by J. C. Penney upon retirement.

Ah, but the war was getting to be a drag for everybody. The damn thing seemed to be deteriorating, getting dirtier and nastier and more discouraging; it was no abundance of joy for anyone involved. Even the folks back home were getting sick of it. Some of the participants were getting decidedly sick of it.

DeWayne Ludlow had a brake failure, applied the emergency air brakes, blew both tires, skidded off the runway into the mud, fodded an engine, and received a most Brobdingnagian ass-chewing. Lance Major Slocum mispositioned a selector on the dogbone panel and pickled off a centerline multiple ejector rack with four unarmed bombs attached, which the Cong would recover and use for booby traps. That gave rise to hours and hours of meetings, switchology examinations being administered to all pilots, official promises to pull the wings of the next one to do it, Slocum being grounded for a week, and more than a few pointed remarks, not to say slurs, being uttered by field-grade officers, both privately and publicly, concerning his adequacy as an aviator. Rawlins was being transferred out of the squadron. Hang Dog caught the clap from General Jefferson's maid. Of course the general would not require her services anymore during this war, so rather than quarantining her they could just drive her off the base into the general population. Goldfinger, the

OB/GYN flight surgeon, got a Dear John from the rich J.A.P. whose troth he had elicited in better times, got drunk for a week, and lost seven thousand dollars at poker. It would take a lot of pap smears to make that up. The rains were coming, the club was behind schedule, Nguyen Van Dan, the bricklayer with two assholes, had escaped to rejoin the Cong, where it was safe, and Colonel Creed was beside himself. Goldberg had been assigned to Major Poltroun as his permanent RIO, because Al "Shaky" Morgenkrank knew that Goldberg was a better pilot than Poltroun, even if they had kicked him out of flight school, and Morgenkrank figured Goldberg might be able to keep the major from landing with his wheels up again, and other stupid shit he was prone to do. But what a bummer for Goldberg! C. Ross Culpepper's sister was four months pregnant and he wasn't there to persuade her swain from the next hog farm over to do the right thing by her. Moon Dog was grounded for a week with an ear infection, and aside from the flying he didn't love the war. Jimmy and Torres and Staff Sergeant Sam were still loading bombs by hand, and still couldn't get an R and R approved because they were too vital to squadron operations. Things just weren't going well. And would get worse.

As Captain America, who, incidentally, was the only one in the outfit who seemed never to get depressed and thought the war was going along fine, just as everything else was, turned inbound across the beach toward Vinh, they were above a low overcast, and all that Slick could see of what he knew to be North Vietnam was a layer of gray clouds. R^2 Jones, off to the right of his leader in a combat spread and responsible for continually clearing his blind spots, was asking the general if he knew how many Polacks it took to change a light bulb, or something equally appropriate. The general was beginning to wish he had gone with Poltroun. Very soon he would wish so more fervently than ever he had wished before. Jones, grinning no doubt inside his mask, as he seemed always to do, having delivered the stupid punch line to his stupid joke, was looking in his mirrors trying to catch the general's expression when the first ugly telephone pole slithered out of the cloud bank slightly behind and off to the left of the flight.

The SAM-alert code word for that day was BLIND DATE. When R^2 Jones saw, out of the corner of his eye, already too late, the missile streaking toward his leader, he was stunned, speechless for a microsecond, until the code word popped into his mind.

"BLIND DATE," he blurted, screamed, more like, over the radio. "Break left, break left!" Knowing neither who was talking, nor to whom, every airplane in the northern skies that was up on that frequency wrapped into a shuddering, hard-as-possible, descending port turn. Captain America, knowing the voice and for whom the message was intended, responded as gamely as was possible. He bent it into a seven-g pull, condensation boiling off the wings, Slick plastered down into his seat like the cornerstone of the great pyramid. But it was too late. The missile was already tracking on a rendezvous bearing and Captain America could not get enough sustained g on the airplane to elude it. He turned right into the telephone pole, and it reached out and touched someone. Touched them amidships and detonated the Phantom into a fulminous blizzard of debris, some metal, some composite, some flesh, some bone. Slick and Captain America had gone to that unremitting harvester that all the science from Hippocrates to Freud, with Cyrus McCormick thrown in, could neither displace nor deny. Their war was over.

The thing that R² Jones had not seen at all was the second surface-to-air missile that was homing on his aircraft even as he broke sharply off to the right. That telephone pole had slipped out of the cloud deck a few seconds behind the first one. Jones had a little more of a lead on that one and almost dodged it. Almost. But as he wrapped that hog of an airplane into a buffeting right turn there was an explosion slightly below and behind him, off the starboard wing, much of which was blown to pieces. Shrapnel smashed into control surfaces, fuel tanks, hydraulic lines, and engine sections. Smoke and fire appeared almost immediately, the dials on the instrument panel went crazy, every red light in the cockpit came on, and the airplane began to lurch and skid, and began a slow roll to the right despite Jones's frantic applications to the controls.

"I guess we'll have to get out, General. Get yourself ready and eject before this thing blows up." In some quirk of human nature that defied explanation, perhaps known only to Grampaw Pettibone, Jones was still grinning even as he spoke those fateful words.

General Jefferson was in a state of disbelief. As he straightened his back and put his feet together, his mental apparatus refused to compute this development at first. He reached for the face curtain, readying himself to yank it down and trigger the propellent that would shoot him out into the cold, unfriendly atmosphere, above a solid overcast, well inside the territory of the Democratic Republic of Vietnam. At the beginning of the pull on the curtain, the general muttered: "Oh, no. Oh God, not again."

The maintenance duty officer found Rawlins in the ordnance shop. "Report to the XO ASAP, Jack."

So it was time for the final negotiations. He was getting fired officially. When Rawlins walked into the hootch, Major Poltroun was almost gleeful. "So. You just can't obey the rules, can you, Rawlins?"

"I guess not, sir." Rawlins knew that he was only being prepped to talk to the CO, that this annoying bullshit was just Poltroun's unofficial attempt to insert himself into proceedings that really didn't concern him, to be assertive in the workplace and establish that, by God, he was the Executive Officer of this outfit, in case anyone had forgotten, and he had a thing or two to say about what went on. Rawlins bore it.

"So you've gone against squadron operating procedures again, and nearly lost us an aircraft, not to mention the unauthorized expenditure of Zunis. You just won't learn, will you?"

"I guess not, sir."

"Well, this time you've gone too far. It won't be tolerated. The skipper wants to talk to you, Rawlins, and I assure you, it's not going to be pleasant." Poltroun had to be very formal and severe about all this, it was deadly serious business; but he could hardly keep the grin off his face. This troublemaker was going to get his. Poltroun thought he would try to stand unobtrusively by the door and enjoy this masterful ass-chewing.

Which he didn't and it wasn't.

"Leave us alone please, Major," was the first thing Al "Shaky" Morgenkrank said. The next thing, still in Poltroun's hearing, was "Sit down, Jack." That was no way to conduct an ass-chewing, inviting the recipient to sit down and make himself comfortable! Poltroun was livid as he left the room.

Al "Shaky" Morgenkrank looked up from the papers on his desk, looked Rawlins straight in the eye, a thing Poltroun could not do.

"You fucked up, Jack."

"Yes sir. I know that."

"I know why you did it, and I know the results. And you pulled it off, though just barely. But you very nearly lost a two-million-dollar airplane. I'll say it again, there is *no* target in this war worth the cost of an airplane. We just can't have this shit, Jack."

"Yes sir. I know that." There was no use mentioning the hundreds of planes that ran into trees and mountains, that were blasted out of the air by missiles and cannon fire, that flew into their own bomb fragments, or were put into unrecoverable spins by over-eager would-be jocks. In a combat situation, there was bound to be some property damage, but that was not recognized in the operation plan.

"There are other units in this war, Jack. Somebody else would have got in there and rectified the situation. By staying on that target too long you recklessly endangered not only your own life, but your RIO's as well, and also government property."

There was no point in trying to explain that the members of Zulu Company who were still alive would not have been so in five minutes if Rawlins had not stayed. Airplanes cost more money than people did, it was that simple. Why ask if this was a fucking war, or a drill? It was a drill. No, you can't buck the system.

"You fucked up, and I've got to do something about it." The colonel fixed Rawlins with a pointed but not unkind stare. A look as much of sadness as of anger. "You understand that, don't you?"

"Yes sir. I know that."

"Well, I'm transferring you to Group. They always have billets for warm bodies. They'll find some stupid thing to occupy your time for the rest of the tour. Maybe after things settle down you can come back and fly some TPQs with us. But by God, if you ever squeeze off another unauthorized Zuni or land low state I'll have your fucking wings."

During the formal, disciplinary part of this discussion, Morgenkrank had been all colonel, leaning aggressively forward, shoulders squared, eyes intense. Now his expression softened ever so little. Possibly he sagged a bit, and gazed, unseeing, at a point roughly where plating joined wall stud and rafter.

"God, I hated to lose that boy, Jack."

"Captain America?"

"Of course Captain America. Who the hell else? He was my finest young officer. That boy could have gone so far in this Marine Corps. And him a nigger, too." In death he was remembered differently. Senses and awareness were heightened. He was already taking on mythic status. "This is a dirty little war, Rawlins."

"Yes sir. I know that."

"Dirty little war. Yes, well. You can pick up your orders at S-1. Good luck."

It being an ill wind indeed that "blows no man to good," Rawlins was assigned as the group awards officer. His predecessor had rotated back to the States some weeks before, leaving all his paperwork in confusion. The first thing Rawlins came across was the request for Bronze Stars for Staff Sergeant Sam, Torres, and Jimmy. He gave those documents highest priority and entered them into the pipeline. The next paper to catch his eye was the case in which Poltroun and Creed had written each other up for DFCs for dropping their bombs through an overcast, not knowing whom or what they hit, although it wasn't explained just that way in the citation. That one he filed rather permanently. Rawlins found he had unlimited power in his new bureaucratic situation, if only the counterfeit power of paperwork. The first thing he did was declare a moratorium on medals for all field- and general-grade officers. He would look rather carefully on a case-by-case basis at his fellow company-grade citees before deciding whether to have them decorated or not. Next he began compiling a master list of all the enlisted swine, the real heroes of the Air Group. He would get them all Bronze Stars, with an occasional Silver Star, Navy Cross, or Medal of Honor for somebody who actually saved buddies' lives, or gave up his own trying to. This could be fun. The Marine Corps was, true to its bandied lore, giving him "one good deal after another," but maybe he could turn this one to the promotion of some justice and goodwill. Decorate the troops and give them grist for their sea story mills!

As for flying, Rawlins spent most of his time driving an ancient but honest DC-3 from base to base, delivering cases of red death, snow shovels, United Way pledges, and displaced autochthonous peasants, and usually returning with a cargo of much the same stuff.

Of course Rawlins's participation as a combatant was effectively over, but the larger war was going on, and going downhill. Most of the participants were beginning to think the whole thing was a mistake and just wished it would get over with, so they could return to pleasanter pursuits.

Barbi and the SLURniks back home wanted it over *raht now*, peace without honor, unilateral withdrawal, and imprisonment for all the perpetrators. The peasants knew things would be just as bad as ever no matter who won, and they just wished the bombing would stop. Random five-hundred-pounders from a TPQ mission are just the worst kind of toxic waste to a rice farmer.

Vo Nguyen Giap was already beginning to draw up contingency plans for the Tet offensive up in Hanoi, and the residents of that fair city were *damn* sure ready for the day when they could walk down the boulevard to the park, with their children in tow, to have a picnic of fish heads and rice, or cabbage soup or whatever, and not have to dodge shrapnel and jump into manholes en route.

The whole world deplored the slaughtering of one bunch of Homo sapiens by another bunch of the same genus and species, because it reminded them just how closely we are all related. Where might this aspect of the nature of man rear its not-so-pretty head next? No, the world at large wanted this awful war to stop, and no two ways about it.

But Rawlins, among others, sensed that it wouldn't stop, that it had a long period of worsening to get through before it began to get better. Had not Talleyrand observed that war is much too serious a matter to be entrusted to the military? And that was only the war on this immediate level. The ramifications and repercussions of it would last for generations, would rupture societies and turn brother against brother, maybe forever. The hatred, the oppression, the divisiveness, the enmity, the disgrace, the cloud over society would remain, both here and abroad.

So maybe Rawlins's war was over, but the rest of it wasn't. As fabled barkers on midways in perpetuity are wont to bark, "Folks, you ain't seen nothing yet."

27

California, 1980s

It was only a small thing at first, but it was a beginning. As such it was to loom larger as life and health and circumstances continued in decline for Smilin' Jack Rawlins. He quit drinking. Oh, only for ten days or so, but he showed himself that it could be done. The first couple of days were tough, with the demon circling, grinning, smacking his lips, but Rawlins had the tranquilizers, and he had made up his mind. So with that resolve he doped himself up to a state of advanced relaxation, a touch on the sleepy side, and discovered that life could be maintained without alcohol.

It began, not oddly, with a Friday lunch. Rawlins powered down four of Chez Ramon's most generous martinis and floated through the afternoon. He didn't have much to do that day, so when 4:42 rolled around he made a straight shot to the Mexican restaurant down the street and had three or four more. Now he was on the step, chock full of chemically induced elation and false prospects for a night of good old-fashioned grade-A fun. Like it used to be. Pub crawling and partying, in search of that elusive new girl, that fascinating conversation.

He managed to get home untrammeled by either the murderous traffic or the legions of MADD-inspired police agents, who seemed to lie in wait every damn where for the innocent citizen, minding his own business, merely meandering his way homeward. Or to the next bar. Rawlins parked his car in the garage, considered it a job well done, went inside, and poured a beaker of scotch. His pocket was full of money, he had on one of his nattier outfits with a new five-star rep tie he especially fancied. He was still on the step at that time, filled with good humor, seemingly heightened awareness, and a heady, though false, sense of well-being. This was a state that, in his younger days, he could maintain all evening, all night on occasion, then sleep some, detoxify, and wake up ready to go again, feeling few or no ill-effects. Times had changed. Any time now he would begin a quick slide into the oblivion that claimed him nearly every night. While he would never acknowledge that pattern, still he knew it to be true, and felt an anxiety to get out amongst 'em while yet he was witty and articulate and lively. To have the magic encounter, to charm, perhaps to score; to relive the past, if only for a time.

Rawlins set out for his walking-distance saloons, full of jollity and expectations that were not quite as high as he tried to make them seem. Way in the back of his mind, where the outlook was still a little sober and sick and pessimistic, an unpleasant memory chafed. He had joined in a heated disagreement with McKinley Mortadella over yet another piece of that literary starburst's redolent and purple prose that was so festooned up in layers and drapings of self-congratulatory, extraneous hyperbole that it didn't manage to say anything. Harsh words were exchanged and Mortadella alluded to the possibility of Rawlins being replaced as the lead editor on the HOGASS project, should he persist in his illegitimate and unqualified attempts to debase the pure, effective, technical and scientific language of the Executive Summary, which was Mortadella's volume. That was fine with Rawlins, except it boded ill for work generally. He did not like his job and his job did not like him. His work situation sucked, and Rawlins did not belong there; it was smothering him.

But he pushed those worries further back in his mind and pressed on into the welcome night. At McGillivray's Pub he found a stool between the cocktail waitress's station and two youngish, cheaply but fashionably dressed secretaries—administrative assistants—telephone operators—whatever. They were at least subliminally engaged in shop talk, while scoping out the action. They gave Rawlins a cursory glance. He was well dressed, probably moderately successful, and looked intelligent and nice enough. But the bags under the eyes, the crow's feet, and the balding head made him a little old. Or a little not-with-it—you could have those things fixed if you could afford it. A small danger signal was the arching of his eyebrows. Unconsciously gearing up for when the lids would gradually slide down to half-mast, Rawlins had involuntarily drawn his brows up into peaks, to take up the slack. One who knew him well would have detected just the beginning of a glaze in his still lively eyes. All in all, though, he was presentable. They gave him fleeting smiles and exchanged quick glances.

Rawlins flashed an ingratiating grin and said, "Hi. Nice day for a flaming hooker, wouldn't you say?"

The girl nearer him drew back in a defensive reaction, eyes widening. His remark suggested to her some sort of untoward allusion to a flamboyant prostitute, possibly meaning herself. "What are you talking about?" she asked rather coldly.

"Oh, please. No offense." He smiled again. "It's an old fighter-pilot drink. You take a shot glass of brandy, light it, and pour it down still flaming."

"You a fighter pilot?" She eyed him suspiciously.

"Used to be. The trick is not to spill it. If you gulp it down clean, the fire goes right out. Doesn't even burn you. I don't really want one, though. I was just, ah, making conversation, as they say. It's too hot, anyway. My name is Jack."

"What do you do now?" This dude was weird, but kind of funny, and maybe cute in a way. For an older guy.

"I, madam, am a sort of hack. Jack the hack. I write mendacious proposals to selected despots here and abroad, designed to entice them to buy lots of lethal weapons from my company. I once knew a lad who spilled one. Burned all the hide off his lower lip and chin."

"What?" He *was* weird.

"Flaming hooker, of course. Let himself recoil slightly from the flame, just as he was pouring it down. Poor bastard had to fly home from his cross-country at low level. Couldn't put his oxygen mask on."

"Scotch, Jack?" The bartender knew something of his habits.

"By God, Barney, now that you mention it, maybe I will have a touch. Better pour these ladies a back-up while you're at it."

The girls, it turned out, called themselves "account executives": One sold wholesale plumbing supplies, the other cemetery lots. That would have struck Rawlins as odd, but nothing was odd any more. There was further small talk, but no remarkable chemistry. Like most American rockets these days, the conversation did not seem likely to reach a scintillating orbit.

"Are you into crystals?" asked the grave executive.

Rawlins, who had been leaning rather heavily on the bar, sat up straight and refocused his attention. He pursed his lips and thought for a moment.

"The crystals. Hmmm. Is that a band?"

"No, no. Natural crystals, you know? Like rocks."

"Oh, rocks. No, excepting diamonds and emeralds and what goes into whiskey, I'm not much for rocks."

"Well, you know, they have healing powers and all. Amethyst, rose quartz, obsidian, that stuff. My girlfriend had this awful fungus infection and nothing seemed to help, but she had crystal therapy and it went away in less than a week. It really works."

"Ahhh," said Rawlins with a studious look. "Healing powers, eh? Well, now, in that department I tend to subscribe to the doctrine put forth in The Gospel According to Old Saint Luke, which is to say, 'Physician heal thy ownself.' And, acting in concert with young Barney here, I'm fixing to do that right now. Barney! Faithful dispenser of nectars and what have you. Another dollop of your most efficacious elixir here." He pushed his glass toward Barney, who had already fished the Dewar's bottle out of the speed-rack and set it on the bar.

Rawlins eyed the tulip glasses in front of his newfound semiterrestrial friends. "I reckon you better give my ladies some more of that sad little white wine too, my friend. Though it does seem a bit on the weak side for a libation, generally speaking, and likely won't heal much." Rawlins was pensive, then he broke into a rueful grin. "But I guess two such healthy young specimens as these don't need the kind of healing that I do, eh, Barney?"

Barney polished a glass and gave him a wry smile. "Jack, the word is, around the saloon circuit, that if you keep medicating at the rate you're going, one of these days you're going to heal yourself to death."

"Oh, nobody ever dies," said the girl who sold reservations for single-occupancy holes in the ground. "You just go on to other lives, new episodes."

"Well, now," said Rawlins. "I surely must admire your pluck for going into the cemetery business when you're convinced that nobody ever dies. And that's the real skinny, huh? There's no such thing as death?"

"No. Not of the spirit. There is no death, there is no such thing as time, and there are no accidents. The interment site or sepulcher are just ceremonial resting places for the physical trappings that are associated with this one earthly incarnation. The spirit, the real significant you, just rejoins that incredibly strong and timeless field of cosmic energy that makes up the universe. You get the right trance channel and you can talk to almost any dead person you want."

"I thought there was no such thing as a dead person."

"Oh, you know what I mean. The essence just reenters that timeless spiritual spectrum of being and sometimes chooses to reappear in the body of a channel to advise us. Like I talked to Mafu and he told me I had once been a Nubian slave girl in the court of Pharaoh Thutmose III in Thebes. That kind of stuff. It's rilly awesome."

Rawlins gave her a most approving glance. "Well, if I may say so, you don't appear to have lost your touch. No sir, you could be a Nubian slave in my harem any old time."

"Don't you wish." She laughed. "Sorry, I'm not in that line of work any more."

The purveyor of bidets and toilet seats was into New Age too. "Where did you go for harmonic convergence?" she asked her friend.

"I went to Chako Canyon in New Mexico. I wanted to do Machu Picchu, but I couldn't get the time off." They talked at some length about the lack of time, death, and accidents, throwing names and concepts around like independent film producers trying to put together a deal.

The conversation became somewhat confusing to Rawlins. Maybe some contradictory. He had understood so far from the discussion, or thought he had understood, that these spectral wraiths, these celestial guides and lecturers, agreed to a man that there was no time—that the concept of time was specious, merely an empty dimension born of the earthlings' conceit about the relative positions of earth, sun, and moon. It was a false obstacle that lowly humankind had created out of its ignorance—real energy and spiritual being were eternal. Well, okay, Rawlins could go along with that for a while. Only what about the so-called time that she couldn't get off to go to the high Andes, fetching along her parcel of distilled, hand-selected, and New Age–packaged harmony that she would unleash, along with a very Handel's *Messiah* of OM chantings, to obviate the destruction of the world during that particular season, be it time-oriented or no? What about that conception of time? And what about this fellow Arguelles, a self-described art historian who sat up in his own variety of cave somewhere with a stack of ancient Mayan calendars and wouldn't deny that he understood all their secret meanings a little better than anyone else did? It was from these calendars that Arguelles, in his special wisdom, derived the notion that the sure-enough end was near unless a whole bunch of shamans and charlatans and mediums and astral frequent-flyers assembled at preselected places and spread around an abundance of, well, harmony.

It occurred to Rawlins that the business of calendars—*all* calendars, *per se* and *de facto*—was time. If there *was* no time, how could the cat get any message from his funky old calendars? And what if all the faithful, because of the constraints of nonexistent time and other trifles such as coin of the realm, couldn't get to Ixtacihuatl or the great pyramid or wherever their harmonies were required; what if they could only do harmony in Central Park on their lunch hour or groove out in the backyard while keeping an eye on a couple of preschool harmonizers, and it didn't work? What if they didn't get their harmony spread around just so, and the world was destroyed anyway? Wouldn't that appear suspiciously like an *accident?* And didn't every mother's son of a spirit, every Lemurian and Alpha Centaurian, every Tom, Dick, and Ramtha who offered otherwordly insight to the initiates, hold absolutely, *insist*, that there were *no* accidents? Of course anyone who had read Bierce knew about accidents.

No, Rawlins thought the New Age might need a little work. Of course the point was likely a moot one. If there was no such thing as death, then the end of the world wasn't a very big deal. Everybody could just pure-energize and boogie off into some fourth or fifth dimension and continue to truck. All the multipoint-sensory and polyperspicacious spooks, be they only former denizens of this mortal coil come back to visit and profess, or full-on spectral presences from a whole 'nother fucking *density*, man, seem to agree that we are all God. They all assure, through channels as it were, in their, well, whimsical lingo, usually approximating either feigned British, B-movie Indian, or inscrutable Oriental detective, that we are all co-creators, little chips off the old God-block, continually creating ourselves and everything around us, including time. Well, to a bunch of resourceful folks like that, what is the loss of a little thing like a world? We could just slap together another one and, again, keep on truckin'.

Rawlins, not yet nodding, but close, raised his left eyebrow a little higher than the right, imperceptibly shook his head, and noted that the conversation between his newfound friends had again swung around to the recently celebrated convergence of proportionate congruities. The effort had been successful, the globe still twirled on its implied spindly axis, and the Fibonacci Ratio, as expressed through the exponential medium of the Elliot Wave Theory, correctly predicted the crest of the third-wave rally, and subsequent crash of the stock market. Rawlins did not know of these machinations and did not care. He was no more concerned with primary-wave market corrections than he was with the advent of Kaposi's sarcoma in the heterosexual, low-risk segment of the population. Rawlins owned no stocks, and had not been laid in several months; he could not remember just how many. It was hard enough to stumble through this earthly wasteland without lugging a baggage of paranormal terrors along. He was scared enough as it was.

"It was beyond belief," said the agent of pre-dug cubiform vacancies in hallowed ground to the agent of elimination, the Rita Lavelle, the Superfundsperson, the account executive of human waste disposal. "Un-*bee*-lievable. Everyone was like ecstatic while we were chanting."

"Well, you know. Ecstasy is just another frequency. All you have to do is learn to tune it in."

"*Ecstasy and Me*," said Rawlins. "Hedy Lamarr. But I don't think she chanted."

"The vibes were so strong," said Graves Registration, paying no attention to him.

"Vibes," said Rawlins. "Lionel Hampton. There's you some vibes."

"The chakras were just opening in everyone's body like humming antennas," she went on, "and the pure, flowing, harmonic energy was indescribable. It was like the perfect union."

"Harmonic energy," mumbled Rawlins. "Now you take the Harmonicats back in the fifties. They had a song called 'Just One More Chance.' They should have a reunion. A perfect reunion. Now those boys could blow some real harmonic energy." Rawlins was by now nodding, his eyelids had slid down a notch and he was starting to slur. An untouched drink sat in front of him, ice melting. A cigarette burned in the ashtray.

"Always liked the harmonica, myself," he mumbled to no one in particular. "Used to have one when I was a kid. Learned three songs, too. 'Red River Valley' and . . . uh. I don't remember the other ones. But liked the harmonica. Marine Band, too. 'Just one more chance,' " he sang. "Take the accordion, though. Infernal machine. Should be dismantled and buried in the toxic waste dump with nukes."

The account executives had begun to politely ignore his strange mutterings, and Rawlins was talking mostly to himself.

"Copper bracelets too," he said. "Worthless. Put 'em in the nuke dump. Maybe crystals too. Pyramids. HOGASS. Put 'em all in the nuke dump. Herbs and flutes, too."

"But the *reception*," said Plumbing Supplies. "When all that energy converges you can just *feel* the magnetic attraction in your arms. It's a, like, divine experience."

Rawlins perked up a little. "Reception? Yes. Divine. The immaculate reception. Was it Stallworth or Swann? Don't remember. Maybe somebody else. But the magnetism was there all right. We're talking *full-on* convergence in the end zone that day. Yes sir."

Sometime later Rawlins became aware that he had been dozing. He sat up straighter and noticed the cup of tepid coffee that had replaced his drink; Barney's signal that he had had enough. The women had finished their Chardonnay and moved on to more alluring scenarios and more with-it Lotharios. He sipped some of the coffee.

"New Age is bullshit," he said to no one. "Cop-out. The laughing philosopher thought we should create new gods and myths. Creative process. Elevate at least a few to be *higher men*. Oh, 's hard. Dangerous; gotta be willing to perish in the act of creation, but that's the only hope. Must be willing to sacrifice all for the creative process. Let it all hang out." This thought seemed momentarily sobering to Rawlins, and though his eyelids drooped, he spoke, to himself or nobody, with that urgent clarity that drunks sometimes summon.

"Ah, but these yuppies, pissants, New Agers. They want it all, want it easy. They want it right now. They hire some interstellar used car salesman to beam up a few gods that will tell them anything they want to hear. Instant gratification. They want a magic shortcut. Scared of man's insignificance in nature and scared of dying. Health and happiness and safety, but no effort, no waiting. So for two or three hundred bucks Doctor Feelgood tells them they're all part of God and therefore invulnerable to the ravages of nature and the pedestrian conceit of time, which does not exist on higher planes or affect the pristine force, the wavelengths, the pure, universal energy field of which they are all, each and every one, an integral part. And there are no accidents and nobody ever dies. Hah! That's rich."

Rawlins sucked once more on the lukewarm coffee, shoved a couple of dollars across the bar, and initiated his combined shuffle and glide toward the door.

The night air braced him up some, and restored a little spring to his step. He negotiated the forty-four well-traveled paces around the corner to the Blue Dolphin, his choice for that all-too-early, but final, last public nightcap. He had another scotch. Two. It was warm. He was again slumped on a barstool, one of his more frequent points of repose. This time he was at the end and had a wall to lean up against. But he didn't need it. Smilin' Jack had a phenomenal sense of balance, and had slept many an hour on freestanding barstools without falling. But it was an embarrassment to him and to his friends the bartenders, so he tried not to practice it. As he caught himself once more flirting with the arms of Morpheus, Rawlins detected the softest warning signal from a data recorder, a black box stashed somewhere way back in his mind, in a section that still played host to fleeting manifestations of sanity. The message was that when next he slipped into a trance it would be a deeper one and more likely to cause official indisposition, banishment under the "86" rule, even arrest and incarceration. In short, he had better get his ass home, where it was safe.

Rawlins drained his drink, stood up, stretched, blinked, and shuffled out of the cheery barroom without a word.

Earlier in his unexamined life he would have jumped into whatever overpowered speedster he and the finance company owned at the time, and thrown caution to the winds and the car into gear, defying the odds. No more. A couple of recent nights in the drunk tank, with thousand-dollar-plus fines, lawyer's fees, and the threat of losing his license for a year or two had got through to him.

So this night he did not drive; he staggered. And made a pretty good show of it for the most part. He proceeded under the uncanny three-axis autopilot system he had developed over a thousand-and-one nights like this. It kept him upright and headed generally in the right direction, but the control inputs were erratic. There was evident in his track considerable drift and course correction, with intermittent stops, starts, and lurches. His gait resembled that of Gung Hay Wong on an icy sidewalk.

Rawlins paused to lean on the bench at a bus stop and gazed through the lighted window of a drug store, at the magazine rack. Polly Esther Proudbird winked back at him from the cover of *Mademoiselle*, but he didn't know it was she.

So he tripped along toward the safety of his one-bedroom cave and sweet oblivion. Until he got to the four-lane arterial street he had to cross to get to his building. It was a long block, with the nearest signal and crosswalk about a hundred yards down the street. His objective was straight ahead. He noted the traffic stopped at the light, judged he had enough time, and pushed on. But he miscalculated. The street was wide and his locomotion at that point was something shy of an Olympic-class sprinter. He was ambulating all right, it was just that his progress described anything but a straight line, and that, being the shortest distance between him and his front door, was what was wanted. Rawlins's pattern of advance might put one in mind of the running back who reverses his field three times and rushes forty-seven yards east and west for a gain of three. He just wasn't getting there. And he had no more than entered the street when the light changed and the traffic rushed toward him. Lights flashed, horns honked, and brakes squealed. Rawlins tried to run, staggered, stumbled, lurched, and reeled for the curb. Just as he thought he had eluded the pack of irate drivers intent upon his murder, just as he neared the sanctuary of the sidewalk, one of the cars stopped. It was then that he remarked the ample illumination of the scene by flashing red lights. "Oh, great," he muttered. "Now I'm probably headed for that fucking jail again."

One thing Rawlins knew better than he knew his name, would likely remember even when dead, was that the surest way to gain entry to the local hoosegow was to argue with a cop. One must be strictly polite, deferential, compliant, and speak only when spoken to.

After the cop had checked his identity, warned him about jaywalking, and lectured him about public intoxication, he said he thought he'd better take him in, for his own safety if nothing else.

Even in his stupor, Rawlins's heart sank as he recalled the niceties and refinements of drunk tanks, where the guards are wont to punch you and push you around, the other drunks vomit on you or want to fight, and as the pen fills up through the night, things just get worse. And he would have no pill for the morning. That would be the worst of all. Rawlins figured he had one shot.

"Sir," he said in a voice intended to sound businesslike, matter-of-fact, and respectful, though that was hard for Rawlins, as he had no love of police and respected them less than the drug dealers and prostitutes they sometimes tried to arrest. But he forced what he imagined to be a grave, sober tone into his voice.

"Sir, I live right in that building, not twenty feet away. In deference to public safety, I wouldn't consider driving on a night like this; that's why I was walking. And I have to piss like a racehorse; that's why I was hurrying."

The cop made a snap decision. There are those who would attribute it to the candles of understanding that burn, and quarts of the milk of human kindness that flow, beneath every badge. A more likely influence was the policeman's reluctance to breathe the bouquet of urine in his patrol car for the rest of the shift.

At any rate, he said: "Mr. Rawlins, if that is in fact your domicile and place of residence, I suggest that you gain entrance to it at once, without saying another word and without delay."

"Color me gone," said Rawlins. And he was. And, boy, he *did* have to piss. That was lucky. It may have been the inspiration that delivered him from free lodging that evening.

The brisk night air and the sobering experiences of the last few minutes had uplifted him to a temporary state of reasonable consciousness, so, yes, he fixed a drink. Fixed it, stirred it with his finger, turned on the RCA, and settled, if not with grace at least with gratitude and relief, into the warm, familiar, uterine comfort of the recliner, the encompassing, reality-defying, modern-man-conjured cavity of the contemporary lotus eater—the chair before the set.

Once in place he cradled the drink in his lap and let the alpha waves flow. Did alpha waves come from Alpha Centauri? He must remember to ask a channeler if ever he encountered one. Kim Novak, although built like a flat-chested locomotive, still had the cheekbones, the haunting, chilling smile, and those Gargantuan, or perhaps more correctly Pantagruelian, eyes that told everything. And Rawlins grooved, and the gyros wound down, pumps and generators slowed, pressures and voltages lessened, relays and valves opened, and the machine decelerated into inertial torpor. The images on the lighted screen were his own version of New Age color healing.

And he slept there, basking in the eerie glow of the perceived reality of modern man. Slept and snored and expelled noxious gases. And the liver, that great filter of the dross and dregs and lees of human folly, worked through the night. Slept and reconstituted himself and did not spill the drink until first light, when he came to semiconsciousness with a start and sloshed some of the whiskey on his groin.

Rawlins came awake slowly, somewhat in concert with the rising of the sun and the increasing light entering the room. At first the only thing that he could perceive in his dark, womblike chamber was the flickering images and shadows on the electronic screen. All sound, too, came from the shadow box and was therefore only a reflection of the sounds made by real things and creatures. He was observing a children's program, populated solely with exaggerated caricatures, clowns, and hand puppets, which served to accent the distortion of reality. He mused that the world was willingly confining itself to the unthinking habit of basing concepts of truth and right on appearances; on images of images. We were so constantly bombarded with shadows and reflections of reality that we no longer recognized knowledge, the essence of truth.

He changed to the cable news channel and was struck by its similarity to the puppet show. Was the fulminous potentate of some two-bit Third World country mesmerizing his rabble with exhortations about "The Great Satan" any more real or immanent than a crotchety old hand puppet raising hell with the turtle caught red-handed, flippered really, now a shade remorseful, who had converted the oatmeal cookies to his own use? Or take the political candidate who tried with every fiber of his being, when in public, to convince the people that he was absolutely, utterly sincere. He never laughed or spoke lightly of anything. His off-camera peccadilloes, however, suggested another character: "Human, all too human." Whether womanizer or wimp, plagiarist or canting proselyte, black or white, he still pretended to sincerity and honesty. How much of the Good, of truth and reality, could there be in that enactment? Was the image anything but phony?

As more light filtered into the room, Rawlins began to observe objects other than the screen. He saw the cable that went into the wall and far, far away somewhere, to an antenna that received its signals from satellites and transmitters that got their messages from other transmitters and cameras and projectors, and where did it all end? How far removed from reality was the message of the medium.

He made out the tomahawk that he had fashioned years before while he was on survival training. High in the California Sierras the Marines were released in groups into the wilds to practice escaping, evading, and surviving. The exercise was to simulate their having bailed out over enemy territory. The "enemy" were permanent-personnel grunts at the camp who were assigned to harass and attempt to capture the fugitive airmen. Each man had a survival knife, each team was given a parachute, a map, a compass, some fish hooks, and nothing else. With this issue they were to prowl around the mountains for four days, hiding out from the enemy and attempting to make contact with "partisans" at designated times and places, who might give them some sort of aid; a bag of rice, or something. Supposedly, if you were caught, you failed and would have to repeat the course. That turned out not to be true, because several laggards were captured and dragged back to the simulated prison camp, where they were detained, harried a little, and then graduated just like everybody else. It may have been the better course. They were subjected to the "torture" of being tied up for long enough periods to create some discomfort, being locked in boxlike cells where they couldn't straighten their legs or lie down, and being awakened at all hours of the night for interrogation by a Mexican corporal who spoke enough Spanish to keep most of the prisoners confused and half-spooked as he yelled and ranted at them while they dutifully recited only name, rank, and serial number, in accordance with the Code of Conduct and the Geneva Convention. On the other hand they were given some watery oatmeal and a crust of bread each day and they didn't have to run their asses off in the mountains.

Those who continued to evade *did* have to run their asses off, or thought they did, because there were rumors of enemy troops all over the place trying to catch them and they did not want to get captured, fail the course, and have to do this bullshit all over again. And they got nothing to eat except the occasional squirrel or rattlesnake. Well, with the exception of one bunch. Moon Dog looked over his map a little closer than the other group leaders did. He discovered that just a few miles away, maybe half a day's march, was a fishing camp and bait shop. It was outside the perimeter of the training base, where they were not authorized to go, but, he figured, in uninhabited mountains, who the hell would know where they went? Besides, if they got caught they could just claim they were lost; and they would not get caught anyway because the troopers who were supposed to be chasing them did this week in and week out, knew the authorized training area, and would never leave it because it was against the rules and they would be technically AWOL. So Moon and his men marched over to a ridge overlooking the little store and café, off-limits to be sure, but who was to know? They found a deep ravine surrounded by thick timber, set up camp, and sat back to live off the land. When things got tough they would just walk down the hill and order two cheeseburgers and a six-pack. Their money was as good as anybody else's. And they never saw the enemy.

It was later conjectured that, in fact, there wasn't much enemy after you got more than a mile or two from the base camp, and the more gung ho elements probably did a lot more escaping and evading than was really necessary. It was a moot point, however, because on the fourth day everybody was instructed to meet a partisan, at a time and place, who would guide them to safety in friendly territory, and the ordeal would be over. These partisans turned out to be double agents who delivered their allies into preset ambushes, allowing everyone to get captured, tortured, and interrogated. Then the ordeal was over.

Of course Rawlins didn't know that when they scattered into the hills and, while perhaps less foolhardy than Moon Dog, he was still a practical strategist. He reasoned, correctly, that the poor stiffs who were stationed in that godforsaken wilderness had probably lost some of their zeal for running up and down mountains, and likely did as little of it as was required. Furthermore, this was a game. They would not get much to eat nor be inundated with amenities for the next four days, and then it would be over. He could see no advantage in snooping and pooping through the boondocks all that time foraging for food, reconnoitering the enemy, and trying to contact the elusive partisans. That would be hard work and they would probably get caught and have to do this bullshit all over again because wherever the partisans were, the enemy would not be far away. No, the thing to do was find a good hiding place and wait this thing out. To that end he picked a high, rugged peak some distance away and then humped on up to the top of that sucker and sunbathed for the rest of the week. Rawlins's four-man team never saw the enemy either, but they did get pretty hungry.

But somewhere up on that mountain Rawlins found his axe. It was a nearly perfectly chiseled piece of flint, maybe lost there by an Indian centuries ago. There was just the stone, but Rawlins, seeing that it was meant to be a tomahawk, set about finding a suitable branch for a handle. After some searching he found a piece of aspen that was about the right size and had the nice curve of an axe handle. Painstakingly, over a couple of days, he shaped the branch to fit the stone, with only his knife for a tool. He bound them tightly together with strong nylon cord from the parachute. Having little else to do, he became quite involved in the project. He carved intricate designs and patterns into the handle and smoothed and balanced his handiwork. He found what he figured might be an eagle feather and attached it to the head, thinking he had read somewhere that the Indians considered that pretty strong medicine, and the best sort of spiritual augmentation for your implements of war. Rawlins practiced throwing his axe against a dead tree trunk, and got pretty accurate. It usually didn't stick, but did measurable damage to the stump, as it would to foe or prey.

One night there was a commotion in camp. A porcupine had wandered in and brushed against one of the sleeping pilots. This produced a yelp of fear, a great sucking of wind, and greenhorns skying out in several directions, not knowing by what feral creature of doom they were pursued, but electing not to sit by and calmly determine its species and the relative danger to life and limb. Most of these boys had never been stranded in the wild mountains in the middle of the night before; they were a little skittish. Rawlins jumped up with his trusty tomahawk and dispatched the critter with two or three blows. It was a *young* porcupine. In the morning they cleaned and skinned it and roasted it. But they ate sparingly. For one thing, it didn't seem to cook uniformly. Their fire was too hot and their spit too low and too high by turns; every bite they got hold of was either charred to ashes or raw and cold. Also, they had no condiments or side dishes, but the truth was that these boys weren't really hungry yet. If they had been out there a month, their appetites would have improved markedly.

But Rawlins had made a weapon with his own hands. It was effective: It could protect him from harm, and to an extent feed him. He liked the axe, was proud of it, and had kept it all these years, perhaps as some kind of totem, a sign of his direct relationship with nature. As he looked at it in the gradually increasing light, hanging on the wall not far from the television, the axe was far more real to him than the counterfeit likenesses flashing on the screen, purporting to be the reality of the world. With his own ingenuity and dexterity he had created the axe out of nature, in the wilderness, unassisted. It was simple, but it was something utterly real to him, that he knew well, not someone else's idea of something, depicted in arbitrary shadings and colors.

Below the axe, on a speaker cabinet, sat a large handcarved figure of a hugely fat, smiling Buddha that Rawlins had bought in Japan. It had been fairly expensive and was his favorite piece of artwork. As the illumination in the room slowly intensified, he began to make out the fine detail of the carving. It was of hand-rubbed teak, and the expression on the Buddha's face, every wrinkle and smile line, each hollow and protuberence, every cleft and curve of the icon, had been slowly, carefully, even joyfully crafted by the artisan, surely a disciple, practicing in a sense the teachings of Buddha in his humility, cheerful devotion, and presumably, sensibility of the concept of "I am you," at least in part. These feelings about the piece gave it tangible reality to Rawlins.

As he contemplated the carving, in his phantasmal state of intuition, and only partial wakefulness, the news channel was summarizing the current predicament of the Christian television evangelists. To Rawlins the coincidence appeared, in only a vulgar sense perhaps, as a minor epiphany. What truth could there be in the mincing, posturing, prating rhetoric and bombast, the exhortations, entreaties, and supplications of foppish, tawdry television personalities, inventions of the medium and of the credulity of the confused masses? This was alpha-wave religion, baby, the devotional stuff of a populace that no longer read, studied, thought, or even had to wonder. It was so easy that folks just couldn't leave it alone. All you had to do was turn on the set, tune in, and drop out. They made it available twenty-four hours a day; any time you needed a little fix of guilt, penitence, or sanctimony it was as close as your tube. And these were no hayseed country preachers or Sauls of Tarsus, either; they were Holy Rollers with razor cuts and eye shadow, Firebreathers with MBAs, the Account Executives for God Almighty & Son, doing BIG business for the Lord. There was only one catch. Once they got you saying "Amen, Brother" back to your Zenith and just brimming with beatitude, you were instructed to go to the sugar bowl, take out three or four dollars of the Social Security money, and mail it straight off to old Reverend Hardblow, for God's Work, lest he miss his quota for this accounting period and be called back from his earthly mission to serve the Creator in other, unspecified ways. And we wouldn't want that, would we? Mercy! Since the Almighty has no conceivable use for cash, it may have been suspected by Pettibone, Chaplain Gaylord, and Rawlins, among others, that less of that money went for God's Work than did for Hardblow's Work, which appeared to consist mainly in the acquisition of property—more television stations, amusement parks, Rolls-Royces, and other Christian necessities. These folks were not exactly Carthusians. Just one little vow of silence would have shut the whole enterprise down. No, they were show folk, pietistic Thespians in the entertainment business. Their wardrobes, jewelry, and props cost more than the pope's did, and the *mise-en-scène* they erected, whence to preach humility and moderation, would have made the Sermon on the Mount look like it was shot on a soundstage in Culver City amidst papier-mâché boulders and potted plants. "Vanity of vanities, saith the Preacher, vanity of vanities; all is vanity."

They lived and breathed and affected the Bible. But they didn't read it very well. Who among them could quote the psalm, saying, "Put not your trust in princes, nor in the son of man, in whom there is no help," and then in the same breath ask you to send him some money? That was the rub. They all could. And with a straight face and a beatific smile.

No, there was more religion in the Buddha than in all the gauche, garish, rhinestoned ministries of the air lumped into one Jerry Lewis Moral Dystrophy Telethon.

Somewhere along in these surrealistic musings, Rawlins began to get it. He was living with too much illusion and too little truth. He was drunk half the time, and brain sick the rest of it. That scared him a little, and pissed him off. He figured then that he had to adjust his attitude a touch—force himself to begin to make some sense—find some truths in his mess of a world.

The morning's hangover was bad in every sense of that word. The fear of the anxiety attack was already upon him, the angst, the anginaphobia. The demon was up early. Rawlins dragged himself out of the chair, stumbled into the bathroom, hacked, spat, coughed, drank water, took two Valiums, and vowed seriously that he would not drink for a week. He looked into the mirror. It was not a pleasant sight.

So that was how Rawlins stopped drinking the first time. It wasn't easy. He shook. He could not eat anything all day. He watched television all that Saturday, old movies, "The Love Boat," any nonthreatening mush that would shelter him from the harsh reality of withdrawal. He died some small deaths and suffered a hundred hallucinatory ills. He found tears coming to his eyes frequently, summoned by nothing more than the bathos and sentimentality of bad movies. A rerun of "M.A.S.H.," late in the afternoon, was so poignant that he had to blow his nose several times. The Valium kept the demon at arm's length, though he howled in the background, but the heart attacks, the suffocation, the imminent dread were kept at bay. But he had no composure; he wallowed there in maudlin self-indulgence, giving rapt attention to the drivel of the television in order to stave off the multitude of fears, to escape the terrible unreality of his current reality. He was uncomfortable, but his mind was made up, and he struggled through, drinking ginger ale and not thinking at all.

It got worse in the evening when he really began to crave the drink itself, not just the peace of mind. His hand craved it, and shook; his taste buds craved the reassuring flavor; his nervous system craved the accustomed touch of euphoria, the sense of well-being, however false. Habit demanded compliance; this was what you did in these circumstances, and there were thirty years of positive reinforcement to insist on it. In a moment of particular weakness he almost tricked himself into allowing himself just one. Just one wouldn't hurt anything. Ah, but he knew that only one would destroy his resolve. He took another Valium and resisted. He was *not* going to drink. He was prepared to call in sick Monday if necessary, but by God he would not drink for a week. He had called in drunk so many times that it would be a nice irony to call in because of abstinence.

Rawlins hardly slept that night. He was afraid to go to bed; he took another pill and became so relaxed he was sure he could sleep. But he lay there and worried that the anxiety would come. He vowed that he would not think the unthinkable, would not allow himself to worry about worrying. He would sleep. That was that. Then, when he drifted off, something in his resolve seemed to relax, and the demon would find an opening. He would be jerked violently awake, gripped in some terror that lurked in the dream state and did not reveal itself, certain that he was dying. He continued through the night in that pattern, starting awake in fear, then slowly dozing off. There were alternating night sweats and chills. Finally, sometime in the morning, he fell into a deep but troubled sleep and didn't awaken until after noon, soaked with sweat.

The second day was better. Having made it for twenty-four hours, he began to take some pride in beating this thing. There arose the hint of a mental attitude that did not want to take that first drink and spoil the success. He ate something, went for a long walk in the fresh air, and began to get control. Sleep was a little easier that night, though still frightening. He dragged himself up in the morning and went to work.

His vision of Saturday morning had, of course, been focused mainly on television, only one symbol of society in general. Still, he wondered, was not the Vulcan V-belt and Avionic Pilotage System Corporation, in a sense, just a big-screen television show, populated by lies and half-truths, myths, misdirected loyalty, rumor and error, folly and foible, hyperbole and synecdoche, sinecure and blind ambition? And the whole thing sponsored week in and week out by the government of the people. For that matter, what was society itself but the ultimate wide-screen production? Television was nothing other than a reflection of society, perhaps in some ways distorted, but in many ways deadly accurate. Everything bad about television had to be engendered by what was bad about man. If television lacked honesty and truth, then it must be that society also lacked these qualities.

As he became accustomed to this long-overdue revisitation to sobriety, Rawlins found himself less troubled by pain and self-pity. He began to look around him with a sharper and more inquiring eye. The chronic, low-grade depression gradually lifted and a spark of the old enthusiasm returned. He was again able to envision life beyond mediocrity. His mental lethargy and resignation began to abate and he once again considered the realm of the possible. Though he might stumble many times, reenter the closet of despair and ennui, of drink and the contemplation of his own navel, it would never be the same. Because for this one illuminated period he had been out of the cave. Had been up, out of the cave, had seen some light, and knew that by struggling he could go again and see more.

After three dry days the demon was pretty well banished. Oh, he would threaten to come back and do mischief about six o'clock in the evening, cocktail hour, or again at bedtime, but one of the pills would chase him in a few minutes. And Rawlins felt stronger each day. By Friday he didn't even need the pills. If the fiend reared his ugly, warted little head, Rawlins could chase him away by sheer will.

As courage and confidence returned, he found the daily business of business at VVAPS less odious and painful to perform, but the more deplorable because he saw with clarity that he was wasting what remained of his life. He knew without question, and was brave enough to accept without equivocation, that there had to be something more; something more difficult, but better and truer than the endless shuffling of meaningless paperwork, the prevarication and procrastination of government-subsidized bureaucratic bungling.

He noticed that on Electra Gunhammer's desk, in addition to the small portrait of Cleveland Amory, her idol, were scattered a few crystals of varying shapes and sizes. These fetishes were, no doubt, to ward off the negative energy that seethed throughout the plant. Rawlins reckoned that there weren't sufficient crystals in the whole of the Rocky Mountains to counteract the "wicked falseness among those who will beyond their capacity . . ." as the German said. Electra's little energy field wasn't even strong enough to keep McKinley Mortadella out of her cubicle. And wasn't this today the mob's? And wasn't it true that "in the market place one convinces with gestures. But reason makes the mob mistrustful." And wasn't he, Rawlins, part and parcel of this charade, this industrial sham on the grandest scale? What of this society of "small people," these mild-mannered, orderly, cowardly little men who would never be in battle, could not survive in battle, but who banded together in their vast, safe war plant to create instruments of doom, from the use of which they would be completely removed, much as Rawlins had been removed from his war, high above in his sterile capsule, raining death on unseen vulnerable mortals? Was this reality?

No, crystals wouldn't do it. There must be a higher calling, a state of cognition where the mind could discover truth out of reality. Although he wasn't yet fully aware of it, Rawlins was beginning his quest. He was not consciously committed, but, as Caesar remarked before crossing the Rubicon, the die was cast. He had no choice but to remove himself for a time from the counterfeit mummery that passed for society. And that certainty, slipping in almost unnoticed, was the most important factor in the later life of Smilin' Jack Rawlins, citizen of the world.

He called the accounting department and requested a printout of the monies he had amassed in his company savings account and the employee retirement fund. He began toying seriously with the idea of walking away from VVAPS and never looking back.

Doctor Lieutenant Colonel McKinley Mortadella had 'elt right along that the success of the HOGASS project would propel him into that eighty-eighth vice president's spot. The sixty vice presidents, already effectively and efficiently managing the program, each felt that the success of HOG-ASS would certainly move him a square or two beyond the competition toward being selected as the next company president if ever the prosaic, arm-twisting firebrand who now ruled were to contract an ulcer, stroke, cardiac infarction, or other debility, take his $232 million dollars in stock, and step down. Those concerns had caused some corners to be cut. It appeared that there was evidence of overpayments, underpayments, under-the-table payments, nonpayments, deferred payments, and, finally, suspension of payments by the Pentagon, who suspected fraud, mismanagement, and misprision, among other things. And the congressional committees were circling and wheeling, led by none other than . . . yes! Congressperson Barbi Belheur. Barbi had introduced legislation making it a felony to manufacture anything that would explode, but even she and the rabid gun-control lobby couldn't get that past the rabid National Rifle Association lobby and its bulldog congressional supporter, ranking Republican on the Senate Armed Services Committee, Senator General Jefferson, decorated war hero. Well, anyone who could spend seven years in the same cell with R^2 Jones and his brother C^2 should have been decorated. Some things never change.

But now everybody in Washington—Democrat, Republican, or Independent; hawk, dove, or fence sitter—had the scent of corruption in the HOGASS program and they were jockeying for position to close in for the kill. Corruption was wonderful stuff because no politician could ever lose while probing it unless he had his own hand in the till. So far it appeared that the HOGASS scandal was contained entirely in the stygian infrastructure of the VVAPS Corporation and its labyrinthine network of suppliers, procurers, and subcontractors. Nobody in Washington figured to get burned, so the hunt was on.

The reason they were willing to fight fang and claw over this still-undead corpse was that every person in Washington wanted more than anything in God's world to see his own likeness up there on the monitor being interviewed on the six o'clock news. Or, best of all, televised hearings! Every Senateperson and Congressperson and what have you was rubbing his or her or its hands together in gleeful anticipation of an appearance on that national forum—the opportunity to practice his, her, or its look of *absolute* sincerity, and to spout the dull homilies and bromides about leadership, honesty, and new ideas that would assure re-election.

Management at VVAPS was rooted in the twin foundations of the good-old-boy network and the buddy system. The first concern of every manager was to watch his own six o'clock position. That quarter secured, his next inclination was to protect his buddy. Each manager had to, by dealing under the counter, using unauthorized sources, falsifying records, by hook or crook, make himself shine, while at the same time eliminating any indication that he had used irregular or unapproved procedures to do that shining. By extension, the good old boys of the network did not scruple at eliminating any source of embarrassment to their asshole buddies. The result was a management of obscurantism. Things were not recorded, dates and times and names not written down. Deals were made by phone. There was surreptitious comingling of assets. Inferior components were used, in desperation, to meet unrealistic deadlines, and then authorization forged. Monies were secretly diverted from one contract to another. It was not so much that the right hand didn't know what the left hand was doing as that it didn't know *how* it was getting it done. Or want to. The concept of "What did he know, when did he know it, and why didn't he tell someone else?" as popularized by certain watchdog committees had become a very touchy one for anybody having access to government resources. The upshot was that everyone stemming from McKinley Mortadella, both up and down, was so paranoid and so busy erasing trails and distorting facts that the whole project was beginning to look like layers and layers of cover-up. When the auditors swooped down, they would find it very tough going. But eventually, heads would roll.

Rawlins thought he could see a shadowy parallel between the state of the HOGASS program and, by implication, the whole VVAPS community, perhaps society at large, and the decline and fall of South Vietnam. It seemed that before the war everything had been logical and, well, *worthy;* since the war nothing had. In the fifties and early sixties, human relations had been an orderly business; everybody went by certain rules, even the bad guys. And there were always bad guys; there were two forces at work in the world, one good and one evil, but they were easily distinguishable. It was a Cold War planet and you knew where you stood. And the Shining Soldiers of Freedom worked in concert to keep the bad guys in their place. And, oddly enough, it worked for ten or fifteen years. It even worked in Korea, and everybody was lulled into thinking that as long as we were strong and vigilant, things would go on that way indefinitely. Grampaw Pettibone and the savants of his ilk would have seen the Cuban missile crisis as a signal that the times they were a-changing, but no one else did. No sir, we scared them Ruskies. We had more missiles than they did and they had too much to lose, so old Khrushchev backed down. Packed up and went home, and the Western Hemisphere was safe for democracy again.

What the pundits failed to figure out was Ho Chi Minh. "He Who Enlightens" had nothing to lose and everything to gain, and he wouldn't back down. Never. And old Ho wanted to be friends, too. He liked us lots better than he did the Russians; he even borrowed the opening paragraph of the Declaration of Independence of the United States of America to announce his own country's independence in 1945. Verbatim. And we would have done well to back him, too, because it took thirty years, but he did win the fucking war. The only trouble was that every time he mentioned a dirty word like "socialism" or "Communism" or "Marx" or "Lenin," Washington experienced a 7.0 tremor. We could have thought it over more carefully and considered the consequences, but we didn't. Like Mr. Bumble's LAW, we were "a ass, a idiot."

If Pettibone had bothered to formulate a LAW, Rawlins thought it might be, simply stated, this: You had better watch your step very carefully out there or something will bite you, because the world is rife with, abounds in, folly, perversity, and misadventure.

That seemed to be the case. Around the globe, whether it was Protestant or Catholic, Arab or Jew, born-again charismatic, Sikh, Sandinista, Communist, Contra, liberal, conservative, Sunni or Shi'ite, Pentecostal or Palestinian, the sectarian fundamentalists were at each other's throats. We had the CIA, Hezbollah, KGB, Islamic Jihad, IRA, Mujahedeen, and PLO all hell-bent on destroying each other and/or the moderate majority of Communists, Conservatives, Social Democrats, Laborites, and so forth. There were Libyans, Cubans, advisers and agents from all the major powers, oppressive armies and police forces, terrorists, arms dealers, rebels, guerrillas, zealots, fanatics, and chauvinists of every stripe— all intent on visiting annihilation upon the others.

"Before God! But now this God has died. Oh, nausea!"

What Marshall McLuhan called the "Global Village" had become a condominium development of houses divided.

It was as the Grand Inquisitor had prophesied to the visiting Christ: ". . . the terrible tower of Babel will be built again . . . they have set up gods and challenged one another . . . they will end, of course, with cannibalism."

Well, if all that were true, if the world is rife with folly, perversity, and misadventure, and who would gainsay such an oracle as Pettibone, must not the converse also be true? If those faults were epidemic in the world, must not there also be reason, salubrity, and beneficence? If chaos seems rampant, might not some careful thought reveal a sense of order?

Rawlins figured he had to try to find out. It was getting late and, what the hell, it all seemed kind of worthless unless he could begin to understand some of what had happened and exercise some control over what was left.

Rawlins was so pleased with his newfound sobriety and resulting mental state that he pressed on past his avowed week and held out for ten days. Then he got drunk, and it was truly a wonderful feeling. But the seed had been sown; his brain had been reawakened to an extent; he had proved to himself that when he eschewed the liquids and the chemicals, a positive, upbeat sense of strength and curiosity came over him. It was pleasant and exciting, and he knew that he must avoid the stimulants and soporifics and mind-dulling agents and return to that state more frequently, maybe for good.

He found that during his years at VVAPS he had accumulated several thousand dollars in savings and pension, enough to live on for a year or more if he was careful. By that time he hoped he could learn something of what he wanted in life; where he belonged.

It was a hard choice. He would have to give up the sinecure, the support system, the safety. And for what? Well, some fucking peace of mind, for one thing. Ahah! There may be more to that than is revealed at the first blush of passing curiosity. Still, he hesitated. A gallimaufry of saws and homilies having to do with numbers of eggs in baskets, looking and leaping, flaming bridges, and suchlike wandered through his head. To risk all was heavy on the downside. Instinct told him that, and fear of the unknown, but now there was a louder voice, one with an arm that tapped him on the shoulder and asked, rhetorically, "What is it with you, shithead? Do you think you can just hide until things get better?"

And the teeming mass of society was too confusing. He was weary of the horde mentality, the polarized ideologies, the crowding and demanding, the zeal and the cant. He had to get up above and away from the moil and try to think. So, not unlike the policeman's horse, that distant descendant of the gentle Houyhnhnm, who fled the peace march because of all the racket and guile and turmoil, Rawlins made up his mind to seek some higher ground. He would find himself a mountain; a rock to sit on, a tree to lean against.

He sat down and printed the first and last memo he ever wrote at the Vulcan V-belt and Avionic Pilotage System Corporation. It was addressed to Malcolm "Bud" Malison, Proposals Manager. It said:

> Bud: I quit. Please get my walking papers drawn up by two weeks from today.

He would try to leave the residue behind. The ashes, the emotional flotsam and jetsam of his helter-skelter existence. He would fetch the demon along, at least for a time. Perhaps the monkey had been his benefactor all along. After all, it had been he who drove Rawlins upward, out of the morass, who frightened him into opening his mind just a crack. He would yet carry the fiend a while, but maybe not for long. Fiends do not like clean. They do not like cold. They do not like fresh air. Fiends breed and prosper in fetid slime; they need heat and noxious odors; their lifeblood is decay. Maybe that was why the demon threw his worst fits in the high, thin, clear air of the cockpit. Fiends don't like it there. They thrive on the baser chemicals and liquids and mixtures. Now that Rawlins was learning to take that load off his shoulder, he could also dislodge the monkey. He would climb higher, to where the atmosphere was purity itself, until the fiend was discouraged and could come no farther. Then, at some point, he would kick that baggage back down the loose shale slope, cursing, screaming threats and blasphemies, scrambling, scratching with his grubby little claws, down and down, all the way to his nefarious origins. And be forever free of the hellhound.

He would also take his tomahawk along, and maybe, some day, if he climbed high enough and felt genuinely at peace with himself, he would bury it for someone else to find in some other century.

But he would be free of the monkey, free to search out some old antecedents, understand some whences and whithers, seek some truths, maybe invent some new ones of his own.

So Rawlins walked away from VVAPS and never looked back. He went up to the mountains and found a cabin near the confluence of two swift rivers. He unpacked his books and cut wood. The fall came and it began to snow. He was very much alone, and cabin fever set in early that year. He began to read and to consider and ponder. It would not be easy. "Needs must it be hard, since it is so seldom found." But he began, in earnest, to examine his life. He didn't know what he would find, but at least he would be looking.

Some of us are born posthumously, Rawlins read, and wondered. Yes, it was a time of returning.

> Old Jack Rawlins used to own a grocery store,
> He used to hang his meat upon the outside of the door.
> All the little children used to run and shout,
> "Old Jack Rawlins, your pork is hanging out."